JUN 1 1 2019

P9-AZV-718

ALSO BY ALIX OHLIN

The Missing Person

Babylon and Other Stories

Inside

Signs and Wonders

Dual Citizens

Dual Citizens

Alix Ohlin

Alfred A. Knopf · New York · 2019

THIS IS A BORZOI BOOK PUBLISHED BY ALFRED A. KNOPF

www.aaknopf.com

Knopf, Borzoi Books, and the colophon are registered trademarks of
Penguin Random House LLC.

Grateful acknowledgment is made to Nancy Willard, in care of
the Jean V. Naggar Literary Agency, Inc., for permission to reprint an
excerpt of "Swimming Lessons" from *Swimming Lessons: New and
Selected Poems* by Nancy Willard, copyright © 1996 by Nancy Willard.

Library of Congress Cataloging-in-Publication Data
Names: Ohlin, Alix, author.
Title: Dual citizens : a novel / Alix Ohlin.
Description: First edition. | New York : Alfred A. Knopf, 2019.
Identifiers: LCCN 2018058308 | ISBN 9780525521891 (hardcover)
ISBN 9780525654629 (ebook)
Subjects: LCSH: Sisters—Fiction. | Self-realization in women—Fiction. |
Domestic fiction. | BISAC: FICTION / Literary. | FICTION /
Contemporary Women. | FICTION / Coming of Age.
Classification: LCC PS3615.H57 D83 2019 | DDC 813/.6--dc23
LC record available at https://lccn.loc.gov/2018058308

Jacket photograph by Bauer Syndication / Alamy
Jacket design by Gabriele Wilson

Manufactured in the United States of America
First Edition

for PTOR

Editing—even on a more "normal" film—is not so much a *putting together* as it is a *discovery of a path*.

—WALTER MURCH, *IN THE BLINK OF AN EYE*

Little Red Riding Hood: A wolf and a person aren't the same thing.

Witch: Ask a wolf's mother.

—JAMES LAPINE, *INTO THE WOODS*

My heart is not afraid of deep water.
It is wearing its life vest,
that invisible garment of love
and trust, and it tells you this story.

—NANCY WILLARD, "SWIMMING LESSONS"

PART ONE

Before

The story of Scottie's life—which is, of course, the story of my life too—begins with my sister Robin. It's strange how little we talk about it now. Of the three of us, I'm the only one who dwells on our history, probably because I'm the one who chose and formed it. If I bring up that day in the Laurentians, Robin says she doesn't remember much about it. I find this impossible to imagine. For me, the opposite is true, with every detail lodged unwaveringly in my memory, recorded in detail, like a film I can replay at any time.

It goes like this: a sunny day in June, the leafy heat of summer at odds with my frozen terror as I stood fixed to the ground. The air thick and still as a wall against Robin's ragged breath.

And the wolf my sister had named Catherine inspecting us both with her yellow eyes.

Robin was thirty-eight weeks pregnant at the time, and she'd just irritably informed me that pregnancy lasted ten months, not nine. She was angry about this, as if there had been a conspiracy to keep her misinformed. She was angry in general, because she was hot and uncomfortable and couldn't sleep. We were walking down a trail behind her house that led to a canopy of pine trees, hoping the air would be cooler there. Walking was all Robin wanted to do, although she complained about this, too: her hips hurt, her knees hurt, her ribs hurt. Complaining wasn't typical of my sister, who was stoically, even savagely independent, and it worried me. We stopped every few steps so she could catch her breath, and when we did, I watched her stroke her belly; she wasn't in other ways tender toward the baby inside her, or herself.

She frowned. "What are you doing?"

"Nothing."

"You're touching yourself," she said.

I hadn't realized until then that I was imitating her, making myself a mirror. My palm was flat against my own stomach, though there was nothing to stroke. I flushed with embarrassment, and my sister gave her harsh bark of a laugh.

"It's okay," she said. "I get it."

But how could she get it? She didn't live in my body any more than I could live in hers. We stood body to body, sister to sister, across an impossible divide.

To change the subject, I began telling her about a cache of old films that had been discovered in a permafrost landfill beneath an ice rink in Dawson City, Yukon. Dating from the early twentieth century, the films had belonged to a movie house. Back in those days, I said, movies traveled from California to cities like Calgary and Vancouver before heading to Whitehorse and eventually reaching the mining community in Dawson City, at which point it made no sense to ship them back to their point of origin. So they accumulated there, an accidental archive. The films were made of cellulose nitrate, a material known to disintegrate, melt, even spontaneously combust. If they hadn't been buried below the rink—nestled alongside chicken wire and dirt and bits of wooden debris—they might have burned the whole town down.

"Movies used to explode?" Robin said.

I nodded. I told her how the movie house went out of business and dumped the films, which were found decades later by a backhoe operator clearing the land for a new recreation center. The story fascinated me, with its unlikely combination of flammable film and icy bedrock, of preservation by neglect, how a town had maintained its history by forgetting it. Most silent films of that era have been lost to fire or decay, but abandonment saved these ones. As for my sister, she'd heard me go on about this kind of trivia for years—I was a collector of arcane information, especially anything relating to film—and I suppose she must have been used to it. She was listening now, so quietly that it took me longer than it should have to notice something was wrong.

Her eyes were trained on a point behind my head. "Look," she said.

We saw the wolf trot out of the forest like a lost dog looking for its home. From her strange gait, one leg hobbled, we knew it was Catherine. Her grey-brown fur looked knotted and flat, her body narrow-hipped and sinewy. It was possible, we thought later, that she was searching for her pack. To me it hardly matters; her motives aren't my concern. What I remember is her graceless stagger, and how quickly she moved despite it. How when she bore down on us, so close that I could see her eyes, I couldn't tell whether she recognized us, whether the bond Robin had nurtured with her was sturdy, or significant, or the slightest bit present in her mind.

What happened next was my fault.

The wolf ran toward Robin as if to jump on her, and I pulled my sister sharply to the side, scared for both her and the baby. Robin wrestled against me—wanting to greet Catherine, I guess, or at least to see her close-up. A fit of vertigo washed over me then, the sky and earth changing places; everything solid jellied and spun. I clung to whatever I could grasp as my vision hazed, and inside my ears was the crash and roll of some invisible ocean. I think I grabbed Robin's shoulder, but it might have been her leg—that's how disoriented I was. In the push and pull between us Robin lost her balance, stumbled, and fell. The wolf kept going, running past us as if we didn't even exist.

Slowly my eyes cleared, and the ground assembled itself beneath me. Vertigo passing is like an earthquake in reverse: pieces knit themselves back together, the world unshudders and comes to rest.

Next to me, Robin moaned, a terrible, keening sound.

"Are you all right?" I said.

She didn't answer. Her face was an ashy color I'd never seen before, and she pressed a hand to her belly again, the gesture not gentle this time.

I cradled my sister's head in my lap but she seemed hardly to notice my presence, much less be eased by it. Her body was hot to my touch, her hair sticking wetly to my hand.

Then we heard the rest of the pack begin to vocalize in rolling harmonics, whether in greeting to Catherine or for some other reason. Their silvery howls rose and fell, rose and fell. I thought it was spooky, but Robin's face relaxed and she opened her eyes. What I found wild, she found a comfort, and that had always been a difference between us.

"Where's Catherine?" she said.

I told her I didn't know; the wolf had gone. My sister struggled to sit up, and I could see she was hurting, but there was no stopping her from standing. There had never been any stopping Robin from whatever she wanted to do. She got to her feet, though her knees buckled once and she had to brace herself against me as I tried and failed to coax her back to the house.

Only my sister would have ignored going into labor in order to look for a wolf. Only my sister would have asked, through the pain, "Where did she go?"

PART TWO

Childhood

I.

It seems to me now, as I look back, that my sister was never entirely tame. When we were children, Robin often disappeared for an hour, an afternoon, a day. Our mother, who was rarely home, didn't notice, but I was bothered by these absences. I nursed a passion for regularity; I craved fixed mealtimes and weekday routines. Every Wednesday I went to the pizza parlor down the block from our apartment and, using the crinkled bills our mother left scattered on the counter, bought a pizza, carried it home in a white box loose-bottomed with grease, and waited. I only did this on Wednesdays. On Tuesdays my class had library time and on Thursdays we had art. I liked the library and art, but I loved knowing what was coming next. In my mind each day wore a color—purple for library, orange for pizza, a splatter of yellow for art—that stitched the week into a rainbow, into structure and sense. Even at that age I was a collector of patterns, a magpie in search of scraps.

Our mother, Marianne, was vexed by my expectations. If I asked her when she'd be home, she wouldn't answer, finding the question unreasonable. She considered it a form of imprisonment to say where she was going or why, and as the young mother of two young children she'd already been imprisoned enough. At least that's what I think now. At the time, I thought she resented us, and contrived one reason or another to be away from us as much as she could. Which may also have been true.

Marianne was beautiful. She had long shiny black hair that she wore loose or in a flat ponytail tied at the base of her neck, and either way you could see her high pale forehead and dark brown eyes. Years later, at a museum in New York, I came across Giacometti's tall, spindly bronze sculptures of women and burst into tears, because they reminded me so much of her: thin but not fragile, flesh hard as metal, unembraceable. She didn't enjoy being touched, at least not by us. She came from a rigid Catholic family, the dual strands of Irish and French-Canadian tradition forcefully interwoven, and I suspect her father had laid a hand on her more than once when she was growing up. Her mother was equally severe. When Marianne was fifteen she began fighting with them, protesting that her older brothers were given freedoms and futures denied to her. Her parents wanted her to get married as soon as possible; that was the extent of their hopes. Instead, she left their cramped apartment near the Farine Five Roses Flour sign and moved in with a friend whose parents were more permissive. She dropped out of school and got a job at a record store, where she charmed anyone who came in for a listen. She knew every band and every album. I'll say this for Marianne, whatever her faults: she filled our home with music. She had a Magnavox turntable and a collection of albums she "borrowed" from the store, rotating the stock in her personal library, so we grew up listening to everything from Félix Leclerc to Mahler to the Rolling Stones.

It was at the record store that she met my father, Todd, who'd come to Montreal from Vermont; although the draft for the Vietnam War had ended two years earlier, he maintained conscientious objections to American warmongering. He was, according to Marianne, very handsome and not very smart. She had no pictures to show me, so I was left to conjure him based on her description: a curly-haired puppy of a boy, nineteen years old, who wore plaid shirts and a sheepskin jacket unbuttoned despite the cold. They spent most of their time together with his friends. She enjoyed this, the feeling of being apart from her own background, of breaking ties to the past without even having to leave town. When they discovered she was pregnant, Todd whooped with happiness, she told me, and I have no reason to doubt her; she never once lied to protect my feelings.

They didn't marry, because marriage was a corrupt institution of the bourgeoisie, a fading remnant of the old order, and they put my mother's last name, Brossard, on my birth certificate. Todd stayed in Montreal long enough to bestow upon me his American citizenship and a collection of rare coins he'd brought along from Vermont, thinking he could sell them to support us. They were worth less than he'd imagined and so, I gather, were we. One morning Marianne woke up to find him gone, leaving a garbled and poorly written note that she tore up in irritation and whose contents she could not, years later, remember.

I've never looked for my father. I like to think he has regrets, that sometimes he wakes at night believing someone has spoken to him, a voice he doesn't know but nonetheless recognizes; that sometimes, when he sees a woman my age, he wonders if that's what his daughter looks like, walks like. This is my right, to think about him as I please, since he's never been around to contradict me.

After he left, we were alone together. Another girl of that era, adolescent and abandoned, might have turned to her family for help, but not Marianne. Finding herself a single mother only reaffirmed her break from her background, her stalwart refusal of their judgment and values. Her parents, Cathleen and Jean-Louis, didn't even know she'd had a baby until they encountered her on Sherbrooke Street pushing me in a pram one Saturday afternoon. Marianne was wearing what she called, with the fond nostalgia she reserved for herself, "an outrageous costume": something like a flapper dress, hung with beads that shook when she moved, and platform sandals, and a feather in her hair. She'd come to think of life as performance. Calmly, she kissed them each on both cheeks. Jean-Louis sputtered wordlessly; Cathleen burst into tears. Their reaction seemed to have as much to do with her appearance as with the baby.

Marianne lifted a corner of the blanket one of her friends had crocheted for me and explained that the father was an American, that they'd named me in memory of the summer days they'd spent in La Fontaine Park when she was pregnant, listening to the sounds of birds. So it could have been worse—I might have been a cardinal or a dove—but my name infuriated Marianne's parents, as she must have known it would. The fact that in French it was the name of the Montreal football team only added to the offense.

Marianne didn't care. "That's her name," she announced on the street, "whether you like it or not."

This story was one of her favorites, and I used to beg her to tell it when she was putting me to sleep, knowing it made her tender, that she'd caress my cheek with a finger.

"Mais qu'est-ce ça veux dire, alouette?" cried her perplexed, angry father. "What kind of a name is Lark?"

2.

To keep a roof over our heads and food in our stomachs, Marianne took a number of jobs: hairdresser, waitress, coat-check girl. She was good with people and did well with tips. She was less good at showing up on time, or at being told what to do. Sometimes, when she was between jobs, we ate at soup kitchens or the homes of friends. When things got dire she'd sell her costume jewelry at a stand in the flea market, taking the money to the nearest diner, where we'd devour grilled cheese sandwiches as she filled her purse with oyster crackers and jelly packets. But she was rarely without work for long; her charm always saw her through.

After Todd left, she talked herself into a job as a secretary at a bank downtown, and it was at this position that she met Bob Johnson, of Fox Run, Minnesota, who became her husband and Robin's father.

Bob was older than my mother—at thirty years old, he seemed ancient—and the opposite of Todd. A creature of habit, he ate a seven-minute egg and a slice of buttered toast with the crusts cut off for breakfast every day. I was fascinated by how the perfect rectangle of his bread disappeared neatly between his perfect rectangular teeth. He was quite handsome, with thick, wavy brown hair and high cheekbones that my mother claimed were traceable to his Dakota Sioux ancestry. Although it was 1979 when they met, he dressed like a movie idol from the fifties, in slim-cut pants and collared shirts with sleeves rolled up to his elbows.

After they married in a small ceremony at the Palais de Justice, we moved to a tidy, well-kept apartment in Rosemount. I ought to have been happy, because my mother had, inexplicably, chosen a man whose attraction to routine was even stronger than my own. Bob liked a roast on Sundays. He liked a single glass of whiskey while he watched the evening news. He liked to think he was rescuing us from a life of poverty. He liked gratitude.

But Bob did not like me. I think my very existence troubled him, since it reminded him that my mother had had a life, sexual and otherwise, before they met. He treated me with a tight-lipped politeness that was more uncomfortable than outright hatred would have been. I did my best not to upset him. I tiptoed around the house, I put away my toys, I dressed tidily and combed my hair; but I didn't succeed in winning his love.

A child who knows she is disliked can acquire the skill of invisibility. I learned to spend as much time as I could at school, and I walked slowly there and back, making each block last as long as possible. On weekends I stole change from Bob's jacket pockets, my one delinquency, to buy tickets at the movie theatre down the street from our apartment, always sneaking from one show to the next. Many of these were films for grown-ups, and I could barely follow their plotlines, but I responded in some intuitive fashion to their rhythms, helped along by the brightly flickering images, the swell and fade of the music. I sat cross-legged in my seat, mesmerized, and nobody—it was a different era then—asked what I was doing there alone. I came to prize my invisibility, and to grasp the freedom it offered. I watched couples kissing in the dark, mothers hushing their children, an elderly woman laying her head on her companion's shoulder and falling asleep. There was more to watch than what was on the screen.

Marianne quit her job after Robin was born. Perhaps strangely, for a woman once so fixed on rebellion and independence, she didn't seem to mind not working. She and Bob both doted on my sister, who was an easy baby, fat-legged and dimpled, a happy eater who snuggled against my mother's chest and fell asleep without complaint. Marianne doted on Bob too, greeting him at the door each afternoon with a freshly made drink. I see now that she threw herself into the performance of domesticity with the same intensity she brought to every other role.

I don't know how long she would've lasted in this one. It seems unlikely that she could have endured a whole life like that, or a whole marriage. But she didn't have to try. She and Bob had been married for five years when he sat up in bed one night, white-faced, clutching his stomach. He'd apparently been suffering pain for months, but chalked it up to indigestion and stress. By the time it was diagnosed, the cancer had already spread to his lymph system, and he died two months later at the Queen Elizabeth Hospital. He ordered Marianne not to bury him in Montreal. "I want to go home to my family," he said, by which he meant Minnesota and his parents.

Marianne's grief was as impenetrable to me as her marriage had been. She seemed more nervous than sad; she smoked constantly, and her hands shook. Most nights she fell asleep in an armchair in the living room, with the television on. Bob's colleagues at the bank sent their wives over with casseroles, and they'd put the food on the kitchen counter and get drunk with Marianne, stumbling out the door hours later, trailing vapors of cigarettes and Baby Duck wine;

but after a while, they stopped coming. Marianne had been told she could go back to work at the bank, but when she applied the manager said nothing was available. Perhaps you should be at home with the children, he suggested, and Marianne spat on his desk and walked away. At least that's what she told me she did; even then I understood that her version of events was not always credible.

She found another job, at a company that imported digestive biscuits from the UK. Every week she came home with "mistakes"—boxes that had been dropped, crumbling the biscuits, or whose labels were crooked—which we ate for breakfast, lunch, and snack until the taste made me sick to my stomach. To this day I can't eat a digestive biscuit. She hired babysitters to look after me and Robin during the workday, and increasingly left us by ourselves. While Bob was in the hospital, and Marianne often there with him, I'd grown accustomed to taking care of my sister. Giving up the movies and my long walks home from school, I fed her biscuits and milk and dressed her and played with her. I taught her to sing "Au Clair de la Lune" and to somersault across the couch cushions. I decided that she belonged to me.

3.

My sister grew into a delicate, dreamy girl with Bob's high cheekbones, whether they were Sioux or not, and our mother's shiny dark hair. She had an air of looking a bit lost, even when she knew exactly where she was. People liked to give her things: she'd come home with a box of pastries from the bakery, or a wheel of cheese in a bag that someone had thrust into her hands. Since we were usually hungry, I was always glad to see these gifts. Marianne started dating again, and often didn't come home until after we were asleep. In the mornings, getting ready for work, she'd tell us where she'd been: a restaurant, a party, a night at the theatre. Her stories were tinged with glamour and malice: when she talked about people she'd met, she cut them down to size. She wanted us to know that she saw through everything.

Every so often she brought a man home for dinner, and Robin and I would comb our hair and wear dresses and set the table. Some of the men were jocular, stealing our noses and waving their thumbs in our faces; others were red-faced and tipsy, squeezing Marianne as she brushed past them to serve the lamb or beef. After eating we got ourselves ready for bed, reappearing in our pajamas with our teeth brushed for a final goodnight.

In our shared room, we whispered. Quiet and invisible elsewhere, with my sister I was full of opinions.

"That one was the worst yet," I'd tell her.

"He wasn't so bad."

"His breath smelled like Limburger."

"What's Limburger?"

"The worst-smelling cheese in the world."

"He's nicer-looking than the last one."

"That's not saying much. The last one looked like a walrus."

Robin would laugh. "He did!"

The dinners always seemed to go fine but the men never came back, and I assumed this was because of us, the burden we represented. Marianne moved from one man to the next. All her friends were getting divorced and she declared, "Finally, everyone else is catching up with me." We didn't point out that she had never, in fact, been divorced. She liked to think of herself as a pioneer.

Marianne fed and clothed us, but anything beyond that was our responsibility. If we asked for more of her attention, she might give it, or she might fly into a rage and scold us, even knocking over furniture in her anger. Once in a tantrum she gathered up all our toys in a garbage bag and threw them away. Once she stormed away from the dinner table while we were eating and we didn't see her for two days. Other times she took us in her arms and spun us around to "Superstition" or "C'est pour toi." We never knew which Marianne to expect, so we learned to expect nothing, demand nothing.

Robin's teachers praised her, cast her in plays, and sent notes home suggesting singing lessons, because her voice was so lovely. I was the better student, often placing at the top of my class, but struck silent by shyness, and throughout elementary school I don't think I ever once raised my hand. Sometimes my teacher would turn around and seem surprised I was even in the room, and when this happened I wasn't upset but gratified. I practiced the art of subtracting myself from any given situation. To do what Robin did—to sing "Greensleeves" by herself at a school assembly, for example, when she was in grade one—would have been impossible for me. I would rather have died. I was proud of Robin and not at all jealous. Years later someone asked me about our unhappy childhood, using that word, and I was startled; I'd never thought of it like that. It was strange, yes, in the sense that we mostly raised ourselves, but I wouldn't call it unhappy. My sister and I had each other, a union of separate but conjoined strengths. We were the bird sisters, Lark and Robin, one who could study, and one who could sing.

4.

When I consider the shape Robin's life took later on, the things she chose or refused, I think about the year she was seven and I was eleven. At school her teacher had mentioned Marie-Angélique Le Blanc, the eighteenth-century Wild Child of Songy, who lived in the forests of France for a decade before getting captured by villagers. Historians believe she was from the Meskwaki people of what today is Wisconsin, and that she was brought to France under mysterious circumstances by an older Canadian woman. Some believed that during her time in the forest she lived with wolves; others that she fended the wolves off with weapons she'd fashioned. After her capture, she was assimilated back into society, successfully learning to read and write, and died in Paris at the age of sixty-three.

Some combination of the elements of this story—Midwestern roots, mysterious parent, youthful years of freedom and isolation—must have spoken to my sister of herself. Fascinated with this girl, Robin took to befriending whatever wild animals she could find in our neighborhood—mostly squirrels, feral cats, the occasional dog that had breached its yard—wondering if she could live among them if the opportunity arose. She scavenged berries off bushes, nibbling them as she sat outside in a cutting wind. At home she insisted that I put her food on the floor, where she'd crouch down and eat without using her hands.

I wasn't bothered by her behavior. I was absorbed in reading a biography of Mackenzie King, the prime minister who used séances to consult with his dead mother on issues of the day. Interested in trying this myself, I lay on the floor next to my sister with the book open before me, scribbling notes about how séances could break through the slim barrier between the living and the dead. Unfortunately, the only dead person I knew was Bob, and I doubted he wanted to hear from me. Marianne would step over both of us, shaking her head, and go straight out the door.

When Robin wandered through the neighborhood befriending the animals, I sometimes went with her, less out of a desire to protect her than because I had no other friends. A few streets away was a small house that looked semi-abandoned, its paint faded and its siding streaked with grime. Sometimes we crept up to the windows and stared at the cobwebby innards. We could make out an arrangement of furniture whose use seemed ambiguous—a few scattered chairs and stools, an armchair, a high table in the center of the room. Sometimes these pieces had been moved around, but we never saw anyone inside, until one afternoon, as we were peering in the window, a witch's face appeared before us.

Her nose was round and bulbous at the tip; her eyes were pale and watery and weird; her grey hair lay in a braid that coiled around her neck and trailed down her shoulder like a pet snake. She wore dangly earrings with dusty-looking rhinestones and a long skirt with ruffles that were tearing loose in spots. She looked like she'd gotten dressed for a fancy party decades before and never changed.

She smiled at us and curled a finger, beckoning us inside.

She was, it turned out, not a witch, but a piano teacher named Mrs. Gasparian. She led us into a side room that featured a piano, a rug, and a wilted plant. We'd been told at school to be wary of strangers, but Mrs. Gasparian was as threatless as a person could be. She sat with her legs crossed beneath her long skirt, listening and nodding as we gave her our names. Then she offered us some digestive biscuits, which we refused.

Mrs. Gasparian asked a lot of questions, none of them personal. She wanted to know what we'd learned at school that day, what books we liked, what we thought of the painting on the far wall, and whether we'd rather visit Paris or London. In other words she spoke to us as if we were adults, not children, and this was thrilling. Her low, husky voice was very pleasant to listen to, and one of her eyelids drooped, which made her look a bit ill but also a bit mischievous, as if she were permanently winking.

In a rare moment of extroversion I was telling Mrs. Gasparian about one of my favorite films, *Chitty Chitty Bang Bang,* elaborating its plot intricacies in detail, when Robin slipped off her chair and went to investigate the piano. She plinked around on the high notes and began to sing along, matching the notes with her voice. While still talking, I saw Mrs. Gasparian's face change, the attention leaving her expression even as she nodded and kept her eyes fixed on me. At last I fell silent, and we both watched Robin pressing the keys with her index finger and mirroring the melody with her voice, completely absorbed in what she was doing. It felt like eavesdropping on a private conversation, something very intimate, almost grossly so, and it made me uncomfortable, though I couldn't have said why. I shifted in my chair.

Robin turned around. "What?" she said.

"Nothing, dear," Mrs. Gasparian said. "Keep going."

But Robin could tell that I wasn't happy, and she cocked her head to the side. We had between us a language of signs and gestures, and this one meant *Let's go*.

Soon Robin and I were haunting Mrs. Gasparian's house. She never asked to speak to our mother and didn't seem to care about payment for the lessons she began giving my sister. She told Robin to come over as often as she wanted, to practice, and I often went along. She had a grey cat named Marcel who was grotesquely fat and rarely moved, although he must have gotten around somehow because cat hair feathered the chairs and clustered beneath the furniture in dense, silky drifts. There didn't seem to be a Mr. Gasparian, and she never spoke of her past, at least not that part of it. We heard about a concert she'd been to as a girl, when a Liszt sonata had moved her to tears; we heard that Kafka was the great poet of loneliness, and that cold weather made her crave a particular kind of soup whose name I can no longer remember. She was full of reminiscences that meant nothing to us, and yet we were riveted by them. I think this had to do with her air of conviction, her assumption that we under-stood the importance of culture, and the exoticism of her clothes and hair. Like Marianne, she didn't care what anybody else thought of her, but unlike Marianne, she had time for us and was always home. Though focused on my sister, she'd also lay out books for me in the living room, or old wall calendars she'd kept because she liked the pictures, and I'd sit on the floor there and occupy myself. Sometimes I returned to my old habit of going to the movies, but just as often I preferred to be in the living room while Robin and Mrs. Gasparian played and murmured. This was my ideal situation, to be present and listening in one room while the action happened in the next, and during those long dusty hours I was happier than I'd ever been.

5.

Mrs. Gasparian told us that every pianist must learn to perform. Robin had been taking lessons for over a year, and it was time for her first recital.

"Perhaps you will invite your parents to come," Mrs. Gasparian said gently, writing the date and time down on a notecard in curly, old-fashioned penmanship. Robin and I glanced at each other nervously. We were both thinking, I was sure, about something that had happened earlier that year, when I won an award at school; it was part of a provincial math contest in which all students were required to participate. The results were announced at assembly, and those with the highest marks were asked to walk onstage to receive certificates. Not only did I have the top score in our school, I'd placed fairly high in the entire province. When I heard the math teacher say "Lark Brossard," I shut my eyes in terror and kept them closed until Vivian Hum, who was sitting next to me, pushed me hard and hissed, "Go." My legs shook as I climbed the stairs and stood in front of everyone.

"Well done, Lark," the math teacher said, and gave me the certificate; my hand trembled so badly that I dropped it, and it fluttered down below, making everyone laugh. I ran offstage, not realizing I was supposed to shake the teacher's hand, so that she was left there with her arm outstretched, making everyone laugh again. I ran out of the gymnasium and into the girls' washroom, where I locked myself in a stall. Vivian Hum, who would've been my friend if I hadn't been too shy to allow it, found me there after assembly and handed me the crumpled certificate, which she'd picked up off the floor.

I would never have mentioned the award to our mother, but

Robin was so proud of me that she told Marianne the next morning, when we were drinking our milk and Marianne her tea. "Look," she said, holding the certificate out. "Lark is the smartest girl in school."

Marianne blew on her tea. We hadn't seen her the night before, and this morning she was wearing her bathrobe, which was usually a good sign; it meant she'd enjoyed herself, and wanted to luxuriate in the feeling. She glanced at the paper, then at Robin, as if noticing her for the first time in ages. "Your hair is a disaster," she said. "Where's your brush?"

Robin said, "They made a presentation onstage and everything."

"I can't even look at this bird's nest. Go get your brush. Now!"

It never did any good to argue with Marianne. Some nights, we woke from dream-deep sleep to find her next to one of us in bed, stroking our hair, nuzzling our temples. But she wouldn't be forced into anything, even praise. She gave affection when she wanted to, not on command.

So Robin and I decided that inviting her to the piano recital—especially since we'd never mentioned Mrs. Gasparian in the first place—wouldn't go well.

On a cold Saturday afternoon in April we slipped out of the apartment, wearing ski jackets over our dresses and our Kodiak boots. We spent some time at the pharmacy, where I shoplifted a lip gloss for Robin, and then lingered in the little weedy park next to the dépanneur. Robin was unusually quiet. At night I could hear her fingers rustling across the bedspread as she rehearsed a piece in her mind, and she was doing the same thing now, her hands twitching lightly on her jacket as if flicking away one bug after another.

By the time we arrived at Mrs. Gasparian's we were windswept, cheeks red, hair in knots. If she was surprised to see us unaccompanied, she didn't show it.

"Welcome, my dears," she said. "Would you like something to drink before we start?" She gave us each a mug of weak tea with a lot of milk and sugar, and we stood in the corner, warming our hands. The piano had been rolled into the living room, and Mrs. Gasparian's assorted chairs lined up in front of it. Marcel the cat was seated in an armchair, licking himself with brazen exhibitionism. Next to the piano, Mrs. Gasparian stood chatting with a thin, bearded man wearing too-tight corduroys and a sweater vest over a collared shirt. There was also a stout middle-aged lady with curly hair and a younger woman wearing red lipstick and a fancy black dress. We were the only children.

Mrs. Gasparian clapped her hands in welcome, then invited the younger woman to play first. She clicked forward in high heels and played what seemed to me an impossibly complex piece, flowing and moody, and her hair, which was pulled back in a high ponytail, swished back and forth wildly. When she finished, she pulled the end of her ponytail toward her chest, shyly, and began picking at the hairs while the rest of us applauded.

The stout lady followed, a beginner soldiering through a parade march. Mrs. Gasparian watched with an expression of benign neutrality, and then we all clapped again, the stout lady red-faced with relief.

Robin was next. Though I'd been present for most of her lessons, I hadn't paid much attention and knew nothing about music; I'd taken her progress for granted. It was only when I saw the thin bearded man stiffen, and the young lady scowl in jealousy, and Mrs. Gasparian break into a smile, that I understood something about my sister. She played a piece divided into several small sections—a theme and variations, I can guess now—and I imagine Mrs. Gasparian chose it for the range it offered: one section romantic, one brooding, one violent, one pretty and spring-like. Robin frowned at the piano while she played, as if commanding it to behave. Her performance held the same private quality as it had that first day; again I felt like I'd stumbled into some intimate conversation, as if she were sitting there naked and exposed, and I flushed with an emotion that I couldn't define. When she finished, the applause was slow and bemused. The bearded man whispered something to the young woman, raising his eyebrows. Robin returned to the chair beside me, not looking at anyone; her eyes were still elsewhere.

"I made a mistake," she whispered. "In the adagio."

"No one could tell," I said.

"Mrs. Gasparian could," she said unhappily, her mouth pursed.

After Robin, Mrs. Gasparian stood again. "Our final performer, Leo, has a special piece planned." The bearded man stood, bowed, and sat down on the bench, but did not play. I looked around, trying to understand what was happening. Everyone was still, listening thoughtfully. Robin was preoccupied, going over her mistake. At last he stood again, bowed again, and returned to his armchair. Mrs. Gasparian led us in a round of confused applause, then invited us to join her for cake that she'd baked herself.

Almost no one spoke to us afterward. The others gathered in clusters, making small talk, acknowledging Robin only in sidelong glances. We didn't think much of it; being ignored by adults was normal to us; it didn't occur to us that her talent was outlandish and perhaps even intimidating. The bearded man explained his piece to everyone. "It's about *silence,*" he said. "Didn't it make you feel the room?"

"Sort of," said the young woman with the ponytail. "It was kind of uncomfortable."

"Exactly," said the bearded man.

Only the stout middle-aged lady came over to us, squeezing both of our hands. "Your sister is something else," she said to me ambiguously. "I'm so embarrassed."

Mrs. Gasparian brought us each a slice of chocolate cake on a plate. When I cut into mine, I saw it was downy with cat hair. I ate it anyway.

6.

When I was fourteen and Robin was ten, Marianne got a job selling perfume to department stores. She began traveling for work, and sometimes she was gone for days at a stretch. While she was away, we looked after ourselves. In the mornings I packed Robin's lunch and braided her hair and walked her to her bus stop—we were at different schools now. In the evenings I signed Marianne's name on notes and made Kraft Dinner or grilled cheese sandwiches. Robin set the table and washed the dishes. Then we listened to Marianne's records or watched TV until bleary-eyed, with no one to tell us it was bedtime. We missed Marianne but we were more relaxed in her absence, less afraid of doing or saying anything that might tip her mood into ugliness. When she came home, she'd bring us tube samples of perfume taped to little cards, and we'd douse ourselves until she held her nose and said, "Enough, you fiends."

At night Robin and I lay in bed and talked, mostly gossiping about Marianne. We didn't believe she was always at work when she went away. Sometimes she came home with a mysterious smile on her face, or made us hot chocolate with marshmallows for breakfast, both of which we took as signs she'd been up to something.

"I think she has a boyfriend now," I said.

"You mean that man who called? He was selling vacuum cleaners."

"That's what he said he wanted."

"Maybe he really *was* selling them."

"Maybe she really wanted his vacuum cleaner," I said.

Robin laughed. She was the only person I could make laugh. I told her stories about people at school: how the science teacher and the custodian were having an affair they thought was secret but wasn't; how I'd seen the teacher emerging from the supply closet, straightening her skirt. Robin didn't talk much about her life at school. She never did very well there, because she was like Marianne, paying attention only when she felt like it, learning only what she wanted to, not liking being told what to do. She had difficulty concentrating except when it came to music. And perhaps just as importantly, she didn't mind being scolded; didn't care when her report cards noted that she could certainly do better if she tried harder. She lacked the fear that motivated me constantly, whether in the classroom, on the bus, or at home: I was terrified of being discovered and chastised by some nameless authority. I felt guilty of a crime I hadn't committed yet, and so I constantly atoned. Once another girl stepped on my foot in the hallway at school, and I said sorry. She grimaced. "What are you sorry for? Being born?"

7.

Marianne did have a new boyfriend, a Swiss businessman named Hervé whom she'd met on one of her business trips. At a department store where she was calling on her account, he was buying shoes that cost more than she made in a month. "They were so beautiful," she said reverently, as though it were the shoes she'd fallen for, not the man. In the picture she showed us, his blond hair cantilevered out from his forehead in a commanding ledge, beneath which protruded an equally monumental jawline; he seemed built of powerful structures, tightly girded and trussed.

The two of them met in Toronto for romantic weekends, Marianne returning flushed and languorous, often wearing some new piece of jewelry that she'd turn around and sell. She was in love, but she still believed in cold, hard cash. During these years of their affair, she was almost always happy, and the mood in our apartment lightened. In the evenings we'd watch movies together—*Pretty Woman, The Bodyguard.* We never met Hervé, which was fine with us. We didn't miss the awkward dinners of our childhood, or the obligation of performing for Marianne's suitors.

Robin finally found the courage to tell her about the piano, only because Mrs. Gasparian said that she must look for another teacher, one who specialized in advanced pupils. "You need more training than I can provide," she decreed. She recommended someone, and insisted on speaking with Marianne. On a rainy afternoon all three of us went over to her house. Robin played a piece she was learning, stumbling a bit, which rarely happened. I could see how uncomfortable she was at this meeting of worlds. When she finished, Marianne and Mrs. Gasparian drank coffee in the kitchen, whispering for a while, and then Marianne returned to the living room and picked up her purse. She narrowed her eyes at Robin and said, "If it'll keep you out of trouble, I suppose it's fine. Better this than boys."

So Robin took the bus twice a week to lessons downtown, using Mrs. Gasparian's piano for practice in between. I spent my time studying and did extra work: math competitions, essay contests, science projects. I needed something to fill the hours while Robin and Marianne were gone. One day my history teacher dropped a flyer on my desk for an American standardized test to be held at school the following month. "This could be good practice," he said, not specifying for what. I registered, paying for it with essay contest prize money, and took it without thinking much about it. When the scores arrived in the mail, I didn't even look at them. But I must have done well, because glossy brochures for American colleges began arriving at the apartment. In the pictures, girls in wool sweaters and corduroy skirts walked beneath brilliant autumn trees, while boys in lab coats measured fluids into beakers, their faces intent. Fascinated by these catalogues, I spent hours looking at them, stuffing them beneath my pillow when Robin or Marianne came in.

A letter came from a small school outside Boston, Worthen College, suggesting I might qualify for a scholarship. With my history teacher's help, I filled out an application and sent it off. I'd never talked with Marianne about what my life after high school would be like; I don't know if she ever thought about it. She'd never finished high school herself. Anyway, she was busy with her work and her friends and her trips. When I heard her talking on the phone, she said things like, "At last the girls can look after themselves a bit more, I'm finding myself again," which I repeated to Robin in a mocking whisper while we lay in bed at night. I thought Marianne was selfish and vain and immature. It didn't occur to me that perhaps she was immature because she'd missed out on her own youth; when I was seventeen and spending my nights poring over college brochures, she was only thirty-five years old.

8.

When a manila envelope came from Worthen, including a letter that offered a full financial aid package, I wrote back straightaway to accept, forging Marianne's signature with a confidence borne of years of practice. It's funny how easy it all was. These days college applications seem to take months to complete, with great expense and stress; but in 1993 the process must have been more casual, or perhaps Worthen was just so obscure that nobody was clamoring to get in. In my memory, anyway, a kind of magic took place: a portal appeared, and I slipped through it, simple as that.

I waited until late spring to tell Marianne I was leaving home. She'd cut her hair very short and tufted it into spikes, shiny with hairspray. She ran her hands through it, like a bird adjusting her plumage, and said, "How will you pay for it?"

"They said I don't have to pay."

"What, nothing?"

"Nothing."

She didn't believe me, I could tell, but couldn't come up with a reason why.

"So that's it, then? You're just leaving."

She didn't ask what I was going to study, or what I wanted to do with my life—questions that would never have occurred to her. I could tell she was angry about my rebellion, but she was too used to being the rebellious child herself; she had no words to voice her current position, and was all the more angry at me for putting her in it. At last she threw her hands up in exasperation.

"You and your sister," she concluded. "You just do whatever you want, don't you?"

That evening, in the dark, I told Robin. Over the past few months, I'd shared my obsession with her—the college brochures, my dreams of strolling along cobbled walks, kicking autumn leaves—but for her this was all abstract; she was thirteen, and in her entire life we'd never spent a night apart, had never even slept in different rooms. I myself could hardly believe I was leaving. When I explained that night, whispering, Robin said nothing. The room was silent—or, not silent, but full of quiet terrible noises: the sound of our breathing, the rustle of sheets, the hum of cars outside. It made me remember the piece we'd heard at Robin's first recital, the four minutes of silence, and how awful it could be to listen to a quiet room.

My sister left her bed and padded over to mine, crawled in beside me, and rested her cheek on my shoulder, her tears trickling down my arm. "I didn't think you would really go," she said.

I flushed with guilt. "I'll be back," I told her. "And you can come visit."

"That's not the same," she said.

I put my arms around her and inhaled her familiar scent, Finesse shampoo and sweat and something else that was unidentifiable but particular to my sister, the smell of her skin. "You'll be fine. You'll play piano, you have your friends, you won't even have time to miss me."

"I'll have time," she said.

She burrowed even closer, her hair tickling my chin and neck. I stroked her back, and we both shuddered with crying.

9.

I left for the US on a Greyhound bus, carrying only a backpack puffy with clothes. I didn't realize until I arrived and saw the other students that I was supposed to have brought creature comforts: blankets, a bathrobe, flip-flops, the larger apparatus of a self. A dorm administrator took pity and brought me hand-me-downs from her own daughter, who'd recently graduated, so I soon had a quilt with flowers on it, a shower caddy, and a small desk lamp.

"You should've come early," she said. "We have a special orientation for the international students. To help you adjust to American culture and expectations."

"Oh," I said.

"Don't worry," she said, squeezing my hand, then abruptly letting go as if she'd done something wrong. "It'll be fine."

I wasn't worried. I loved the tiny, forested campus, nestled inexplicably on a hillside behind an industrial park. From my dorm room on the fifth floor I could look down on a mid-sized factory with two smokestacks and a horn that blew every weekday at noon and six. Worthen had once been a teacher's college for women, and it retained an air of modest, slightly shabby, scholarly ambition. Students walked along pathways beneath wrought-iron lamp posts, just as they'd done in the brochures. The two original buildings were lovely Victorians, while the rest—including my dorm—were made of wood and concrete blocks, and smelled of mildew. I didn't mind. I walked through the early weeks of my classes in a kind of trance, clutching my books to my chest as if someone might try to steal them. But no one would steal anything at Worthen; it was a place where everyone smiled at you and then quickly averted their eyes so as not to cause alarm. The school was full of mild-mannered introverts, male and female, who blushed when they raised their hands. It was uncanny the extent to which I felt, for the first time, at home.

My roommate was a girl from Framingham named Helen, who ran track and planned to study zoology. She wanted to go to Africa and save the gorillas, like Jane Goodall, whose picture she taped to the wall above her bed. When she went out for practice runs she wore headphones and listened to gorilla sounds, hoping to become fluent in gorilla communication. It was how Jane had learned, by osmosis. "She crouched and observed," Helen told me. "She didn't even have a formal scientific education at first." She had Jane Good-all's biography memorized.

I liked her, though it was hard to get used to sleeping next to anyone but my sister, and Helen snored in delicate bursts, like tiny thunderstorms rolling past. And she soon drifted into a circle of athletes who met for frosty six a.m. runs and ate egg-white omelettes for breakfast; we had little in common except a willingness not to disturb each other.

Most of my classes had been chosen for me in advance, but I liked them all and didn't find them difficult; the extra work I'd done in high school served me well. I loved the food in the cafeteria, and when other students complained about it, or talked about missing home cooking, I didn't know what they meant. "You eat like a stray cat," a boy once said to me, and he was probably right: the abundance struck me as too good to be true, and I shoveled the food down enthusiastically. His remark reminded me of Robin, how she had pretended to be an animal when she was a child, and I missed her with an ache that flared suddenly and didn't diminish so much as recede, with willed effort, to a back alley of my mind.

I joined the international students' association, and once a week we ate pizza in the homes of different professors who all asked whether we needed any explanation of American customs. We didn't; we just liked the pizza.

On Sunday afternoons I wrote letters to Robin and—nominally—Marianne, in which I tempered my happiness, not wanting to gloat or sound selfish. In return I received postcards from Robin, mostly dumb tourist ones she stole from the dépanneur, showing the cross on Mount Royal or a beaver wearing a Mountie hat, smiling with buck teeth. She said Brahms was giving her headaches and that she'd finally met Hervé. I felt a stab of betrayal: Why had Marianne brought him home now? Was I the only daughter of whom she was ashamed?

I tried not to think about it. I was studying calculus, American literature, and European history. I was equally interested in everything and had no idea what I would major in. I was a hoarder, a collector of facts that I stored in my brain for later use, not knowing what this use might be. In the Netherlands, I learned, 1672 was known as *rampjaar,* the "disaster year," because the Dutch were attacked by England, France, Münster, and Cologne. The Dutch had a saying about themselves in that year: the whole country was *radeloos, redeloos en reddeloos*—desperate, irrational, and past recovery. I loved this idiom, the silly-sounding Dutch words that seemed to balloon, lightly, above the weight of disaster, and I wrote about it to Robin. She wrote back on a postcard of the Quebec flag. *Mrs. Gasparian died. She was in the hospital and I didn't even know.*

I called home as soon as I got the postcard, but no one answered for hours. Finally Robin picked up at ten p.m., sounding forlorn.

"Should I come home? Are you okay?"

I could hear her crying, then a long, mucusy sniffle. "No, I'm all right," she said.

Silence between us on the line, but a known one. The rhythm of my sister's breath.

"She was so nice," I said.

"She was really nice."

"Did she still have that cat? Marcel?"

"No," Robin said. "The cat died a while ago."

"Oh," I said.

"I hadn't seen her in months. I've been practicing at my other teacher's house because the piano is better. She never told me she was sick."

"She probably didn't want you to worry."

"The last time I saw her she said I needed to read Proust. That it would help my playing. I was like, what? I just shrugged and ignored her."

"She loved you," I said.

"Don't you think I know that?" my sister said, her voice squeaking with distress.

IO.

I regret that I didn't take the bus home for the funeral. But I had my first exams coming up, and I had only just integrated myself into college life; I was worried that if I left it, the place might seal up against me and not let me back in. Robin wrote me a postcard about the service later. She said Mrs. Gasparian's students were there—she had no family—and that Robin had played a sonata, and then everyone drank coffee and ate poppy seed cake.

At the edge of the Worthen campus, up the steep side of a hill, was a stand of large trees that students used at night for drug trips or sex. During the day it was empty, and I often took refuge there when I needed time alone. I'd sit on a fallen log and listen to the uneasy swish of branches, the occasional bell of the campus chapel, and the trucks grinding in the industrial park below. On the morning after I spoke to Robin about Mrs. Gasparian, I was startled by a man who entered the woods walking fast and panting hard, punctuating every step by stabbing a walking stick into the forest floor. Crashing along the path, his eyes on the ground, he didn't see me until he almost sat down on my lap.

"Oh!" he said. "I usually sit here."

I stood up, flustered and a little annoyed. "I usually sit here too," I said.

He was wearing khaki shorts, though the weather was cold, and a heavy knit sweater flecked with pine needles and bits of leaves, as if he'd been sleeping outside. He was round and stout, with a reddish beard, and he could have been twenty or forty or anywhere in between. His legs were furry with light orange hair, and I found myself staring at them, wanting to run my hands over them; it was less a sexual attraction than whatever impulse leads a person to stroke an animal's fur.

"I've seen you before," he said, his voice changing. "You live in Marston, right? Your roommate is the Running Girl."

"My roommate is Helen," I said stiffly. "She's on the track team."

"We just call her the Running Girl, because she always jogs past our window in her sweats. We've never seen her in normal clothes."

"She wears them," I said, compelled to defend her. I could sense him staring at me, and it made me more self-conscious than I'd felt since arriving at Worthen. I focused lower down, on his feet, which were encased in old-fashioned leather boots. He was outfitted as if for a days-long hike, though our campus was steps away.

"We call you Looks Down at the Ground," he said cheerfully. "You never make eye contact with anybody."

"Yes, I do," I said, meeting his eyes, which were green and not as confrontational as I'd imagined. Somehow this made me even more uncomfortable, and I sought safety in his shoes again. He leaned against his walking stick and laughed at me—for confirming the nickname, I suppose.

"I'm Gordon," he said.

"Are you Canadian?"

"No! I'm from Jamaica Plain. Why, are you?"

"Yes."

"Do you have a lot of Gordons in Canada?"

"Yes," I said. "There were three in my graduating class. We called them Big Gordon, Little Gordon, and one was just Gord."

"Huh," he said, uninterested in this trivia. "My parents are ridiculous Anglophiles. They drink pots of tea all day long and say WC instead of bathroom. God knows why. Their people are from Rhode Island, probably expelled by the very royalty they now worship."

"Expelled for what?"

"Being thugs," he said airily. "In an early-eighteenth-century kind of way."

I would have liked to hear more about this, but his attention wandered. He gestured toward the trail with his stick and began walking, and I followed him. As he huffed and puffed up the hill—he was not fit—he explained that he was a senior at Worthen, studying history, and he was getting in shape because after graduation he planned to spend six months hiking the Appalachian Trail. "You know, going to the woods to live deliberately and all that jazz," he said, summarizing the jazz with a wave of his hand. He seemed a long way off being able to accomplish a six-month hike, because we stopped every couple minutes for him to catch his breath. Part of the problem, though, was that he was talking so much. Another person might have relieved him of the conversational burden, but it didn't occur to me. I stopped and paused with him and waited for him to continue. He told me about the thesis he was writing about the history of religious violence in the nineteenth century—"People always talk about the separation of church and state," he said, "but this is a country founded by religious extremists and that informs our national character as much as anything"—and about walks he used to take as a child with his dog Coconut, giving each subject equal weight and attention. He talked about music he liked and why David Bowie was better than Bob Dylan ("there's the same degree of musicianship but more intellectually rigorous, you know what I mean?"—I did not) and about how hip-hop was the metaphysical poetry of our time. When, half an hour later, we reached the far end of the forest, we turned around and walked back to campus together as if this had been our plan all along.

In front of my dorm, he asked me if I'd like to have dinner that night, and I said yes, assuming he meant in the cafeteria. But when I came outside at six he was wearing khaki pants, a blue collared shirt, and a corduroy blazer, and we walked ten minutes to a Chinese restaurant in a strip mall on the other side of the industrial park. In contrast to the morning, he spoke little, and silence gaped between us. When we sat down, a waiter brought us a pot of tea, and we each guzzled three or four tiny cups of it, as if slaking desperate thirst.

"Your parents would like this, I guess," I said.

"What? Chinese food?"

"The tea," I said. "You said they drink a lot of it."

"Oh right. I can't believe you remember that. You're a good listener."

"It was only this morning," I said.

He fidgeted in his dress-up clothes like a kid at a wedding. "So, Lark," he said. "Lark, Lark, Lark. Did your parents name you for a joke?"

"What?" I said.

"I don't mean, did they name you that to tease you. I mean, a *lark* can be a bird or it can be an amusing escapade. Are you an amusing escapade?"

"I don't think so," I said. I was fidgeting myself; due to nerves and copious tea drinking I needed to visit the washroom but was too shy to excuse myself from the table before we had even ordered. I was afraid of how it might look. I had no experience with boys, and Gordon, three years my senior, seemed a man.

"So your parents were neither ornithologists nor British roust-abouts," he said.

"Not really," I said.

He nodded, the teacup miniscule in his large hands. They were furry too, I noticed. It was pleasant, his hairiness; once again I imagined stroking them. He reminded me of an orangutan, and I almost told him so, before realizing this might not be received as a compliment.

"My sister's name is Robin," I told him, "so that probably tips the scales toward bird-loving." Robin had in fact been a compromise between Marianne and Bob, who wanted to call her Roberta after himself, a name that my mother declared was only suited for ugly girls.

"Lark and Robin, are you serious?" he said. "Who are your brothers, Duck and Goose? Sorry, that was a stupid joke."

"It was pretty dumb," I agreed.

"Man, you don't make things easy, you know that, Looks Down at the Ground?"

I glanced at him. His face was flushed with anger, or so I thought, but the tone was closer to admiration. Warming to the subject of birds, he told me how a German man brought European starlings to the US because he wanted to introduce to North America every bird mentioned in the plays of Shakespeare. Now starlings outnumbered and outcompeted many native birds; they even stole grain from dairy farms, reducing milk production. "They're invasive pests," he said, folding his palms together on the table. "And that's why literature is dangerous."

"I see," I said. I was happy to meet someone whose enthusiasm for stray bits of information matched my own: another collector, another magpie.

He was more relaxed now, and his opinions on Shakespeare ("the history plays are so much better than romantic schlock like *Romeo and Juliet,* but that's not what goes over in Peoria") and Unitarianism ("I mean, is it even religion, or is it community theatre?") kept us going through egg rolls and chicken fried rice. After dinner, we walked slowly back to campus, along the industrial park. A pack of cyclists passed us, a pizza-delivery car. There was no sidewalk and we kept jostling elbows and shoulders. On campus, I could see other students heading to and from the library and evening classes.

Gordon said, "My roommate is performing at this concert thing on Friday night. His band is frankly terrible, it's supposed to be Buddhist synth-pop, whatever that is, but I should go. To support him."

"I see," I said. I thought it was just more information.

"It's at eight," he said, persisting.

"Sounds interesting."

At the entrance to my dorm he lunged forward and kissed me, wetly, on my cheek; having turned toward him too early, I forced him to make contact just below my ear, and I felt the trail of his saliva there.

"I'll see you?" he said, and I said, "Yes."

It took a conversation with Helen for me to interpret everything that had happened, as she patiently listened to my account of the evening and made sense of it for me. I didn't tell her that she was known to Gordon and his friends as the Running Girl, but she knew who he was as soon as I described him. "He's that burly guy," she said, which was so appropriate that I thought of him that way for weeks afterward. *The burly guy is kissing me,* I would think. *The burly guy is in my bed.* "He lives with skinny Mike, the bass player for Smiling Avatar." This, I guessed, was the Buddhist synth-pop band. I waited for Helen to say more about either of them, passing judgment, but she was too sensitive to do so.

"Are you into him?" she asked instead.

I'd never been into anybody. "I'm not sure," I told her.

"I know the feeling," she said dryly, then went out for a run.

On Friday she agreed to go to the concert with me. It was in the basement of the college chapel, which, being godless, I'd never visited before. We entered a dark, cramped hallway and then filed downstairs into a surprisingly large room. At the far end, the band was tuning up, and continued to do so for at least half an hour. Near us, people were helping themselves to punch from a bowl into which Gordon, *the burly guy,* was pouring a bottle of Everclear. We joined the queue, and Gordon smiled widely when he saw us.

Since coming to school I hadn't drunk much, less out of prudence than pre-emptive embarrassment; I didn't know how to drink or how to behave while doing it. Everyone else, even the bookish introverts, seemed to know how to banter and flirt, how to rehash their adventures the next morning while moaning about their hangovers. It was mysterious to me. But now I gulped down half a cup of punch that tasted angrily medicinal. Gordon was busy with other customers, so I followed Helen around as she chatted with people from our dorm or her classes. I envied her ease. As she spoke, nodding and laughing, she kept lifting her long hair into a ponytail, smoothing it, letting it go, over and over.

"You keep staring at her like that and I'm going to be jealous," said a voice in my ear. I turned to see Gordon with two cups in his hands. He held one out to me and went on, "Do you think there's any slower process than the tuning of a college band? I've seen elephants gestate babies in less time than this."

"Almost two years," I said.

"Exactly," he said. "I knew I liked you."

I smiled at him, waiting for him to segue into another of his monologues, but instead he rattled off a series of questions—what was my major going to be, how were my classes—as if completing a questionnaire.

"Mike says I talk too much," he confessed after a few of my one-sentence responses. "He says girls like it when you ask questions."

I was touched that he was concerned about what I'd like. "I'm happier when other people talk."

"Well, I can't shut up, so that works out perfectly," he said.

At last the band began to play, jangling music with no lyrics and strummed chords that, for all the preparations, sounded out of tune. Gordon kept muttering, "Christ, this is terrible." He circled his arm around my waist, and after a while I realized he was slowly edging me across the room. By the third song we were in the stairwell, my back against the wall, his palms braced on either side. I felt trapped and contained, as if in a cozy coffin.

"Your eyes look bloodshot," he said. "Are you stoned? Which, it's fine if you are."

"No," I said. "A little drunk, I think."

"Too drunk to be a consenting adult?"

I considered. "No."

His ample stomach pressed against me, an insistent pillow. If I fell down, his weight would prop me up.

"So are you consenting?"

"Yes," I said. Then came a hairy flurry of lips and chin against mine. Around my ears he made little snorting sounds, like a pig seeking a truffle. Or how I imagined a pig would seek a truffle. I was enjoying myself enormously. I didn't have to worry about not knowing what to do. His certainty, I thought, would protect us both.

II.

Gordon and I saw each other nearly every day after that, coordinating our schedules with our roommates, so we could be alone in his dorm bed or mine. Sometimes we borrowed a car from his friend Mike and explored local trails. Although he always talked about how busy he was and how much pressure he was under, there seemed to be plenty of time in the days for hiking, talking, and sex. Many of our dates had a scholarly cast. We met in the library to study side by side, reading each other's papers, with Gordon scrawling all over mine in large blue exclamations. *EXPAND THIS THOUGHT!! WHERE IS YOUR SUPPORT FOR THIS ARGUMENT???* Gordon was my first exposure to a certain type of intellectual male—brashly confident, endlessly opinionated—and I was too young to see him as a type at all. I thought his genius was unique. I wrote to please him as much as my professors, and fortunately for me their standards weren't at odds. My grades were high, and so was my confidence; I began speaking up in class and sometimes lingering afterward to continue talking with one or two others. It's hard to explain how much this meant to me, how giddying it was: the sensation of tasting food after years of hunger, of eating freely and knowing there would be more.

I was happy; I was also busy. My scholarship covered room, board, and tuition, but I hadn't understood that a student's life might include further expenses. I needed money for books, laundry, snacks, and contributions to the punch fund at parties. Having told Marianne when I left that everything would be covered, I refused to ask for help, and instead found a job in the college's computer lab, in the basement of the student union building. It was 1994, and although some students at Worthen owned computers, I couldn't afford one, so I outlined my papers longhand, on yellow legal pads, then typed them at the lab, squinting at my own handwriting. One evening while I was working, the attendant there—so far as I could tell, his only duty was to sit at a desk by the front and help people when the printer jammed—opened a bottle of Coke that he must have been carrying around for a while because it sprayed wildly, covering his keyboard with brown foam.

"Shit, shit, shit," he said. "Richard's going to *kill me.*" He made a few half-hearted stabs at mopping up the Coke, then gathered up his stuff and left, the desk still puddled with liquid. I wasn't the neatest person, but I'd always found the lab's quiet sterility soothing and hated to see it disturbed. I went to the washroom for some paper towels and cleaned up the mess, then returned to my work.

A few days later, I went back to finish another assignment, and there was no student at the front. Instead, a very tall man who barely fit at the desk glanced at me, then glanced again. He had big, pale, watery blue eyes made even bigger by thick-lensed glasses, and he moved and spoke slowly, with a strangely weightless grace, like an underwater mammal.

"You're the one who cleaned up after Basu," he said. I nodded, not sure if Basu was in trouble.

"Do you want his job?"

I remembered what the boy had said, how scared he'd seemed of Richard, and hesitated. "Did you fire him?"

"Did I what? No, he quit. Cracked under the pressure of this intensive position."

I wasn't sure if this was meant as a joke, but it absolutely was. The work, if you could call it that, was spectacularly easy; there was almost nothing to do. I loved the lab, starting with the contrast between the student union's old-fashioned brick exterior, with its gingerbread molding and brass door fixtures, and the cool white modernity of the lab in the basement. There were no windows, and all the light was fluorescent. Although Richard was a hulk of a man, well over six feet tall and not thin, his stature seemed to embarrass him, and he did everything he could to diminish it. I sat at the front desk, and his office was in the back of the room. When he needed to talk to me he'd stand a few feet away, so as not to overwhelm me, and speak so softly that I often had to ask him to repeat himself. Even the second time I wasn't always sure what he'd said.

Sometimes Richard and I chatted, him telling me about his weekend—he and his wife were Renaissance fair people, though you'd never have guessed it from his workweek khakis and collared shirts—but most of the time I was alone. When the phone rang, which it rarely did, it was my job to answer it, and I'd often have to clear my throat, because it had been hours since I'd said a word.

I finished the fall semester in a haze of intellectual and sexual satisfaction. When I arrived home for the holidays, I felt like a stranger there. My sister and mother had grown closer in my absence, with shared jokes and frames of reference from which I was excluded. Robin seemed more anxious to please Marianne than she'd ever been before, fixing her attention on our mother in a way I didn't remember her doing in the past, and I wondered if this was to punish me for having left. Neither of them was interested in my stories about Worthen, and I often found myself starting an anecdote only to abandon it halfway. The style of speaking I'd picked up at school, a name-dropping banter that relied on the listener's familiarity, real or pretended, with figures like Foucault or John Stuart Mill, confused them, and they kept saying things like "I don't know him" or "Who's he when he's at home?" I retreated into my silence, watching them from the sofa while they prepared dinner, missing them while they were right in front of me.

The only times I felt at ease were at night, with Robin, in our room. In the darkness, we reverted to our old selves, whispering gossip. Things were going well between Marianne and her boyfriend; Robin thought they might get married. He was very refined, Robin said. "He has his shirts handmade in Italy. It's called *bespoke*. He wants to have some dresses made for me next time he's in Milan."

Like me, Robin mostly wore thrift-store clothes from a boutique in our neighborhood called Mimi La Guerre, whose owner wasn't named Mimi and never explained where the war was, but who liked us and would sell us outfits for less than a dollar. The previous year we'd bought, from an Army surplus store, matching navy-blue pea-coats that were too large for us.

"So you like him," I said.

"He's okay, I guess. I don't know."

"What do you mean you don't know?" It wasn't like Robin not to have an opinion. The silence that followed was hemmed by the famil-iar movements of Robin's body in her bed, the creak of its frame.

"He said I'm beautiful like a spring day when the first flowers come up."

"He said that?"

"Yeah." She propped herself up on her elbow to look at me, her face a serious mask in the dark.

"It sounds like a commercial. *Fresh as a summer breeze that takes you by surprise.*"

"What are you talking about?"

"Like an ad for a feminine hygiene product."

Robin lay down, then propped herself up again. "What's a femi-nine hygiene product?"

Of her own life she said little, and afterward, on the bus back to Worthen, I regretted not asking her more about it. I'd allowed my discomfort to overwhelm me, and I wrote her an apologetic letter asking how she was doing. She replied with a postcard of a Salvador Dalí painting of a melted clock hanging off a dead tree. *I told you everything,* she wrote. I found the note strange, and was unable to decide whether this sentence was reassuring or accusatory. I'd never had trouble parsing my sister's tone before. I showed the postcard to Gordon, who shrugged. "She said everything's fine, so it's fine, right?"

"I guess," I said. Later, I blamed myself for not suspecting that something was wrong. But almost immediately I was swept up in the rhythms of the new semester. I was back at the computer lab and with Gordon, and then I fell in love again, this time academically.

I'd enjoyed all my classes at Worthen, but it was in a film class that something extraordinary happened. I enrolled in the course without much thought or intention; as a child, I'd loved going to the movies, and I wanted to learn more about how they were made. My ambitions weren't much greater than those of the guy who sat next to me on the first day of class, winking as he said, "Who wouldn't want to watch movies for credit, right?"

But we didn't watch a movie. The professor was a dark-haired Russian woman wearing bright red lipstick and a blue scarf that trailed down her back, almost to the floor, and I kept worrying she was going to trip over it, since she was also wearing very high heels. She launched into her lecture without preamble, discussing the nostalgia of the modern. In my notebook, I wrote down: *Nostalgia is rebellion against the modern idea of time. It is a romance with the fantasy of loss.* I didn't know what she meant by this, and nobody asked her to explain; I didn't want to reveal myself as the only ignorant one. *Nostalgia is to memory what kitsch is to art,* she also said, *a homesickness for the home that never was.* As she spoke she passed around strips of film and asked us to examine their material qualities. I had never seen a film strip before, and I held mine by the perforated edges, afraid of the damage I might do. My fingerprints smudged the strip anyway and trying to wipe them off only made it worse. On the strip itself, reddish-black and mysterious, I could make out nothing at all.

Then the professor—her name was Olga Ivanov—fished a reel of film out of a round metal container, fed it into a projector, and then, to my surprise, projected the film against us, the students, not onto the screen at the front of the room. We were bathed in barely perceptible colors that flitted and fell; we could both see and not see. Whispers filled the room. According to my notes: *Cinema is a museum of memory, an artifact that both enshrines and falsifies.*

Then she reversed the projector and showed the same film on the screen: it was of another group of students, sitting slack-jawed in a classroom. They whispered at us; we whispered at them. Then, abruptly, she shut the projector off, packed up the equipment, and left the room, her heels hammering the floor as she went.

"What a gimmick," said the guy next to me who'd just wanted to watch movies.

"She's amazing," I said.

"Oh, you're going to be an acolyte," he said. And I was.

12.

Olga Ivanov had come to Worthen from Moscow via Paris and New York. Whatever pressures of academic job market and personal circumstance had led her to a tiny college in Massachusetts, she didn't act as if the place was beneath her. She treated her work with high seriousness and expected us to do the same. She made no allowances for our youth and lack of sophistication; she showed us Tarkovsky and Deren and Eisenstein, who called montage the *nerve of cinema* and constructed a grammar of film adopted by Hitchcock; and if we didn't understand what she was saying, she looked at us over the rim of her glasses and talked dialectical materialism until we were even more confused, dizzy with our confusion. *Why is it,* she seemed to say, *you think understanding should be easy?* From an enrollment of fifty on the first day, the class shed students week by week until it was down to nine people, all of us who remained entranced by her.

One day in class we were discussing the film *Werner Herzog Eats His Shoe,* a documentary in which the director is shown living up to his promise to eat his shoe if Errol Morris finishes his film *Gates of Heaven.* Olga Ivanov described this as an example of sublimated sexual desire reinforcing the bonds of the patriarchy, "which is not to say that both men are not great filmmakers," she added. "Merely that the camera operates from a position of male hunger and appetite." She made asides like this which I wrote down, word for frantic word, wanting to preserve not just the insight but also her cadence and intonation.

After class that day I worked up the courage to visit her office. I stood at the door, peering in. It was dim—she refused to use the fluorescent overhead lights, and only a single lamp cast a meagre glow—and cluttered. Stacks of books and files leaned on top of cabinets and on the floor, landslides waiting to topple. She sat at the desk wrapped in a shawl and didn't look up when I cleared my throat. I was so nervous that I forgot to knock, instead simply launching into the question I'd rehearsed in my mind on the way over.

"Do you think Herzog eating the shoe is an homage to Charlie Chaplin eating a shoe in *The Gold Rush,* or is that just a coincidence?"

If she expected more of a conversational preamble, she didn't show it.

"There are no coincidences," she said. "Only versions of the image."

Like many of her remarks, this answer was more gnomic than illuminating. It seemed designed to provoke further conversation, and indeed she gestured for me to enter. "Would you like some tea?"

I nodded, and she poured some from a small clay teapot. The mug she passed to me had no handle and burned my fingers, so I almost dropped it. I squinted at her in the semi-darkness. Outside, the sun had already set, the Worthen lamp posts gleaming in the January afternoon, snowflakes visibly churning around students as they passed into the light and out again. She began talking about Herzog and his integrity, a lecture I was barely able to follow but that thrilled me nonetheless. Only in retrospect do I understand that she must have been lonely; at the time she seemed impossibly glamorous and self-possessed. Her talk was a winding path through the world, with signposts of the artists and writers and filmmakers she'd met in her travels. She told me about living in London when she was my age and watching films by experimentalists like Chantal Akerman and Lawrence Wheelock, names that meant nothing to me at the time.

"And you?" she said on that first day. "What do you do?"

Every answer that came to mind seemed inadequate, pedestrian. "I want to make films," I said impetuously.

"Ah?" A smile tilted her red-lipped mouth to the left. "What kind of films?"

I was already in over my head, and I groped for a response that would please her, rendering me worth her attention. "Films with integrity. In which the camera isn't just an apparatus of the male gaze." I had little to no idea what this meant. I was merely throwing back to her words she'd flung out in class, a human echo, vague and faint.

"How will you do that?" she said, and laughed when I told her I wasn't sure yet.

She didn't give me any advice, much less encouragement. But she allowed me to visit her regularly, to share my primitive opinions of the films we'd seen in class, and she talked to me about her work as we sipped tea. I became her unpaid assistant, filing her interlibrary loan requests for items not available in Worthen's library, searching microfiche documents, proofreading her manuscripts. "You check for grammar and spelling *only*," she told me, with the severity of a parent instructing a child. "Nothing else." I wouldn't have dared to consider anything else.

Toward the end of the year, she invited me along on a trip to New York City. She drove a battered old Toyota with a stick shift through the chaotic traffic, muttering what I assumed to be Russian curses, and parked on the Lower East Side in a lot operated by other Russians, with whom she argued violently before handing over her money. We spent the afternoon at a film archive before meeting a friend of hers for drinks at Yaffa Café. I wasn't included in their conversation, but I didn't mind. I was happy that no one expected me to participate, as I was more than a little distracted by the burlesque decorations and zebra-print furniture and strands of lights, not to mention the arguments and flirtations going on all around me. Afterward, as we walked past the record stores on St. Marks Place, Olga asked me to drive home, and I had to explain that I didn't know how.

"Stick shift is not difficult," she said stubbornly.

I told her this wasn't the issue. I didn't know how to drive, period.

Olga, vexed, didn't believe me. "All Americans learn to drive," she said. When I said I was Canadian, she was nonplussed. I understood with chagrin that the drive home was the entire reason that she'd brought me along.

"All right," she said at last. "All right. Your job now is to keep me awake."

She downed an espresso and reclaimed the car. As we jostled over the threadbare highways out of the city, I tried to entertain her with stories about my mother and sister, the devil and angel of my life, exaggerating both the bad and the good. I made Robin and myself sound like orphans out of Dickens, and Marianne an abusive tyrant. We all changed in my telling, squirming into new relief. Olga squinted at the road—I learned later that she hated to drive at night—and gave no responses. I moved on to Gordon and how, though we'd been together for months, I still sometimes called him *the burly guy* inside my head, and this made her laugh. Being with her in the car as the traffic thinned, following the wooded curves of the Saw Mill Parkway, then hitting the almost absolute darkness of the county highway that took us back to Worthen, reminded me of being with Robin at night in our room. I talked and talked, ransacking my life for material—Todd and Bob; Mrs. Gasparian; Hervé of the bespoke shirts—and I was almost sorry when the drive ended. It was past midnight when Olga dropped me by the college gates. It occurred to me, as I trudged the final steps back to my room, that I didn't know where she lived.

13.

The summer after my first year at Worthen, I didn't go home. I'd felt so uncomfortable at Christmas that I decided, dramatically, there was no longer a place for me there. Richard said I could work at the computer lab, and Olga, before departing for Europe, gave me some research projects for which she offered a small stipend. The two jobs added up to just enough money to live on. Required to move out of the dorm, I answered a flyer for a roommate posted by a woman named Emma, who was twenty-four and taught at a nearby elementary school. The room came with a single bed and a card table with a folding chair. It was the first time I'd ever slept in a room alone.

When I told my mother over the phone that I wouldn't be returning, she was indifferent. "If that's what you want," she said with the air of someone who'd washed her hands of the situation. I asked to speak to Robin, and she laughed harshly. "She's never home anymore," she said. "All she does is play that piano. For years I couldn't wait to get rid of you both—and now, poof! You're gone." She sounded less pleased than defiant. As always with Marianne, her emotional reactions were mixed and difficult to parse. I had the feeling she missed us, and also that she wished she'd kicked us out herself.

At graduation, I met Gordon's parents. His father was a larger, stouter version of him, with an even bushier beard shot through with grey, and his mother was a dowdy, fair-haired woman in enormous glasses behind which her eyes blinked owlishly. True to reputation, they showered me with questions about growing up in a Commonwealth country and were gratified that I knew the words to "God Save the Queen." They took the two of us out to dinner at the nicest restaurant near Worthen, an Italian place noisy with other graduating students and their families, where I ordered plain spaghetti and an iceberg salad and sipped Coke with crushed ice from a tall glass. The next morning they drove off with Gordon's things. His roommate Mike was going to drive him up to Maine to begin his Appalachian Trail hike. As Gordon and I kissed goodbye outside his dorm, Mike gazing discreetly at the horizon, I burst into tears. Everything I'd become at Worthen had taken place under his tutelage.

"Hey, hey, Looks Down at the Ground," he said, circling his arms around me. "I'll write you all the time, and we'll meet up later this summer. What do you think my trail name should be? Apparently everybody has one."

"Burly guy," I said, wiping a palm across my wet cheek, and he scowled.

"I was thinking Thoreau," he said. "You know, I really feel like I'm going to find something essential on this trip. I'm going to get boiled down to myself, you know? The inner resources. The measure of a man. I'm going to figure out what's underneath this bluster. Why I'm such a pedantic mess."

"I don't think you're a pedantic mess," I said.

"Well," he said, "I'm a work in progress, anyway." He kissed me again, and got into the car.

After his departure I moped around for a while until the tranquility of the summer restored me. I loved the campus in June, lush, green, and underpopulated, and at a garage sale I bought a second-hand bike, which I rode from Emma's apartment to work each day.

I'd leave home in the morning earlier than I had to, to avoid both the heat and Emma, who scared me a little. She rarely spoke to me or, so far as I could tell, anyone else. Every morning she performed an elaborate breakfast ritual involving ground hemp seeds and soy milk for herself and mashed slurry for her elderly cats, who possessed five teeth between the two of them. The route to campus was tree-lined and quiet, and the lab was fluorescent and quiet. While sitting at the desk I went through Olga's manuscript—a book about nostalgia and the image—making an index, which involved painstaking scrutiny and record-keeping. Fortunately, I was rarely disturbed. The few people using the lab in the summer were mostly other international students, so devoted to their projects that they sat in front of their terminals for hours on end, the only noises the click of keyboards, the occasional sneeze or cough or sigh.

Evenings I often spent in the Worthen library, watching movies in a media room in the chilly basement, then cycling home in the warm, humid air to sleep.

After two weeks I received my first letter from Gordon, which,

he noted on the back of the envelope, he'd given to a hiker nick-
named Hulk to mail in town: *THANKS HULK!!* I was reassured by
the sight of his large, exuberant handwriting, only slightly messier
than usual, and by the affectionate, quite sexual content. He missed
my body, he wrote, and couldn't wait until we were together again.
I kept the letter, carefully folded, in a side pocket of my bag, and
took it out every few hours at work to read it again, until it tore at
the creases.

Almost everyone I knew had left for the summer, but I wasn't
lonely. In a magazine I'd found a list of the one hundred best films
ever made, and I set about watching them. When Richard heard
about this project, he took an interest in it, and almost every morning he'd ask me what I'd just watched and what I thought, con-
tributing his own opinions on *The Searchers* or *Vertigo,* which we
both loved. Richard's favorite moment in *Vertigo* came when Jimmy
Stewart begs Kim Novak, a brunette, to dye her hair blond in order
to resemble his lost love. "Judy, please, it can't matter to you!" he
says desperately. Sometimes, walking past my desk, Richard would
repeat, "It can't matter to you!" and shake his head, laughing.

A week later I received, all at once, four letters from Gordon,
mailed by another trail friend. I spread this treasure out on my
card table at Emma's, sorted them by date, and read them carefully;
they were long and cramped, Gordon concerned about running out
of paper before he could replenish his supplies. His writing, often
edited mid-sentence, escaped the confines of the lines to crawl up
the margins of the pages. He loved the trail, he said, it was the first
genuine experience of his life. His feet were blistered and his neck and
arms were covered with mosquito bites. American masculinity had
gotten divorced from the life of the body, he wrote, and now he felt
his physical self as never before. Our society is so plastic, he wrote,
even language itself is plastic. All we are, he concluded, is animals.

Although I didn't agree with his positions, they didn't bother me.
I was used to his extremities of thought. It was part of the appeal
of Gordon, his willingness to adopt radical ideological postures and

then abandon them without difficulty or regret. I was less comfortable with the language of desire in the letters, each one more fervent and explicit than the last. I'd enjoyed sex with him and now I missed it, but in these letters Gordon's fantasies seemed to have less and less to do with anything we'd actually done together. He didn't dwell on memories of our past experiences as I did. He imagined and described a new future and new ways of being together. When he wrote about things he wanted to do, I began to feel that it was not *my* body he was describing, but *a* body. The more graphic the sex in the letters became, the less it seemed to have to do with me.

Which is not to say that I didn't read the letters over and over, hiding them under the pillow in my bedroom, removing them at night to be read before sleeping, handling them gingerly, as if my fingers might burn.

The last letter closed by saying how excited he was to see me soon. With his friend Mike, I was supposed to meet Gordon when he made it back down to Massachusetts. He would get more food supplies and we'd go to a motel and spend the night together. *I AM GOING TO RIP YOUR CLOTHES OFF!!* he wrote, with a row of x's and o's, incongruously sweet, beneath.

I was excited about this rendezvous, and pleasantly scared; I wasn't sure what being with this new, animalistic Gordon would be like (*I AM PRETTY RANK!!,* he'd also written). But the next group of letters, which arrived soon thereafter, was different. One letter was seven straight pages of sexual scenario, with no preamble or sign-off. Another had been rained on and was indecipherable, but had been sent anyway. *I can't stop thinking,* the last letter began, *about the Apollonian-Dionysian strands in American life.* Though at first this discussion seemed theoretical, it wound back to his thoughts on the primacy of physical experience. He had decided, he wrote, to embrace the Dionysian. *What Thoreau didn't understand was the basic savagery of mankind. We're primates, that's all.* This last sentence made me think of my roommate Helen, who was spending her summer interning at a conservation society. She was always talking about how animals were more intellectual and sensitive than we gave them credit for, how their forms of language and social hierarchies were as complex as our own. She'd moved on from Jane Goodall to Frans de Waal, whose research on primates had shown that animal societies included principles of altruism and empathy. Obsessed with his book *Chimpanzee Politics,* Helen believed that bonobo civilization was superior to the human one. "It's all about love," she'd told me, "and we could learn a lot from it." I would've liked to put her in a room with Gordon, who apparently wanted to dismantle civilization. It seemed to me that his mind was dismantling itself, and I felt sorry for him, going mad with loneliness and exhaustion on a trip that was proving too much—sorry, that is, until I came to the end of the last letter, in which he broke up with me.

Love is a construct, he wrote, *a social invention. I just don't see a future for it.* There were no exclamation marks.

The turnaround from the previous letters was so sharp that at first I couldn't take in what he was saying. If he was going to embrace his animal self, wasn't our sexual reunion part of that? He'd seemed to think of little else—I'd read next to nothing, in the letters, about the scenery of Maine and New Hampshire, or even about the other hikers he'd met. I felt he was unhinged. If I could just stand in front of him, and talk with him and touch him, then surely he would recover himself, and change his mind.

But the letters were a one-sided conversation. There was no way to respond.

In agony, I sat down and wrote him one letter after another—some angry, some pleading. In some I tried to be funny. In others I reminded him, tentatively—I didn't have his freedom with sexual language or imagination—of our physical connection. Then, desperate, I called Mike, who was at home in Boston, and asked him to deliver my letters.

"No can do," he said jauntily. With the blinkered narcissism of love, I'd always assumed that Mike—whom I'd steadfastly ignored and knew virtually nothing about—liked me and wanted me and Gordon to be happy. How could anyone feel otherwise? But it was evident he was enjoying this drama. "Gordo wrote to me too, and I'm under strict orders to protect his decision."

"But why is this happening?" I asked, too upset to be embarrassed by how pathetic I sounded.

Mike's tone softened. "It was always going to happen," he said.

"What does that mean?"

"You know what it means," he said. "Gotta go."

I didn't know what he was talking about; I refused to believe that the intensity of Gordon's attention, which had wrapped itself around me so completely, could be anything but permanent. At night I sobbed so hard that Emma knocked softly at my bedroom door and asked if I was all right. I wasn't all right, I was far from all right. I'd grown used to seeing myself through Gordon's eyes, and now I was invisible to both of us. I would have done anything, changed any part of myself, to bring him back to me. *Judy, please, it can't matter to you.* But he wasn't asking.

14.

Gordon had been the cornerstone of my life away from home and now, in the thick heat of summer, I felt more lost than when I first arrived at Worthen. Noting my swollen eyes and slumped posture, Richard was too tactful to ask questions, but he must have guessed that sitting at the desk, thinking all day, was the worst thing I could have been doing. So he assigned me a project that involved cataloguing and re-shelving inventory in a back room, moving boxes of printer paper and old floppy disks, work that was tedious, physical, and perfect. I stopped watching so many movies; instead, I went for long bike rides on the industrial roadways surrounding Worthen, watching forklifts load and unload their freight with mechanical grace, trucks arrive and depart, the men operating these machines small and insignificant in comparison.

By late July, I was still miserable, but I'd begun to collect some shards of self again. Richard, who was a very sweet man, went on vacation to San Francisco and returned with a gift: a mug featuring the original poster from *Vertigo,* the figure of a man in black falling into a swirl of red. I placed the mug on my desk and went back to working on Olga's manuscript, wanting her to be pleased when she returned in August.

The days were unrushed and uneventful, and I had no reason to expect otherwise when the phone rang one afternoon and a woman said, "Lark, someone's here for you."

I tried to speak, croaked, coughed, tried again. "Who is this?"

She let out an irritated sigh. "It's Emma."

She'd never called me at the lab before. Since moving in I'd avoided her, as she was almost always in a bad mood. She worked up so much irritation during the school year that it was taking her all summer to clear it out. When we spoke in May, she asked only about my social life—did I have a lot of friends, would I want to have them over—and nothing about my finances. She kept saying she needed peace and quiet, "inside and out." I *was* exceedingly quiet, but even my footsteps in the hallway bothered her, even the sound of my shower in the morning. Later, she moved to the Berkshires to make cheese. But she hadn't yet discovered cheese that day, was off all dairy, in fact, and I could tell she was annoyed. "There's a girl here asking for you," she said. "She wanted to come in but I don't know her so I had her wait on the steps outside. You know about the cats. They're not used to strangers."

She used the cats as an excuse for everything. The cats needed the shoes to be cleared out of the hallway. The cats needed lights out by ten. I wanted to tell her that the cats were nocturnal, and they rarely moved anyway; they were bony, fuzzy lumps who sat by the windows gazing reproachfully at a world they weren't allowed to explore.

"She has *luggage,*" she added.

I couldn't imagine who it was. Everyone I knew was at home or traveling or working somewhere else for the summer.

"Who is she?" I said.

I heard Emma set down the phone—even the clack of the phone on the table sounded peeved—and go outside to ask the girl her name, then come back in.

"She says she's your sister."

How this information hadn't come out earlier, I wasn't sure. "Could you put her on, please?"

Another annoyed clack, another pause.

Then: "Hi, it's me," Robin said. At the sound of her voice I burst into tears; I'd forgotten how beautiful it was. My own voice, which I hated, was flat and nasal, and whenever I had to leave a phone message I rushed so fast it was practically incomprehensible. But Robin's was a musical instrument, making even three words a song.

"What are you doing here?"

"I came to visit. I'm sorry I didn't call you. I didn't have your number."

I'd given the number to Marianne, but it didn't surprise me that she hadn't passed it on. I'd been too mired in heartbreak to wonder how Robin was doing, and now I felt guilty and purely, simply, thrilled to see her.

"Wait there," I said. "I'm on my way."

When I rode up to the apartment fifteen minutes later, my sister was still sitting on the steps, with a threadbare brown suitcase next to her, like a street urchin in an old movie. She was wearing a boxy red flowered shirt that didn't quite fit, a jean skirt, and Converse running shoes. I was startled to notice, as I got closer, that she'd pierced her nose with a tiny gold stud. Her dark hair was in a messy ponytail and I felt, seeing her, the pride that had warmed me throughout our childhood. To me she was the loveliest person in the world.

When she stood up she leaned against me and hugged me so hard my spine cracked, a violent, happy pressure. When we pulled away, I saw she was crying.

"What's wrong?" I said. I could see Emma and her cats at the bay window in the living room, all of them staring.

"Can I stay with you?"

"Of course," I said, glancing doubtfully at the window.

Inside, on my single bed, we sat together and whispered. My sister said she'd come to visit, that she needed a break, things weren't good at home. I nodded; I knew how our mother could be. But when I pressed for details, Robin was evasive. Expecting our usual late-night gossip sessions, in which we analyzed and dissected Marianne endlessly, I was surprised that she had no anecdotes to offer. She seemed less angry than uncomfortable, ill at ease in her own skin; she'd always carried herself with grace, and now her posture was slumped and awkward. She crossed her arms over her chest and crossed her legs twice, both at the knee and ankle, rope-twisted.

"I just need to stay here a little while," she said at least twice, adding, "please?" as if I needed to be persuaded, which I didn't.

After a while I went to the kitchen and made us peanut butter sandwiches. Emma had gone out but the cats still stared at me suspiciously. When I came back to the room with the sandwiches, my sister was asleep in my bed.

15.

In the week that followed, I brought Robin with me everywhere. She rode with me to work, doubled on my bike, and ate lunch with me outside under a tree; afterward we watched movies in the Worthen library, curled with our knees up to our chins in the freezing basement media room. At night we took our shoes off, tiptoed silently past Emma's closed bedroom door, and took turns sleeping in the bed or on the floor. After a while I hit on the idea of giving her my student ID and showing her where the practice pianos in the music building were, and soon she was happily occupied there for hours each day. I knew Emma wasn't pleased about my houseguest, but she was attending a wedding in New York on the weekend, and I'd long ago agreed to take care of the cats, who required a complicated regimen of liquid food and medicine. One was diabetic and the other arthritic; Emma had given me extensive training in their care and written out a list of instructions that was two pages long.

"Don't worry," I told her on the day she left. "Beowulf and Grendel are going to be fine."

She came over and held my hands in hers. She'd never touched me before. She was a strawberry blonde with eyebrows and eyelashes so pale they were invisible, offering her eyes no protection; she always looked as if she'd ordered something in a restaurant and was unpleasantly surprised by what arrived. "I've had these cats since I was fifteen years old," she said. "I've had them through my parents' divorce, my first boyfriend, my eating disorder, my second boyfriend, my disappointing my father and deciding not to go to med school, my third boyfriend, and my realizing that I didn't want any more boyfriends because I like girls. The cats have been with me through all of that. Do you understand?"

I told her I did. I squeezed her hands and she scowled at me dubiously, then said she had to go.

The night she left Robin and I celebrated with Kraft Dinner and a dance party in the living room, the cats hunkered down on the window seat, turning their backs to the festivities. To be with Robin in an empty apartment, to listen to music and make dumb jokes and eat junk food and watch television, felt like releasing a breath I hadn't realized I'd been holding for months. I told her about Gordon, editing out the sex in his letters, and she listened intently. Then I told her about Olga, how I wanted to think like her and act like her and maybe make films. Robin told me that the piano was going well and her teacher thought she should get serious about it.

"Aren't you serious already?" I asked her. "Marianne told me you practice all the time."

At the mention of our mother's name, she flinched so briefly only I would have noticed it. "More serious. Go to music school."

"Do you want to?"

"Yes."

The only awkward moments came when I asked her about home. She kept changing the subject, with increasingly obvious excuses, and when I asked her directly why she wouldn't talk about it she only shook her head and said she didn't know what I meant. "I'm not telling you anything because there's nothing to tell," she said, and the lie hung in the air between us, a single discordant note in an otherwise harmonious song.

In the morning, when we woke up, one of the cats was dead. At first I didn't notice—the cats, being elderly, didn't move that much to begin with, and I was used to seeing them as still as statues by the window—but after I had prepared their morning "soup," as Emma called it, and carried the bowls over to them, I saw that Beowulf was lying on his side with his mouth open and his eyes staring straight ahead, his legs rigid. The other cat ate her soup, accepted her medicine, and did not seem perturbed.

I swore, long and loud, bringing Robin out to the living room. She was always groggy in the morning, her hair in chaos and her eyelids thick with sleep; she moved around a lot while sleeping, sometimes walked and talked too, and when she woke up she often seemed exhausted from her labors.

"What's wrong?"

"Look," I said, pointing at the cat. "My roommate is going to kill me."

"Oh, no," Robin said.

"I know!"

"Is it our fault? What did we do wrong?"

"I don't know!"

"You gave him the medicine last night, right?"

"Of course I did."

"Then it's not our fault."

"She's still going to kill me."

Robin sat down by the bay window next to Beowulf's body. Even his fur looked stiff. "Poor sweet baby," Robin said, gently rubbing the cat's head. "Poor sweet little thing."

"What are we going to do?"

When Robin looked up, there were tears in her eyes. "Make a coffin," she said.

I found a shoebox and lined it with a couple T-shirts. After we nestled Beowulf inside, we debated whether to put the lid on or not. Closure seemed cruel, somehow, even though the cat wouldn't know the difference. Then we talked about the weather: it was hot and humid, and the apartment didn't have air conditioning. What if the cat began to decompose before Emma got back? So we covered the shoebox and put it in the fridge, next to the eggs.

Almost immediately I felt better, and I tried to talk Robin into a plan for the day: we could bike to the Goodwill store, I proposed, or have a picnic on campus. But the death of the cat had unsettled my sister.

"I think we should stick by Grendel," she said. "What if he's lonely?"

"Grendel is a she," I said.

"Oh, you're right," she said, examining the cat's grey underbelly. Grendel was also blind, and almost as stiff in life as Beowulf was in death. Every once in a while she lifted a paw and craned her neck as if to go somewhere, then gave up. Though she'd always bared her two teeth at me, she allowed Robin to stroke her head and closed her milky eyes in something that looked like pleasure.

"I'm not sure she can tell anything's different," I said.

"Don't be ridiculous! Of course she can." Robin's tone was aggravated. She seemed to find me pitiless. Growing up, we rarely fought—united as we were against our mother's unpredictability—

and I couldn't remember her ever snapping at me. Now I found her judgmental, and thought she was posturing; there was no reason for her to act heartbroken over an animal she'd only just met. It was a *cat,* an old cat, and not *her* cat.

"Come on," I said. "Beowulf had a good long life and Grendel will be fine."

"I bet she got them together," Robin said, sniffling. "I bet they've been together their whole lives."

"They never seemed to like each other all that much," I said.

"You never pay attention to animals."

I was hurt. "That's not true."

"You always complained about having to be quiet for the cats."

Always seemed a strong statement from someone who'd been visiting for just a few days. It was true I'd made fun of Emma to my sister, mocked her attachment to the cats and how she used them as mouthpieces for her own complaints; *feline ventriloquism* I'd called it, but I was only trying to entertain.

"So you want to sit here and pet the cat all day?"

"Yes," she said. "I do."

"Okay, then," I said, stalking off. "Suit yourself."

I rode my bike to the Worthen library and tried to watch *Fantasia.* I thought the movie would be a welcome distraction, but it only seemed dated and weird, and cycling past Gordon's dorm on my way did nothing to lighten my mood. I wanted something darker, and checked out *All About Eve* instead; the story of two women plotting against one another struck closer to home, but it also made me shift in my seat. I've watched the movie many times since then, and each time I see it differently; sometimes its wit makes me laugh, other times I've shuddered at the meanness of it, its smartly directed blows. On that day, which was my first viewing, it made me feel as if something had been taken from me, though I couldn't have said what; like all films, it showed me a reflection of myself, and the reflection was injured and dented, open to theft.

I gave up and got home a few hours later, to find my sister on the couch in Emma's living room with Grendel on her chest, the cat purring in blind pleasure.

Robin was crying, a steady stream of tears and snot coursing down her cheeks. A snowbank of crumpled tissues next to her testified that she'd been crying the whole time I was gone. Her shirt and hands were whiskered with cat hair. I lay down next to her, pushing her over slightly to make room, and the cat put out a feeble paw in protest.

"Tell me what's wrong," I said. "Please."

Robin sighed and wiped her nose with the back of her hand. Staring at the ceiling, her voice a low-throated murmur clotted with snot, she explained the real reason she'd come to stay with me. It didn't have to do with Marianne, at least not directly. The problem was Marianne's boyfriend, Hervé. When they'd first met, he was charming, with genteel European manners. He took the two of them out to dinner at an expensive restaurant, and when Robin faced a menu filled with choices she didn't recognize, he smoothly ordered for her. He was always telling Marianne she couldn't possibly be old enough to have a teenage daughter, and as a sort of elaborate courtesy he would pretend that Robin was ten years old, that she was seven, that she was four. "Are you learning your multiplication tables?" he'd ask in mock severity, raising an eyebrow. "Are you working on your finger-painting technique?" It became a running joke, at which Robin and Marianne would laugh excessively, anxious to please and be pleased by him. Although odd, it seemed harmless, and gratifying to Marianne. Otherwise Hervé seemed to have few flaws, except that he could be fussy. When Marianne served him dinner at the apartment, examining his face nervously, he would lift his knife and frown, ever so gently, at its smudges.

Marianne preferred to meet him at his hotel or at a restaurant, but Hervé said he liked to come to the apartment, "to play the family man," he said, in a tone of ironic amusement, "to dandle the young one on my knee."

Whenever he visited he brought gifts: jewelry and scarves and perfume for Marianne, clothes for Robin. He thought her outfits were slovenly. He instructed Marianne to take Robin to a seamstress and have her measured, and then took the measurements to Milan and returned with silk blouses and shirtwaist dresses, beautifully made and classic, not exactly unfashionable but certainly nothing like what other girls were wearing. "I couldn't just walk around in them like I'm Audrey Hepburn or something," Robin said. She put them on only when he came over or they went out to dinner, and while the dresses were not revealing she noticed that men paid her more attention when she wore them; heads turned on the street; waiters hurried to fill her glass. It was as if Hervé had unlocked some secret to her appearance and chosen to share it with other men without her consent. She felt like a marionette. Worst of all was the look on Marianne's face when this happened: desperate and greedy, grieving and tentative. "I hated to see her so sad," Robin said. "Like I was taking something away from her. And I didn't even want it."

My sister escaped to her piano practices, and when Hervé came to town she often made excuses as to why she wasn't free to see him or to go out to dinner. "Hervé missed you," our mother would say. "You're hurting his feelings." And Robin would promise to be around the next time, would play up to our mother with jokes and sweetness, watch movies with her, cuddle next to her on the couch. During this period the mood in the apartment was tense, and yet somehow, perversely, they were closer than they'd ever been before. The unspoken was papered over and the papering had a force of its own. "She's not so bad, sometimes," Robin said. "Remember when we were little and she'd play Stevie Wonder for us and we'd have dance parties and hot cocoa? She can be fun."

One day in the spring Robin arrived at her piano teacher's home after school, as usual. The piano teacher finished her lessons for the day by six p.m., and after Robin's lesson she was allowed to stay and practice on her piano for several hours. This agreement had been reached years earlier, through the intervention of Mrs. Gasparian, who'd connected them in the first place. On this particular day the teacher acted strangely—giddy and unusually complimentary of Robin's performance—and when Robin finished, at nine in the evening, Hervé was sitting in the living room with her teacher, drinking tea. "Not bad," he said approvingly, raising the cup in her direction. "Not bad at all." Marianne was not there, and Robin felt chilled. The message, she felt, was clear: there was no place she could go where his gaze wouldn't follow.

Of course he'd charmed the piano teacher. He even offered to buy Robin a piano, and only the space limitations of our apartment—"Where would we put it? In the bathtub?" Marianne said—prevented him.

Once Robin came out of school to find him there in a car with a driver, offering her a lift to her lesson.

Once she came back from practice to find that all her clothes, the T-shirts and jeans and running shoes she favored, had been removed from her dresser, and replaced with the tailored Italian clothing he preferred.

Once she woke up in the middle of the night to find him sitting on my bed, looking at her.

I didn't have to ask why she didn't turn to Marianne, knowing the answer already: because she would have received no help at all.

He never touched her; he never raised his voice.

I held my sister's hand as she cried. "You see why I couldn't stay there, right?" she said, and I said, "Yes."

Robin was more like Marianne than I was; she didn't have my meekness or my fear. She did three things. She pierced her nose, so that when he looked at her face he would see a choice she'd made. She threw out the beautiful clothes, stuffing them in a dumpster behind our building, the colorful silks flapping from beneath the lid. And she stole all the money she could find in the apartment and used it to buy a bus ticket to the United States.

16.

We decided that Robin wouldn't go home. Like me, she was a dual citizen—why couldn't we just stay together? The hazards and difficulties of this plan we pushed aside. We spent the rest of the weekend relaxed and happy. On Sunday we cleaned the apartment and settled down to wait for Emma's return. Grendel cuddled on Robin's lap; if she felt any grief over the death of her longtime companion, she didn't show it. Maybe they'd been enemies all along, just like their namesakes, but had grown too old and tired to fight.

When Emma came in, sweaty and red-faced, with her backpack heavy on one shoulder, my sister carefully lifted Grendel off her lap and stood up.

"Emma," she said, and gathered my roommate in her arms, pressing her close. I could see Emma's face melt into worry. "What is it?" she said. "Oh, God."

Robin whispered the cat's name in her ear and Emma began to shake, dropping the backpack on the floor.

"I'm so sorry," I said, "I promise we gave him his medicine." I'd prepared myself for shouting and blame, steeled myself to mount a defense, but no accusations came. Instead, Emma's shoulders quaked and she leaned into Robin, who guided her to the couch, her arms circling Emma's neck. I don't know if they'd even had a conversation before.

"Please, where is she?" Emma said.

Robin gestured to the fridge. Emma got up, opened the door, and looked inside the box. "Oh, God," she said again. "He looks so peaceful." She wiped her nose with the back of her hand. "He was eighteen," she said to no one in particular.

"That's a long life," Robin said.

"Just like Beowulf," Emma said. She took a glass out of the cupboard and poured herself a shot of tequila, then another one, her shoulders still shaking.

"Why did you name him that?" Robin asked.

"I don't know. I read a comic-book version of the story in elementary school. When they were kittens they wrestled all the time so it seemed like Beowulf and Grendel fighting." She swayed a little. "My dad and I picked them out at the shelter."

"Emma," I said. I went into the kitchen, but I lacked Robin's ease with people; I put a tentative hand on her shoulder, waiting for her to flick it away.

"'His soul left his flesh, flew to glory,'" she said. "I still remember that line, from the story."

Then Robin was in the kitchen too. "How did Beowulf die?" she said.

"He ruled as a king for a long time, and then died an old man. They gave him a huge funeral with a pyre."

"Then that's what we should do," Robin said.

Emma nodded. Her hair was matted with sweat; she looked frail and drenched with grief. "You're right."

Robin took charge. She made Emma sit on the couch with more tequila and got her to phone some of her friends. She sent me out to the store for snacks and candles. By the time I returned, Emma's friends Julie and Suvarna were there, looking sombre. Grendel was on the window seat, ignoring us all.

The shoebox sat on the coffee table. I arranged the candles I'd bought around it, and lit them. Robin raised her hands like a conductor, and we all stood up at her bidding. Then she nodded at Suvarna, who opened a book I'd had to buy for English class. She read the poem by John Donne that begins, "Death be not proud." As soon as she said the word *death* Emma sobbed, and Julie hugged her.

"This is about love, and remembering what's left behind," Robin said softly. She seemed completely comfortable in her role, as if directing cat funerals were something she did all the time. "Beowulf, we'll never forget you."

Then she sang quietly, by herself, "In My Life," by the Beatles, and by the end we were all sobbing. We were also all drunk, except Suvarna, who was the designated driver. A few miles away there was a small, pretty state park with a pond where Gordon and I had gone for hikes, and we piled into Suvarna's car and drove there. Emma sat with the boxed cat in her lap, tears running freely, as miserable a person as I'd ever seen. Robin held her hand.

At the pond, Robin asked Emma if she was ready, and she nodded. Julie poured lighter fluid on the box, then held a lighter out.

"I can't, I can't," Emma said, sobbing. She passed the lighter to my sister. "You do it," she said.

So Robin lowered the box into the water and then set it on fire. The box flared up brilliantly but wouldn't float away, instead hugging the shore as if it didn't want to leave us. Finally I found a stick and poked the box until the wind carried it a few feet away; then it bobbed and rollicked beneath a footbridge, and the water extinguished the flames and it was invisible, wherever it was.

There was no one else around, only us and the dark pond water and the summer night, warm and dense and intimate.

I kept waiting for Emma to accuse me, to throw me and Robin out of the apartment in retribution. But she never did. Robin had somehow caught her anger and released it as the sadness it had always masked. The cat funeral was absurd, but it was also magical, and the atmosphere in the apartment was different afterward— thanks to my sister, who knew to join Emma in her grief and comfort her there, without mockery or self-consciousness. Years later, when Robin fell in love with wolves, I remembered Beowulf and the ceremony she'd given him, how I both envied the intensity of her attachment to animals and felt estranged from it, a gap between us that I could never cross over.

After the cat funeral, Emma and Robin were friends. They huddled in conference, Robin listening as Emma talked about the cat, her unhappiness with her work, her lack of love life, her lack of anything life. Within a few weeks, Emma decided it was time for a change: she gave notice at her job, and registered for a culinary program in Great Barrington. She helped us figure out how to establish me as Robin's legal guardian and register Robin at the local high school. At the end of the summer, she moved out, leaving the two of us her apartment, and we hugged goodbye tightly, as if we'd known one another for years.

17.

I was watching a film called *Close-Up,* by the Iranian director Abbas Kiarostami, and it was unlike anything I'd seen before. In the film, a man presents himself to a family as an acclaimed director, and they welcome him into their home, even going so far as to rehearse with him for a film he tells them he'd like to make. As it turns out, he's an impostor: separated from his wife, underemployed at a print shop. He's a melancholy figure, this man, more pitiable than villainous. Once his charade is discovered he is arrested and put on trial, and the film cuts between his gentle interrogation by a bemused judge and scenes of his deception and discovery. Other than money for a taxi, he has taken nothing from the family except their credulity, and their time.

The strangest thing about the film is that it's both a documentary and a fictional feature; actual footage is combined with reenactments in which all the people involved play themselves, and Kiarostami is part of the film as well. In court, the judge asks the imposter whether his contrition is genuine. "Aren't you acting right now?"

"I'm speaking of my suffering," the impostor says.

All his answers at the trial are like this—curiously articulate, he never says yes or no, and delivers statements about the nature of art that seem sophisticated yet humble. His teeth are crooked and overlapping. He confesses to dying his hair to look younger. "You *are* young," the judge tells him, and he shakes his head sadly, denying it.

Watching him speak, I found myself crying without knowing why.

I cycled home in the cold October evening, thinking about the film. I loved the idea of a story that was both true and not true, documentary and fiction, art and artifice so intertwined that you couldn't tell the difference between them. Since Robin had come to live with me, I'd begun to make films—or, not really films so much as very short experiments with light and sound. One was mostly close-ups of Grendel, Emma's surviving cat, which we still had while Emma got settled, trying to capture the texture of her stiff elderly fur and her rheumy eyes. I called it *A Cat Considers Her Mortality* and it was not well-received by my Intro to Filmmaking professor, Alice Boryn, or my fellow students. "*Why* are we looking at this?" said a woman in my class, twirling her hair around her finger, while others nodded in agreement. Olga, for whom I still worked as an assistant, said it was interesting, but she said everything was interesting, in a non-committal tone that seemed to suggest both that I'd failed and that I was capable of better.

After watching *Close-Up* I began to film my sister. I had the idea to interview her about our childhood; sometimes I asked her questions about her memories, and sometimes I asked her to play the role of someone other than herself. Most often, I asked her to pretend she was our mother. She was an excellent mimic, and it was curious and fascinating to hear her voice take on the cadence of Marianne's. She could inhabit our mother simply by shifting her posture in a chair and narrowing her eyes; she captured Marianne's vanity and her laugh and the lift of her left eyebrow. It helped that they looked quite a bit alike, with the same dark hair and wide-set eyes. It didn't help that she would only maintain the fiction for a few minutes before she'd get tired of the exercise or collapse into laughter, saying she felt ridiculous, or that she didn't want to be Marianne in the first place; she wanted to get away from her, not *become* her. Eventually I cut together several takes of her pretending to be Marianne and then giving up, her face serious and then creased with laughter, serious and creased, a looping repetition of composure and its opposite. I called the film *Robin Giggling,* and Alice Boryn said it was purposelessly inscrutable and the other students frowned with distaste and Olga, of course, said it was interesting.

Robin laughed often, whether I was filming her or not. That fall, my sophomore year, our apartment was a cheerful place. She rode the bus to high school and came straight to campus every afternoon to practice the piano. At the beginning of the semester, I'd approached a faculty member in the music department and begged him to hear my sister play. He explained that he was very busy, but once he listened to Robin, his expression changed and he agreed to take her on as a pupil. Robin and I had no money to pay for lessons, but this teacher—his name was Boris Dawidoff, and like Olga he was a Russian émigré; I don't know how it happened that Worthen had attracted them both—suggested that I could register under my name, and Robin could show up instead. It was unethical and inappropriate, possibly grounds for expulsion, yet we didn't think twice about doing it. If anyone at Worthen questioned why piano classes began to appear on my transcript, I didn't hear about it. The generosity of this teacher, the risks he took to help my sister, the ease of his solution: we took all of it for granted, not understanding the potential consequences or costs.

Marianne accepted Robin's decision to live with me with frosty dignity. At Robin's insistence, we didn't tell her anything about Hervé; all we said was that we missed each other, and thought being together would make us happy. I still don't know how much she suspected of the truth; her pride, and Robin's discomfort, made the subject impossible to discuss. Marianne agreed to the guardianship and then proceeded to give us the silent treatment, never calling or writing to see how things were. We were unperturbed. If anything, we were glad to be free of her temper and moods. What she intended as punishment felt to us like relief.

Our main issue was money. Now that I was living off campus, we needed to pay rent, and although Emma's apartment was cheap by most standards, it cost more than I was bringing in from the lab. This was how we came to be employed at the group home.

Robin was the one who saw the flyer, handwritten in blue ballpoint, on a community bulletin board at the Stop & Shop. *Need part-time help with simple tasks:* a job description so basic even we seemed qualified for it. She tore a strip off the bottom and called the number, and the next day we both had interviews.

The group home—it was technically the Freedom Within Limits Residential Program, but nobody called it that—was located on a quiet street behind a strip mall that housed a pizza place and a dry cleaner. The couple who ran it introduced themselves as Mr. and Mrs. Dean Smith, and I never learned whether Dean Smith was a hyphenated name, or the husband's name, or if the wife had a first name of her own. Harried and brusque, they hired us immediately, dispensing commands in terse sentences that made it clear they had no time for small talk. Mrs. Dean Smith was the director and looked after the house and meals, and Mr. Dean Smith looked after the grounds.

Downstairs there was a kitchen and a living room filled optimistically with books and board games; in all the time we spent there, I never saw anybody take them off the shelves. Instead the residents huddled in front of an old television that received three channels clearly and two more blurred with snow. Upstairs were four bedrooms, each with bunkbeds. Some kids stayed for a week, others for months. Once they were eighteen, they had to leave; some treated their coming birthday like a release from prison, while others dreaded it, as it meant they'd soon be homeless.

Robin and I worked ten hours a week. The contrast with the computer lab, where I still worked also, was severe: instead of white-roomed silence, the group home was all jangled disruption, screaming laughter of teenagers, the clatter of dishes and endless chores. Much of our time was spent assembling meals: squishing tuna fish and mayonnaise in a giant vat, or layering lasagna noodles and sauce and cheese into sheet pans. We'd show up on a winter afternoon, stomp the snow from our boots, and take our instructions from a chore list posted on the yellowing refrigerator. If there wasn't cooking to do, we'd sweep and vacuum, or wash and fold laundry, or do piles of dishes.

When cooking we wore hairnets and gloves, but that didn't deter the boys in the home from acting like we were superstars. Once they learned our names they called us the Birds, and greeted us with whistles and songs. "What did you bring us, Birds?" they'd ask, though we never brought them anything.

One of them, Bernard, wouldn't speak to us but stood on the stairs or in the hall, watching as we worked, sometimes braving a smile. He was tall and thin, with big brown eyes and frizzy brown hair like a dandelion gone to seed, and so quiet that for the first few months I couldn't tell whether he was brain-damaged, or mute, or just shy.

As for the girls, if they noticed us at all it was to roll their eyes at our thrift-store clothes and ponytailed hair. They wore bright sweatshirts and jeans appliqued with flowers and painted their nails fluorescent colors and teased their hair to great heights. A girl named Kristina told Robin she'd be pretty if she fixed herself up a little. Robin stopped on the staircase—she was carrying a load of dirty sheets and towels down to the basement—and said, "I don't have time for that."

It was true. We hustled between school and work and piano and the library. We grabbed dinner at the group home, making ourselves sandwiches from the leftovers and devouring them as we trudged back to the apartment in the cold. Sometimes I saw my old roommate Helen between classes and we'd wave to one another and make vague plans to get together that neither of us followed up on.

"So you're off campus now?" she asked once, and I nodded.

"Is it lonely?" she asked, and I shook my head.

On campus, I knew, there were parties and jokes and people falling in love and breaking up, but all those activities seemed to take place in an alternate dimension, from which I was now separated by a barrier, very thin but nonetheless real, like a cell membrane. That Worthen wasn't mine anymore, and I didn't cross back into it; I had no urge to do so.

18.

In a physics textbook I read that Marie Curie's papers were, decades later, still radioactive. She and her husband Pierre had collected numerous dangerous elements—thorium, uranium, plutonium—in their home laboratory, and the elements glowed at night; Curie wrote in her autobiography that they were beautiful, "like faint, fairy lights." She carried them around, glowing, in the pockets of her white lab coat. I found a lab coat for sale at the thrift store and had Robin wear it while she made coffee in the kitchen. I turned off the overhead lights and slipped travel flashlights into the pockets.

"But what should I do?" Robin asked.

"Don't do anything," I said. "Think about something else."

The resulting film, *Marie Makes Coffee,* was grainy and out of focus. I used black-and-white film which I damaged by singeing it in places with a Bic lighter, feeling the thrill of destruction as the tiny flame licked the edges.

"I don't see the point of this," said the woman in my class who never saw the point of anything.

"Is this about the reclamation of feminist role models?" Alice Boryn asked.

I nodded, thinking it seemed like the right answer, but it wasn't really true. I mainly wanted to capture the radioactive fairy lights, to put them on film as I'd seen them in my head while reading. She sighed. In her class, we were supposed to defend and dissect our projects, to be articulate about film theory and technique, and although I was an enthusiastic maker of films, I said nothing during critiques of my own work or that of others. It wasn't because I had no thoughts. Rather, it was because I had *so many thoughts,* and they jostled inside my head as I planned and rehearsed them; by the time I was prepared to speak, the discussion had moved on to someone else, leaving only my silence behind.

Alice Boryn asked me to come to her office hours. She was a redheaded woman from the South, given to cursing in class. Although I didn't realize it until later, she'd recently been denied tenure for never finishing her own film, a documentary about the Triangle Shirtwaist Factory fire, and her freewheeling attitude probably arose from the fact that her time on campus was coming to an end.

"Olga thinks you're talented," she told me. I was standing across from her desk—she hadn't invited me to sit down, and I was too shy to do so anyway. I was late for a shift at the group home. "I'm not so sure, myself."

For moment my mind went blank, overwhelmed by the thought that Olga had praised me. As much as the praise itself, I was amazed that she'd thought about me enough to discuss me with someone else, that my existence had registered on her at all. I still thought of myself as invisible, as I had striven to be for most of my childhood. I remember Alice Boryn was wearing bright red lipstick that had worn off in the middle, and her cheeks were clouded with freckles that darkened her face as if she'd been slapped. I craved her approval and was also scared of her, and the only way I could keep going with my films was to say as little as possible to her, lest I humiliate myself.

Now she was waiting for me to speak. I considered, discarded, paused. Finally I said, "I'm not so sure either."

She grimaced, and tented her fingers beneath her freckled chin. "I'm going to give you some advice," she said. "I get that you've got this persona going, this outsider artist thing or whatever it is."

"It's not a persona," I said, confused.

"Olga says you're bright, and I know you work hard. But life isn't just about working hard. Trust me, I know. You're going to need more than just your work. You're going to need to sell it. Sell yourself. Do you know what I mean?"

I didn't. I scratched the back of my head, which I often did when I was nervous. After a stressful class my hair would be tangled in knots. Once Robin had to cut a whole section out, because it had grown too matted to fix. In this moment I felt not just nervous but accused, without understanding the accusation or knowing how to defend myself.

"I'm just kind of shy," I said finally, my throat constricted.

Again she sighed. "I'm trying to tell you something bigger," she said. "You're interested in self-invention, I can see that. You're interested in postures of greatness. You need to take these fascinations and put them to work for you. Don't be a *mouse*."

I stared at her. I had never articulated these ideas before and felt myself swamped by them, by the possibility that she knew things about me that I hadn't known myself. Though I had happily made my films and shared them with the class, even listened to the critiques with interest, I'd never thought much about others interpreting the images in such a broad fashion, finding strands or themes. It's strange to think about it now, the innocence of my self-absorption, which I didn't recognize until it was taken from me, a door swinging forever open on its hinge.

"Am I getting through to you at all?" Alice Boryn said.

"Yes," I said. "Of course."

It was clear to both of us that I was lying. She sighed irritably.

"Anyway," she said. "Try to talk more in class."

19.

The conversation had the opposite effect than she intended. Her attention made me so self-conscious that I stopped going to class at all, and almost failed; it took an intervention from Olga, and a paper I wrote for extra credit, to rescue my grade. Later, when I heard Alice Boryn had left Worthen to teach at a community college on Long Island, I was relieved.

But Boryn wasn't the only reason I had trouble with school that semester; I was distracted by other events as well. One afternoon in March I walked to my shift at the group home. The day was unusually mild and sunny, and remnants of soot-encrusted snow were collapsing on the sidewalk. As I neared, I could see two residents standing on the porch smoking, and two more below them, throwing melting snowballs at each other in a front yard turning rapidly to mud. Only when I was almost at the building did I understand that it wasn't a snowball fight but an argument with snow as prop; also, it wasn't two residents, but one resident—Bernard—and my sister. The smokers, Kristina and Jennifer, stood with their arms crossed, expressions slightly bored, as if watching a TV show that was only semi-entertaining. Every few seconds one of them would lean forward to tap ash from her cigarette, then cross her arms again.

"Why would you do that?" Robin yelled, her face contorted. She threw a clump of snow that disintegrated halfway between them. For a second Bernard looked like he wanted to laugh, but stopped himself. Though he was very thin his clothes were still small on him, pants an inch too short, sleeves shrunken above his wrists, which made him look younger than he was. They stood almost ten feet apart, facing off, as if in some ceremony or ritual.

"I had to," Bernard mumbled, without conviction.

"Oh, come on," Robin said. She was wearing an old blue ski jacket of mine over a flowered sundress and rubber rain boots, an outfit for three different seasons, and her hair was in two long braids. Braids made it easier to put on the hairnets Mrs. Dean Smith required in the kitchen.

"What's going on?" I said. So far as I knew, they'd never had a conversation that extended beyond hello. It embarrasses me now to remember how oblivious I was, especially when I consider what Bernard's life was like then, and how much he meant to each of us later on.

"He's leaving the home," she said without looking in my direction.

I couldn't see why it was our business. The mid-afternoon sun had slipped behind the house, casting the yard in shadow, but Bernard, wearing no jacket, hugged his arms around himself. "My moms has a place now," he said. "I can stay with her."

"Great," I said.

"It's *not* great," Robin said. "It's the opposite of great." She was crying, and when I stepped closer, she waved me off as if whatever were happening were my fault. Kristina and Jennifer stamped out their cigarettes and opened the door to the house with its telltale squeak; Mr. Dean Smith was supposed to oil its hinge but never got around to it.

"What the hell is going on?" I said, and Kristina called helpfully, before disappearing inside, "They in love."

That night, after we finished our shift, I confronted my sister, who confessed that she and Bernard had been seeing each other since November. When I was at the computer lab or the library or in class, they'd go for walks; he sometimes met her at school and rode the bus with her to her piano lessons. From beneath the dresser in her room she drew out a shoebox and showed me, with tender, fluttering pride, a pile of drawings he'd made for and of her: Robin in profile, her eyes focused on something in the distance; Robin at the piano, her fingers a blur of movement. They were pretty good, I had to admit. Robin said Bernard was gentle and sweet. Once they went to the Museum of Fine Arts in Boston; he liked Titian, she said. She'd been taking him to the public library to look at art books. She'd even been giving him some of her group-home wages—money she'd told me she'd spent on sheet music and school supplies—so he could buy things. When I asked what kind of things, she said, "Amenities."

It turned out "amenities" meant Cokes, bags of chips, and comic books. Why, I asked her, had she kept all this from me?

"I didn't think you'd approve."

"I *don't* approve," I said immediately, though I wasn't sure why. Bernard was fifteen and I'd barely ever heard him speak. I didn't know if he went to school, or where. My objection was largely to the secrecy itself, which excluded me from her life after she'd moved to Worthen and changed so much in mine.

"You can't tell me what to do, you're not Marianne."

The thought was repulsive. "Of course I'm not Marianne!" I said.

Robin burst into tears. She was upset, she told me, because his mother's new apartment was in Baltimore and Bernard planned to join her there. "It's my *mom,*" he kept saying to Robin, and no matter how much she reminded him of the things his mother had done—drugs, never having food in the house, asking him to steal things for her—to get him placed in foster care originally, he wouldn't be dissuaded. Robin couldn't believe it, and neither could I. She and I had left our mother behind and found ourselves happier for it; nothing, we thought then, would ever bring us back to her. We hadn't even gone home for Christmas that year, lying to Marianne that we'd been invited to the home of a wealthy classmate in Connecticut; raising no objection, she mailed us drugstore chocolates and *Joyeux Noël* cards.

"And now I'll never see him again," Robin concluded, twisting her hands.

I recognized her distress. How could I not? I had just lived through it myself. I cradled her head in my lap and told her I understood, her tears wetting my shirt, her long hair tickling my arms. Sometimes I can still feel the weight of her body against mine, damp with heartbreak, beautiful Robin, sixteen.

20.

A month later Mrs. Dean Smith phoned us, yelling, her spittle making static on the phone. She called Robin and me liars and thieves. She'd always known we were strange and couldn't be trusted.

"I don't understand," I said. "Are we fired?"

"You bet your behind you're fired," she said. "And don't be asking for references, neither. You're lucky I don't go to the police."

"Okay," I said.

"You should *thank* me for not calling the police!"

"Thank you," I said.

"Don't ever show your weirdo faces around here again!" she added, and hung up.

It was nine in the evening, and Robin was sitting on the couch with one leg curled beneath her, bent over geometry homework. Her piano lessons were going well, but she was barely passing her classes at school. She seemed to study, but I think she just stared at her books while her mind wandered. Whenever I looked at her papers or tests the first section was done perfectly until the letters or numbers loosened around the edges as she got distracted, with the bottom of the page always blank. *Nice start,* her teachers sometimes wrote, *what happened?* Others, less sympathetic, assigned poor grades without comment. Now I could tell, from how hard she appeared to be concentrating, that she was faking.

"Do you know what that was about?" I asked.

She put her pencil down. "Bernard needed some help for his trip," she said.

"Some help."

She wouldn't meet my eyes. "They keep some cash in the kitchen cupboard—you know the one where that big coffee pot is?"

"Robin, did you *take* it?"

"No, of course not!"

"But you told your boyfriend about it."

She didn't say anything. I was furious, and told her so, and we argued. How were we going to pay our rent? Robin's teacher had recommended her for a special summer program—how would we pay for that? We needed this job, badly. Robin had no defense; she told me to stop yelling, that she knew it was a problem, and she'd fix it, somehow.

"How?" I said cruelly. "By calling Hervé?"

Once I spoke I heard how mean it was, and wished I could take it back; I could see the imprint of the words on my sister's face, as clearly as if I'd slapped her. She ran out of the apartment. It was a warm night and the lilacs were blooming, a sweet and wistful fragrance that carried through our open windows. After a few hours I pulled on my jacket and went looking for her. More than anything I was afraid that she'd gotten on a bus to Baltimore and I'd never see her again. I'd orbited my life around hers and if she left, all that remained would be an empty circle. I checked the convenience store, the campus, the piano studios: she was nowhere. On a bench by the bus stop a man slept under newspapers that rustled with his breath. At the factory, trucks began rumbling into the parking lot. The sun came up, and she was still nowhere. After long hours without sleeping I eventually went to class, though I sat through my lectures in a daze, and when I returned to the apartment she was sitting on the couch, studying, as if the previous twenty-four hours had never happened. Her face was pale and set. She told me that she'd found a job washing dishes at the Chinese restaurant at the strip mall, and that she'd collected a few job listings for me. She planned to work full-time until the end of June, and showed me her calculations for what she would earn: enough to pay for her summer program and half the rent.

"Please don't send me home," she said.

I was stricken; I'd never meant her to feel so threatened. "You never have to go back there," I told her, and she sighed like a pardoned prisoner.

21.

My junior and senior years at Worthen passed quickly, in a density of work and classes. My mind was engaged by my studies, stretching itself so palpably that it felt physical. I worked for Olga on her book, and I made a series of short films. Olga encouraged me to find a different subject than my sister, a good idea because Robin was so busy herself. Instead, I approached my old roommate Helen, who greeted me with casual warmth, as if I hadn't completely absented myself from her life. My films were a study of the women's track team, and I spent hours at Helen's practices and meets. I wanted to capture the strength and grace of these athletes, the exactitude of their movements; in one film, I intercut them with stills from Eadweard Muybridge, the nineteenth-century photographer who had been hired by a wealthy patron to figure out whether, when horses run, their four feet ever leave the ground at the same time. (They do.) "So you're saying we're like horses?" Helen said, amused.

Flustered, I tried to explain that no, this was not the point, it was about trying to capture the fluidity of movement itself, but Helen interrupted me, laughing. "I don't need to hear the theory," she said. "I was just giving you a hard time."

However much footage I shot of the women in their tracksuits, laughing and stretching before and after the meets, the images I found most entrancing were their faces as they ran, furrowed and intense, cheeks flattened and rippling, teeth bared, stripped of all self-consciousness. In retrospect, I see that I was trying to capture the same concentration I'd observed on Robin's face when she was playing the piano, but at the time I thought that I had found an entirely new subject, a departure. In my senior presentation I talked about Muybridge and the camera's male gaze and how I wanted to position these athletes, in their physical prowess and ambition, as running away from that gaze; I stammered with hesitation but kept going, and Olga was pleased.

In those two years Robin and I rarely went to Montreal, and Marianne didn't visit us at Worthen. We settled into distance from our mother as if this had been our home all along. In fact we rarely even talked about her, no longer finding her life as fascinating as we did when we were children. In spite of all the time we spent working and studying, we nonetheless grew part of a social circle; we were invited to parties thrown by Helen and her friends, who treated Robin as a kind of mascot. "I wish my little sister could come live with me," one of them said sadly at a party, "our parents are assholes too," and for the first time I could tell that some people envied us. Robin's friends from high school were Laotian twins who bonded with her over their ignorance of American history; they were all three close to failing civics and often gathered in our living room to go over the basics, sometimes receiving tutoring help from the track team, who sang them the song from *Schoolhouse Rock* about how a bill becomes a law. At Helen's urging I went on two dates with a very tall boy on the track team, Billy, who bent down to kiss me from his great height, the milliseconds before he made contact ticking by in frightening slow motion. The kiss was not unpleasant, but it sparked nothing in me. In melodramatic moments I confided to Robin that I was forever scarred by my experience with Gordon, and would never fall in love again, and she nodded, feeling likewise permanently broken. We were tragic heroines together, undone by love, but steadfast in our bond.

In the fall of my senior year, two things happened. One day when I was at work at the computer lab, talking to Richard about Scorsese—I confessed that I'd fallen asleep during *Mean Streets,* and he was teasing me about it—Professor Boris Dawidoff came in. He was a middle-aged man with red-veined skin and a significant stomach who nonetheless carried himself with an air of elegance; he always wore a blazer and scarf knotted in the European style. Robin didn't think he liked her; he'd told her she didn't practice enough and that her interpretations were amateurish. *More technique, less show,* he would tell her, rapping on the piano with a conductor's baton he kept for that purpose. She said she felt like he was restraining himself from tapping her on the fingers directly, that he knew she felt this and did it to instill fear in her, to make her cower. "I won't let him get to me," she told me, in a tone that suggested the opposite was true. Because of him she practiced more than she ever had, although she complained about the dryness of the music he made her play, steering her away from the Romantics she loved and toward the Baroque.

Now he stood in front of me in the lab. We hadn't had a conversation since I'd first approached him about teaching Robin, two years earlier. Richard discreetly went back to his office, and Dawidoff sat down next to me.

"Have you thought about where your sister will go to school?" he said.

I hadn't. If I'd considered the future at all, it was to panic about my own. Worthen had been my whole life, and in seven months it would eject me. All I knew was that I wouldn't go back to Montreal.

"We need to start setting up auditions," he went on. "Blooming-ton, Cincinnati. Juilliard."

Seeing my blank face, he ran his hands through his grey hair and nodded as if my reaction had confirmed his suspicions. "With your permission, I will take over," he said. "I have friends at these institutions. There are financial aid packages as well, if that is your concern."

"Okay," I said.

He sighed, and pursed his lips. "Your sister," he said, "should be supported in her aspirations."

I was offended. "I *do* support her," I said. "I support her all the time."

"I'm sure you do," he said condescendingly. "But what you offer may not be enough."

Before long, Robin began to come back to the apartment later and later at night, as they spent long hours together rehearsing her audition pieces. It was Dawidoff who took her to Juilliard and Berk-lee, navigating the process with assurance. As he shepherded her into the future, I built my own in line with it. I applied to film schools in New York and Boston, asking Olga for help. She offered little advice, only agreeing to write me a letter of recommendation, and I under-stood that I was not the prodigy to her that Robin was to Dawidoff. I wasn't surprised by this. It seemed only right that the world found my sister as exceptional as I did, and myself as ordinary.

"Holy shit!" Helen said when we told her that Robin had been accepted to Juilliard. "That's amazing!" The track team threw us a party, where we drank Red Stripe and danced to the Fugees. At three in the morning Helen and her friends requested a concert. Robin blushed and declined, but they persisted, pestering her good-naturedly until she gave in, leading us over to the music building; it was locked, but Robin produced a key that Dawidoff had given her, and we sat on the floor while she splayed herself across the keyboard, lushly, loosely playing Mendelssohn's *Songs Without Words*. She was wearing a New York Mets T-shirt that had belonged to Bernard and the same jean skirt and Converse shoes she'd had on the day she arrived at Worthen. She looked like any other teenage girl, but when she began to play her features settled and her face became suddenly more adult. Although I knew how much she practiced, I was still sometimes surprised by her intense, almost devotional seriousness; it was like realizing your sister was a nun, betrothed to God. The music flooded the room: ripples of sound that spread out from her in waves, cresting and ebbing; the waves hit me in my chest and kept going, a tidal force. The word that came to my mind was *gigantic*. Next to her talent, anything I had ever made or would make was a miniature, of tiny and passing import. From the movement of my sister's hands came something enormous and majestic, big enough to fill us all, and when she finished, the silence in the room still seemed to bristle and quiver. One of the girls was crying.

"Jesus Christ," said a hurdler named Samantha. "That is freaking unbelievable."

My sister stood up from the piano bench and curtsied, drunkenly, before pivoting sharply to the left and leaning against a music stand, which fell over with a clatter. Knowing what was coming, I grabbed a trash can and ran to her, feeling her collapse into my arms. She sat on the floor and threw up into the can as I held her hair out of the way. Her hands clutching mine were clammy and cold, and she moaned a little, wordlessly.

"You'll be okay," I told her.

"Oh, God, I'm spinning," she said. "Don't let go."

"I won't," I said. In my pocket was an envelope I hadn't told anyone about yet, an acceptance; I was going to New York too.

Marianne finally did come to Worthen, for my graduation. When she stepped out of her rental car in front of the apartment, we were so shocked at her appearance that we didn't know what to say. She'd gained a great deal of weight, and for the first time in her life she looked frumpy and old, though she was only forty. Her unstyled hair hung limply to her shoulders above a blue button-down shirt and a baggy pair of pants with an elastic waist. She stood in the center of our living room, taking in our furnishings with some of her old imperiousness. "That couch is hideous," she said. We were reassured by this, her meanness a constant from our childhood. She'd brought us presents, clothes of hers that didn't fit anymore and, for each of us, a fancy bookmark of thin, flat gold.

"They were gifts from my grandmother," she said, "when I was a girl. I used to get high marks." Her eyes glimmered with tears, and Robin and I looked at each other, confused. Robin stepped closer, as if to hug her, but Marianne shook her head. "Is there a decent restaurant," she said, "in this stupid American town?"

We went to the Italian place where I had once eaten with Gordon and his parents. Marianne ordered a bottle of wine and drank it all herself. She didn't mention Hervé. She did say that she'd switched to a new job as an account manager at a small firm and no longer traveled, and when we congratulated her on the promotion she raised an eyebrow and said, "Let's not get ahead of ourselves."

We didn't discuss the future or the past. We'd told her on the phone that we were moving to New York that summer, having cobbled together enough in the way of scholarships and student loans, and she'd said only, "Fine."

She asked if we wanted dessert and then seemed aggravated when we accepted. The tiramisu we chose puddled on our plates in a congealing sauce. I sat on my hands; Robin tapped the sides of her seat with her fingers.

Marianne's eyes watered when she looked at the bill. "You girls," she said, "you've always sucked me dry."

I saw Robin stiffen, and it was her discomfort that made me speak, more than my own. Or perhaps, I think now, I was emboldened by Marianne's weakness, her middle-aged ugliness, which made her seem vulnerable as she never had before.

"We've taken nothing from you," I said. "You've given us nothing. All you think about is yourself."

If Marianne was shocked by this attack, so uncharacteristic of me, she didn't show it. She rolled her eyes as if it were an argument we were in the habit of conducting, as if she'd heard it all before. This made me even angrier.

"Someday you'll understand," she said condescendingly. "Perhaps when you have children of your own, you'll know what sacrifice being a mother is."

"What would you know about being a mother?" I said, raising my voice. If the restaurant hadn't been crowded I would have attracted attention, but all around us families were laughing, bantering, congratulating their children with noisy praise. "I've been more a mother to Robin than you," I went on, surprised to hear my own voice snapping off each word with clear articulation.

I felt Robin's hand on my arm, but what shut me up was Marianne's laughter, which filled the restaurant even above the noise of the other tables; it came in gales, loud and fake, like an actress in an old movie. She laughed and laughed, and other people looked at us; the waitress approached to collect the bill and timidly stepped away.

Then Marianne stopped, as abruptly as she'd started, picked up her napkin, and fussily folded it into a neat, perfect square. Her expression was no longer angry or upset, but simply neutral; she seemed to have forgotten the entire conversation while we were still in the middle of it. She looked very strange. I noticed that her neck had developed a wattle beneath her chin, and the skin there was twitching with her pulse. The weakness that had emboldened me now shamed and confused me. I felt like a cat that had leapt on a mouse, thrilled to play, only to be disappointed because it died too soon.

Marianne paid the check and drove us home in silence. She sat through my graduation the next day and made it clear she wouldn't be attending Robin's from high school, which was the following month. When she left, she kissed us each on both cheeks, formal as a stranger, her lips pursing the air.

Better in every way was the farewell party we threw at our apartment. Emma drove back from Great Barrington to celebrate with us, bringing with her a large block of milky homemade cheese; Richard and his wife came, wearing identical khakis and blue polos, and only after they left did I discover an envelope they'd addressed to me, with an astoundingly large check inside, more zeros than I'd ever seen in my life, and a note that said, *Use this for your future.* The track team came and so did a couple of people from my film classes and the Laotian twins and the Chinese family who owned the restaurant where Robin still worked. Olga and Boris arrived together and stayed for fifteen minutes, smoking cigarettes on the porch and speaking only to each other before departing, as mysterious to me as they'd always been. At midnight, gathering empties into a garbage bag, I sobbed at the thought of leaving Worthen, which seemed to me then the most perfect place in the world.

22.

Robin and I moved into a place in Hell's Kitchen we called the Tunnel. It was a railroad apartment, skinny as a snake: you entered into a hallway, and from there into a combined living room and kitchen where the two of us could just barely sit down on a futon. Then there was my bedroom, which you had to walk through to get to Robin's bedroom, which was no bigger than the mattress we put in it. The apartment didn't matter much, because we were hardly ever there. In order to make ends meet I enrolled in classes part-time and worked full-time at the campus store, where I stood behind the cash register and rang up overpriced sweatshirts with the school logo. I often grabbed a few hours of sleep on the couch in the student lounge rather than bothering to take the subway home. Nobody thought this was weird; nobody paid any attention to me at all. In film school everyone seemed more confident and sophisticated than I was; they argued for hours about Jim Jarmusch, could dissertate on Wong Kar-Wai. I was back where I'd been as a first-year student at Worthen, listening to Gordon's speeches, acutely conscious of all I didn't know.

Robin picked up new friends with whom she shared impenetrable inside jokes about "J-yard," as they called it; a mention of twelve-tone scales sent them into spasms of giggles and groans. They sat around listening to CDs and rating the performers as "Rach 2" or "Rach 3." Some of them had done nothing, it seemed, but play the piano since they were four years old. They were like veal calves who'd spent their lives in cages, fattened to bursting with musical technique; they could barely walk on their underdeveloped legs, but their Chopin could make you cry.

Maybe in response to this atmosphere, or maybe not—she didn't talk much about her decisions—my sister dyed her hair blue and wore men's clothes. To her existing nose piercing she added another hoop, and one at her eyebrow; one day I noticed bloody bandages in the trash and learned she'd gotten a spiral tattoo on her ankle. Later she added others—a heart, a flower—on her bicep and the small of her back, doodling on herself as if she were a notebook. Nowadays these kinds of tattoos are common on young women, even expected, but at the time I was mildly shocked by them, less by their appearance than by her belief that these symbols were worth carrying permanently. What did a spiral mean to her, or a rose? When I asked, she shrugged casually and said it was something to do. She dated a woman named Sheri who accused her of "using lesbianism as a fashion accessory" and then dumped her, leaving my sister sobbing and bereft, just as she'd been with Bernard. She drowned her sorrows in rum and I'd wake up to hear her retching as she ran through my bedroom on the way to the toilet.

She spent as much time at school as I did, and sometimes a week passed without us speaking. Our lives overlapped at the edges, never the center.

Even with all these changes, I was cautiously, timidly happy. The city confessed itself to me, as if in secret confidence. My New York was a study in negative space. It was Washington Square at five in the morning, mostly deserted except for me and the addicts and the early-waking joggers, or the view from the editing lab at midnight, when the streets were full of NYU undergrads heading to bars. It was a man walking with his head down, cigarette in hand; another reading a book on a park bench; a woman I saw on the bus, looking out the window, tears rolling down her face. The bulk of my time I spent alone, the quiet of my work-study job with Richard now tuned to a professional frequency. The membrane I'd felt before in college, separating me from everyone else, still endured, but now I considered it protective, and I hummed with activity behind it, purposeful, unseen.

23.

In my second semester of grad school, I took a documentary film course. In class we screened *Titicut Follies* by Frederick Wiseman, about life inside a prison for the criminally insane. Produced in the sixties, it had been banned for decades and released only in 1992. I watched it with horror-struck fascination; at times I covered my face with my hands and then peered through my fingers. What I was seeing was terrible—abuse, violence, illness, degradation—and the fact of seeing it felt transgressive and monumental and implicating. I wrote an essay about it, twice as long as the assignment was supposed to be, receiving for my efforts a failing grade and a note from the professor that said, *I asked for analysis, not fan mail*. My cheeks burning, I planned to drop the class, too embarrassed to face him again. But when I looked at the syllabus, I noted that the following week was scheduled to feature as a guest speaker a filmmaker named Lawrence Wheelock.

At Worthen, Olga had talked to me about Wheelock's film *The Habit of Despair*. We were sitting in her office on a typically dark winter afternoon, the wind making the walls of the building creak. She tipped back in her chair and looked at the ceiling, speaking more to herself than to me. When she first saw *The Habit of Despair,* she was around my age. The title came from Camus—"the habit of despair is worse than despair itself"—and Olga, who loved Camus, recognized the quote immediately. Other than this, she knew nothing about the film. She had the habit herself, at that time, of wandering into films she knew nothing about. In fact she purposefully wouldn't read about them in advance, would sometimes even buy a ticket to a showing that was halfway through, or leave before the film was over. It was, she told me, a test of her own receptivity to the image: whatever was projected, she'd make sense of. "Or maybe," she said, "it was just a silly game of chance."

Wheelock, she'd learn later, was just twenty-five when he made this, his first film. Intending to watch for a few minutes, she stayed for the entire thing. She was the only person in the theatre, and at one point she looked up at the projection booth and saw there was no one in it; afterward, when she exited to the lobby, there was no one working there either. The whole experience was so vivid and odd that it felt like a lucid dream.

In the film, a woman goes about her daily life. She feeds her children breakfast, kisses her husband, cleans the house, then goes off to work at a paper factory. She answers the phone and types letters while behind her, on the factory floor, massive rolls of paper spin from machines and are pulled from conveyer belts into bins. These industrial movements are so noisy that the woman's voice can't be heard at all. At night, she puts her children to bed, lies in bed herself reading a magazine, turns out the light. She doesn't complain. She doesn't speak to the camera or give any sense of being watched. The narrative is artless, seemingly unshaped. When it finished, Olga was sobbing. "It was the saddest film I had ever seen," she said.

Slowly she lowered her gaze from the ceiling to me. "So you see," she added, spreading her palms.

I didn't see. I didn't understand the point she was making, and yet it was probably the most intimate confidence she ever shared with me. I remember she was wearing a red scarf and brown lipstick, which was fashionable then, and a bulky navy-blue turtleneck sweater that fell just below her hips. Somehow, this blanket-sized item of clothing looked chic on her and not ridiculous. In the semi-darkness of her office the planes of her face tilted into shadow. I lingered there, hoping she would say more, but the moment passed, and she turned to the book manuscript on her desk and chided me for some sloppiness in the proofreading.

Because of Olga, there was no way I'd miss Wheelock's lecture, so I returned to the class and hid at the back. When he entered the room, accompanied by my professor, I had the rare experience of seeing a person who was more uncomfortable in front of an audience than I was. And perhaps it was for good reason: his appearance made the two students seated in front of me, a couple who worshipped Hal Hartley and wore matching Doc Martens, snicker. I flushed with vicarious embarrassment and hoped he hadn't heard.

Wheelock was wearing frayed khaki pants belted high at the waist—just under his ribcage—and a thick white shirt gone yellow at the armpits. The clothes were stained, not with romantic paint splatters but with what was clearly food, coffee, and dirt. His glasses were thick and his dark brown hair hadn't been cut for months. He squinted at a point above our heads while our professor fussed with something at the lectern. He kept wiping his hands on the seat of his pants, then staring at whatever residue he couldn't get off his palms. Dark-eyed, very thin, he resembled the physicist Robert Oppenheimer. Looking at him, I remembered reading that Oppenheimer only learned about the Wall Street crash of 1929 six months after it happened, in a conversation with a friend. He was that removed, as a young man, from the things of this world. Wheelock had an air of absent-mindedness that made me imagine he, too, lived at some incalculable distance from the mundane reality the rest of us shared.

I expected him to stammer and pause, but in fact once the projector was set up Wheelock was confident and articulate. I thought he was brilliant. He didn't discuss his own films, even in passing. He showed a scene from Renoir's *The Rules of the Game* ("predictable," sniffed the couple in front of me) and took apart its composition, comparing it to Velázquez's painting *Las Meninas.* He talked about the camera as a kind of mirror held up to the content of the scene, making its presence felt even though the equipment is itself unseen. He said any filmmaker embodied the Heisenberg uncertainty principle, affecting the proceedings by observing them, and that the best filmmaking embraced this complication rather than attempting to smooth it away. He discussed how Errol Morris's *The Thin Blue Line* led to a man being released from prison, and how in it Morris used re-enactments *except* for the scene he argued had really taken place, and in this way the truth, if there was such a thing, lived in the viewer's mind instead of on the screen. Then, abruptly, almost mid-sentence, he stopped. He'd been talking for an hour, and our professor, flustered, noted that we'd run out of time for questions. Seeing the flicker of a smile pass over Wheelock's face, I understood that he'd talked too long on purpose.

Students from the next class were already filtering in, taking their seats. I walked over, drawn as if magnetized, to where Wheelock and my professor were standing in the hallway. "Espresso?" the professor was saying, and then, laughing nervously, "or whiskey?" It was eleven in the morning, but Wheelock looked interested.

"I know a good place for whiskey," I said. This behavior was so uncharacteristic of me that I can't, even now, explain it. My professor looked startled; I never spoke in class, and I'm not sure he knew who I was.

"Well, if you know a good place," Wheelock said. I noticed his lips were chapped and there were circles beneath his eyes. I didn't, in fact, know a good place; I knew no bars at all. But New York was full of bars, and surely they all had whiskey. I led the two men down the elevator and out of the building, operating on bravado alone. When we reached the street, I remembered a bar I'd seen on the way to the subway during a snowstorm; a man and woman had been sitting at the window, their heads bent close together, cozy and romantic. Now we walked there through the kind of characterless March day that was cold but not biting, wind flinging trash around the street like a child bored with its toys. I opened the door and said, "After you."

Inside it was dim and cold, not at all cozy or romantic. One man sat at the bar with his coat on, drinking what looked like a glass of milk, an empty shot glass next to it. The bartender came out from the back. He had a shaved head and a bruised lip and didn't seem pleased to see us.

"Perfect," Wheelock said behind me.

We settled into a booth. The professor went to the bar and came back with three whiskeys, and a Coke for himself, explaining that he had to teach in an hour. Ignoring him, Wheelock lowered his head to a glass and slurped carefully, smacking his lips. Then he picked it up and drank the rest, his fingers flailing. The professor's eyes met mine. He slid his whiskey over to Wheelock, who drank it, too, then sat back in the booth, his relief palpable. Up close, his chin was graveled with stubble. "I don't sleep well," he said to no one in particular. "I'm not much of a public speaker."

"I thought you were amazing," I said, and the words evaporated in the dark bar, ignored. I remembered my professor's comments on my essay: *I asked for analysis, not fan mail.* I started to talk about Werner Herzog's film *Fitzcarraldo,* about a man who wants to build an opera house in the Amazonian jungle. I'd watched it earlier that semester because other students were talking about it. They loved to use the word *Fitzcarraldian* as a casual adjective. "I have a Fitzcarraldian ambition to write this paper," they'd say. The film was famous and I hated it, feeling, as I often did, conscious of my failure of taste. Wheelock didn't seem to be listening, and my professor was rifling through his backpack, muttering about missing lecture notes. This freed me to talk without any expectation of being heard. I said the movie made me angry, that it collapsed male ambition and high culture as if the two were one and the same; I said—and these were Olga's positions more than my own—that the camera's male gaze supported this vapid ideology, in which there was no self-questioning. "What I want in a movie is more uncertainty," I said, having no idea what I meant. "More room for randomness and chance."

But somewhere in the middle of my musings Wheelock had begun to pay attention, and he interrupted me with questions. What did I mean by *uncertainty*? Could I give an example of it in a film? By this point I'd drunk my whiskey—the first of my life, I think—and it was burning in my stomach and brain. I talked about Sophie Calle, a French artist I'd recently learned about and by whom I was fascinated. She'd once asked her mother to hire a detective to follow her around Paris. The detective recorded her movements as she recorded her experience of being watched. She was both in control of his gaze and not; both observer and observed. Wheelock rolled his eyes. "A stunt," he said. "Artificial reality, no better than the formula of a studio film."

Soon we were arguing. Wheelock raised a finger, and more whiskey appeared. At some point I noticed my professor was gone. I was very drunk. I began ranting about the movie *Pretty Woman* and Wheelock, to my surprise, was laughing. There were more people in the bar now—all men—and he was so loud that they turned around to look at us. It wasn't the kind of bar where people laughed. It was a quiet hovel for daytime drinking, but I didn't have enough experience of bars to know that. When I saw Wheelock laughing, I knew I'd embarrassed myself. But I also knew he was transformed;

he had a beautiful smile, with two dimples that sucked his stubble into sweetness.

When we stumbled out of the bar into the bleak windy afternoon, Wheelock handed me his card. He lived and worked in a farmhouse in Pennsylvania, and he promised me a summer job.

"Are you going to remember this?" I asked, swaying on the sidewalk.

"I forget nothing," he said.

24.

Perhaps if I'd been less wrapped up in my own life, I would have noticed Robin's troubles, but it wasn't until much later that I understood how much she struggled. At Juilliard, there was nothing but rules. Robin's technique was considered sloppy; it was said that she'd been allowed too much freedom and her playing was inexact. Her teachers raised their eyebrows at her interpretations and she was given to understand that her bad habits would have to be unlearned. They wanted to break down her technique at the most basic level; they were teaching the Taubman approach, which was supposed to reduce injuries. So they would make her play—over and over again—the first three measures of a piece she'd learned when she was ten years old. They stood beside her and made her tuck in her chin; they worked on micro-rotations of her elbows and wrists; they changed her fingering and pressed their hands on her shoulders. Everything she did was *too much*. Sometimes she caught them rolling their eyes, and rather than hastening to please them, as I would have, she went in the opposite direction, playing her pieces with mannered exaggeration. "Is it possible to play the piano *sarcastically*?" one of her teachers said. "Because I think that's what I just heard."

Unlike me, Robin never retreated into herself. Charismatic and opinionated, she made friends easily, and they went out for coffee after class, complaining about their workload, their teachers, the theory courses that made Robin's head ache with boredom. But after coffee, her friends would go back to work, and Robin wouldn't. She went out for drinks or dates. She went dancing by herself and didn't come home alone.

Then, in December of her first semester, Dawidoff called. They'd never spoken on the phone before, not even at Worthen, and for a moment his low, thick, familiar voice warmed her, until he said, "I'm not hearing good things."

"No?" she said. "Your new students can't live up to me, is that it?"

"Don't be cute," Dawidoff said. In his Russian accent, which Robin imitated later in telling me the story, the word came out long and icy, *quooot*. "You are there because of me," he said. "I realize you do not know this. You think everything comes to you because you are so special and lovely, pretty Robin with the beautiful music, la la la. You are a talented girl. But you are not as special as you think. *I* made this happen. I called in years of favors for this. When you fail, it looks very bad for me."

Robin buttoned her lips.

"I didn't ask you for anything," she said finally. "I could just go to community college or whatever."

"Fine," Dawidoff said brusquely. "Do that." He hung up. Robin held the receiver with shaking hands, the dial tone humming A and F notes, a chord she couldn't unhear.

She was determined that if she left Juilliard it would be her own decision and no one else's. So in the spring semester, around the time that I met Lawrence Wheelock, she changed her playing style. She broke herself of all her old habits—what she considered her entire personality as a musician—and assumed new ones. She obeyed every instruction. She found the performance style dry and limiting but not, ultimately, difficult. She made of herself a perfect robot. When her teachers smiled thinly, still not convinced, she pressed on, stripping everything away, all color, all spontaneity, all romance.

"It's nice to see you maturing," a teacher told her at last. "We'll make a Glenn Gould of you yet." People at school were always making Gould jokes because my sister was Canadian. She wished they'd find some better material.

"Excellent, I'd love to be a disturbed shut-in who dies at the age of fifty," she said.

"Still," her teacher said. "We like to see you moving away from all that self-indulgence."

Robin thought it made no sense that indulging the self was considered a bad thing. What was there in music besides the self? And if you took out the self, where was it supposed to go? When she told me this story, years afterward, I could see how she still bristled at the memory, how she was both proud of her ability to give her teachers what they wanted and resentful of their demands.

"Do you wish you hadn't given in?" I asked her.

"I didn't give in," she said sharply. "I only pretended to."

Pretend or not, Robin made a great success by the end of that first year. She was invited to a prestigious summer festival in Aspen; her grades were excellent. At school one day she received a bouquet of flowers, and tucked among the daylilies and roses was a small card. *I guess you aren't going to community college after all. Boris.* Robin carried the bouquet, pink and yellow sprays tickling her nose, through the hallways and down to the street. She walked across Lincoln Center and west on 66th Street, the wind flapping her hair into her eyes, so that she was half-blind but unable, because of the flowers, to push it aside. If people stared she didn't see them. She kept going until she hit the Hudson and there she set the bouquet down. She tore the flowers into pieces and flung them into the choppy water. When she ran out of flowers she threw the vase, which bobbed briefly before sinking below the surface with a disappointing lack of fanfare.

A man in a business suit was eating lunch on a bench, his bento box perched on his thighs, and observing her with a smirk. Holding a piece of salmon between his thumb and index finger, he waved it at her while a seagull eyed it jealously. "Don't worry, baby," he said, "there are a lot of other fish in the sea."

Robin turned on him. "What an incredibly wise saying! I've never heard anyone put it that way before."

He wasn't fazed. "So we're in *that* mood," he said, still smirking.

His name was Saul and he was a management consultant. Robin followed him back to his apartment on the Upper West Side and had sex with him but only, she told me all those years later, still percolating her rage, to get rid of that smirk.

25.

Robin and I spent the summer apart. She went to Aspen and then Chicago for a summer intensive program, returning to New York and the Tunnel before I did. She earned scholarships and stipends, enough to cover her share of the rent, and I took this to mean that everything was on track. I had no doubt that she'd become famous, performing in fancy gowns and recording music that would be listened to for decades, just as she and I had played countless albums on Marianne's Magnavox turntable. Because of this certainty, some tension that had gripped me for years—the pressure of being responsible for her—lessened. I went to central Pennsylvania to work for Lawrence Wheelock, who lived in an old yellow farmhouse decorated with peeling hex signs the previous owners had left behind. When I arrived, he came to pick me up at the bus stop in a dark blue pickup truck scabied with rust.

"Pleased to have you," he muttered as we rumbled along the gravel road, "I look forward to your contributions." He showed me to a garden shed behind the house, where I would be staying. "For your privacy," he said, raising his eyebrows awkwardly. The shed had been fixed up by some previous occupant: there was a four-poster bed with surprisingly nice sheets and blankets, a nightstand, and a little bookcase. It was wired for electricity and had a small sink and toilet in the corner, like a deluxe cell.

Wheelock's house testified to his immersion in his work. There was almost no furniture; the living room was a mess of an archive, with filing cabinets and shelving units on which were stored reels of film, and the long kitchen table was stacked and scattered with newspapers and yellow legal pads crammed with enigmatic notes. Though the arrangement of papers seemed chaotic and random, if I got anywhere near them he would say quickly, "Don't touch that," from which I gathered there was some system only he could understand. Against one wall, beneath the windows, sat a series of glass urns filled almost to the brim with cigarette butts swimming in a dingy, dark liquid. I never saw him smoke.

On the second floor were Wheelock's bedroom and two other rooms he used for editing. The kitchen he used for drinking. Sometimes, lying in the garden shed at night, listening to the wind throwing pine needles down on my roof, I saw a light shining in the kitchen well past three in the morning. The shed itself creaked and juddered, with tiny scurrying movements across the roof I couldn't identify, and I took some comfort from this light even while knowing that I wouldn't see much of Wheelock the next day. Other times he went to bed early—by eight o'clock—and rose at five, working for hours without stopping.

From our correspondence, I knew Wheelock was making a film about farms. He wanted to capture the life of the small farmer still trying to make a go of it in an era when corporate agriculture had taken over almost everywhere. And he was particularly fascinated by farming equipment, the rhythm and noise of it; the whish and hum of milking machines, say, or the throttle sound of a tractor plowing a field. The film, he said, would be wordless and black-and-white, with close-ups so tight the machines would become abstractions. Before I arrived, I'd thought that I would be traveling around with him to farms; I'd imagined myself lugging equipment and setting up shots, perhaps sharing a cup of tea with the farmer's wife in the kitchen while Wheelock talked crop yield with the farmer outside. Maybe, I'd thought, Wheelock would give me a sequence to edit; we'd confer over footage late at night, watching one version and then the next, squint-eyed with exhaustion but determined to continue, denying our fatigue in the service of art.

In reality my duties were mostly custodial. Wheelock had me clean the kitchen and buy groceries. He asked me to tidy up the basement and sort his tools. Sometimes he asked me to make coffee. Most of the time, he asked me for nothing at all. If I pressed him for work, wanting to make myself useful, he'd rub his face with the heel of his hand, his eyes watery and squeaking, and say, "Lord, I'm tired." If he didn't say, "Lord, I'm tired," he'd say, "Well, listen to you." Most of our conversations consisted of these two phrases. I felt as if we were a married couple whose fights of many years had worn him down.

Wheelock gave me the keys to the pickup truck, and I learned to drive by edging cautiously out his driveway and gingerly nosing my way along the country roads. Once I felt comfortable I ran errands in town, mostly for something to do; I waved to the guys at the hardware store and chatted about the weather with the ladies at the supermarket. Out of boredom more than anything I decided to make a film, having brought with me a hand-held camera that I'd bought second hand from a graduating student who was giving up film and going to law school. I called it *Summertime, PA,* and I filmed the men who chatted on benches in the town square; I set up long shots filled with nothing but gnats swirling in the yellow glow of a porch light, while the sound of cicadas rolled by in waves like an engine trying to turn over. I filmed the teenagers who gathered at the ice cream parlor, the girls flirting by pressing their hands quickly to the boys' arms and then recoiling from their muscles as if burned; the boys yelling insults to each other or calling out from the rolled-down windows of passing cars, everyone performing, summertime a stage. I was recording an adolescence I'd never had. In the garden shed I cut the film together, cicadas and girls, old men and moonlight. All my life I'd gathered tidbits—things I read, a picture that lingered, the memory of an afternoon in a movie theatre, the face of my sister as she laughed—and sometimes my head felt cluttered as an attic with them. But stitching a film together satisfied this collector's itch perfectly, my magpie treasures woven and spackled into a nest.

At the grocery store I met a guy named Brian who claimed to be home from college for the summer, though when I asked him where he went to school he said only, "Elsewhere." Tall and rangy and fair, with an angry-looking sunburn on the bridge of his nose and the back of his neck, he liked to wear loose tank tops and long basketball shorts. He had a job at a feed store and we'd meet up at seven or eight when he was done, the sky still light, to drive around, or park and make out, or listen to scratchy music on the truck radio. The feed store, it turned out, doubled as Brian's drug-dealing headquarters, and he often came to meet me with a bag of wizened shrooms or some quality weed. On a hot night in early July we took ecstasy and went for a hike on Wheelock's rambling property, stopping to have sex in a field, and when I woke up in the morning I discovered my ankles and calves were lashed with red wounds from stinging nettles I'd walked through without noticing. Wheelock, passing me in the kitchen, said nothing. But later that day, as I sorted and filed some of his mail—he hadn't dealt with his mail for years, and I kept finding letters and contracts and invitations to festivals that had taken place long ago—he suddenly appeared in front of me with a bucket of hot water.

"Here," he said. I was so startled by it I didn't say anything. He bent down and lifted my feet, one at a time, into the water, which was cloudy white. As he knelt before me I could see thick patches of dandruff in his hair.

"Baking soda," he said. "The alkaline neutralizes the sting."

"Thank you," I said, and he nodded and went back to work.

That evening I made spaghetti and jarred sauce, the extent of my cooking repertoire, and knocked on the door of the editing room. I could hear indeterminate rustling noises. "I made dinner," I said, and went back downstairs. I wasn't expecting anything, but five minutes later Wheelock came downstairs and served himself from the stove, then sat down at the table. We didn't speak. Outside the kitchen window a couple of swallows were dive-bombing the eaves. We watched them, or I watched them and Wheelock stared into space as he chewed.

I began working on another film, this one called *Brian Driving*. I told him he was my muse, and he laughed and asked if I wanted him to pose naked. "Maybe," I said thoughtfully, and he got a queasy look and changed the subject. I never asked him about his family, or where his friends were, or what he did when we weren't together; but I shot hours of footage of him at the wheel of his car, close-ups in which I focused on his ear, the dashboard, his hands on the steering wheel, while he talked about what he'd do when he became rich, which was one of his favorite topics. He wanted a Cadillac Escalade and a McMansion. "Not a real mansion?" I asked him, and he shook his head. "I want a normal life in the suburbs. But also better than most people. *That's* a McMansion."

Wheelock and I ate dinner together more and more, still without much conversation, though every once in a while he'd swallow and speak, usually a sentence or less: "Wasps' nest outside, gotta deal with it," he said once. Or: "They say thunder's coming." He spoke to no one, and I didn't know who "they" were. Though I couldn't have taken any credit for it, I did notice that his hours, as the summer passed, grew more regular. He didn't stay up until three in the morning as often, and he usually materialized in the mornings as soon as I'd brewed coffee and in the evenings once I'd made dinner. The smell of alcohol was less pronounced, and his fingers didn't flutter as they had in the bar on the day we'd met. Maybe what he'd needed all along, I thought with disappointment, was a housekeeper.

. . .

In early August, Brian told me he'd be heading back to school before long. It turned out "Elsewhere" was MIT, where he was studying mechanical engineering. I asked him why he'd never mentioned this before, and he shrugged. "Around here I'm just your friendly neighborhood drug dealer who works at the feed store."

Knowing that our time together would soon end lent it a sweetness that was sharp and concentrated and lovely. We touched each other tenderly, freed to act out romantic gestures that we knew would have no consequences. Nights he spent with me in the shed, rolling out of bed at the last possible moment before heading to the store for work. One morning I looked up and saw Wheelock watching from the upstairs window of the farmhouse, his expression impossible to read. Was he always watching us? I shivered, but told myself defiantly that I didn't care.

That night, Wheelock opened a bottle of wine with dinner. He'd brought it up from the cellar, shaking off the dust, and poured with care. I drank the glass he gave me nervously, wondering what was coming, but he stopped when the bottle was finished and asked me to come upstairs. For the first time that summer, I was invited into the editing room. Unlike the rest of the house, it was fastidiously tidy. Everything was neatly labeled in his block-letter handwriting, dates of footage shot, cuts made. On the table was a black composition book in which he kept neat, detailed notes. He flipped through the notebook, outlining the work he'd done so far. "This is from the shoot in Lancaster. This is from the shoot near Centralia."

"Isn't Centralia where the coal fire has been burning underground for decades?" I said. "I didn't think there were farms there."

"Anthracite, yes. It burns very slowly. Could last hundreds of years. You're right, it's a ghost town. But there's a potato farm nearby I've been visiting. I like the idea that something's growing underground not far from the fire."

"Maybe they'll come up French fries," I said.

He didn't laugh. "They aren't that close together," he said, as if I were an idiot.

"I know. It was a dumb joke."

"I keep forgetting," Wheelock said musingly, "how young you are."

Mortified, I fell silent. I was concerned that I'd broken the mood irrevocably, ruining my one chance to garner access to his work; but he continued to show me around the space, at last feeding a reel into a projector and turning off the lights.

"Here," he said, "watch."

I held my breath. What he showed me was a piece of a film, *Potato,* which was released two years later, but not widely seen. It's not hard to understand why. The film is slow, densely composed, exquisite. Every shot shows how he labored over it, and this is perhaps part of the problem: his fingerprints are on every frame, urging the viewer, *Look how beautiful this is.* It's as if you're not allowed to see anything for yourself. The other problem (besides the title, which encouraged bad behavior among writers, unable to restrain themselves from headlines like *Spud Flick a Dud*) is the film's level of abstraction. The tight composition focuses on the threshers, the planters, the rolling escalators in which the trembling potatoes are fed into the gaping maw of the processor, the camera so close to the equipment that it becomes difficult to tell what the machines are doing. The whole experience is aestheticized, and for all the nearness, there is no intimacy.

I didn't necessarily understand this at the time. In the moment, I was overwhelmed by the privilege of seeing his work in progress. And I know now that he showed me some footage that didn't make it into the final film: three minutes of Isaac Hoberman, the potato farmer, talking about his work while holding a potato in his hand. One end of it is clustered with wart-like shoots. There is no sound. As he talks, he keeps rubbing the skin of the potato with his thumb, with gentle familiarity, as a man rubs the cheek of a child or a woman he loves. And then, without warning, he suddenly throws it over his shoulder and walks away, the camera gazing without judgment at his back. This sequence was so comic and unexpected—like something out of Charlie Chaplin—that I gasped and laughed. Wheelock grinned at me. I still don't know why he didn't put it in the film. Sometimes, when I'm being vain, I imagine that he left it out as a secret between us—a gift. That he saved it for me.

Another thing about the footage he showed me that night: the relentless tightness of composition, so many close-ups without a break, and the level of abstraction, all of it was unusual for Wheelock. The change in his style was notable and strange. Strange because the film I'd made of Brian had been shot in more or less the same way. I knew he hadn't seen my footage, nor had I seen his. Had I picked up something from Wheelock by osmosis, simply by sleeping in a garden shed next to his yellow farmhouse? Or was it possible that we'd simply arrived at the same destination by chance? Later I would read about simultaneous invention, the notion that scientific discoveries are often made independently at the same time, as calculus came to both Newton and Leibniz, or evolution to Darwin and Wallace, or even the crossbow, which was invented over and over again in countries around the world. Not that I considered myself a Newton or a Darwin or even an inventor of a crossbow. I was a girl in a garden shed, and I figured I must have plucked his ideas from the air, without even knowing how I did it.

After that night, Wheelock invited me into the editing room regularly, and those final weeks of August became what I'd hoped the entire summer would be. He needed my eye, Wheelock said, and I was happy to give it to him. He'd show me two sequences— sometimes as brief as ten seconds—edited slightly differently, and we'd discuss them for hours, well into the night, drinking bitter coffee gone cold. At two in the morning I'd go to the shed, where Brian was sleeping, wake him up to have sex, and then lie awake after he fell back asleep, my nerves buzzing from adrenaline and caffeine.

Besides the editing, I went through Wheelock's correspondence and blocked out a plan for the next year: which invitations he should accept, which deadlines he could meet, which could be ignored. I mapped his future. "This is perfect," he said. "Are you sure you have to go back to New York?"

I laughed and told him I did, gratified by the look of disappointment on his face.

Brian and I said goodbye on a clear night lavished with stars made blurry and thick by the ecstasy we'd taken. We stayed up until sunrise, when he said he had to go home. "My mom always makes me pancakes on my last day."

I pictured a middle-aged woman in a flowered apron, spatula in hand, a vastly different mother from my own. I hadn't spoken to Marianne all summer; when I'd told her I was going to Pennsylvania, she'd said, "Watch out for vampires." I realized later she meant *Transylvania,* and I wasn't sure if she was joking; I knew her that little. "You never introduced me," I said to Brian.

"I know. You're welcome."

He kissed the tip of my nose and drove away. Then for the last week it was just me and Wheelock. Emboldened by the screening of *Potato,* I asked if I could show him some of the work I'd done that summer, and he agreed. I showed him *Summertime, PA* and *Brian Driving.* All together the films were twenty-six minutes long, probably the longest twenty-six minutes of my life to date, sitting in a dark room with Wheelock watching his profile, listening to him breathe. "Hm," he said, and nodded. "I see what you're doing," he said, and nodded again. He didn't say he loved the work; he didn't say he hated it. He knew—he must have known—how terrifying it was for me to show him the films. He could have chosen to cut me down. But he didn't, and from this I deduced there was something of worth in what he saw. So he bought my allegiance, not with praise but with silence. That's how cheap I was.

26.

I came back to the Tunnel in a frenzied mood, convinced that the summer had changed my life. I wanted to show my sister the films I'd made, to recount the twisting course of my time with Wheelock, sharing each detail, from the unexplained vats of cigarette butts to the day he cured my nettle stings with baking soda to the nights we spent talking. So often in my life events did not seem real until I'd narrated them to her. She'd sit on her bed with her knees tucked under her chin, her eyes fixed on mine, listening, drawing from me the confessions I couldn't make to anyone else.

I burst into the apartment, calling her name. Her shoes were by the front door, her jean jacket hung on a peg in the hall. But she didn't answer me. The door to her room was closed. I called her name again, thinking she might be asleep—though it was two in the afternoon—and knocked lightly. I could hear movements and maybe low music; she had a little CD player on which she played her repertoire, often falling asleep to the pieces, so that her mind would absorb the rhythms even while she was unconscious. I knocked again. Then I opened the door to see Robin sitting up in bed in her T-shirt and underwear, next to a boy who was, like her, rubbing his eyes sleepily. Though he was older and his shoulders had broadened and his hair was shorter and now in braids, I recognized him right away. It was her old boyfriend from high school: Bernard.

"What are you doing here?" I said stupidly.

"Lark, what's up? Long time."

When I looked at my sister, she smiled at me emptily and leaned against him, pushing hard until he got the hint, gathering his clothes and putting them on under the covers. The air in the room smelled skunky and stale. Bernard kissed her on the lips and took his time with his clothes and shoes. They said goodbye calmly, without making plans to see one another again, which I took to mean they already had such plans, regular plans, a routine.

After he left I sat down on my own bed and Robin joined me

there, knees up, shirt pulled over them. On the front of her shirt was a picture of Snoopy and Charlie Brown, both of their faces swollen and distended by her knees. "It happened a few months ago," she said.

"*Months* ago? When I was still here?"

She didn't answer. "I was walking across Washington Square Park on my way to see you. I'd had a bad day at school and I had this idea that I could surprise you. It was really cold out and I just wanted to find you and we'd maybe drink some hot chocolate or something. Go to a movie."

"Months ago?" I said again.

"Then this guy in a Rasta hat said *Smoke, smoke* and I shook my head but then I doubled back. He was wearing a hooded sweatshirt that said 'Worthen' on it and that made me stop. I didn't even see his face but I recognized him, Lark. Something about his shoulders. His *feet*. I said his name and we hugged, for a really long time, until we were just standing pressed up against each other. I was so happy. I couldn't remember the last time I felt happy like that. Like finding a hundred dollars in the street—something really good happening that you never expected."

"Like getting into Juilliard?"

She shook her head. "Something without strings attached," she said. We were lying next to each other now, stretched out head to head, Robin telling her story to the ceiling. When we were kids we used to sleep in each other's beds if we got lonely or sad or scared. We never minded being on top of each other.

"So instead of finding you I went to a bar with Bernard. He has his GED. He lives in Jackson Heights with his aunt and he works at Foot Locker."

"And sells pot in the park."

"Retail doesn't pay anything, you know that."

"What happened to his mom?"

"She's back in jail. Of course. I could have told him that would happen—I *did* tell him that would happen—but he always said she was his mom and that was that."

At this, she and I exchanged looks. We were the opposite of Bernard; we were mother fleers, self-chosen orphans.

"Anyway, we made out in the bar for a while."

"I don't need this level of detail," I said.

"I know you probably think it's weird, but he calms me down."

"Of course he does. He's a pot dealer."

"It's not that," she said. Her face was creased with sleep but her eyes, it's true, looked calm and clear. Her fingers weren't drumming her thighs in spastic practice of whatever piece she was committing to memory. I thought about Glenn Gould, whom everyone brought up to my sister, and the chair he always sat in to play. His father had sawed off the legs to give him the perfect height from the ground. The chair was shabby and often the subject of jokes, even from Gould himself. He could sway back and forth in it, balancing. By the end of his life the stuffing was falling out and you could only sit on one wooden plank that bisected the seat, but Gould wouldn't part with the chair. It must have brought him so much comfort. Or maybe it was just an eccentric attachment. My sister, I knew, needed both comfort and attachment. I should have made her a special chair, I thought.

"You can disappear into the editing room for days and not think about anything else," she said. "It's not like that for me."

"What's it like, then?"

She flopped down on her back again and stared at the ceiling. She put the palms of her hands on her ears, then her stomach, then crossed her arms to rest a palm on each shoulder. "It's like . . . everybody's pulling at me," she said. "I have no control. I'm not allowed to feel what I *want* to feel." Her hair was growing out from a short punk asymmetrical adventure; one side of her head was severe, with a blue streak getting paler with time, her natural color re-emerging at the roots, and on the other a new tuft of baby hair was curling out shyly below her ear. She looked so pretty; trying to blunt her beauty only made it more obvious.

"I know school is stressful," I said, feeling how unhelpful it was.

"My teachers say my craving for drama is holding me back. That I should aspire to be a vessel without ego. That if I focus on technique expression will follow. That I need to have faith in the piano, not myself. One of my teachers, Stanley, he stands next to me while I'm playing and whispers over and over, *More fingers less brain.* I can't even listen to him anymore, Lark. I hear his voice and I want to strip my own skin off. I want to be naked, more than naked, I want to be stripped down to the bones. I want to be nothing."

"Smoke, smoke," I said, and she nodded as if I understood her at last.

27.

Bernard did seem to mellow her, or maybe it really was the weed. Whichever it was, she spent less time at school and more at the apartment, the two of them lounging in her bed. Learning that they'd been together for months without my knowing it had startled and alarmed me; I felt that I'd abandoned my responsibility to take care of her, and I too began keeping more regular hours, coming home for dinner a few nights a week. Sometimes we even cooked together while listening to music, never classical but bootleg hip-hop that Bernard bought somewhere in Queens. The bands were from Slovenia or Senegal or Israel, and they sampled American songs while simultaneously playing the accordion or the drums or the kazoo. Bernard could repeat all the words, though he didn't speak the languages, and would bop around the kitchen singing along as he chopped vegetables or opened cans of Tecate. When I asked what the lyrics meant, he'd shrug. When I asked why he liked the music so much, he'd say, "How could you *not* like it?" He had no answers for anything and no interest in the questions. He was happy all the time. He had no edges, he was completely rounded; he seemed to have decided the world would bounce off him and he'd made himself into something ragged but buoyant, the personality equivalent of a rubber-band ball.

He loved my sister, I could see that much. He brought her gifts from the street: books scavenged off stoops, little shoplifted toys. She lined these totems up on the shelf above her bed, where they spent hours together, Robin going over her sheet music, Bernard smoking a bowl and staring at the ceiling, apparently thinking about nothing. Fingers without brains.

He made her happy, but I couldn't bring myself to like him; I was forever suspicious. One time he tried to pour some Coke from a bottle into a glass and the cap was still on and this made him laugh for five minutes. He was a clown.

Maybe it was also true that with Bernard around Robin didn't need me as much. At night I could hear them rustling, like two animals in a terrarium. Sometimes Bernard would get up in the middle of the night to go to the bathroom and his knobby-kneed legs would brush past my bed, close enough that I could have touched them if I wanted, although I didn't. He was very thin and his legs were hairless and stringy. Robin never woke up in the night. When she slept she dove far beneath the surface of consciousness, fathoms deep. I lay awake, turning problems over in my mind. I knew Bernard often lay awake too because I smelled the pot he smoked after he came back from the bathroom. He and I were like two sentries, vigilant by my sister's body, standing guard over the temporary dead.

Bernard more or less lived with us that year, still working at Foot Locker and selling in Washington Square Park. He wanted to enroll at John Jay College of Criminal Justice and study fire science. When I asked him why he said that fire was a holy spirit and to control it was the greatest challenge known to man. Then I asked if he was doing more drugs than just pot and he didn't answer. I said, "You know being a fireman is hard, right?" He didn't answer that either.

Besides fire science his other life dream was to take care of his mother, on whom he still doted, despite the thousand times she'd disappointed and betrayed him. She was getting released in six months and he wanted to bring her up to New York and find her an apartment. He was saving all his drug money toward this goal. Like a lot of things Bernard did or hoped to do, it seemed both commendable and misguided.

Robin's asymmetrical hair grew out to a bob, and as the weather turned warm she wore short, flowered dresses and combat boots. Once, coming back to the apartment at five in the afternoon, I saw a beautiful couple dancing in the street ahead of me: as they held hands, the man lifted his arm into an arch and the woman twirled beneath it like a ballerina in a music box until she landed against him and he dipped her. It was Robin and Bernard.

In April Robin performed in a recital at school, and to my surprise, Boris Dawidoff was there. She played a baroque piece I didn't enjoy, a sonata in which her fingers picked and stabbed at the keys with tidy, dry precision, the music folding and turning back on itself in intricate, nearly mathematical variations. But when she finished she was flushed, and her quick side smile to the audience showed me how hard she'd worked. In the lobby afterward she was surrounded by friends and other performers and I stood off to the side, clutching a few shortbread cookies in my left hand. Boris was in front of me before I knew he was even close.

He'd left Worthen, I learned, for a position at the Manhattan School of Music, and he gleamed with success. He was beautifully dressed, in a blue shirt, pressed wool pants, expensive loafers. A navy silk scarf coiled around his neck. He looked like a playboy millionaire on a cable TV show. I asked him how Olga was—although I thought of her often, I hadn't written to her much, mostly for fear of imposing on her time—and he shrugged and said he didn't know. Their relationship was, as ever, a mystery to me.

"The performance was not bad," he said. "Whatever you're doing, keep doing it."

I'd just popped a whole cookie in my mouth, and it took me an awkward second to get it all down. When I spoke, I spat some crumbs on his shirt. "I'm not doing anything," I said.

"If you say so," he said. "But she's growing up, our girl."

I said nothing, unhappy at his proprietary *our* but unwilling to contradict it; so much of Robin's life we owed to him.

"She seems happier these days," he said.

"She has a boyfriend," I blurted, instantly regretting it.

But he nodded without surprise. "Yes, Bernard," he said. "Not the brightest man I ever met, but therefore no threat to your sister's confidence. A smart choice, if an obvious one."

I stuffed another cookie in my mouth. To hear Robin spoken of like this, dismissively, as if she tabulated her needs and insecurities on some kind of sheet, made me queasy.

"She's like all artists," he said. "She's the top part of the stool"— here he hovered his palm over the floor, to illustrate—"always looking for the legs that will prop her up." I thought, inevitably, of Gould's chair, which was now on display in a glass case in Ottawa, no stuffing left. I pictured Bernard sitting in a glass case, cross-legged, smoking a bowl while arts-minded tourists checked him out.

The cookies were turning to grit in my fist. "I should go congratulate her," I mumbled.

"In a minute," he said. "I need to talk with you."

I waited. A space cleared around my sister, and she looked at me across the room, raising an eyebrow to ask, *What's going on?* I shook my head slightly in answer, as in, *Don't worry.* Then more well-wishers came up, blocking her from my view.

"I have an opportunity for her," Boris said. "Some performances in Europe, this summer. Do you know Leda Makarovich? Lovely pianist and a good friend of mine, but unfortunately she's having some health problems and had to cancel her Scandinavian tour. They're looking for a replacement and I suggested Robin."

"Isn't she a little unknown?"

"The tour is a little unknown itself," Boris said. "Small venues with local orchestras. Let's say it's no frills. They need someone without a big ego, who can ride a bus and carry her own bag. Someone cheap and available. It's a perfect opportunity for her. Wonderful experience."

"Why are you asking me?" I said. "Instead of her?"

"Because she will listen to you," he said. He held his palm above the floor again. "You are the legs of the stool."

"I can't go with her," I said. "I have my own thing."

"Of course you do," Boris said impatiently, as if he had explained everything to me long ago. "She'll have company with her the whole way."

"Who?"

"Bernard, of course," he said.

It was as if he'd orchestrated all of it, perhaps even plucked Bernard out of Baltimore and set him up in Washington Square Park, just in time to intercept Robin. I pictured the two of them in some European city, holding hands as they gazed up at the churches, strode down cobblestoned streets. Robin, I knew, would love the travel, a different city every day; she'd joke with all the members of the orchestra and come up with nicknames for them, even the mustached guy who played the clarinet, and they'd all fall in love with her, especially the mustached guy, but the existence of Bernard would protect her from the adulation; and every night she'd play before rapt audiences, smiling her sideways smile, and everyone would love her. I could see it all.

"It's time," Boris said, but he only meant that the lights were blinking on and off. Intermission was ending. I could see Robin drifting out of the room, still flanked by an admiring crowd. We made our way back into the auditorium. I dropped the fistful of cookies, now sand, into a trash can, and found my seat, wiping the residue on my dress. Later, at the apartment, Robin would burst out laughing, and point at the stain across my abdomen, a spray of butter and oil that made it look as if I'd soiled myself. Washing it only made the stain worse, and I never wore the dress again.

28.

On a Monday morning in June they left from JFK on a flight to Reykjavik, where they'd connect to Oslo. I'd seen Bernard's luggage—a backpack with two T-shirts, a pair of rust-colored corduroys, and a copy of *Siddhartha* he'd found on a stoop—and it didn't inspire confidence. I packed Robin's things myself, with care, like the replacement mother I still wanted to be. We rolled her dresses instead of folding them, because they'd take up less space, and bought travel-sized shampoos and a little first aid kit with Band-Aids and antibiotic ointment. It seemed inadequate. I sewed a hundred American dollars into the lining of her backpack, and then I sewed a Canadian flag on the outside of it. We said goodbye in the doorway before they went down to the car. My sister threw her arms around my neck and squeezed me quickly but hard, whispering, "See you soon," and then I went to the window and watched them fling their bags into the trunk of a black Crown Victoria that had seen better days. I waved at them, but there were bars over the window, and I don't think they saw me, or even looked.

The following week I too left the Tunnel, exchanging the city's spitting air conditioners and hot gusts of subway air for the easier humidity of Pennsylvania. Brian had an internship with an aeronautics company in Seattle and didn't come back home, I was told by one of his former customers at the feed store, who lamented the absence of quality "product" and raised his eyebrows hopefully at me, disappointed when I couldn't step in to fill the void. I moved back into the garden shed, noting that a few things had changed while I was gone; there were new books in the bookcase (*Ways of Seeing* by John Berger, which had been read, and Plato's *Republic,* which hadn't) and a little plastic pot of African violets that had wilted from neglect. Whoever the interim occupant had been, Wheelock didn't mention her. (I assumed it was a her.) He was hard at work on *Potato,* and now that I had more distance from the film I could see how little our work had in common, and how superior his was to mine. I was retroactively ashamed that I'd shown my work to him. Still, he treated me with respect, listening to my opinions so intently that it took me weeks to notice how thoroughly he ignored them. We settled back into our routine of early-morning coffee and shared dinners in the kitchen, and once I noticed that he wasn't drinking, I didn't drink either. The only other difference was that the vast urns of cigarette butts had been removed. One day I asked him where they'd gone—thinking that the answer might reveal why he'd had them in the first place—and he only looked at me as if he had no idea what I was talking about.

Though I'd brought my camera and sometimes drove around in the truck looking for things to shoot, nothing seemed to spark my attention as it had the previous summer. Instead I wrote email messages to Olga, with whom I was back in touch; she'd expressed interest, in her offhand way, in hearing about my time spent working with Wheelock, and so I began to record notes about the days, his work on *Potato,* his method in general, typing them up at a computer café—Wheelock didn't have internet service—in a town forty-five minutes away. I never felt I quite captured the experience of living next to his yellow farmhouse with the fireflies that blinked in the evenings as if attempting to communicate with the larger glow of Wheelock's upstairs rooms. What I would have liked, really, was to film him, the S of his spine as he slouched in the chair in the editing room, gnawing at a pen until the plastic turned white. But Wheelock would never have allowed that; he never even let his picture be taken in interviews, and when magazines profiled him they often had to resort to photographs from decades earlier, a vastly younger Wheelock with shaggy hair that fell in waves around his sensitive, unlined, handsome face.

While finishing the current film, Wheelock was planning the next, which was to follow a group of scientists working on animal cloning. He was obsessed with the subject and often talked about it while we ate dinner, feverishly wiping his hand on the tablecloth, a tic of his. To finance the film he had to apply for grants, a task he largely deputized to me, although I had no experience writing them and little idea how to approach it. I went through his files, looking for previous proposals to emulate, but generally getting lost in the minutiae of his personal archive—typewritten letters on onionskin paper, old carbon copies, tax records, ancient check ledgers. He trusted me to look through all of it, which I knew was less a mark of high esteem for me than low esteem for the papers. Once I found a check for a thousand dollars he'd never cashed. It was ten years old. When I showed it to him, he shrugged. "Too late now," he said without apparent regret.

I did my best. I wasn't particularly skilled, but I learned how to do what he needed, because I wanted to please him.

In addition to his work at the farmhouse Wheelock had accepted a number of speaking engagements, only because he needed the money. He asked me to travel with him, and since he hated to drive, we took the train to Albany and Boston, flew to Chicago and Denver. On all these trips I stayed by his side carrying two notebooks: one a calendar with all his engagements, and the other a diary, in which I noted people we met and what Wheelock said. I had no official job title, and he usually introduced me awkwardly as "my . . . Lark," the words blurring together. Once at a reception I found *Mylark* printed on a name badge.

At the end of each evening he'd thank me gravely for my work and disappear into his hotel room. In the morning he'd order coffee for breakfast—room service was one of his few indulgences—then meet me in the lobby, always showered and shaved and dressed neatly, if shabbily, in his old collared shirts and frayed pants, like a farmer come uneasily to town.

The many hours we spent together, on trains and in airports and in the yellow farmhouse, cocooned us. I mentioned in passing my sister, our mother, my own shyness and sense of estrangement from people, including my fellow students in the film program. Wheelock neither encouraged nor discouraged these confidences; he always seemed to be listening, but rarely asked follow-up questions or expressed opinions. Because of this, I felt more comfortable with him than I did with other people; talking to him was like talking to myself.

Although he didn't reciprocate about private matters, he did talk about his films, muttering under his breath about the editing or camera work, or the scenery we passed on the train. Once on the way to Albany he spoke about the Hudson River School for fifteen minutes straight, describing in great detail a particular mountain scene in a painting he admired. I came to think that these talks were as personal as he got simply because his work was his life. I believed that we were very much alike, in that we were both at ease with solitude; we both preferred watching other people from a distance. It made me feel special to believe this, affiliated with his genius.

Once, as we waited in an airport security line, watching bags feed themselves slowly into the maw of an X-ray machine, he said, "Were you sickly as a child?"

We hadn't been discussing sickness, or my childhood. "No," I said, "not especially."

He didn't elaborate, only pushed his bag forward, so that I had to say, "Why do you ask?"

"You seem like you were."

"I seem sickly?"

"You seem like someone who spent their childhood watching other kids play out the window."

I took a moment to digest this. Wheelock removed his belt, dropped his keys in a waiting basket. The security agent frowned and scrutinized the camera equipment in his bag as it went through.

On the other side I said, "Were you? Sickly?"

"Pretty much," Wheelock said. "Sometimes. Well, not that much." Then he picked up his bag and strolled over to examine the tourist souvenirs for sale at a kiosk. He was always wandering off in airports, his attention drawn by some object for sale or the view of baggage handlers from a window. In Cleveland one day he was so absorbed in a display about Amelia Earhart and the International Women's Air & Space Museum that we missed our flight and had to spend the night in an airport hotel.

At the end of the summer, Wheelock asked me to leave school and work for him full-time. He'd received some financing from a private foundation, he said, and he could afford to pay me a decent wage, he said, not specifying what "decent" meant. I could take breaks when I wanted to and continue to make my own films, but thirty or so hours a week I'd continue to help him as I had the last two summers. In the year to come he would begin shooting the cloning project, and I would accompany him to interviews, get the releases signed, organize everything else. "You could even talk to the people for me and save me the trouble," he said, his mouth set in the especially grim line I understood by now meant that he was joking.

I was flattered, I told him, but I had to finish school.

"You'll learn more from me in three months than in that entire misbegotten program," Wheelock said, which was the closest thing to braggadocio I'd ever heard from him. "Also, you hate it," he said. "Which is a mark of good taste on your part." This drew me up short. I wouldn't have said that I hated the program, and I was surprised that Wheelock had been listening closely enough to have an opinion about what I felt.

I wasn't about to leave my program, however uncomfortable I felt there at times, because of Robin. She had two years left at Juilliard and our plan had always been to live together until she graduated; I paid two-thirds of the rent and bought the groceries. I couldn't leave her behind.

Wheelock didn't seem offended when I declined. "You're a careful sort," he said. "I wasn't like you. Probably should've been."

We were sitting in the kitchen after an evening meal of cheese and olives and bread. I remember Wheelock was wearing one of his ragged button-down shirts, and his beard, three days grown, was black and white as static. In his upturned palm he cradled three small green olives, like eggs in a nest. The sky was dark and hot and in the distance thunder was rolling in. It had been a summer of intense mugginess broken but not relieved by intense storms, and I'd grown to love them, even as the rain hammered the roof of the garden shed and kept me up at night and formed mud patches that squelched underfoot as I walked to the farmhouse in the mornings. I would miss it here, the focused, energetic quiet, much of which emanated from the man sitting across from me.

"What were you like?" I asked him.

He tilted his head back and stared at the ceiling, which was splotched with peeling paint and water stains. He never felt the need to answer any questions I asked. Instead, he popped an olive in his mouth, chewed it carefully—he'd once broken a tooth on an olive in Italy, he'd told me earlier that summer, one of the few personal anecdotes he'd ever shared, and had to visit a dentist who used tools that had belonged to his great-grandfather—and said, "You let me know if you change your mind." I was sure I wouldn't.

29.

In New York, I waited for Robin's return. I hadn't heard from her during her trip, and I'd had to imagine her summer for myself. Now I was restless with anticipation, wanting to know how closely the reality would conform to the pictures in my mind.

But Robin wasn't doing any of the things I'd imagined. She wasn't testing the keys of a ramshackle piano, feeling its bones shift as she rehearsed before rows of empty red velvet seats in an auditorium that had been resplendent a hundred years ago. She wasn't nursing a coffee at an outdoor café, steadying herself for the evening performance, or sipping some aromatic liqueur the owner insisted she should try at least once. She wasn't dipping her toes in foreign rivers. She wasn't playing Rachmaninoff—I knew now that she was a Rach 3 pianist—to adoring crowds. She wasn't holding Bernard's hand as they walked over a footbridge in the early morning, his hair skunky with potent local hash, their eyes pleasantly glazed. She wasn't thinking about me, back in New York, in the Tunnel. She wasn't getting ready to come home.

Instead of Robin, a postcard came, bearing a picture of a little blond girl wearing flowers in her hair. Above her head was the word *Ytterby*. Robin's usual taste in postcards was kitschy; she liked to find the tackiest one available, with cartoon animals or neon lettering, and I couldn't tell if this little girl was cute or too cute, in Robin's opinion, or merely the only postcard available.

I spent a long time dwelling on the image because the message on the back made so little sense. Robin had written only a short sentence: *Don't look for me.*

I was confused. Why would I look for her when she was on her way home?

On a Tuesday morning, the phone woke me. I'd had trouble falling asleep the night before, and the ringing filtered only gradually into my groggy brain. When I picked up, the man on the other end sounded annoyed.

"It's about time," he said, vexed. "Where were you?"

It seemed a rhetorical question, and I said nothing in response.

"Are you there?" he said.

"Yes."

I recognized the low register and unconcealed impatience as belonging to Boris Dawidoff. I wandered into Robin's room, the only one with a sliver of window. Outside, the day was spectacular, the kind of sleight-of-hand morning only New York can provide. Yesterday had been oppressive and terrible, but this day was fashioned from different material. The last of the summer flowers clung bountiful in the trees, but fall had snuck into the air. The sky was a wide and cloudless blue. There was for a brief moment no traffic, no yelling, and no car horns: a pocket of perfection.

"Can I speak to Robin?" he said.

"She's not back yet." I was puzzled.

"Have you heard from her?"

"I got a postcard," I said.

"I received a call last night from Nils Anderssen."

"I don't know who that is."

"Hold on and I will tell you," Boris said, his tone even more vexed and irritable. "He's my contact who set up Robin's trip. He had been trying to reach me for days but I've been in Durban, working with a composer on a commissioned piece about the new South Africa." I said nothing during the pause he left. "Anyway, we finally spoke last night. Robin walked off the tour."

"Walked off?"

"She told Nils one night after the performance that she couldn't *feel the music*. He asked if she needed more practice time, less practice time. It wasn't his first encounter with a diva. She said she was very sorry, but she had to go. He reminded her that she had certain obligations. She said *her heart wasn't in it right now*. He suggested perhaps her heart could get in it with the aid of a small financial bonus. She shook her head and said something about her soul. Nils is furious with me, and I will have to bow and scrape to him."

I shook my head. The picture I'd held in my mind, of Robin and her shabbily elegant touring life, was so vibrant that I couldn't dislodge it even in the face of this new information. "What about Bernard?"

"Nils said the boy departed separately."

"Do you mean they broke up?" I said.

"I cannot emphasize how little I care whether they did."

"But is she okay?" My voice rose higher, an anxious squeak.

"Your guess," he said, "is as good as mine."

"But this happened a while ago? So where is she?"

He said nothing, and I understood that he wasn't worried about

Robin; rather he was angry, deeply and perhaps permanently angry, and since Robin wasn't available he was prepared to be angry with me instead. "I don't know," he said, "but if I don't hear from her soon——"

Rather than let him finish the sentence I hung up, and sat in the quiet of my sister's empty bed, looking at the beautiful morning in my pajamas.

30.

I didn't know what to do. Call our mother, call the police, get on a plane to Europe and look for Robin myself? Maybe my sister was heartbroken; maybe she'd lost her mind. I'd read that after Agatha Christie's husband fell in love with somebody else and asked her for a divorce, she disappeared for eleven days. Some people think she was trying to frame her husband for murder, or at least embarrass him, but others believe she was so traumatized by heartbreak that she lapsed into a dissociative fugue and forgot who she was. She was found in a hotel in Yorkshire, registered under the last name of her husband's mistress, and never spoke publicly about what had happened during those eleven days. It's possible she didn't know herself.

I could call all the hotels in Scandinavia, asking if they had a young Canadian woman staying there who didn't seem to know who she was.

I could look for Bernard, but I had no idea where to find him. I didn't know his aunt's name, or his mother's.

In the end I called home, not having anywhere else to turn. My expectations for help were low, and still weren't met.

"So, she's gone off somewhere," Marianne said without distress once I'd explained the situation. I could hear her heavily exhale, then inhale.

"Are you smoking?"

"Of course not," she said, and the exhalations stopped. She was a terrible liar, probably because she didn't care very much whether anyone was fooled.

"I'm worried about her."

"And you want me to do what?" she said.

Standing in the Tunnel's tiny kitchen, I closed my eyes in irritation and wished I'd never called.

"Your sister *fait comme elle veut,* Lark. She wants to be famous, she tries to be famous. She has enough, she leaves. She's a narcissist."

"She's an artist."

"She gives herself permission to do whatever she wants, if that's what you mean," she said.

It seemed to me that she was describing herself. We lapsed into silence, stalemated. "I can't believe you aren't concerned," I finally said.

"She left me, and now she left you," Marianne said, and I could hear the satisfaction in her voice. "Now you know how it feels."

I looked up Ytterby and found it on the island of Resarö, in the Stockholm archipelago. Pioneering research in rare earth minerals was conducted there. If you go, you can view the historical marker commemorating the Ytterby mine as a landmark where four periodic elements were isolated from the black stone gadolinite. Ytterby, I learned, is to the periodic table what the Galápagos Islands are to evolution, a small place that birthed great scientific knowledge. I remembered making Robin dress as Marie Curie for my film at Worthen, the sparkling fairy lights of radiation in her lab coat, and tried to picture her now, wandering the little village of Ytterby with gadolinite in her pockets.

The mine was not on the postcard that she sent.

Don't look for me.

I taped a map of Sweden to the kitchen wall. I drew a circle around the area of the archipelago, the uneven clusters of rocky islands braced in the Baltic, and added lines from Resarö to other islands and cities, to Norrtälje and Stockholm. A line that cuts across a circle is called a chord. I imagined Robin crisscrossing the archipelago, from one chord to the next, a musical geography only she could hear. Before she left, we'd watched Bergman's *Summer with Monika,* in which two teenagers from the city run away and spend a romantic idyll on the beach before the realities of life bring them back home. Robin thought the movie was boring. She said it should be called *A Not Very Interesting Vacation.* But maybe, I thought, the movie had made a bigger impression on her than she'd revealed.

When I contacted the police, they said that since she'd gone away of her own volition, since she was an adult, there was no action they could take. They suggested I monitor her credit cards. "She doesn't use credit cards," I said, and they said nothing.

As the fall progressed I imagined Robin shivering in the cold. Of course there was no reason she should have stayed in Sweden; she could have gone south; she could have traveled to Italy or Spain. She could even—I realized with a swift, sharp sting—have returned to New York without telling me. So far as I knew, I was the only person Robin had written to; I was the only person she'd told not to look. Maybe, I thought, the only person she wanted to hide from was me.

Weeks became months and Robin did not return. I slept poorly, each footfall in the building's hallway waking me with the hope it would be her. Unable to concentrate, I fell asleep during screenings at school, failed to hand in papers. I rarely ate and never felt hungry, though I was often light-headed. At the campus store I scowled at customers and gave back the wrong change. My boss put me on notice. My fellow students gave me an even wider berth than usual. I was in a fog, neither present nor absent, some part of me traveling with Robin despite not knowing where she was. I forgot to shower, slept in my clothes, walked to work the next day still wearing them.

"Jesus, girl," my boss said. "You reek."

"Sorry," I mumbled. She sent me home. I walked down Broadway, the October wind whipping my hair in my eyes with a force that felt personal, and I was so dazed that I didn't realize until I had already passed her that a woman on the street was saying my name. Through some uncanny coincidence, it was Olga. She was wearing over-the-knee boots and a long grey cape with large brass buttons, and she looked like a general in a fantasy army. Her lips were red and her eyes were wide with concern.

"Are you all right?" she asked me, and I burst into tears. Olga had never been maternal, but she swept her arm around my shoulder and shepherded me into a coffee shop, muttering dismissively to her companion, a man in a tweed sports coat who brought us a large pot of heavily sweetened tea and then disappeared. I told Olga about my sister, in brief incoherent phrases, and she nodded. "I see your worry," she said. "It is very strange."

After I had calmed down a little I asked Olga what she was doing in New York, and she explained that she was on leave from Worthen, doing research. When I asked her what her project was, she laughed and shook her head. "Let's not talk about that now," she said. "But look, I have something for you."

She bent down to a leather satchel between her feet and pulled out a book, which she laid on the table between us. *The Rise of Nostalgia and the End of the Image.* It was her monograph, the one I'd worked on at Worthen. "Here," she said, and flipped the book open, her painted fingernail resting on the pages like a drop of blood. All I saw were wavy lines on the pages, and only gradually did they come into focus, the list of names on the acknowledgments page, which included my own. The tears came again, and Olga withdrew the book before I could cry on it. I sensed her suppressing a sigh.

She began telling me about a film she'd just seen, *Tokyo Story* by Ozu, one of her favorites. It was showing at Lincoln Center and she left the library early to watch it, even though she'd seen it many times before. I didn't interrupt her to say that I had seen the film too, in college. I let her talk. The film depicts an aging couple who travel to Tokyo to visit their children, who are busy and neglectful, but their daughter-in-law is kind to them. Ozu's style is very quiet; the story is simple, and the audience is left to infer much of the unspoken emotions. Even the camera movements are quiet. I waited for Olga to make an argument about the film, to somehow connect it to her interest in nostalgia, or to draw a parallel between the family in the film and my own predicament. But she didn't do any of these things. Instead she described the film, almost frame by frame, as if we were watching it together in the coffee shop. We drank the tea. She talked. I listened.

My meeting with Olga cheered me, as did her suggestion that we meet again in a few weeks. Because of this, and because I was so embarrassed by the condition in which she'd found me that day on Broadway, I tried to pull myself together. I did my laundry. I washed my hair. Still, worry about my sister preoccupied me, and I continued to lose weight, and couldn't concentrate on my classes. The program wasn't Worthen; it was large and I was only a part-time student, barely known to my professors, who didn't care if I passed or failed, if I stayed or left. I stopped attending class, and I stopped watching films, too. Most of the time I lay on my bed in the Tunnel, feeling the invisible membrane that had long separated me from other people enclose me, and now it was thick and suffocating, and yet I could do nothing to break through it.

On a cold rainy Tuesday in November I came home from work and opened the door to find Robin inside, sitting on the couch, her dark hair slicked to her cheeks. She was wearing clothes I didn't recognize, a dirty white fisherman's sweater and jeans ripped at the knees, and she looked sickly and exhausted. I rushed to her, and then stopped: I wasn't sure she would want me to touch her. I wasn't sure of anything. But when I sat down she laid her head on my shoulder as if she'd been waiting for nothing but that, and I put my arms around her.

"Your clothes are wet," I said, and she nodded. She stood up, leaving a damp moon on the couch cushion. I tugged off her sweater. I pulled down her jeans. She was so thin that she looked like a little girl again. We had no bathtub, so I stood with her in a hot shower until her cheeks were pink. I washed her long hair, untangling it with my fingers. Then I dressed her in pajamas and put her to bed. It seemed too soon, she seemed too fragile, to ask her where she'd been.

When I did ask, the next morning, she shook her head and said she didn't want to talk about it. She said she needed some time. She used mundane phrases like that, seemingly designed, in their blandness, to discourage further questions. When I asked why she had come back now, she said it was because she was ready to. I couldn't solve either mystery: the drama of her disappearance or the puzzle of her return. Again and again, I came up against her mute refusal, and it dug a gap between us that deepened by the day.

When I brought up Bernard, she shrugged. She seemed alternately vulnerable and roughened by her time away. Most consistently she was irritated with me. She complained that I woke her too early in the mornings. She complained about my hair in the bathtub. She didn't like the food I bought. When I asked whether something awful had happened to her in Europe, she answered, sharply, "The only awful thing is having this conversation with you."

When I called Marianne to say that Robin was back, she said only, "I knew it would be fine," in a tone that implied I was neurotic and Robin was careless; I was so furious that I hung up before she could say anything else.

I told myself to be patient. I poured all my energies into caring for her, and we spent Christmas together, the two of us, in the Tunnel, drinking hot chocolate in our pajamas. I gave her an intentionally hideous sweater I found at our favorite thrift store, the kind of thing that once would have made her laugh, and she said, "It's scratchy."

"Yes," I said, "that's kind of the point," and she frowned.

In the new year, Robin informed me that she wasn't returning to Juilliard. "It makes sense that you'd need a break," I said, although none of what was happening made sense to me.

Robin shook her head. "It's not a break," she said. "It's over."

She'd gained some weight and she was as beautiful as ever, but now there was a glossiness to her I hadn't seen before. She had her hair done at a Brazilian salon in Brooklyn and started wearing lipstick. She also got long fake nails in brilliant colors; when playing the piano she'd never been able to grow her nails, and now I sometimes caught her studying her hands with pleasure. She started wearing tight jeans and a black motorcycle jacket she'd found at a restaurant; someone had left it behind, she said, with a sly smile that made me wonder if she'd stolen it. She got a job as a bartender and began working late nights, sleeping until early afternoon. She hardly ever spoke to me. It was as if I didn't exist. I didn't know what I had done to be so rebuffed, and when I begged her to tell me she would only look confused, as if I were speaking a language not our own.

This continued for months. On my own during those long nights in the Tunnel, Robin out at work, I sat and cried, and one day when we met for coffee Olga put her hand over mine and said gently, "This is not good, your life, Lark," and I knew she was right. It was my turn to go. I wrote to Wheelock and asked if the job was still available, and as soon as he said it was I dropped out of school. When I told Robin, she hugged me, but mechanically, her arms stiff with obligation, and I knew she could hardly wait for me to leave. I left her my key to the apartment, and I didn't see her again for five years.

PART THREE

Motherhood

I.

The village of Briar Neck perched at the edge of the Susque-
hanna River like a child gingerly dipping its toes in the water. In
summers it was dense and picturesque, with an explosion of tangled
greenery—including the shambling, prickly shrubs that gave the
place its name—extending from the town below to the rolling hills
above, and tourists came to eat ice cream and shop for antiques
along Main Street. In winters it was deserted and lovelier, a sepia
postcard of stark tree branches and milky snow. The few restaurants
closed early, and people hunkered down in their homes, their plea-
sures turned silent and internal. These were my favorite months. I
lived in a small brick house with red shutters and a tiny front lawn
girded by a picket fence, as if mail-ordered from a catalogue of
Americana. I'd been in Briar Neck for three years, ever since the
runaway success of Wheelock's film *Hello Dolly* had enabled him to
procure office space there, and I knew the florist, the baker, the best
mechanic, and the cheaper but less trustworthy mechanic. Every
morning I drove twenty-five minutes along winding roads to a nondescript office park that had been constructed in the late nineties for
a high-tech company that was born, spectacularly metastasized, and
died all within five years, leaving the buildings well-appointed and
empty. It was a company that promoted local bands by researching
them on the internet and then emailing people in their towns who,
it turned out, knew about them already. Wheelock purchased the
entire property for a song, assuming there are songs about bargains
in real estate. When we were moving in I came upon a room full of
doomed company swag emblazoned with their musical-note logo—
T-shirts and fleece vests and mugs—that Wheelock and I, along with

a rotating cast of interns and assistants, wore and used whenever we were working long hours and didn't feel like doing laundry or dishes.

I was Wheelock's editor and right-hand man, his permanent Mylark, a job that had grown over the years along with his reputation. I no longer made my own films or dreamed of doing so. I was unburdened by ambition, too busy for it. When *Hello Dolly* came out, following the practices and ethics of cloning from scientists in their labs to the bleating of an artificially made sheep, it won awards and accolades and was nominated for an Oscar, though it didn't win, and then Wheelock was invited to turn the film into a series for public television, which was widely viewed and adopted by schools across the country, and something similar happened with his next project, a documentary about climate change. These new projects were less aestheticized than his previous work, though still beautifully shot and composed; they were viewer-friendly, issue-based, and Wheelock had become less of a filmmaker's filmmaker (as *The New York Times* called him) than a documentary corporation. The Wheelock I'd first met as a student—fragile, shy, and prone to drink—would have been overwhelmed by this change; but the Wheelock I worked for now was prosperous and confident. His personality had shifted so gradually that only when looking back could I see what a distance it had traveled. *It's funny to remember,* I emailed Olga, who was now teaching in London, *what a mess he used to be.* She wrote back, *Like all men, he believes his success was fated,* which struck me as bitter and not entirely untrue. Wheelock himself had been generous, both financially and otherwise; he always credited my editing work on the films, and in interviews would talk about how much he owed to my eye. But it was Wheelock whose name had become a brand, Wheelock who won a "genius" grant, and Wheelock who was invited to speak at schools and film festivals and symposia—all of which, to be clear, was fine with me.

. . .

When he was in Briar Neck, Wheelock and I lived in the same house, in separate rooms. He also had a studio apartment in New York, but he spent much of his time on the road, at residencies and conferences and meetings. Usually I traveled with him. In the third year of my full-time employment, we were on a train in Italy. We'd attended a biotech conference in Milan on genome sequencing—Wheelock was often the only non-scientist invited to conferences like these—and were heading back to the States, where he was speaking to film students in Chicago. We did much of our work on planes and in cars, comfortably in suspension between the task just done and the one ahead. Wheelock was using a voice recorder while I made notes on my laptop, which sometimes rocked against the window or his shoulder as the train sped up or slowed. This, too, was comfortable. As colleagues we inhabited a bodily rhythm together. We each spent more time together than we did with anyone else.

As he spoke his thoughts into the recorder I typed a smoother, cleaner version onto the computer, easing the transitions and clarifying his points as he went along. I never worried about upsetting him by making changes or suggestions, assuming that this was why he'd hired me in the first place. The train lurched, shuddered, stopped. We weren't at any station. The landscape out the window was hilly and light green, terraced with vineyards. As soon as we stopped moving the air in the car grew dense and close, and people opened the windows to invite a non-existent breeze. Wheelock undid a button on his shirt, his face unhappily flushed.

I pressed Save on the document as the conductor barged past us down the aisle, trailed by two squabbling engineers. "I think we hit something," Wheelock said. "They're arguing about how to fix it."

"I didn't know you spoke Italian."

"I picked some up this week."

Around us in the crowded car complaints gathered steam. A child spilled his drink and burst into sobs while his mother scolded him, whether for the spilling or the sobbing I didn't know. I took off my sweater and pressed Save again, although we hadn't changed the document. I didn't want to lose anything.

"I wonder what we hit."

"Either a herd of sheep or a round of cheese," Wheelock said.

"A round of cheese?"

"My vocabulary's pretty limited," he said.

I closed the laptop to preserve the battery. My mind looped ahead to Chicago, and then to Berlin, where Wheelock was to present *Hello Dolly* to German audiences, and where my sister had briefly lived, working as a painter's assistant. *Not an art painter,* her postcard had clarified, *a guy who paints houses. His name is Aksel and he looks like Don Cherry.* She'd left New York soon after I did; she never graduated from Juilliard or anywhere else, and she traveled a great deal, working just enough to cover her expenses. Marianne said, "She was never suited for regular life," as if she could have predicted Robin's path all along. Her complacency annoyed me and yet, perhaps to make up for Robin's absence in my life, I began calling her every once in a while, to share whatever news I had, though we argued more often than not.

What frustrated me the most about Marianne, in these conversations, was when I mentioned some aspect of the past; I talked about movies we'd watched together, or about how she used to play us Stevie Wonder on her Magnavox turntable.

"I don't remember that," she said. "I was never a big admirer of Stevie Wonder."

"You loved 'Superstition,'" I insisted. "You knew all the words." I hummed a little of the song, though I was embarrassed at how off-key it was and quickly stopped.

"I don't believe that," Marianne said, as if insulted. "Now, Donna Summer I liked. 'Hot Stuff.'" Her voice thickened with nostalgia. "My girlfriends and I used to dance to it at a club." Her fondness for the past, I felt, was restricted to a version without us in it, and I changed the subject. I asked how the weather was in Montreal, about which she harbored endless comments. In those years I often knew more about the forecast there than where I lived.

Meanwhile Robin bussed tables in Spain, sheared sheep in New Zealand. She never said how long she planned to stay or where she was going next. Once, Wheelock and I attended a film festival in the Stockholm archipelago; we boarded boats late in the evening, as the sun finally set, and watched images projected from the shore, rippling in the wind. Afterward I made a trip to Resarö, as if following in Robin's footsteps. I saw the plaque at Ytterby and bought a cinnamon bun at a café. There was no trace of her there, of course; she'd left no mark behind. Every so often I imagined running into her at the Berlin Hauptbahnhof or Orly airport, the two of us just happening to pass through security at the same time or to use the ladies' room and suddenly, while washing hands, catch a glimpse of the other's face in the mirror above the sink. But my fantasies never went any further than that, because I never knew what I would say.

"Now I think it's birds," Wheelock said beside me.

"Our train hit birds?"

"Possibly ducks," he said.

I opened the laptop again and clicked through our itinerary. We had a three o'clock flight, which the train delay was bringing uncomfortably close.

"We're going to be late."

Wheelock shrugged. He was never anxious about travel arrangements, having effectively annexed all his worry in me.

"It'll be fine," he said, and put his hand on my knee, which he'd never done before. He had always made me feel simultaneously essential and invisible. I said nothing, shifting in my seat. The backs of my legs were sticking uncomfortably to the plastic.

"Lark," he said. "Lark."

"Why do you keep saying my name?" I said. The train was too

warm, and we were sitting too close together. An announcement gibbered over the loudspeaker. The laptop was hot on my thighs and heavy and I bent over in our tiny space, angling it with difficulty into my backpack. He moved his hand to my shoulder.

"Lark," he said again, his voice taut and insistent, and when I sat up, he kissed me.

We were less a couple than a unit of force. We didn't date; we didn't eat in restaurants or go to the movies. But we lived and worked together, we breathed the same air, and we reached for each other when we needed it, in his bed or mine. To my surprise, Wheelock turned out to be good at sex; he was both attentive and casual, in the sense that there was never any pressure. His expectations of me were nil, other than that I enjoyed myself. If I was tired or not interested he didn't seem upset. In bed he was playful and we sometimes tussled like puppies or children, rolling over until we were knotted in the sheets, short of breath, and laughing. It was a side of him that I would never have guessed at, and this was one of the things that drew me to him, and kept me there. Every year I knew him unfolded some new aspect of his personality. Every year he turned into someone else.

2.

Not all the revelations were easy to take. Just before we outgrew the yellow farmhouse and moved forty miles over to Briar Neck, I found out who the other occupant of the garden shed had been. We were packing boxes—or I was packing boxes, while Wheelock was doing something upstairs—on a bald, lusterless day in late March. Spring was slow that year; the trees had yet to bud and the yard was still glazed with the last dirty remnants of ice. I heard an engine rumble down the gravel driveway and I assumed it was

UPS; nobody else ever came to the house. But some movement out the window caught my eye, and I saw a slender, dark-haired girl in a motorcycle jacket emerge from a black SUV, cross the yard, and open the door of the shed. For a second, my heart plummeting and then rising, I thought it was Robin. I wrote to her every few months, first by mail at the Tunnel and then at an email address she seemed to check only sporadically. I confined myself to brief and concrete particulars about my life. In return I received occasional postcards and, once, a clipping from a gossip item in an Italian newspaper with a picture of a marginally famous American actress sitting at a fancy party next to a man in a silk scarf. The man was Boris Dawidoff. Robin had drawn on the photo, giving him devil horns.

Outside, the shed door slammed. Wheelock came running down the stairs, blitzing past me without a word, faster than I'd ever seen him move. In the windy yard he talked with the girl, who was now facing the house. It was not my sister. She looked quite young, maybe college-age, wearing dark lipstick and a leather choker rimmed with silver spikes, and she was beautiful. Wheelock was speaking to her animatedly, but I couldn't hear what they were saying, or tell whether his hand gestures were angry or pleading. I wasn't surprised to see how he occupied myself when I wasn't around; some part of me even expected it. I did feel uncomfortable at how young she was, and how tiny; she barely came up to his collarbone. Wheelock threw an arm around her and kissed her black, shiny hair, guiding her into the house. She was crying, burying her head in his armpit. An unlovely gob of snot hung from her nose, and she wiped it on his sweater.

When they came into the living room their cheeks were livid from cold.

"This is my daughter," Wheelock said. "Min."

"I hear you've been sleeping in my bed," she said. "Like fucking Goldilocks." Her accent was obscurely foreign, hints of British melded with something else.

"I'm Lark," I said. "The—assistant."

"Jesus, I know. Your presence has been *explicated*."

"Easy, Min," Wheelock said.

"Easy," she repeated, mocking him. "Is there any booze in this shithole?"

"If I'd known you were coming I would've laid in some grain alcohol and barbiturates."

"Ha ha," she said. "You're the only dad in the world who thinks rehab jokes are funny."

They interrupted this seemingly angry repartee to grin at each other with undisguised delight. In that moment I saw the resemblance between them. Min flung herself down on a chair, spread her legs over the side of it, and sighed with exaggerated weariness. "This poor woman. She probably thought you were normal up to now."

"I doubt that very much," Wheelock said.

I produced one of my typical dinners, a sorry affair of gluey rice and rubbery chicken. As we ate, Min told me she was "on a break" (duration unspecified) from "school" (location unspecified), and she and her mother "needed space" (reason unspecified).

"Also I got my heart broken by some moron," she said, tears welling up to contradict her scornful tone, "and last time I got my heart broken I self-medicated to excess."

Wheelock put a hand over hers. I'd never seen him like this before, solicitous and paternal, and I was impressed by how natural he was at it.

Min's mother, Soo Jung, was a wardrobe designer who worked at a theatre in London. "It's not as glamorous as you think," Min confided, though I hadn't said anything. "It's a lot of sniffing people's smelly armpits while you're sewing them into decrepit velveteen dresses." She was even younger than I'd thought, maybe eighteen, her sophistication spackled over her nervous energy. After dinner Wheelock said calmly, "I'd better call your mother." Min and I did the dishes, or I did them while she leaned against the counter and talked.

She told me all about her school, how she planned to be a painter, that she was the product of a "brief flirtation" (length unspecified) between her parents and had never known them together. She and her mother had moved abroad when she was ten, first to the Czech Republic and then to England, which accounted for her accent. Her Korean grandparents were scandalized by her patchy academic performance and time in rehab. Wheelock had no living parents to be scandalized. His only brother had been killed in a factory accident when they were both in their twenties. "He never talks about it," she said. "But if you watch carefully in his films there's almost always a moment when industrial machinery suddenly, like, looms. It'll go from normal to really threatening and scary. He can't help but see it that way. It's like a ghost he doesn't realize is haunting him." In the two hours Min had been around I'd heard more about Wheelock's life than in the previous two years. I rinsed out the saucepan and deposited it in the rack, drying my hands on a grubby dish towel Wheelock and I kept forgetting to wash.

"So," Min said, peeling a strip of black polish off her thumbnail, "what do you do for fun here in Hicksville, anyway?"

"There used to be a guy who dealt drugs out of the feed store," I said. "But he's in grad school now."

"Aren't they all," she sighed, with more of her fake worldliness.

"I guess we could play Monopoly," I said. By the time Wheelock came back downstairs she owned all the hotels and had hundreds in the bank.

Min stayed for six weeks. She slept until noon every day, seemingly unwakeable by any amount of noise. She turned out to be a skilled cook who could turn out everything from bulgogi to bangers and mash, and I gladly ceded the kitchen to her. She'd sit in the living room while I worked and ask me questions about my personal life, which I answered as blandly as possible. The version of myself I told her was stripped down and sedate. My sister lived abroad. My mother worked in marketing. I'd lost my father young and didn't remember him.

"You're the most boring person I ever met in my life," she told me once. "How do you stand it?"

"I get by somehow," I said.

"Is that why you've glommed on to my dad, because he's so much more interesting? You feed off his interestingness like those parasites that live in sharks' mouths."

"Sharks?"

"I seriously just learned about this in zoology. The resemblance is uncanny."

During the days Wheelock was as occupied with his work as ever, so it fell to me to entertain Min. I took her to the feed store and the ice cream parlor; we swam at the quarry; she pronounced all of it dull and stupid and yet she could have left anytime she wanted to, and she didn't. On her last day she called Wheelock "Daddy" and burst into tears at the thought of leaving him. And she must have enjoyed herself somewhat, because she returned every six months or so for a visit, often picking up a conversation as if we'd just broken it off the day before. She gossiped indiscreetly about her mother's love life and her own. She knew every single one of Wheelock's films by heart and to my irritation could correct me on minor points about them. She was always right. She deduced it immediately once Wheelock and I "became intimate" and she often said "became intimate" to torment me, knowing how uncomfortable I was made by the phrase. She also loved to call me "Stepmom" in a voice drenched with irony, and in a salute to the Julia Roberts movie of that name would insist on singing "Ain't No Mountain High Enough" at the top of her lungs whenever we went anywhere in the car. She finished high school and was accepted to a prestigious art program in London. She once left, on my bed, a portrait she'd drawn of me in charcoal, so quickly that I hadn't noticed her doing it. In the picture I was staring down at my hands, my hair falling across my cheeks. She'd made me more angular than I was in life, and, as a compliment or taunt, more beautiful.

3.

Min inspired Wheelock's next project, on the cheery subject of rising global plagues. During one of her school breaks she and a friend traveled to Southeast Asia, through Thailand to Vietnam and Malaysia. Unlike my sister, she was an excellent correspondent, sending long, chatty emails about their drunken escapades on beaches and close calls they'd had weaving mopeds through chaotic traffic. It wasn't until she was on the plane home that she started to feel ill, and by the time they landed at Heathrow she was unconscious with fever and had to be transported by ambulance directly to the hospital. The virus she'd contracted turned out to be a strain of bird flu not previously known to leap from animals to humans. Wheelock, grim-faced and mute with worry, got on a plane to be by her side. He was terrible at keeping in touch, and answered my questions over the phone with one-syllable answers. I was stuck back in Briar Neck by myself, researching the history of the flu. I read about how the 1918 flu epidemic killed nearly thirty million people, more than had died in the First World War. From its origins in China it coursed around the world, following every trading route and path. Children sang a rhyme: *I had a little bird, its name was Enza. I opened the window, and in-flu-enza.*

Min herself emailed me the first update of any length. *Guess what, I'll survive to bug you for a few more years. I look like a skeleton but my cheekbones are amazing. My career as a supermodel starts now.*

Despite the flip tone of this message, she emerged from the experience changed—more serious, even rigid, in a way that reminded me of her father. Though she recovered with a speed that impressed her doctors, her body was different after the flu; she'd always been thin, but after the illness she was almost skeletal, permanently so, her body whip-like and wiry. She developed a slight hunch, her shoulders forever pushing forward as if against a world that had robbed her of her invulnerability. The next time she came to Briar Neck, she threw out everything in the garage and converted it into a studio. She'd work there for hours at a stretch, making charcoal sketches I never saw because she ripped them up at the end of each day, dissatisfied, and burned them in the fireplace. But she didn't seem to mind. She said transience was part of her process. "If I leave here with nothing," she said, "it's perfect. Because that's how we leave this planet, right? With nothing. I'm like one of those monks with sand art that gets destroyed as soon as it's finished."

Wheelock didn't care for these remarks, finding them callow. He called her a ten-cent Buddhist, whatever that was, and the two of them argued regularly over dinner, Min having cooked a curry or stir-fry using spices she'd brought in her luggage, because the Pennsylvania supermarkets never had what she wanted. After she left, for lack of a target Wheelock began to argue with me, picking fights over everything from American foreign policy and the war in Afghanistan to the future of nuclear energy. I wasn't a satisfying partner in these debates. I folded instantly, and anyway we held most of the same positions to begin with. I was less a combatant than an echo chamber. Wheelock grew ever more frustrated and irritable. He withdrew into his office and then went off to New York for a spell, and when he came back he informed me that we'd be working on a ten-part series about plagues, epidemics, and global health. It would take years.

"All right," I said.

But I'd had enough of travel. I liked Briar Neck and no longer enjoyed the endless days of airport meals and waking in hotel rooms unsure what country I was in. I told Wheelock he had to learn to look after himself, and he consented. Over the next year we spent more time apart than usual. I spent my days with two assistants I'd hired fresh out of school, Bikram and Javier, who lived together in a tiny apartment behind the Elks Lodge. The two of them bickered endearingly and then hushed when I came in; they were obedient and a bit fearful, and as I taught them what to do, it was odd to realize that I was no longer the youngest or least knowledgeable person in the room.

In the evenings, I went back to my college habit of patching gaps in my education in classic films, making notes in a small Moleskine Wheelock gave me for Christmas. I watched all of Kurosawa and Tarkovsky and Fellini, keeping myself company with the flickering images. I wrapped my solitude around myself like a blanket, and I was cozy in it; which isn't to say that I wasn't overjoyed whenever Wheelock came home, laying his footage, that dubious gift, at my feet, like a cat presenting a dead bird.

I watched so many hours of the footage that it grew emptied of content, and I became inured to the horrifying facts—pestilence, epidemics, antibiotic-resistant bacteria rampaging the earth—being presented. To be an editor is to systematize. To stitch and cut. To observe and connect, layering one idea on the next. I was good at it. By this point Wheelock and I communicated in shorthand, using terms no one else would have understood. "We need a bridge here like Texas," he'd say, by which I knew he was referring to a montage from a piece about offshore drilling in Galveston several years earlier. We'd built a language together; we'd built worlds. Whenever I showed him a preliminary cut, he nodded curtly, but I could tell—having learned years earlier that he wouldn't provide compliments, I'd gone scavenging for them myself, in the lift of an eyebrow or a tilt of the head—that he was pleased.

4.

After she graduated from art school in London, Min moved to New York, where she worked as a gallery assistant and went to parties with fashion designers and internet-famous indie musicians and then returned late at night to the apartment in Bushwick she shared with three roommates. When the city got to be too much, she'd sublet her bed—it was a loft apartment, so she didn't have a room, just a mattress in a corner—and come to Pennsylvania for a month, making art in her studio and cooking meals for us, bringing with her a charge of energy that was both invigorating and exhausting. She showed up whenever she wanted, without asking permission or giving notice, and she didn't care whether her father was there or not. She treated us both with a boisterous aggression that I understood was her form of love. She liked to mock Wheelock to his face for entering what she called his "sellout years," joining the "tote bag tribe," by which she meant anything that involved public television. Wheelock never seemed hurt by these accusations, though occasionally I caught him glancing at me, as if wondering whether *I* was hurt by them. I wasn't. What did make me uncomfortable was when Min allied herself with me—sometimes because we were younger; sometimes because we were both women—and then switched to Wheelock, calling him Daddy and referencing trips they'd taken when she was a child, toggling between the two of us with ferocious speed. I don't think she cared as much about playing us off each other as she craved the instability of the switch itself. Too much tranquility made her uneasy; she didn't feel at home in it.

I almost preferred when it was just Min and me. We'd drink tea late at night and she'd tell me about her boyfriends, past, present, and future. She claimed she could envision the men she'd fall in love with before she even met them.

"First there's going to be a dangerous guy with maybe a speed or credit-card problem," she'd say dreamily, mangling a bag of chamomile against her spoon. "Then, like, a sweet nerd to settle down with, maybe pop out a kid or two. Then when I'm sixty I'm totally going for hot young guys who want to use me for my connections in the art world. Turning that old male-lecher paradigm upside down." So far as I could tell, this was all just talk. Her only dates in New York were hookups, guys in their twenties who made as little money as she did and had nothing to offer but their opinions. They seemed to bounce off her like billiard balls, colliding quickly before they rolled into pockets and disappeared from the table.

"But what about you?" she asked me once. "Are you going to be my dad's concubine forever?"

I let the insult pass. "I'm married to my work," I said.

"You're married to my dad except there's no pre-nup or job security," she said. "My mum says one day you'll wake up and find out he's living in Paris with a new *assistant*. That's what happened to her."

"I thought it was just a fling with them."

"It was to him," Min said, raising her eyebrows at me with a look of significance. She wanted so badly to find a wound in me she could poke. But I was impervious, a lacquered surface, a rock worn smooth by water; Wheelock had washed over me, and I was clean. I liked my quiet life. I'd seen a documentary about a group of Carthusian monks in France who took a vow of silence, living together in the Alps for years. They communicated in a system of hand signals and moved through their days in a routine that never varied: eight hours of labor, eight hours of sleep, eight hours of prayer. Their lives were empty of noise, music, speech. They lived in small cottages and mostly prayed alone. When a visitor from the outside world was asked what he found most remarkable about his time there, he said it was that the monks lived without fear.

When Wheelock and I were alone we often talked about Min. He worried about her health and her professional future, and he went to New York more often, to see her. Her mother wanted her to find a backup career, like art therapy or law school. Min pointed out that both her parents had been able to survive in artistic professions. *Survive,* Soo Jung said, *is the operative word.* Min complained about this to Wheelock, who discussed it with me, all of us a daisy chain of concern for her, circling around her future.

The pace of his work was wearing on Wheelock; his hair turned grey, and he kept losing weight. Once I found him outside punching an extra hole in his belt with an awl. His face was sallow and lined from overwork, but he never took vacations.

"What, and leave all this?" he'd say when I brought it up, gesturing at the office. I didn't point out that leaving all this was something he did constantly, for work. He wrapped his arms around me and set his pointy chin on my shoulder, digging in, so hard it hurt. "I like being home," he said, and it was true, until the time came for him to leave again.

I took my own trips. I flew to Costa Rica for my old roommate Helen's wedding—she was a zoologist at a field site there, studying white-faced capuchins—and stood in the sand drinking a syrupy cocktail and making strained conversation with people I hadn't seen since college. "Remember that guy Gordon?" one of her track team-mates said to me. "Didn't you date him?" I admitted I had. "I ran into him in a bar in Atlanta." She lowered her voice, and I braced myself to hear what had become of him: he was a professor, he was a farmer or a beekeeper, he'd gone insane. All seemed plausible. "He runs a hedge fund that cleared five hundred million last year," she said. I tried to reconcile this information with the burly guy of my memory, and failed. Seeing my face, the woman laughed and squeezed my arm. "The one that got away, right? Don't feel too bad. He's fat and bald."

Later I went to London to visit Olga, and we spent the week in movie theatres and cafés, arguing pleasurably over the films we'd just seen. At a repertory cinema we sat through *All About Eve,* which I enjoyed more with Olga because she loved it so much, often muttering the dialogue along with the actors. She claimed that as a dissection of how misogyny pits one woman against another it was vastly ahead of its time. When Lloyd Richards called Margo "a body with a voice," Olga clucked her tongue; and when he said, "It's about time the piano realized it has not written the concerto," we both hissed so loudly that the people sitting in front of us turned around to glare. The line made me think of Robin, inevitably, and of Boris Dawidoff, who was every bit as imperious as Lloyd. Afterward, at a bar, I told

Olga about the clipping Robin had sent me, showing Dawidoff with the actress, and she said, "Women are necessary instruments to him."

As I was packing to go home, she kissed me on both cheeks and told me she was moving to Germany.

"Why?" I said stupidly. It was the first she'd said of it. She smiled at me, her eyes bright. She'd gained quite a bit of weight, her face and her body rounded and soft, and I wanted to lean into her and burrow there, though I refrained. She was, I see now, a kind of mother to me, though she would probably have found the idea laughable, and often, by instinct, I concealed from her the depth of my affection.

"Berlin's very exciting at this moment," she said. "Not everyone stays in the same spot like you."

I took it as a rebuke, and I was about to respond when she pressed my hand and told me the taxi was outside. Later, I wrote her an email defending my life in Briar Neck. *I'm pleased you are so happy,* she wrote back. *To me it sounds very dull. Come see me in Berlin.*

5.

When Robin ended her travels, she didn't return to the US, whose post-9/11 political climate she declared unlivable. Instead, to my surprise, she moved back to Montreal, settling in a small apartment in Mile End, and took a waitressing job at a resto on St.-Laurent.

This news came to me from Marianne, who was herself living in a new place, an apartment in Laval that belonged to her boyfriend. He was a dentist and, "in spite of that," she told me over the phone, "very kind." She said Robin looked terrible, skinny as a stray cat. "When she comes over she stands in front of the fridge and eats everything with her hands. She's a savage."

In Briar Neck, in the early mornings, when I heard noises outside—birds, dog walkers, a slow-moving car from which news-papers were tossed onto porches and driveways—I sometimes imagined it was Robin walking up to the door, luggage in hand, as she had all those years ago when I was at Worthen. But she never came, and for that matter I didn't invite her. We'd learned how to live without each other. After she'd been back a year, I went to Montreal for Christmas, and the three of us sat in Marianne's living room, making polite conversation with the dentist about gum disease. He put packages of floss for us under the tree. I stole glances at my sister, who looked both the same and yet so different; it was hard for me to take in the entirety of her presence. She wore a bulky red sweater pocked with white snowflakes, dirty at the cuffs; her hair, once dyed and then left to grow out, was dark brown from scalp to ears, then blond to her shoulders, all of it an ashy tangle. Marianne had been right: she was thin and raw-boned, skin peeling and lips chapped, stripped and weathered like a house untended.

Marianne, by contrast, looked well-kempt; her hair had been cut and colored, and she wore a turtleneck and pearl earrings, like a proper middle-aged lady. We ate tourtière and watched snow fall outside as if it soothed us. Robin took two helpings of everything, sometimes three. The dentist stared at the wall and spoke about recent advances in fixed partial dentures. Marianne rolled her eyes and pulled her coat on over her shoulders, arms free, standing outside in the cold to smoke; the dentist wouldn't let her smoke inside because he wanted her to quit. Among other things, he remarked, it was terrible for your gums. While she was outside with her cigarette the three of us sat at the table in silence, strangers connected to one another only by the thin filament of Christmas.

Robin gave me a book about maps. I gave her a scarf.

On Boxing Day I kissed everyone goodbye and drove back across the border and home to Briar Neck. My sister and I had had no conversation of consequence. When I was leaving she clutched my arm tightly, her fingers like talons on my sleeve, but said nothing. She was bony and strong. She clutched her coffee cup with that same grip, pulled her boots on with it too. If I'd responded in kind, if I'd pulled her close, I was convinced, she would have pushed me away.

6.

I never thought about whether I'd live in Briar Neck for the rest of my life; time passed without remark, in the flow of the editing room, and never stopped long enough for me to take its measure. I was thirty-two years old. At work I supervised Bikram and Javier, along with a few others. The woman who ran the bakery invited me for dinner and walks, and I grew fond of the elderly couple who lived next door, looking in on them during cold snaps and power failures. At home, I hosted "plague nights," when people came over to see movies like the 1950 noir *Panic in the Streets* or *The Omega Man* starring Charlton Heston, from 1971. Nothing relaxed me like watching the last few survivors on earth cling to life against shattering odds. Word got out about these movie nights to the point where I had to start holding them at the community center, though I refused to give introductions or do what the woman there called "talk backs." Wheelock, who flitted in and out of town, still an enigma to most people, teased me that one day I'd be mayor.

His plague programs were widely viewed on public television and received awards, a success that both Wheelock and I now took for granted. His travel schedule, always busy, became constant, so I hired him a personal assistant while I stayed in Briar Neck to edit and supervise the staff. Our lives both knitted together and unraveled. When he was back, he often slept in my bed, without sex; sometimes I woke to him holding me around the waist, his head on my lap or hip, gasping in his sleep, slipping down the bed as if about to drown. Though he kissed me less, he confided in me more. Sometimes he talked about his childhood in Pittsburgh, where his father had worked in a steel mill and his mother cleaned houses. Because their parents were at work so much, he and his brother had raised themselves, filling the hours after school with games of stickball. It was strange to discover, after so many years, how similar our childhoods had been, as if we'd been drawn to one another for this reason without knowing it. When Wheelock was seven his brother almost died of pertussis, and he had a strong memory of seeing his brother hooked up to machines to help him breathe, his body thin and wasted, his face almost blue. In filming the plague project he'd seen countless children suffering and at night he dreamed about them, their expressions gone flat, ravaged by contagions they couldn't understand.

This was yet another new side of Wheelock: sensitive, openly injured, strangely and suddenly forthcoming. I knew I was the only person in the world to whom he said these things, and it bound me to him even more.

One weekend we traveled to a fancy awards ceremony in New York. It was 2008, and I hadn't been back to the city in years; I thought how different it looked, with chain stores and corporate coffee shops on each block. You could buy frozen yogurt everywhere. Of course we were in different neighborhoods than where I'd lived, and I wasn't a student anymore. Wheelock fidgeted in a suit he'd had for decades, broad-shouldered and out of fashion, and I wore a black dress I'd bought in Briar Neck. It was a vintage black shirtwaist with a white lace collar that had looked shabby chic in Pennsylvania and in New York looked only shabby. I blinked at the city lights like a mole. Circulating in the theatre lobby, I was surprised to note how comfortable Wheelock was speaking with people, his hand pressing casually on the small of my back, steering me from one conversation to the next. He no longer needed me to whisper in his ear and keep him steady; instead, he kept me steady. I wasn't used to this kind of event, and I labored to keep up with the banter. I excused myself to the restroom, and when I came back, I paused at the top of a staircase, surveying the lobby. Below me, Wheelock was chatting with a woman in a red cocktail dress, her hair coiled in a wispy bun at the nape of her neck, revealing a serpentine tattoo that crept up from her spine to lick her collarbone. Below the cocktail dress she wore knee-high combat boots. Wheelock, towering over her, tilted his head at something she said, and they both laughed.

He and I had an understanding; he was allowed to do anything he wanted. We were both allowed. But only one of us could make a woman like that laugh. Only one of us was famous.

Wheelock won the award and—despite the confidence I'd noted earlier—was awkward before the microphone. He read a speech I'd written for him, speaking so quickly that the words ran together, incomprehensible if endearing. I hadn't included my own name among those he thanked for their contributions, because it felt narcissistic, and as he got to the end of the speech he wrinkled his forehead before shaking the trophy in my general direction and hastily departing the stage. Afterward, we skipped the party and went to dinner with Min.

"You guys clean up nice," she said, kissing us. She was still living in Bushwick, but the loft had emptied down to her and her boyfriend Jake, a financial analyst from Schenectady. On weekends now they went to farmer's markets and baked their own bread. The economic downturn had given Jake some doubts about his profession; he was, he told us over pasta, "really getting into artisanal ice cream" and the "alternative comedy scene."

"It's alternative because it isn't funny," Min said drily. She loved to bait him, and in response he'd only push his glasses higher up on his nose and blush. I mentioned my old roommate Emma, whose cheese-making empire in the Berkshires had now expanded to include yogurt and ice cream, and he leaned forward excitedly.

"Emma from *Emma's Dairy?*" he said. "You're *friends* with her?"

As it happened, Emma had recently sent me an email, and we'd begun writing regularly, finding in our small-town lives points of connection. "Today I bought tampons at the drugstore from a woman who bought pumpkin ice cream from me yesterday," she wrote. "Is it claustrophobic or reassuring to have no privacy in your life? I'm not sure." *No membrane,* I thought. She asked about Robin, and I shared what news I had without mentioning how little I saw her myself. Emma was married to a goat farmer named Gretchen.

She had another pair of cats, Itsy and Bitsy, and a four-year-old child, Oak, who'd named them. I told Min and Jake the story of the cat funeral and how it prompted Emma to change her life. It was rare for me to tell a long story, and I could sense Wheelock watching me, a small smile playing around his lips.

"It's funny," Min said when I was finished. "You hardly ever talk about your sister."

I took a bite of my food. I'd been talking while everyone else ate, and the other plates were empty. "We aren't close," I said.

"But she lived with you all that time."

Wheelock put his hand on my knee, beneath the table, and I leaned against him, grateful for his weight and warmth. "She's back in Canada now," I said.

"Does she still play the piano?" Min said.

Wheelock shot her a look. I noted his protectiveness with surprise—I was surprised both that he'd been paying enough attention to think I needed it, and that I did, in fact, need it. I put my hand on top of his. "I don't know," I said, and turned back to my food.

Later, at the apartment, Wheelock said, "Thank you."

"For what?"

"I didn't get to say it in the speech," he said. "So I'm saying it now."

Wheelock's studio had just enough room for a couch that pulled out into a bed. He had one of everything: one small table, one chair, one cup, one plate. One fork. But the apartment wasn't spare. It was cluttered with trademark Wheelock touches: tin cans filled with pennies and buttons; pictures cut out of the newspaper and taped to the walls; by the door, a pair of men's shoes he'd found on Fifth Avenue. They didn't fit him, but they were "such nice shoes," he said. It was true they were beautiful, the leather a burnished cognac color, and a stamp on the inside said they were made in Italy. Perhaps they were bespoke, I thought, thinking of Hervé. On the windowsill was a lineup of pebbles in various shades of grey. The apartment made me nostalgic for the old yellow farmhouse, and even those urns filled with cigarette butts I'd never understood. He was a collector of things; he loved weighting his pockets and emptying them at home, spilling the contents of his day on the table, his progress through the world made visible. Perhaps this as much as anything else was what I loved in him.

I lay down on the pull-out couch, which maintained the lumps where it was used to being folded, like a person unable to fix his bad posture. Wheelock placed himself on top of me, his feet on my feet, his hands on my hands, so we were splayed together. His breath smelled of marinara. Although his hair was grey now, his eyes had the same feverish energy I'd seen in the dark bar when we met almost ten years earlier.

"Aren't you going to say anything?" he said.

"Like what?"

"Like *You're welcome,*" he said. "Like *Lawrence, these have been the best years of my life.* That kind of thing."

I frowned at him. I never called him Lawrence. Nor did I ever think about whether the past decade had been the best of my life, though I never regretted it or doubted my decision to join him in Pennsylvania. It would have been like doubting the decision to breathe oxygen, or walk upright. The choice had been made long ago, and not by my conscious mind. "You're welcome," I said.

"Min thinks I've done you a disservice, keeping you tucked away in Briar Neck. She thinks I should at least marry you."

"I didn't realize she was so conventional."

Wheelock laughed, then sighed. He rolled off me and rubbed his chin. "It's that Jake," he said. "I wanted her to find stability, and now that she has it I'm afraid she's going to move to Schenectady and become a housewife."

"It might not be the worst thing."

"Is she right, though? About you?"

"I like Briar Neck," I said.

"And the other thing?"

"I never thought about it," I said.

Wheelock put his head in my armpit and nudged me until I was on my side. He wrapped himself around me, arms and legs everywhere, his cheek scratching my ear. At three in the morning I woke up to the sound of car horns outside, and he was still wound around me, so tightly I could barely breathe.

7.

It was Min who got married, three years later, and she wanted to do it in Briar Neck, which she insisted on calling her "ancestral home," in a tone somehow both archly ironic and sentimental. Because I lived there, I was pressed into service for the logistics. With Wheelock away traveling, filming a special on the aftermath of the tsunami in Japan, Min, Jake, and I looked at venues together, eventually settling on a renovated barn.

"People from New York are going to think it's twee," Min said, and I nodded, not sure whether this was a good thing or not. "What do you think, Jakey?"

Jake, who spent most of his time outside taking work calls on his cell, smiled and gave a thumbs-up. He gave a thumbs-up to everything. The only part he had strong opinions about was the food. He and Min had spent two hours deliberating over a pea-shoot appetizer. They'd had a very intense whispered argument that involved ricotta salata. They didn't ask me to weigh in; Min said I was a nonbeliever, a food atheist, and she was right.

Min designed the floral arrangements and the invitations, and her mother sewed her wedding dress, hand-embroidering it with tiny freshwater pearls.

The morning of the wedding, Min, Soo Jung, and I had breakfast at the house while a hairdresser wove flowers into Min's hair. Wheelock and Jake were off at the barn, overseeing final decorations, and two of Min's rowdier bridesmaids were passed out on the couch after drinking too much the night before. Soo Jung spoke to her daughter as if I weren't there. I don't think she was jealous of me; she just wasn't convinced that my presence was important enough to acknowledge. Fidgety and fretful, Min kept asking over and over how she looked.

"You're gorgeous, you egomaniac," Soo Jung told her. "There will be a million pictures of your perfection, don't worry."

"I feel bloated."

"You look divine," her mother said impatiently. "You have the face of an angel. Et cetera."

"My face is an oil slick," Min said. "And I have a zit on my chin the size of a kumquat. I think I might throw up."

"Here, drink this," her mother said, holding out a flask. She was wearing a purple silk dress, and over it a canvas apron decked with pockets, from which she'd been producing useful items all morning—a makeup brush, safety pins, tissues, and now booze.

"Mom," Min said. "I haven't had a drink in a decade."

"Maybe it's time to reconsider," her mother said.

"I *can't*," Min said. "I'm pregnant." Suddenly in tears, she smeared her face with her palms, twisting her eye makeup into Cubist lines. "I'm pregnant and it's twins and Jake wants to move to Schenectady for the schools."

Soo Jung and I stared at each other. With slow deliberation she held out the flask to me, and I took it. We drank the whole thing, the two of us, before the ceremony began.

In the end Min looked lovely, walking down the aisle on Wheelock's arm, with no sign of nerves or other distress. Her face had been repainted; her hair was exquisite. Everyone said the food was delicious. I waited for Jake to give her a thumbs-up after the vows, but he didn't. Wheelock, at the reception, gave a funny toast in which he managed to avoid the topic of marriage completely and spoke instead about Min as a little girl, her appetite for adventure and art.

Min listened, her eyes shining with unshed tears. Outside the barn fireflies freckled the night. His job done, Wheelock paced outside in the gravel parking lot, examining the tiny rocks and picking a few to store in his pockets.

"God love you," Soo Jung said drunkenly, materializing by my side. "He is one weird dude."

"I guess," I said.

Inside the barn Jake's family was leading everyone in the hora, Min laughing as she was lifted above them.

"I suppose you don't mind, being high priestess of his cult."

I blanched, edging away, and she grabbed my arm. "Jesus, I'm sorry. Weddings make me so mean."

"Because you never had one?"

"Fuck no," she said. "I just hate them."

We stood for a moment watching Wheelock meander around, peeking under the wheel beds of cars on a hunt for who knew what treasure. Inside the guests hooted and danced, the klezmer horns rioting in the night. The next day Min and Jake left for the Amalfi coast and Soo Jung and I packed up all their wedding gifts and shipped them to Jake's family in Schenectady, which Soo Jung insisted on calling, with the heavy irony she'd bestowed upon her daughter, "the promised land."

At the UPS store she briefly put her hands on my cheeks and leaned toward me as if for a kiss. "You are not a non-person," she said. "You deserve better than this."

I was irritated by her judgment of my life. "Than UPS?" I said.

"Don't pretend you're stupid," she said, and then she got into her rental car and drove away.

We met again seven months later, at the hospital in the promised land, where Min's twins, a boy and a girl, were born premature and confined to the NICU. They lay in their ventilators under lights, their yellow skin pinking more each day. I was fascinated by their tiny bellies and perfect fingernails and thatches of fine dark hair. The labor was difficult, and Min spent the days after it weeping with hormonal rage and post-operative pain. No one could calm her.

Soo Jung and I held the babies, sang to them. We knew the nurses by name, the mean daytime one and the nice night-shift one. We took turns fetching sandwiches and coffee. Jake's parents were there too, Sarah and Artie, and the four of us sometimes went out for dinner after visiting hours ended, sitting in the warm neon bustle of the Schenectady Olive Garden. For this moment, suspended in the orbit of the hospital, we acted as if we were all one family.

Wheelock, who was in Japan, took almost a week to arrive. When he did, he held Min's hand and tried to show her footage of the Fukushima power plant until I took his laptop away. "What?" he said, puzzled. I dragged him to the NICU and showed him the babies, and he and Soo Jung smiled and shook hands, congratulating each other formally, as if concluding a business deal.

Then Min was ready to go home, to the house she and Jake had bought, where the nursery was decorated in buttercup yellow. Soo Jung had painted a mural on the wall, bunnies and squirrels and birds, a lovely tamed wilderness. Wheelock and I prepared to say goodbye and return to Briar Neck. At the last moment Min grabbed my wrist hard, with a strength that reminded me of my sister's, and whispered in my ear, "Don't leave me to this hell." I laughed, thinking it was her typical irony, but she was serious, her eyes panicked and wide.

"It'll be okay," I told her.

"Will it?" she said.

As we drove away from the suburbs, I felt sick and sad. Soo Jung, who stayed behind for another month, emailed pictures of the babies, now released from the NICU and swaddled at home, arranged in Min's too-full lap as she bared her teeth in a wan smile. Wheelock immediately went back to work, and I surprised myself by falling apart.

I went to sleep crying and woke up crying. In the mornings I got up, drank coffee, and then went back to bed. Sometimes I lay there the whole day. At night, unable to sleep, I watched talk shows on the couch. Wheelock asked me what was wrong; I told him the truth, which was that I didn't know. I said I missed the dinners with Sarah and Artie and Soo Jung, and he offered to take me to Olive Garden anytime I wanted. I shook my head, still crying. Wheelock gave up and returned to the office. He wanted to help but he needed me to tell him how to do it; this was both fair and impossible.

One night I called Soo Jung. "Just wanted an update," I said with forced casualness, as if I'd ever called her before. "What's going on there?" I could hear an odd squeak in my voice, lurching with still more tears.

Soo Jung's voice was brisk as ever. "Sleeping and pooping, mainly," she said. "You sound weird as hell."

"I'm fine. How's the jaundice? Did the belly buttons fall off yet?" At the hospital I'd learned that the umbilical cord, once cut and tied, left behind a stump that would eventually dry up and drop away; I'd been fascinated by this information, and disappointed to leave before it happened.

There was a pause on the line. In the background I could hear a baby's wail rise and then drop into silence, then another wail, either the same baby or the other one.

Soo Jung said softly, "And finally it happens."

"What happens?"

"You're feeling it. Life is crashing down around your ears. Poor Lark. I'm sorry for you, honey, really I am."

"I don't know what you're talking about," I said.

"The babies," she said, her tone minus its usual acidity. "The babies."

8.

She was right. It was the babies who wrecked me. I was thirty-five years old. I had no desire to be married; I'd lived for years in happy monasticism with Wheelock, wedded to my job. I'd declared myself content in Briar Neck, with my friends and my routines, my days in the editing room, imposing order on hours of footage. It was the perfect life for me, until it wasn't.

A space opened in me that couldn't be filled by work. I can't explain how the desire for motherhood had lain inside me, dormant and unfelt, for so long, only to wake up in a cataclysm that demanded I take action. Had I lacked interest because my own mother was so disinterested? Did I want a child now to fill some past void? Or was it because of Marianne that I'd suppressed the urge so long, believing that you couldn't imitate something you'd never known yourself?

I don't know the answer to these questions. I can only say that once I wanted a child, the want became overwhelming and undeniable, an ache in my body like a permanent migraine. I was never a little girl who dragged around a doll, pretending to bathe or nurse it; I'd never imagined the children I would have, giving them names or imagining their faces. Yet it was also true that I'd thought of myself as a mother to Robin, had taken over from Marianne who had no passion for the task. And now, as an adult, I knew exactly what I felt; however unexpected it was, the feeling was accompanied by certainty.

Soo Jung said it was because of my age, that I saw the window closing and knew that soon it would be too late. "The time is now, my friend," she told me on the phone.

There was a clatter on the line and then Min came on. "Don't do it," she said. "It'll ruin your life." One of the babies started babbling, and the other joined in; according to Min, they were forever waking each other up. "Seriously, though, you'll be a great mom, Lark. Come join our tribe."

I hung up. When Wheelock came in from the office, I was showered and dressed. We ordered a pizza and ate in dull, mechanical quiet, until I told him I wanted to have a child.

"What, now?" he said.

"Yes."

"All right."

"Really?"

"I want you to be happy," he said.

I smiled at him. We were sitting on the couch, wiping the grease from our hands with delivery napkins. Wheelock swept one across his mouth and crumpled it into the pizza box. He was clean-shaven and healthy; in the past month he'd mostly been home in Pennsylvania and taken up hiking, returning from his ventures with pockets full of pine cones. His hair, which had gone almost completely white, hung below his ears. He looked weathered and distinguished and athletic, like an old-fashioned sportsman aristocrat—say, Edmund Hillary. I remembered that Hillary, during his lifetime, was voted the most trusted man in New Zealand. His first wife died in a plane crash, and his second wife, June Mulgrew, was the widow of his close friend Peter Mulgrew, who died after having replaced Hillary as speaker on a sightseeing flight to the Antarctic, which also crashed. I'd read a long biography of Hillary one winter in Briar Neck, following him around the world, on all his perilous journeys, while I nestled safely at home.

"So what are you doing to do?" Wheelock asked politely.

I folded my hands in my lap. Then I folded my knees under my chin and crossed my arms around my shins. I was making myself smaller and smaller. I hadn't realized until that moment that for him the discussion was theoretical. He didn't expect to be involved. It might sound strange that—after all the weeping of the previous days—I didn't cry, but I didn't.

I remembered Richard, my old boss at the Worthen computer lab, and how we used to laugh about Jimmy Stewart in *Vertigo*, making his crazy demands of Kim Novak. *Judy, please, it can't matter to you.*

"Would you ever——" I said.

"My Lark." Wheelock's voice was firm. "I already have a child."

Nothing in my life with Wheelock had prepared me for the look on his face, which was one of great and radiant pity. Pity mixed with love. I couldn't stand for him to apologize to me. To describe his self-absorption, with which I was already intimately familiar. I couldn't bear for him—a person I knew better than I knew myself—to tell me that he'd stolen my youth, when I was perfectly aware I'd given it to him freely, had thrust it, with despairing enthusiasm, into his hands.

9.

I quit my job with Wheelock as abruptly as I'd started it. When I left Briar Neck, I took only samples of my editing work and a suitcase of clothes. In all the years I'd worked for him I'd never paid rent, so my bank account was full. While he was at work I wrote him a note saying I'd be using his apartment for a while. Since Min moved to Schenectady the place had mostly stood empty, and I knew he wouldn't object.

In New York, I threw everything out of the apartment except the sofa bed. All of Wheelock's flotsam and jetsam, the record of his walks through the city, the men's shoes, the pennies and pebbles: I got rid of it. I tried to extinguish him from my thoughts, but at night I often dreamed of him and us, dreams in which we were perpetually in transit, strapped into airplane seats, or leaning into each other as trains veered away from the coast, never arriving anywhere. The meaning of these dreams was obvious and mundane, and I was irritated at my unconscious brain for not generating more arresting imagery. Once I'd cleaned the place out, I began walking the city myself. I visited museums and meandered across bridges and climbed to the tops of buildings that were said to have noteworthy views. I didn't call or email anyone I knew; I wasn't ready to tell the story of what had happened, and I felt suspended between the old life I was mourning and a new one whose form I couldn't yet see. The few calls I received, mostly from Min, I didn't return. The only time I used my phone was in a Gristedes where I'd gone to wait out a rainstorm. I was leafing through some magazines when I came across a picture of Boris Dawidoff, on the right side of an image separated via lightning bolt from his actress girlfriend, who was now quite famous. They'd broken up, the caption said. Boris's face was round and pink, his tousled hair grey. I took a picture of it and texted it to Robin.

The text didn't go through and I thought I'd resend it later, but then I forgot about it as I continued my wanderings. New York was drab and rain-struck, the dull brown of early spring gathered around the city like a trench coat. One day I went to see our old apartment, the Tunnel, and was surprised that I didn't remember the number of the building. The neighborhood itself was unrecognizable, shiny with expensive clothing stores and Asian fusion restaurants. The place where we used to order egg drop soup for two dollars a bowl was now a nail salon offering hot-stone pedicures for forty. At a Starbucks I sat watching two children fight over a hand-held gaming device while their nanny vainly protested. She saw me staring and hustled them out quickly, sneaking a glance back at me over her shoulder. I wasn't sure whether she thought I might yell at them or abduct them, and I flushed with sad self-consciousness at the idea that I was a threat either way.

Outside the Starbucks I waited for the light to change. As I stepped into the street I heard one of the children cry out, and turned my head toward the sound; at least that's how I've reconstructed the events. I don't in fact remember what happened. I only know I wasn't looking when the taxi turned the corner, entered the intersection, and struck me. I heard as if from a great distance the sound my head made against the curb. I noticed my odd, sharp landing on the ground as you might notice a funny noise in your car just before the brakes fail or the engine catches fire.

I woke up feeling weightless. The lights in the room were very bright and the television was on, playing a show about animals, though the reception was fuzzy and pixelated. Two lion cubs wrestled on a savannah while a voice said, "Playing teaches the young about hier-archy." The TV was at an odd angle, much smaller than I remem-bered it, and partially blocked by a white expanse of pillow. At last I understood that I wasn't in the apartment, but a hospital room, and an IV—surely the reason for my weightlessness—snaked along my arm. The pillow that blocked the view of the TV was in fact my foot, bulbous in a cast.

"Their father will teach them to fight while their mother will ignore them," the voice said. "The cubs will grow up as enemies until one of them establishes himself as the alpha male of the tribe." This narration continued as the cubs rolled around, climbing on their father's back and then falling off. "Their father will abandon them and the kids will be like, *What the hell, Dad?* But he has to do his own thing. That's the way of dads. The kids will grow up, fight, hunt, have sex, produce cubs of their own, and fuck those cubs up. That's the way of cubs."

The narration didn't seem scientific. I tried to move my hand to find the remote and change the channel, but found I couldn't.

"Don't worry, you're not paralyzed," the narration said, "just super doped up. You have a broken ankle and a pretty serious con-cussion." I wondered how a nature show knew so much about my personal foibles. My mouth was lint-filled, tongue-scraped, and I had no voice.

"The nurse is going to bring you some water," the narration said, coming closer, and a head swam into my view. It wasn't the television speaking. It was Robin.

10.

I was in the hospital for a week. Because it was a teaching hos-pital, many people observed and inspected me, a troop at a time, ducklings parading behind their mother duck. Because of the con-cussion, I suffered from double vision, so there seemed to be not five ducklings but ten, or even twenty, their ranks swelling each time I blinked. In spite of their number they weren't very helpful. They reduced my medication, and pain blazed at my temples; I tried to press my hands against my forehead and missed, palming empty air. I told them the lights were too bright. They told me to close my eyes. I told them the sheets were scratchy, and they told me to lie still.

My room was semi-private, which is to say that a blue curtain hung around my bed and when the ducklings entered they swept it aside as if performing on a stage. Across the room, behind a separate blue curtain, was another patient, who never spoke or watched television or made a sound. The ducklings visited her too and discussed her case among themselves, but they never asked her any questions. Once a day a machine was wheeled in and parked next to her, making industrial pumping sounds. I was at least as interested in her condition as my own. Why did no one come to see her? Why did she never speak? I asked the ducklings, but they didn't answer. Answering questions was not their job, and I wasn't sure if I'd even asked them out loud.

The ducklings on their rounds provided my only sense of time passing. Otherwise the hours twirled without markers, merely a vague feeling of days turning to nights and then back again. They'd switched my television off and taken away my remote. I wasn't allowed any screens. In addition to my concussion I had vertigo, which turned out to be far less entertaining as an experience than it was as a film. It came and went unpredictably, and during the worst of it the bed spun around endlessly, never coming to rest.

"Try to sleep," the nurses said, and I tried.

But there's no worse place to sleep than a hospital. Even in darkness the hallways whispered with intent. The sounds of rolling wheelchairs and gurneys. Muttered conferences and beeping phones. It was a place where bodies labored and were repaired; this was work, not rest. Whenever I tried to sit up in bed, my temples ached and the room swam. I lay back with my eyes closed, and lay back again, and again, and again.

Because I complained so constantly about my headache they upped my dosages, and eventually I floated above the hospital noises, noting the smells and voices of the various orderlies and nurses, ranking them. I didn't care for the ones who made chit-chat; I preferred to be ignored. There was one who held my wrist to check my pulse and I saw that her nails were bitten and ragged. Therefore I didn't trust her; couldn't she even take care of herself? There was another who had long nails painted in complex and brilliant patterns, and I didn't trust her either; wasn't she frivolous? I felt very sorry for myself, and I was starting to believe I'd been imprisoned and would never be allowed to leave.

I understood I'd hallucinated Robin, that she'd never been there. The nurses asked if there was someone they should call, and I thought of Wheelock and then dismissed the thought; I couldn't turn to him now or I might, I knew, go back to Briar Neck and never leave again. Helen was in Costa Rica with her capuchins and Min had the twins and Olga was too far away in Berlin and Emma was busy with her family and dairy business. There was no one I wanted to call. But then Robin came back.

"Sorry I haven't been around the past few days," she said casually, coming into the room and flicking on the lights, which had been strictly forbidden by the ducklings. "I've had a lot to do."

I squinted at her. My vision was not quite blurred and not quite normal. Parts of her were sharply, overly focused while other parts looked squeezed and stretched. None of her proportions made sense to me. "Are you real?" I said.

She laughed. "Sometimes I wonder."

She swung my curtain all the way to the side and then swung the one beside me, too. For the first time I saw an old woman, or at least a small body topped with a puff of white hair. "How are you holding up, Mrs. Krugman? Still fighting the good fight?"

Mrs. Krugman didn't answer. Robin fished something out of a plastic bag, and I heard a quiet pop. "Don't tell the nurses," she said to the room in general, and started feeding Mrs. Krugman with a plastic spoon. "She loves pudding," she told me. "But who doesn't?" Every once in a while she raised a paper napkin to Mrs. Krugman's lips and wiped.

I was jealous of Robin's attentions. Was she Mrs. Krugman's sister, or mine? I wouldn't have minded some pudding. I lay quietly stewing, observing my sister. At the age of thirty-two Robin was both ragged and beautiful, lovely in her self-neglect. She was wearing dark purple corduroys and brown, thick-soled work boots, and a blue sweater marbled with black and brown threads. When she came closer, to throw the pudding cup in the trash can, I saw that the black threads were animal hair. Her own hair hung down her back in a braid that seemed to have been made some days earlier and then left to fray. Her face was thinner than it had been when I'd last seen her, and her eyes seemed larger and even wider-set. Around her neck was a pair of glasses on a red string. I watched her move around my side of the room, bent on tasks of her own devising. She tossed some hospital brochures into the trash, wiped dust off the television with the sleeve of her sweater, went out to bring me a glass of water, then left the room and came back with another cup and a toothbrush. Until I saw these things I hadn't noticed that my teeth were slimy, my tongue gritty and sour. I brushed, rinsed, spat, and she took everything away. Then she came back and pressed a button on the side of my bed until I was sitting almost upright. I'd been lying down so long that even this simple adjustment made me dizzy.

"You'll be discharged soon, they tell me," my sister said, pulling a chair up beside me.

"Who tells you, the ducklings?"

"Yes, the ducklings," she said, unruffled. "I want to show you some pictures." Over my lap she spread some color photocopies: wood floors, white walls, a bathroom. I didn't know what to do with these images. I thought it must be some kind of memory test, one I was bound to fail. All I saw were empty rooms.

"I found you a place," she said. "In Brooklyn. It's a garden apartment with a little outdoor space in the back. The landlady says you can have a cat, if you want to, but no dog. I said I didn't see you wanting a dog."

I was confused. "I'm moving to Brooklyn?"

"Min and I agreed it's not good for you to keep staying in what's-his-name's place."

"You talked to Min?"

"She's sorry she's not here too, but she's got her hands full. As you know." Here Robin placed another picture on my lap: the babies, red-faced and unsmiling, wearing knitted hats. Min had named them Alma and Alvin. I reached out a hand to touch the pictures and somehow missed; I couldn't orient my body in space, couldn't make contact where I wanted. My head throbbed and I blinked back small hot tears. I thought I sensed Robin watching me, but when I opened my eyes she was bending over to stuff the photographs into a back-pack on the floor. "Are you going to stay?" I asked her.

"For a while," she said.

"How did you know I was here?"

"The nurses found me in your phone and called me. They said I was the last person you'd tried to contact. Something about Boris? I guess you don't remember."

I didn't remember. "Will you bring me some pudding?"

"Maybe," she said.

II.

The apartment was in a quiet, distant neighborhood. It was a ten-minute walk to the subway and a ten-minute walk to the super-market, and not in the same direction. The yellow brick buildings were old yet charmless, and there weren't any trees. The landlady, Elena Brown, explained that there used to be large, leafy elms on the block, but they'd all succumbed to disease and the city hadn't planted new ones. "We're on some kind of waiting list," she said. "Can you believe there's a waiting list for trees?"

She was an Italian woman of uncertain age, her hair dyed a brilliant orange, her eyebrows drawn with a firm hand. I knew she was Italian because she told me so immediately and brought it up every time I saw her. She'd married an African-American man named Ed Brown, and the loss of her maiden name, Caputo, seemed to pain her more than the loss of Ed, who'd died of heart disease decades earlier. "I used to be a Caputo," she'd say longingly, "back in the day." After Ed's death she'd raised their three children alone, and they'd shown their gratitude by moving away to Boston, Milwaukee, and Chicago, respectively. "I hardly even see my grandchildren," she said. "Can you believe this world?"

The world was full of things that Elena Brown couldn't believe. She couldn't believe that Robin and I, such pretty girls, didn't have husbands and children. She couldn't believe that UPS wouldn't deliver her package to the back door when she'd explicitly directed them to in a note handwritten on paper torn out of the phone book. She couldn't believe America had a black president. Ed would be amazed, she said. Never thought he'd see the day. "Next we need an Italian," she said.

Whenever Robin and I were in the little garden, Elena would stand on the exterior staircase above us, arms folded, watching and talking. We'd always invite her down, but she shook her head and said, "That's your space, I'm not going to invade it," then continue with her commentary.

I liked her. I liked that in my apartment I could hear her moving around above me, the thud of her footsteps, the scrape of furniture across the floor, occasional staccato thumps whose cause remained a mystery to me. Sometimes, when it was very quiet, I could hear her sneeze.

Robin slept on the couch we'd bought at IKEA along with a mattress and bed frame. The rest of the apartment we furnished from Goodwill and Brooklyn itself, lugging home kitchen carts and end tables and bookshelves that people left out on the street. That is, Robin did the lugging, as I was still on crutches. When she was done the place was a motley patchwork, with the new couch sitting spotless in the center of the living room like a queen among plebes. In a thrift store on Atlantic Avenue she'd found a box of old postcards and she bought a number of cheap frames and covered the walls with them, pictures of Paris, Los Angeles, Havana, Detroit. On the back of a picture of coastal Maine someone had scrawled, *Came here to get away from you.*

As my ankle mended, my mind also began to heal, shifting from concussion into clarity. My vision returned to an almost painful focus. The world felt too brightly contrasted, too finely grained. I was sometimes transfixed by Elena's face, her one crooked tooth or the ring she wore, which was purple and gold and didn't fit her well, so that she twisted it over and over again with her other hand. My mind would scream, *Please stop!* and she noticed me staring and only did it more, whether to torment or entertain me, I didn't know. My ankle ached, but worse was the vertigo, which robbed me of my footing and tilted the world on its axis at unpredictable moments, so that I found myself collapsing sideways onto couches, or bumping into doorsills, clumsy with disorientation.

Quite some time passed before I remembered to thank Robin for her help.

"It sounded bad when the nurses called me. They said you were slurring your words and not making sense. They asked you if you'd been drinking and you said, 'I do not accept drinks from gentlemen who disapprove of me.'"

It was a line from *Breakfast at Tiffany's*. Why I'd quoted it to the nurses, I couldn't say.

"I pictured you keeping some rough company," she said. "Which didn't seem like you. So I left everything and came down."

We were sitting in the garden—which was composed of concrete slabs, framed by narrow strips of dirt—on two old lawn chairs we'd found in somebody's garbage. They'd been grimy and mottled but Robin had washed and bleached them and arranged them at right angles to each other, with an overturned milk crate in between, and on the milk crate she'd placed a potted geranium. We sat in this civilized plastic tableau, drinking tea. The afternoons were getting warmer and the sun hit our faces with tentative light.

"What did you leave?" I asked. "I mean, what kind of life, is yours like?" At times I had trouble speaking; words evaded me or slithered into the wrong places. That morning I'd stood in the washroom after using the toilet, trying to remember the words *handle* and *flush*.

"What's my life like?" Robin repeated.

"Yes," I said.

"I moved up to Sainte-Agathe, you know that." A few years earlier, Robin's American grandparents—the Johnsons of Fox Run, Minnesota, whom she'd met a mere handful of times—had died, willing her a sum of money. With it she'd bought land in the Laurentians, two hours north of Montreal. On the phone Marianne had said that Robin left the city to spite her. *Came here to get away from you.*

"I mean," I said. "What kind of place." With effort, my head dully throbbing, I turned to focus on her. She was wearing the same pants and sweater she'd had on in the hospital. She wore the same thing every day, more or less. Sometimes she rebraided her hair.

She filled her cheeks with air like a puffer fish, then let it out in a long sigh. "It's a cottage," she said. "On some land. I have animals there."

"Animals?" I pictured her riding horses, or raising chickens. "What kind of animals?"

She stretched out her hand as if to say, *All kinds.* "I like the woods. I had enough of the city. I waitress at a place in town. There's so much money to be made in tourist season. You wouldn't believe what some people will pay for a hamburger in the middle of July."

"Hamburger," I said musingly. There'd been a larger sentence attached to this inside my head, but by the time it reached my mouth the rest of the words had evaporated.

The one-word remnant made my sister laugh. "We could have hamburgers tonight if you want," she offered.

"Okay."

"I remember you always liked A&W cheeseburgers. With root

beer. You used to dig through the apartment for coins, in the couch cushions, in Marianne's pockets, and when you finally collected enough money you'd take me out to A&W."

I'd forgotten this, but as she spoke the memory came back to me with startling sensory detail: the lint and grime of the couch where I groped for pennies and dimes, the clink of the coins when I deposited them in my little plastic purse, my sister at my side watching me, as she was watching me now.

"Are you—do you live alone?" I asked her.

"Not exactly. I have a lot of friends. You should come meet them."

I was silent. I knew I should say that I would like that, and to tell Robin how grateful I was that she'd come to the hospital at a moment's notice, that she'd set up the apartment, that she was staying with me now. And yet for some reason I couldn't; the words caught in my throat. So I sat in the sun and folded my hands in my lap, feeling another fit of vertigo approach.

Robin was still watching me. "You'll be fine, you know," she said, and I nodded and gripped the arms of my chair as the world around me fluttered, slid sideways, and flew.

12.

The savings I'd accumulated in Briar Neck were considerable, and Wheelock, I learned, had paid the hospital bills, which had been mailed to my old address in Briar Neck. He must have considered this charity a gift, proof of his integrity, but it felt more like a net that still bound me to him, and I wanted to be released. While the doctors said I'd eventually be able to resume my editing work, for now I was forbidden to look at any kind of screen. My vertigo ebbed, but effects from my head injury lingered. Sometimes the world was clear and sometimes it was not; sometimes I was attacked by headaches so vicious that I threw up.

Min came to see me in Brooklyn, with the children in tow. She was as thin as she'd been before pregnancy, though the angles of her face were ever so slightly softened and there were light purple circles under her eyes. Her twins were a perfect mixture of their parents; they had Jake's nose and round cheeks but Min's dark hair and mischievous eyes. Somehow they were toddlers already, and they climbed on all the furniture and jumped off, banging their heads on the tables and floor, then howling and starting it all up again. Though Min looked the same to me, her gestures were all new: picking up her daughter, she placed a pacifier in her mouth, then took away from her son a wrought-iron candlestick I'd neglected to put away. I apologized and she shook her head, unbothered. Motherhood had channeled her nervous energy into constant action. She opened a plastic container of crackers for one twin, sniffed the backside of the other. Robin said, "I don't enjoy young children," and left without saying where she was going.

Min laughed. "I wish I could just walk out sometimes," she said.

As I limped around the apartment making tea she told me that she and Jake were moving to California to open an artisanal donut shop. It was Jake's dream, one Min was willing to indulge if it meant getting out of Schenectady. When I heard the news my face crumpled. I hadn't seen Min much lately, and now I'd never see her at all.

"Oh please, please," Min said anxiously, reaching out her hands. She wanted to hug me but the toddlers were grabbing her ankles, trying to pry them apart into a tunnel.

"It's okay," I said. Turning away, I poured the hot water into two cups and missed, scalding my hands. "Stand back," I said sharply, not wanting to hurt the children too.

"Lark cry!" said Alma, interested in me for the first time since their arrival. "Lark cry!" Alvin came over to investigate. He grabbed my leg to steady himself, his grip surprisingly strong; they were both strapping children with round healthy bellies, no trace left of the tiny preemies they'd been at birth.

"Yes," I said, wiping my face. "Lark cry."

My fingers stung. The pain distracted me. Also, Alvin was pulling so hard on my pants I was afraid they might fall down.

At last we were settled in the living room with our tea, and the toddlers amused themselves ripping pages out of a magazine. Alma sat on my lap, surprisingly heavy, comfortable with me as with furniture. I smelled her sweet-sour skin, touched the hair at the nape of her neck, like a person exploring a new neighborhood where she might buy a house; when I placed my palm on her back, I couldn't believe how fast her heart was beating. Min watched me without comment. We spoke for a while about California and their life there. The conversation funneled down into the minutiae of real estate prices and school districts, calming in its tedium, and I stifled a yawn. "We'll go soon," Min said, and I apologized again.

She asked how long Robin was staying, and I said I didn't know. She asked if I'd made plans for what to do next, and I said I didn't know. We didn't talk about my desire to have a child, though it remained inside me, low-burning and constant as an underground fire. I wanted it as much as ever and yet in my current condition I could hardly take care of myself, much less another person. I'd lost the momentum of my new life before it had even gotten under way, and whenever I thought about it I felt seized by failure. Min must have sensed something of this. She'd teased me for years, searching for a sore spot; now that she'd found one, she kept her distance from it, and I loved her for that.

"You'll find something," she said instead. "My dad never gave you enough credit, you know. You practically made his work for him."

"You think things will fall apart now?" I said, hating the hope in my voice.

She shook her head. "I think he'll hire ten people to take your place."

"I don't know what I'm going to do, Min."

"Awesome! A midlife crisis. You should buy a convertible and start sleeping with twenty-five-year-olds."

I frowned, and she laughed. "Don't listen to me. I haven't had a decent night's sleep in two years and I'm not sure I'm wearing underwear."

"I didn't need to know that," I said. We sat smiling at each other, lingering at the end of our friendship. "I'll miss you," I said.

"Mama cry?" her daughter said excitedly.

"Just a little," Min said.

For days after they left I kept finding reminders of their visit: Cheerios under the couch, a tiny plastic dragon behind the toilet, a red splatter of juice on the baseboards in the kitchen like a miniature crime scene. As if the children had been determined, in their chaos, to leave a mark behind.

13.

Robin, too, was getting ready to leave. I could sense her distraction, an ever-greater restlessness. Even on rainy days she went for long walks, without an umbrella, and returned soaked, pink-cheeked. She'd found a cemetery she liked and spent hours tramping around it, looking at birds. She told me about the woodpeckers there, how she'd spotted one defending its territory, swooping aggressively over and around another, then returning to chisel its tree with holes. One evening she talked about a woman named Phoebe Snetsinger who'd been diagnosed with terminal cancer and was spurred to become a competitive bird-watcher. She traveled the world and became the first person to spot over eight thousand species.

"And seeing all those birds somehow healed her?" I said.

"Actually, she died in a bus crash while bird-watching," my sister said.

I laughed, and she frowned. New York was making her cranky. A few doors down from us lived a professional couple in their thirties with a subscription to *The New York Times.* On recycling day Robin would pick up their newspapers and every morning I'd find her head in hand at the breakfast table, a cup of tea at her elbow, reading the events of the previous week and shaking her head in dismay. She ranted about Obama's weak environmental policies and the American military-industrial complex. Her disagreements with Thomas L. Friedman's views were intense and long-winded, and I had a hard time following them. Mostly, I understood, she thought America was violent and corrupt and the president was all style and no substance.

"You'll notice he *still* hasn't closed Guantánamo," she said. "Even though it was one of the first things he promised to do. Not to mention the secret CIA prisons in Europe. Remember that old slogan— *Yes we can!* What a meaningless slogan. Yes we can *what*? Continue the ways of the old regime?"

I wasn't used to thinking about regimes. "He says change takes time," I said tentatively. Words came more readily to me now, and I could manoeuver them into simple sentences, but I wasn't sure I could advance a complex argument.

"His notions of change are completely superficial," she said. "All he does is make beautiful speeches."

"I like his speeches," I said, and my sister sighed heavily.

"You don't even notice the emptiness. You've been living here too long," she said. "I don't know how you stand it."

"It's not that bad," I said.

"Not that bad," she echoed, shaking her head again.

Sometimes I thought we argued about politics because, fraught as they were, these debates were easier than talking about personal realities. I knew there must be more to her life in the Laurentians than she was telling me, and I withheld from her the pit that chasmed in my stomach when I considered the possibility that I might never have a child. The subject was too tender; if she'd mocked or questioned it, I couldn't have withstood the conversation. So we spent each day together, and yet evaded each other too.

Sometimes I thought she picked arguments on purpose, cleverly, to pave the way for her departure. To make me glad to see her go.

Spring came to Brooklyn, and despite the lack of trees in the neighborhood there were flowers everywhere, sprouting in medians and

window boxes. On the street Robin found a broken charcoal barbe-
cue, two of its three legs collapsed like a half-killed spider, and she
repaired it with wooden splints and a hefty round of duct tape. She
called to Elena, who as usual was watching us from upstairs, and
Elena came down with a macaroni salad and two bottles of homemade wine given to her by a cousin in Queens. "He says it's a merlot
mix," she said doubtfully, handing them over. "All's I know is it'll get
you drunk, same as any other wine."

Robin used old copies of the *Times* to light charcoal briquettes,
producing large startling flames that flared and then died, over and
over. When the coals finally caught she went inside the apartment
and emerged with several garlands of Christmas lights, which she
strung from the fire escape over to the back fence. People kept
showing up: the man who owned the thrift store where Robin had
bought all those postcards; the couple whose newspapers we'd been
reading; a guy I was never introduced to but who sat happily on an
overturned garbage can, strumming a guitar and humming songs
none of us could hear over the chatter.

I sat on the steps, sipping a cup of tea and watching everyone. A
middle-aged woman with curly brown hair settled herself next to
me and asked how I was feeling.

"I'm fine," I said, "how are you?"

She smiled oddly. "I mean really, though. How are you *really*?"

"Really fine," I said. "Would you like some wine?"

"Got some," she said, leaning down between her feet to pick up a
plastic cup. She was wearing a purple T-shirt that said *I Am the King-
dom and the Glory* and I wondered who she was, where Robin had
found her. She followed my gaze and settled on my sister. "Robin's
so great," she said.

I agreed that she was.

"You're lucky," she said. "My sister's a crack addict who lives with
her fourth husband in a van in Florida. The only time I hear from her
is when she needs money."

I said I was sorry to hear that.

"Yeah, well," she said. "Nobody's family is perfect, am I right?"
I nodded.

"You don't know who I am, do you?" Her question wasn't hostile, but informational. She was a short stout woman with intelligent eyes that looked straight at me, gauging my response.

I shook my head.

"I'm Karen Madorsky."

I wasn't helped by this, and she knew it. She patted my knee, and as she did I noticed for the first time her long fake nails, decorated with yellow daisies on a blue background. She'd been one of my nurses in the hospital.

"You'll get back to normal," she said. "At some point." Then she heaved herself off the steps and went to pour herself more of the homemade wine.

Robin was busy turning food on the grill and serving it on paper plates. Later she and the guitar guy sang a duet of "Four Strong Winds," her voice as sweet and soaring as ever. At midnight people were still there, at one o'clock and two o'clock, and finally I went to bed. The last I saw of her, my sister was sitting in a corner of the garden sunk deep into a conversation with Elena that looked private and intense, Elena talking urgently, Robin nodding. When I woke up I saw that Robin had left me a note: *Had to catch my bus, didn't want to wake you.* The backyard was clean and the recycling full to bursting with paper plates and plastic cups. The holiday lights were still strung across the space, invisible in the morning sun.

14.

Without Robin in it, the apartment seemed both quieter and noisier; I heard creaks and scraping sounds I'd never noticed before, and even traffic and conversation from outside seemed louder, as if her body had cushioned it. I had a hard time sleeping. I'd read once, I couldn't remember where, that people who grow up by the ocean can never sleep well anywhere else. Its rhythms can't be reproduced. Robin's presence was something like that for me. In the evenings, my headaches came back, and I'd lie flat on my back as the room swayed, wishing she hadn't gone.

Sometimes I called her, but she rarely answered her phone, and I felt she wanted a break from me in any case. So I called Min or Marianne, but it was painful to hear the abundant, chaotic background noise of Min's house, her exasperated laughter as one child or the other ran amok, the soundtrack of a life so far from my own. As for Marianne, she always greeted me with a tone of surprise—"Oh, it's you," she'd say—and then she'd launch into lengthy, impenetrable commentaries on local news stories I wasn't following. I didn't mind this; but invariably she'd come around to asking, "So—what are you going to do now?" It was a question I had no answer to, and in response I'd end the call, feeling even further adrift.

I still wasn't allowed to watch movies or television; it was the longest I could remember ever having gone without films in my life, and this, too, made me feel unmoored, detached from the habits of the past. In an art class at Worthen I'd learned about an American pilot who was injured during the Second World War. Mostly paralyzed, made to lie flat, he spent the years of his hospitalization teaching himself to paint, and went on to become a well-regarded Abstract Expressionist with exhibits throughout Europe and Japan. At the end of his life, suffering from cancer, he continued to work, painting very small pictures using only his left hand. I wished I could paint; I even tried to draw a cat, but the result was stupid and distended, a monster with crossed eyes and the belly of a whale.

Instead I went for slow, ginger walks. Step by slow step I explored the neighborhood, limping past playgrounds and hardware stores and diners. The next day I repeated the route, and the day after that. I began to see the same people at the same time of day—a man sweeping the sidewalk; a woman herding her children to school— and when they nodded at me with recognition, some part of my brain that had been scrambled was straightened.

Eventually I was able to read the newspaper, look at a computer, and use words in the proper order. I was anxious to return to work; my life needed scaffolding, and work had always provided it. Over my years with Wheelock, despite living out in Briar Neck, I'd come to know a fair number of people. I was nervous to contact them at first, mostly because I feared having to explain my current circumstances, but once I did, I found that everyone already knew about them. One ripple effect of Wheelock's reputation was an enduring interest in his personal life. When I emailed people that I'd moved to New York the responses were immediate and enthusiastic. Everyone wanted to have lunch. Everyone wanted a drink. What they also wanted, I found out at the restaurants and cafés and bars where we met, was gossip. After twenty minutes of small talk the person would lean on an elbow and ask, voice lowered, what *really* happened. I offered the dullest possible answer—"It was time to move on," I usually said— and changed the subject.

There was no work; everyone was out of work; that was why they had so much time to meet for cocktails and coffee. Film jobs were non-existent because no one went to films anymore. I was an hour deep into a sushi lunch with a producer I'd hoped might hire me when she leaned over and fished *her* resume out of her bag, flushing a little. "Maybe you'll have something for me sometime," she said, smiling grimly.

I sent my editing reel to a guy who'd been involved in public television before moving on to commercials. I'd once done him a favor, recommending him to a network executive, and when I didn't hear back from him I pressed him. "I loved your work," he said on the phone, without apologizing for his failure to respond. "I don't get to see that kind of languid beauty anymore."

On I went, crossing names off my list, until I reached Javier Fernandez, who'd been my assistant in Briar Neck. I'd given him his first job and taught him how to edit and argued with him about Baz

Luhrmann, whose films he worshipped and I thought represented mediocrity with the noise turned up. Javier was now working on a reality TV show about circus performers. It was called *American Freaks* and best known for the tattooed lady, its star, who was dating a rock musician and often featured in gossip magazines.

"You finally got around to me," Javier said on the phone, his tone arch. "I heard you've been making the rounds."

"I'm looking for work," I said.

"And you're asking *me*? But you're *the* Lark Brossard, muse and manager of the great Lawrence Wheelock, and I'm just little Javier."

"You don't have to be snide," I said. "I bought you bourbon and taught you AutoCAD."

"I'm not being snide," Javier protested. "I just don't understand what's happening here. You're basically famous in the editing world."

"There's no such thing as famous in the editing world," I said. "Can you help me?"

"You hate all spectacle, and this job is basically crafting spectacle."

"Knowing *Moulin Rouge* is unwatchable dreck doesn't equate to hating all spectacle."

On the other end of the line he paused, cleared his throat, making up his mind. "Lark," he said quietly, "I was always scared of you."

I held my breath. He gave me an address.

15.

When last I'd seen him, Javier wore tight button-down shirts over an emerging belly and cultivated a slight facial scruff that he must've thought made him seem more mature but was too sparse to be convincing. It always looked like a smudge I was tempted to wipe off. Now he greeted me in the lobby of a renovated office building in Chelsea, thinner and fitter, and his skin was so clean-shaven it looked polished. He wore dark skinny jeans and black shoes with shiny square toes. In Briar Neck I'd never dressed up for work and of all the items Robin had procured for me, none were clothes. I was wearing brown pants and a light blue sweater that, I'd been pleased to note that morning, lacked stains or holes. I saw Javier register this outfit, which was clearly an aesthetic offense to him, and politely set his reaction aside. He kissed me on both cheeks and said, "You look the same," a diplomatically stated truth.

"Yes," I agreed.

"You're ready to do this? Dip in your toes in the bananas world of reality television? You know it's insane. Bikram worked here two days before he quit and went back to school for library science. Now he lives in Asheville and blogs about home brew."

I wanted to reassure him. "I can take it," I said. "I come from documentaries, the original reality TV."

He looked pained. "Please don't say that upstairs."

"Okay," I said. I followed him into a rickety elevator with an accordion gate that groaned and fought when he tried to close it.

"People here love the gate, they think it's so *authentic,*" he said. "I think it's a pain in the ass." After he got the door shut he leaned against the wall with his legs crossed at the ankle, as if posing for a magazine. "So," he said. "You're sprung from your cage. Did you jump or were you pushed?"

These questions were the price I had to pay. "Both," I said. "It was time for a change."

"Hm," he said. "I'm not sure I believe you."

I looked down at his feet, and then at mine, in running shoes with thick, rubbery soles. Although my vertigo had mostly dissipated, once in a while I still had the sensation of falling over, as if the earth had suddenly skewed 90 degrees, the floor of a room gyrating into the wall. In these, the only shoes in which I felt steady, I looked like an elderly American tourist prepared for a museum tour.

"I heard a rumor that the mad genius was stepping out on you," he said as the elevator crept slowly upwards. "That you finally had enough."

"Javier," I said warningly.

"That's what people say," he reported, raising his palms in disavowal. "*I* said I always thought you guys had some kind of understanding. A co-dependent, dysfunctional understanding."

I would not be baited. "I had enough of Briar Neck, that's all," I said sweetly.

Disappointment made his chin jut out. The elevator stopped and he tugged at the gate, muscles rippling beneath his shirt. It stuck. "Let me," I said, and pulled it aside with a clatter.

"You bitch," he said, which was a compliment.

Upstairs, Javier and I met with a producer, who brought me up to speed on the storyline to date and outlined my initial assignment. I was given a brief tour of the office by a young woman with her hair in pigtails who cracked her knuckles every two minutes. "I know, it's gruesome," Javier muttered in my ear as he handed me off. "She's related to somebody important."

I sat down in the editing bay she showed me, the door closed. The producer had told me to take an hour of footage from a tattoo parlor and get it down to forty-five seconds. "Forty-five interesting seconds, obviously," she added. I watched the hour with earbuds in, making notes on a piece of paper, then set to work. The doctors had told me to limit my time with electronic media lest the headaches and vertigo return, and I hadn't spent more than ten straight minutes in front of a computer in months. I had fasted, and now I returned with a greedy appetite. I replayed and clicked and sorted, ignoring the pain that crystallized around my eyes. In the restroom I took some medicine and then went back to work, the familiar pixilated buzz soothing my brain. Wheelock had always maintained strong preferences about his editing; he thought the transition from one shot to the next should emulate, as organically as possible, the movement of the human eye, which itself emulated the movement of human thought. When we tire, we blink; when we want to know more, our gaze lingers. He hated any transition that called attention to itself. To replace one field of vision with another, he'd explained, to jump from one place to another, or from one moment to the next, was to journey through consciousness. Viewers shouldn't notice they're being taken on a voyage; they should believe they're navigating themselves. In Britain, he'd told me, filmmakers talked about joining frames, not cutting them. What he wanted was joining.

As his editor, the invisible executor of his ideas, I'd striven to please Wheelock while at the same time following instincts of my own. His desire for unobtrusive editing worked well for informational sequences, but didn't always bring out the drama in human subjects; sometimes a sharp cut was what you needed to locate the tension in a moment, to shape it as an emotional experience. The hour I was contending with now was pretty dull. The show's star spent it getting yet another tattoo on her already well-inked back; she lay on her stomach, her face almost completely hidden from the camera. When she talked to the tattoo artist, she mostly grunted. The artist was an ambiguously gendered person with bleached-blond hair grown out to dark roots, wearing jeans and a black T-shirt with a skull on it. The tattoo itself was of a bulldog, and it was disturbing to see the round contours of its face drawn on a shoulder blade, the skin stretched and weeping blood. I cut from the bulldog to the star grunting, as if she and the dog were having a conversation; after she grunted I jumped to the tattoo artist sighing, as if they judged her for showing pain. "What?" she said, and I made it sound as though she were prickling with defense. (She'd said, "What are you doing later? I might grab a burrito.") The tattoo artist's answer—"Nothing"—became a jab back at her. Editing was the art of heightened reaction. By the time I was done with the first part of the scene, the two of them came off as sworn enemies, the crosscutting a kind of warfare, each passing moment barbed and tense.

At one point during the hour she said, "I need a coffee. I'm so tired. I didn't sleep well last night." I showed the tattoo artist pressing against the small of her back, and looped in the star saying "I'm so tired," and the moment became tender, as if the needle were dispensing medicine instead of ink. With her head lowered she seemed crushed by the world. I cut to the reaction shot: "I know," the tattoo artist said, relenting, seeming to pity her, and wanting to make her well. At the end, finally, I offered release: I showed her looking up, and lingered on her face, giving significance to her glance, as if the two of them had bonded, although in the raw footage she was just asking for a break to visit the restroom. I added some soft music, and the scene was done: it had become a love story between them, the tattoo a narrative of conflict, then care.

When I looked up again, it was five in the afternoon. Javier was behind me, examining my work. "Not bad," he said, and in his voice I could hear the young man he'd been in Briar Neck, the one I'd taught and sheltered. "I guess you figured out they used to date, before Mickey transitioned."

I shrugged. Around me the office was silent, everyone working behind closed doors. I swiveled in my chair, cracking my neck. Just then the floor sloped and I grabbed the desk to steady myself as pinwheels hurtled across my vision, a neon parade. I closed my eyes and kept them closed. When the lights subsided, I walked carefully down the hall to the windows and stared out at the black rooftops and the distant river. Below me traffic crawled and silently blared. My eyes and ears and wrists and back hurt. I would do anything, I thought, to get this job.

16.

The producer was pleased. I was given a contract and told to review all the previously aired episodes. I memorized the back stories of the tattooed lady and her several children and ex-boyfriends and ex-friends and current ones. Javier stopped asking prying questions about Wheelock and instead treated me with the casual brutality that, I learned, was his manner with everyone. He was beloved at the office. People brought him treats that he refused to accept, citing his low-carb diet. "I'm not going back to pudgeville," he'd declaim. "No matter how you guys try to sabotage me!" Later he'd eat them anyway, unable to resist, angrily airing his regrets. He called me Grandma and made fun of my outfits, but the cruelty had evaporated from his voice. The pigtailed woman, whose name was Kenzie, asked if the knuckle-cracking bothered me and, before I could answer, explained that there was nothing she could do about it if it did. "I have OCD and it's a calming behavior," she said matter-of-factly. She told me all about her diet, which was gluten-free and dairy-free, except for hard cheeses. Every morning in the kitchen she'd say hello and wave a cheese stick in my direction, saying defensively, "It's a hard cheese!" as if I'd accused her of eating soft. All the other editors were men, and they bantered in the office kitchen about sports without bothering to try to include me. Sometimes we talked about the weather, or who'd buy the next batch of coffee pods. Our conversations petered out after three to five minutes. I found that I could navigate these small bursts of interaction. I could mention the rain, describe something disgusting I'd seen on the subway. Say good morning at ten and goodbye at six. Almost as if I belonged.

With the question of work settled and my head healing, I still had to reshape the rest of my life. I wanted a child, and this meant looking for someone who wanted a child too—didn't it? It was hard to imagine myself with any man other than Wheelock; my body continued to fit itself to his, moved automatically to make space for him in the bed. But I was intent on retraining it. Elena Brown informed me that nowadays everyone met online. That was how she'd met her new boyfriend, the local butcher, even though they lived in the same neighborhood. "You can't just go out there *at random* anymore," she told me. "You have to *select*." She helped me set up a dating profile and took a picture of me with her phone. "This one's not terrible," she said, holding it up. "You could pass for thirty-five."

I told her I was thirty-six.

"Oh, chicken," she said, "you can't say that."

On the dating sites I scanned and clicked. I indicated my interest. I went on dates. One was with a man who'd said he was six feet tall and turned out to be five foot five. Height wasn't a requirement of mine, but I was curious about the tactic. Did he not think he'd be discovered?

"I figured once we met in person I'd win you over with my charm," he said, shoving a fistful of olives in his mouth. I quite liked him. He was dark and ferocious, with glittering black eyes and hair that shone with styling gel. He'd picked a restaurant he knew was terrible so we could bond over complaining about it, a strategy I could see the wisdom of. The waitress brought us the wrong drinks and sighed heavily when we pointed out her mistake. "Whatever," she said, and took them away, not returning with replacements.

"Keep up the good work, Maggie!" the man called after her. "I come here all the time," he said. I was enjoying myself, but then he cracked a tooth on the olives—reminding me of Wheelock—and left in a hurry, cradling his jaw in the palm of his hand. I didn't hear from him again.

Then I dated a man named Martin Dax. His name was so pleasing to me that I often repeated it to myself just to enjoy the sound, and he had a very short haircut that showed off an attractive skull. He was a scientist from Germany who spoke very plainly and directly, always concerned about whether or not he was being understood. When he said, "Do you know what I mean?" he paused for the answer before going on. He spoke about his childhood afternoons spent wandering in drizzly forests outside of Hamburg, and I furtively allowed myself to imagine family trips we might take there, hand-crafted German ornaments on our Christmas tree. We saw each other five times, and on the last evening, I yawned—I wasn't used to working all day, then going out at night—which stung him deeply. "I wasn't interesting enough for my ex-wife," he said sorrowfully, "and now I see the same is true for you."

"It was a long day, that's all," I said quickly.

"You don't have to be polite," he said. "American women are so evasive. One never knows where one stands."

"Where you stand is fine," I said, but he kept shaking his head sadly and soon left the restaurant, leaving a crisp hundred-dollar bill on the table. I rode home on the subway, slumped and bleary-eyed. When I got there, I found Elena sitting on the stoop outside our building, smoking.

"How'd it go?"

I shook my head.

"Well," she said, "at least you're out there."

"I'm out there," I said, my voice wavering.

"Oh, cupcake," she said. All her endearments were food-related. I leaned my head against her shoulder, and heard her sniff. "Did you have something spicy? I smell spicy."

I nodded, wiping my nose.

"You might want to change your order," she said. "A little tip from me to you."

I wondered if I'd lost Martin Dax to the excesses of spice. That night I emailed Robin an account of the latest fiasco. I tried to be amusing. I wanted the thread that had recently unspooled between us to remain intact, a string between two cans. *No loss,* she wrote back the next day. She wrote *No loss* to everything, every canceled meeting or failed date. Sometimes I wondered if she knew what *No loss* meant.

17.

On a quiet Saturday I was sitting at my laptop drinking tea with five sugars in it, a habit I'd picked up from Javier, when Marianne called. Lately she'd been calling me more often, and she often seemed distressed, though when I tried to figure out why, the reasons remained unclear.

"The problem," she said when I answered, "is that the squirrels and the birds are competing for the same resources and I can't keep them apart."

"Who's doing what?"

"Everybody wants more than I can provide," she said. "I'm not the grocery store, *tu sais?*" Her voice was phlegmy, raspy from smoking, or maybe she had a cold.

"Start from the beginning," I suggested.

"The beginning! What's a beginning?" she asked angrily.

I took another look at my screen and then reluctantly closed it. Without an image to distract me her voice was even harsher, and I moved the phone away from my ear. "I'm not sure I understand why you're so upset," I said.

"Of course you don't. No one understands. I'm here on my own. Always on my own, from when I was young."

"Have you talked to Robin?" I said.

"*Robin,*" my mother said, like a swear. "She's away with her animals in her zoo."

"What zoo?" I said.

"Oh, you know," she said. The conversation was escaping me, speeding away like a missed train. I listened to Marianne ramble for a few more minutes, until she abruptly hung up, as angry as when she'd started.

I called Robin. Her phone went to voicemail—it always went to voicemail, and I wasn't sure she ever listened to it—and I left a long-winded message that didn't make much sense. When I hung up, the air in the apartment felt cloistered and dense, more prison than refuge. The season of *American Freaks* I was editing was wrapping up, and soon I'd have a break. Before I could change my mind, I opened the laptop again and booked a flight to Montreal.

August in the city of my childhood was torrid and festive: everyone outside, drinking and smoking, sucking in as much summer as they could fit in their lungs. On Duluth, where I was meeting Robin for a drink, I saw a couple trip over the cobblestones because they were kissing instead of looking where they were going, and they tried to keep kissing even as they tripped, clutched each other, and righted themselves.

Robin showed up late, wearing jeans, work boots caked with mud, and a faded red T-shirt two sizes too small. Her hair hadn't been combed that morning, or recently. Before even saying hello she took a cigarette out of a pack and lit it. She had a new line of tattoos on her right arm, a series of dark blue circles that looked like barbed wire.

"Since when are you smoking?" I said, a question that came out sounding judgmental, although I hadn't meant it to. I was just surprised.

"De temps en temps," Robin said, shrugging. She ordered a beer and gazed at the street, the passersby seeming to interest her more than I did.

"I wanted to talk about Marianne," I said. I hadn't seen her yet; I'd checked into a hotel first and made plans to visit her apartment the following day.

"What about her?"

"She keeps calling me. She sounds upset."

"Upset," Robin said. "When is she *not* upset?"

"I guess. But lately she doesn't make a lot of sense."

"She's getting old, that's all." Robin put down her cigarette and rubbed her right eye with the palm of her hand, hard, like a window washer working on a stubborn streak. When she opened her eye again, all the white was red.

"She's not old," I said.

My sister extinguished her cigarette, sighing out the smoke. "She's always been dramatic, you know that. She indulges herself in moods. Right now she's feeling badly because the dentist left her."

The dentist had been having an affair with one of his hygienists, with whom he'd moved to the South Shore. At the time Robin had said *No loss.*

I sat back in my chair. She met my eyes now, her red eye verging back to white, her gaze direct and unblinking. I wished I smoked; I would have asked her for a cigarette, or taken one. "You never talk to me about what's happening here." In my words I heard an echo of Marianne, a hum of complaint.

My sister shrugged again.

"Robin."

"You seem to have enough trouble taking care of yourself," she said. She caught the waitress's eye and tapped her glass.

"I'm better now."

She looked at me more closely then, as if sizing me up, and then nodded, her manner relaxing slightly. "I'm glad," she said.

"What will we do about Marianne?" I asked. "Is she okay?"

"We won't do anything. I have things going on, you know. Summer's the most hectic time at the restaurant. I have my business."

"You have a business?"

"I have a life," she said, "that's what I meant."

She reminded me so much of our mother in that moment: her quickness to irritation, her insistence on her freedom. I knew she came down to the city regularly to see friends and looked in on Marianne; what annoyed her was to be asked about it, to be drawn into anything except on her own terms.

She lit another cigarette, and the waitress brought her another beer. The city around us was dressed for a good time, women in bright earrings and high-heeled sandals, men in sharp-angled suits exuding clouds of cologne. Two guys strolled by, one with a boombox on his shoulder, listening to some beats as if he hadn't been told the eighties had ended long ago. Or maybe they were back again. Across the street a woman sat on a fire escape, trying to coax a kitten into her lap. When it wouldn't obey she lunged forward, picked it up, and dangled it in the air as if trying to threaten it into good behavior. The kitten was nonplussed, and when she set it back down it licked itself as if nothing had happened.

I reached over and moved a strand of hair out of Robin's eye. She smiled at me then, absently, but still a smile. Her hands, I noticed, were weathered and scratched, with bits of red around the nails I'd thought at first were chips of polish but now saw were dried blood. She looked like a wild animal, and later I decided that was exactly what she wanted to be.

I'd chosen the hotel for its low price and not its comforts and I didn't sleep well. In the morning I read the news at a café, my eyes scanning the same lines over and over, the manifold facts of disaster and want. There was a typhoon in Asia, a volcano eruption in New Zealand. The situation in Syria was worsening. Another chunk of ice had disappeared in Antarctica. After too much reading and too much coffee, my nerves jangling, I walked along Saint Catherine Street, the strip joints and neon-lit bars of my youth mostly subsumed by shopping mall stores. A group of teenage girls wearing short skirts crowded the sidewalk in front of me, each of them making tiny adjustments as they examined themselves in store windows, straightening the fabric over their hips, slouching to hide their breasts or stretching to show them off.

I stopped and picked up some pastries for Marianne, the chocolatines that were her favorites. Since her breakup with the dentist she'd moved back to our old neighborhood. When I rang the doorbell at her building, there was no answer. At last a man came out and held the door open for me without inquiring who I was.

The entryway was musty, with a humid seep, the scent of cleaning fluids not quite victorious. Her apartment was on the third floor, facing the back, and when I knocked, I heard noises inside. She came to the door looking confused, as though we hadn't spoken the day before, as though I hadn't just rung the bell. She was very thin. She was wearing a blue shirt-dress and holding a feather duster, like a housewife from 1954.

I kissed her on both cheeks.

She stepped back to let me in, making no comment. In the past she'd been prone to messiness, draping scarves over the furniture, abandoning her shoes wherever she'd happened to kick them off, but this morning her home was the neatest I'd ever seen it. Not just neat: empty. The living room held a couch and a coffee table and little else. The walls were bare. There were no rugs anywhere. I handed her the box of pastries I'd brought, and she set it down on the coffee table, murmuring polite thanks. "Would you like tea?"

I said I would. In the kitchen, also neat and spare, I opened the fridge, and when she made a hiss of displeasure, I closed the door, but not before noticing how little food was inside. She pulled down two cups, filled each with water, and put them in the microwave. Once the water was hot she dipped a tea bag in one after the other, and then left it on a small plate by the sink. I arranged the pastries on a plate and followed her back into the living room.

We sat across from each other with our hands folded in our laps. She didn't ask me how I was or why I'd come.

"The last time we spoke, you seemed upset," I said.

"Did I? You always overreact. Displays of emotion unnerve you. You get this from your father."

This surprised me; she'd very rarely talked about my father, apparently not wanting to admit that I even had one. This more than anything made me worry about her state of mind.

She tilted her head and eyed me, her expression darkly mischievous. "I used to hear from him, you know," she said.

"Who?"

"Your father. Todd."

"Really," I said. I had no reason to believe her. She'd been erratic since my childhood, alternately hurtful and tender according to her own purposes, and I knew better than to trust any revelation that would come from her now. "What did he want?"

"To know how you were. To be reassured that you hadn't suffered from his abandonment. I told him you were so special that you didn't need a father. And this was true. You never did."

"Thanks."

"You've never understood how special you are, Thérèse."

"Who's Thérèse?" I said.

"I meant to name you Thérèse. It's a beautiful, pious name. Your father wanted otherwise." She shook her head. She'd placed the feather duster on the couch next to her and now she palmed it, fondly, like a pet. "Names are acts of domination, and you and your sister are proof of that. I should never have given in."

The conversation was like standing on a boat and watching the shore recede: for a moment, as you watch, it's impossible to tell whether it's you or the land that's moving. All you know is that distance gathers. It had always been like that, with Marianne. There was no point in trying to pin her down. I looked out the window at the bird feeder she'd hung, the presumed site of the squirrel-versus-bird battles. No animals fought there now; maybe she'd chased them all off.

"Who's winning the resource war?" I said.

She looked at me like I was crazy and didn't answer. We sat for a long time in uncomfortable silence, the chocolatines untouched on the coffee table.

I searched my brain for something to say. "Let me help you."

"Help me with what?" she said suspiciously.

I looked around at her spotless home. "I can help you clean," I said.

At this she brightened. She gave me a broom and together we swept away invisible dirt, wiped invisible cobwebs. Afterward we shared the pastries and drank the weak, cold tea she had made.

18.

I stayed in Montreal for a week. Walking around our old neighborhood I recognized no one; the block had shifted, now occupied by sushi places and tea shops and thrift stores with dusty merchandise artfully displayed in the windows. Mrs. Gasparian's house had been torn down, and in its place was a Mauritian restaurant with no customers. When I was a child this block had been a universe to me, its borders unknowable, and it was unsettling to see how finite it was, how easily escapable.

Some days Marianne greeted me with wary diplomacy, like a visitor from a previously hostile nation. Other days she seemed not to react to my presence at all, and began speaking in the middle of a sentence as if picking up a conversation we'd started the day before, although we hadn't.

On one of my walks I stopped into an electronics store and bought, impulsively, a small hand-held video camera. The next time I returned to Marianne's apartment I asked if I could film her. I'd thought she might protest but instead she seemed to preen a little, straightening her shoulders. She left the room and came back with her face powdered, lipstick crookedly applied. Looking at her through the lens, instead of face to face, felt natural to me, and she also seemed to relax. With the camera between us we spoke comfortably, though the conversations were hardly substantial. She talked about Montreal, her neighbors, a newspaper article she'd read about arsenic in rice. I didn't labor over the composition of the shots or the lighting in the room. In some respects the filming was a pointless exercise—and yet it wasn't, because it put us both, strangely, at ease.

On my last morning in Montreal, when I went to her apartment, I found a box of dishes outside her door.

"I'm giving them away," she told me when I asked.

"But what will you eat on?"

"The table," she said, as if it were a stupid question.

"But—"

"I'm not throwing dinner parties. I'm not that woman. I eat take-out now like everybody else."

She stood with her arms on her hips, her chin jutting out, waiting for me to argue with her: she was the same Marianne she'd always been, refusing demands I hadn't made. I kissed the air next to her cheeks and said goodbye.

At the hotel I packed my bag, preparing for the flight home. And then, without deliberation or permission, I changed my mind. Instead of heading to the airport I got on a bus and rode north, into the cool air of the Laurentians, where I disembarked at Sainte-Agathe, called my sister, and announced that I'd come to stay.

Robin picked me up in a red truck splattered in mud. Her property, which was forty-five minutes outside of town and down a long dirt road, had once been a farm; it included a small white house and, a few hundred feet away, a weathered barn that used to shelter dairy cows. Inevitably I thought about Wheelock's farmhouse, and the day he picked me up that first summer; it seemed both recent and for-ever ago, at once someone else's life and my own.

The previous owners of Robin's property had given up on farm-ing and moved to the city, Robin told me, and when she discovered it, both buildings were almost falling down. "It's taken some time, but everything is solid now," she said. I had the impression she'd done the repairs herself, and wondered where she'd learned these skills. There was so much about her adult life that I didn't know. When I complimented her, she shook her head dismissively, but I could tell she was pleased.

Her house had a small kitchen and sitting room with a fire-place downstairs, and a warren of small bedrooms upstairs. The one she showed me to was cozy, with a rag rug on the floor. Through the open window came the crackling rupture of trees. My sister extended an arm in the general direction of the view. "Make yourself comfortable," she said. "I have things to do." Before I could ask what those things were, she was gone.

19.

I opened my laptop and imported the footage of Marianne. With the volume down I examined the cracked, pale landscape of her face; I watched her lips silently move. She was better at meeting the camera's eye than she'd ever been at meeting mine. Seeing her this way, present and yet at a remove, was oddly lulling, and I lay down on the bed with her next to me and dozed off. I woke up shivering, with a crick in my neck. Outside was the thin high light of summer, but the breeze through the window carried fall. I could smell food cooking and hear voices, and I pulled on a sweater and went downstairs.

In the kitchen, Robin was stirring something in a big pot. With her were two men, one taking a loaf of bread out of the oven, while the second set the table. The table-setter was tall and spindly and bald, with large brown eyes. The combination of his youthful eyes and pocked skin was jarring; he looked like one of those tragic children with an aging disease that makes them accelerate in years. When he saw me, he smiled broadly, revealing brown and jagged teeth, and he came over and wrapped me in a hug that smelled of pine trees and cigarette smoke. The first man, the baker, nodded at me quickly but said nothing; he was staring at the loaf with a critical eye, as if his handiwork had fallen short of expectations.

"What can I do?" I said.

Robin nodded toward the cupboard. "Open the wine," she said.

I poured glasses for everyone. Robin and the baker drank their wine quickly, taking turns stirring the soup in between going outside to smoke. The door kept banging as they went in or out. Meanwhile they kept shouting back and forth, continuing a conversation that seemed to have been going on for a while—about politics, the rise of ISIS, and conflict in the Middle East. They argued about the Palestinian Authority and the possibility of a two-state solution. The bald man said little and smoked a lot, also going in and out to smoke. "Robin doesn't like the smell of smoke in the food," the bald man said to me by way of explanation, though I hadn't asked for one. Outside it was seven and still light, the sky a strong, variegated blue that extended over the tall pine trees surrounding the house as if the day would last forever. It made me think of Frida Kahlo's famous blue house in Mexico City, where she'd lived and painted and been confined to her bed, and which I had seen a film about but never visited personally, as with so many things in my life. I remembered in particular the shots of her bed, which had a painting of a dead child at the head, and at the foot a montage of Stalin, Lenin, Marx, Engels, and Mao. I wondered how she slept in a bed like that, but then again, given the pain and suffering she endured almost all her life, maybe Kahlo didn't sleep well anywhere.

Finally we ate, and talked. At least Robin and one of the men, whose name was Derya, talked, while the bald man and I stayed silent. My sister's fingernails were livid with dirt, her eyes red-rimmed with fatigue and maybe wine, yet she seemed alert and vibrant, her attention shifting and yet complete wherever it landed—on us, the food, the conversation.

"So you're sisters," Derya said, shoveling soup into his mouth. He gripped his spoon in a fist as if it might slip loose, and bent his head low over the bowl, raising his eyes at me as he ate. I nodded. He looked at her, then me, then back again. "You're older," he said.

"True," I said.

"I'm a twin," he said.

"You are not," Robin said.

"You don't know this about me, but it's true." He sat back in his chair and smeared a napkin across his lips, then patted his belly, as if complimenting it on a job well done. "It was in the womb. At the beginning of my mother's pregnancy there were two of us. And then one day my mother went in to the doctor and the other one was gone." He bared his teeth, grinning. Robin was shaking her head. "The doctor said I consumed him. So he's inside me now."

"You seem proud of it," I said.

"You always eat too much," my sister said.

"I'm a man of appetites," he answered.

The light had gone. Preoccupied with the conversation, I didn't notice night arriving until all of a sudden a series of cries arose outside, in thin pained whistles, like babies abandoned or sick, and a shiver rippled across my skin, raising the hair on my arms. No one else reacted.

"What's that?" I said, and my sister answered calmly, "The wolves."

We ate dessert and drank coffee while the wolves howled. No one but me seemed to pay them any mind. I couldn't stop imagining a pack of them roaming ever closer, drawn to the smell of food. Their cries were harmonic and irregular, slowing to periodic silence and then resuming, like choral singers engaged in a round. Each time I thought they'd finished, they started over, the ghostly music distant and then closer and then distant again.

The two men went out to smoke. The open kitchen windows let in the cigarette smoke along with the cool evening air. Outside, the baker laughed, whether at us or something else, I couldn't tell. Robin shifted in her seat, her mouth a flat gash of purple, and I thought she expected me to explain myself, my abrupt visit.

"I wanted—" I said, then noticed her fish a cigarette out of her pack, tapping it on the table, ready to head outside. The two men came back in, and I stopped talking; I hadn't really known what I was going to say anyway. I began clearing the dessert dishes, and the quiet man reached out a hand. Backing away from the table, I shook my head that I didn't need help, and we jostled against each other. Two plates dropped to the floor and broke. In a mess of apologies we both crouched down and began picking up the pieces, piling the shards on the table. For one quick moment, down by the floor, he held my right hand in his. "It's all right," he said mildly. His eyes were wide and familiar, and at last I knew him: Bernard.

· · ·

The next day Robin took me on a tour. The soft late-summer morning was still and dense. Drowsy, laconic birdsong, branches barely moving, the lax contours of clouds. At her suggestion we patrolled her land in the pickup truck, at times veering off the road onto dirt roads or no roads at all. As she drove, she explained: the wolves we'd heard the previous night weren't exactly wild—they were rescues. Of all her property Robin only occupied a tenth; the rest she'd designated as a preserve. Three different grey wolf packs lived there, separated by sturdy wire fencing to keep the peace among them, as well as foxes, bobcats, falcons, and other birds of prey. The packs were small, three or four each; when I looked surprised, she explained that they howled in varying pitches to make it sound as if there were more of them. She talked about how wolves required large territories, because they were travelers by nature and needed to move, and about their unearned reputation for violence.

"The fact is, they have roles and personalities. Some wolves are sweet and some wolves are jerks."

"And you know them? Their personalities?"

"Of course I do," she said.

She talked for fifteen minutes about a particular species of turtle that was endangered in Quebec and whose habitat she was intent on protecting. A speck of foam bubbled on her lips as she talked. She was writing a will that would ensure that the land would remain undeveloped in perpetuity. I didn't see any of the animals; we were parked by a fence behind which the land rose and fell, pocked with boulders and pine trees; anything could have been hiding there.

I asked her why she'd never mentioned the wolves to me before, and she shrugged. "I didn't think you were interested," she said.

"I'm interested. But how did this start—all these pets?"

Her eye-roll made clear I'd said the wrong thing. "They aren't *pets*. I'm returning this land to them. The wolves have been here longer than people."

"But *you* live here," I said. It was yet another question that came out sounding like a judgment, and I winced at myself.

"We coexist," she said.

The truck bumped across a muddy field and I held tightly to the armrest, bracing myself. With the windows rolled down the truck's exhaust and engine noise surrounded it. Suddenly Robin stopped again, got out, and started walking. I followed behind her. So far as I could tell there was no trail; I saw no path, no directional marks on trees. But she stayed sure-footed, never stumbling. She opened a gate in the wire fence and we passed through it, strolling beneath a pine canopy where the air was startlingly cool, like a cave. I kept expecting to see the wolves stealing out from the cover, to greet us or warn us away. But there was no sign of them.

My vision narrowed to Robin's back as I followed her, the dark fabric of her shirt, the waves of her hair. Her shoulders, her neck. Then she stopped walking. The trees thinned, and we found ourselves at the top of a bluff on large slabs of granite rounded by water and time. Below us was a narrow creek running clear. Above, a vulture circled high and dreamily over some invisible carcass. Robin didn't say anything. We sat down and watched the creek flow down the jagged bed it had cut through the rocks and disappear into the woods. I could hear my sister breathing, and noticed that I was trying to match her rhythm with my own. We sat for a long while without talking as the sky changed from pale morning to the deeper blue of day. Bright clouds clustered cleanly at the horizon. There was no darkness anywhere. *No loss.*

20.

That evening, Robin and Derya made dinner again. While Bernard and I set the table, he told me his life story in a version so brief there was almost nothing to it. After he and Robin broke up in Europe, he returned to Baltimore and resumed dealing drugs, for which he was arrested and sent to prison, twice over. During the last stint he joined a twelve-step program, and when it came time to make amends, he wrote to Robin, who wrote back. Eventually she told him about the land she'd bought and invited him to visit. Now he spent weeks at a time here, working as a handyman in exchange for room and board. "And you?" he said.

My version was even shorter. "I had a job, and a sort of partner, and then I moved to New York and started over."

He smiled at me, and his eyes were calm.

"How's your mother?" I said.

"She died."

I told him I was sorry, and would've asked more, but Robin and Derya had begun to argue, and we turned to look at them instead. Derya was shouting about his family: Turks who'd fled their country, first for Switzerland, then to Canada, and fought to establish themselves in a place that spoke of warmth and welcome but in practice provided neither. This is a summary. The actual speech was scattered and angry, and Robin kept interrupting him, defending Canada and Canadians—I think?—and her own life, her commitments, her ideology. "I am open," she kept repeating, as if he should know what this meant, as if her meaning were universal and clear, and Derya would say, "What my family has lived through, you'll never understand," and this seemed to outrage and inflame her, and on top of all this, the lasagna was burning. I looked to Bernard for help, and he shrugged as if to say, *We're not a part of this.* My sister's face grew ugly with defense, and Derya was pointing a finger at her, his spit flecking her face as he spoke.

Without thinking I stepped between them. "Don't talk to her like that," I said. "Stop talking. Leave her *alone.*"

To my surprise, both Derya and Robin laughed.

"You see, Derya?" she said to him. "Yours isn't the only family with loyalties."

He grinned. "I didn't know you two were so close," he said, his tone mocking. I felt myself shaking, like you do after an accident in which you thought you might be badly hurt but weren't.

"Please, the lasagna," Bernard said from the other side of the room, his voice as unsteady as mine, and Robin laughed again, her tone also mocking, and said, "Simmer down now, friend, we're scaring the children."

Though we took our time with dinner, evening had barely fallen. Through the window the light was silvery blue and darkness seemed a long way off. I began clearing the dishes, but my sister said, "Leave them," and gestured for us to go outside.

She took off down the path that led to the barn, which I guessed was an invitation. I followed, with Derya and Bernard a few feet behind; I could hear their low voices but not what they were saying. The smell of cigarettes mingled with the smell of pine trees, a combination that struck me as both pleasant and artificial, like the men's section at a department store.

My sister, ahead, was already sliding open the barn doors, and Bernard sprinted up to offer her help, though I doubted she needed any. I looked around and saw Derya lingering, talking on his cell phone. He waved my glance away as if it offended him.

When I turned back, the barn had swallowed Robin and Bernard. I stepped inside, the building stinking faintly of manure. The air was pale and blue, smoky with dust, and only a few small windows, high up on either side, let in any light. The stalls that once housed cows remained, and they weren't empty; I could see the great hulks of some silent animals in each one. I couldn't see my sister, or Bernard.

Slowly, as my eyes adjusted, I took in more. The windows were open and small birds flitted amidst sloping wooden rafters, busy with their tasks, chattering among themselves. My own footsteps scuffed softly in the dirt, and as if my hearing were adjusting too, I could make out voices.

Soft muttering laughter. The sounds of a private language. At the other end of the barn, Robin and Bernard were sliding another door open, the breeze sweeping through. With more light, I recognized that the shapes in the stalls weren't animals; they were pianos.

I walked past each one in turn, taking them in, somehow feeling as if I were the one being observed. I saw a baby grand, a console, a spinet.

Where the rows of stalls ended was a large space cleared as if for a stage, and two upright pianos sat facing each other. Derya sat down at one.

I looked at Robin, who was conferring with Bernard over a piece of electronic equipment. She said offhandedly, "My other rescues. No one wants them nowadays, so I take them in."

"Ready?" Bernard said, and she nodded.

She crossed to the piano across from Derya's, and the two of them gazed at each other, protracting the pause, their four hands raised over the keys. I was so taken aback by the turn of events that I didn't know what to do—I stood still, balling my hands into fists for some reason. I felt it would be dangerous to move, as if any speech or gesture might bring to a halt something I'd thought I'd never see again: my sister playing the piano. I tried to be invisible. Maybe it sounds precious to say that time seemed to slow down. Maybe it's better to say that I felt time more. I felt each second give rise to the next. No lapses, no jumps. The traffic of birds, the creak of barnwood, the wind.

Afterward, when I exited the barn, the light outside looked exactly the same as when we'd entered, although we'd been inside for ages—as if the evening had been stretched in the sky, indefinitely suspended.

But before that: they played. It was a duet for four hands—Beethoven, I guessed, though I hadn't listened to classical music in years and could easily have been wrong. It began with a sprightly melody, exact and almost priggish, which seemed an absurd contrast to the surroundings. People should have been minueting to it, tiptoeing in fancy dress. The notes sounded gaunt and dry. I remembered that when Robin was at Juilliard, she and her friends used to talk about the acoustics of the rooms they played in: rooms where the sounds reverberated were wet and ones where they were absorbed were dry. Before I heard that, I'd never thought about sound being spatial, tied to its location. Now I stood wondering if the music was dry, or the barn was; I wasn't sure, but I felt obscurely disappointed by it. I'd been expecting something wild, modern and eccentric; perhaps something of Robin's own composition. It would've made sense to me if she'd decided, hidden away in this place, to make her own music. But she was performing as if in a concert hall, her face serious and set.

The theme asserted itself, advanced, revolved. She and Derya were in conversation, though the two pianos weren't in harmony. I don't even know if they'd been tuned. Every few seconds a note would jar and clang. After a while I got used to it, the constant discordance, as if it were part of the score. Then there were the birds, still occupied above us and not at all interested in the music; during the occasional silences I could hear them, and also crickets, and at one point the dull mechanical roar of a plane overhead.

Robin played without the drama or romanticism she'd been criticized for when young. She was restrained, even casual. But I could still hear the training she'd had, the precocity of her playing. The exactitude and fluency of it. How she made each note heard. Derya didn't have her skill, but he mostly kept up, and when he didn't, when he stumbled over notes, neither of them seemed to care.

They played another piece, and then another. When they finished, Robin stood and stretched and nodded at Bernard, who clicked the tape recorder and ejected a cassette, which he labeled with the date and threw into a cardboard box. There were heaps of tapes there. So far as I know, she never listened to any of them.

21.

I stayed with Robin for a week, learning the rhythms of her life. Most days were structured around tasks involving the care and maintenance of her property, and most evenings she waitressed. She seemed to have almost infinite energy. Though her place was secluded, she hadn't isolated herself there. People came and went constantly: a contractor who was helping her build a greenhouse, university students from Laval who were writing a grant to study birds of prey, an entrepreneur from Slovenia who'd detoured from his business trip to Montreal because he was interested in wolves. How he'd heard about Robin's wolves I didn't know. Robin wanted to ask him for money, and she showed him around, fed him, took him to the fenced enclosure to see the wolves. I could have asked to go along—I still hadn't seen the wolves myself, had only heard them howling in the night—but I felt timid about it, no matter how solid the fencing was, and also Robin didn't invite me. At the end of the tour, the businessman wrote her a check whose amount I didn't see but which I took, from her satisfied glance, to be significant. The next morning a sleek black car came to pick him up, juddering down the long dirt road.

At first I thought Robin was involved with Derya; then I thought she was involved with Bernard again. Sometimes I thought she was with both, a shifting set of attachments lacking definition or constraint. I didn't ask; we'd never regained the habit of confiding. Though she seemed happy enough to have me stay, she was also detached, aloof, and I felt there was little distinction between me and the other guests. Since she was busy at the restaurant or working on the property or entertaining people, I didn't see her very much, at least not alone. Strangely enough, the person I spent the most time with was Bernard. In the mornings we made tea, and drank it outside if the weather was good. I noticed that he still drew in a notebook, little sketches of people who came through or the house or the woods, just as he'd done as a teenager. He spent most of his leisure time reading, old paperbacks with tiny print he had to squint to see, so that when he glanced up, his face was crumpled, like a map that had been unfolded but maintained its creases. His selection was improbable. The poetry of Emily Dickinson. *How to Win Friends & Influence People.* A murder mystery called *The Body on Mount Royal,* its cover luridly old-fashioned, a femme fatale in skimpy clothes striking a man in a suit. It turned out these were books he'd found in a summer cottage down the road, when he was helping the new owners renovate. The books smelled of mildew and the smoke of long-ago fires. Reading didn't come easily to him, and he went slowly, occasionally asking me to define this or that word. After supper we did the dishes together, rotating the washing and drying, at ease together in the task.

The night before I left, it was Bernard who stayed up with me. Robin and Derya had both gone to bed, and he and I found ourselves in the kitchen after the dishes were done. I'd enjoyed the easy camaraderie that Robin's house fostered, and was sorry to be leaving.

"Maybe we could email," I said.

Bernard smiled apologetically. "I don't have a computer," he said.

I nodded. "Where do you live usually, in Baltimore? What do you do there?"

He shrugged. "Crash with friends. Make some money. Wait to come back here."

"You could come visit me, in New York," I said impulsively. "I have a couch. Robin stayed there."

"You got work?"

I hadn't thought of it, and I was embarrassed. "I mean, I'm sure I could find something."

"Sure," he said, in a way that meant the opposite. He put his arm around me, and it was companionable, like an uncle to a niece. He'd been working all day, and his body odor wasn't good. For that matter neither was mine. After a couple of minutes, we disengaged. Before Robin drove me to the bus stop the next day, I slipped a scrap of paper with my phone number and address into one of the books he hadn't read, but I don't know if he ever found it. I didn't hear from him.

22.

Back in Brooklyn, I was hired on another reality show. This one, unimaginatively called *The Meat Market,* centered on a group of twenty-somethings who worked at a steakhouse in San Diego and had fights and affairs with one another. They did coke in the bathrooms and spat in the food of rude customers and lived together in groups of two or three, in apartments subsidized by the show, to maximize conflict and romantic entanglements. Also it made shooting easier. I found the drama entertaining and enjoyed playing it up. From the chaos of their lives I sculpted narrative arcs about anger and jealousy and love. The villain was a girl named Mikaela with sharp, expressive brown eyes, and soon I knew her face better than my own, could map her every mood by the raise of her eyebrows, the set of her collagen-injected lips. She was competing against two other girls for the attention of a guy named Chad and I could tell that she would win it, and also that as soon as she had it she wouldn't want it anymore and would break his heart. Despite knowing these things, despite watching the footage over and over again, I was still drawn in. These people were not exactly actors but they were professionals at being themselves and they understood what they'd been hired to do. They were in a performance of real life, heightened for effect.

When I had lunch with Olga, who was visiting from Berlin, I explained how interesting I was finding it. I told her that reality television straddled the boundary between the real and the fictional; that it was not unlike the experience of watching the work of Kiarostami, whose film *Close-Up* had made such an impression on me years ago. I'd recently watched his film *Certified Copy,* in which Juliette Binoche and William Shimell drive through the Italian countryside. She plays an antiques dealer and he plays a writer whose book argues that issues of authenticity are irrelevant, that a reproduction of a work of art has just as much value as the original. Over the course of a day the two of them argue and they seem, during this time, to transform into a couple who've been married for years. Or are they simply play-acting this transformation? The film doesn't explain. You see, I said to Olga at a café, the same thing is happening in reality television. The audience knows it's watching a fabricated reality and both the fabrication and the reality have equal weight.

Olga shook her head over her cappuccino. "It's good you enjoy your work," she said dismissively, and changed the subject.

It's possible that she was right; that I was so happy to be editing again that I found more value in my profession than it deserved. But if so, I didn't care. My headaches were gone and I was able to sit for hours in placid solitude, engrossed. I felt happily unseen. The guys I worked with treated me with indifference. If I stood next to two of them getting coffee, one might bump against me—not rudely, just surprised I was there. I didn't mind. The existence of my own territory—a desk, a monitor, a spot for my mug—was enough. I brought my own lunch and ate it quickly over the keyboard, brushing the crumbs away before resuming my tasks. That I was good at my work, there could be no question.

One day in the break room Matt, an intern, asked me what I'd done on the weekend.

"Nothing," I said.

"Like, literally, nothing?"

"Sat in my apartment. Stared at the walls until it was time to come back here."

He laughed uneasily. "Do you have a cat?"

I glanced at him briefly, then took my yogurt out of the fridge. He was six foot two and gangly, his cheeks a riot of acne scars, his eyelashes long and feminine, the kind of boy who'd been cooed over as a child and still expected it.

"We were, like, taking bets. You seemed like the kind of person who had a cat."

He meant, the kind of woman. A woman without a family must necessarily have a cat. I said nothing.

"Got it, not talking about cats," he finally said, and drifted away, listing with bad posture, like a street sign hit by a car.

I spent long hours at the office, came home late, chatted briefly with Elena—though less so now that the nights were cool and she wasn't out on the stoop as much—and then often resumed work on my computer at home. I was fiddling with the footage of Marianne. I kept editing pieces of her together, a word here, an offhand comment there. Though I lacked a specific aim for this project, I couldn't leave it alone. I worried that it was cruel, a too-unflattering portrait, and yet it made me feel close to her. I felt I was composing a picture of my own memory, documenting my own tenuous relationship with her, the difficult mother I'd wanted so badly to leave behind. Now I found myself craving her, or at least her image, like a ghost I kept inviting to haunt me.

I stopped dating or trying to date. At its root the longing I felt wasn't to do with men, or sex, and perhaps this as much as anything had doomed any potential relationship from the start. My heart had never been in it, because what I most desired was something else. There was an ache in my body that felt physical, and I often woke up in the night to find my palms flattened against my abdomen, as if willing something there. To find a man who felt as I did might take ages, and I didn't have ages. So one day, kneading my hands together nervously, I visited a clinic in Manhattan and told the doctor what I wanted. He waited for me to explain myself with a look of bored patience. The request, so hard for me to utter, was routine to him.

"We can do that," he said.

I could've been buying a bicycle or a sofa. I flipped through information on sperm donors, weighing their educations and career goals and height, though I didn't care about any of those things. All that interested me, all that I looked for in the questionnaires, was a man who wanted a family of his own someday. With Wheelock I'd lived for years in a dispassionate world and I wanted a man who felt warmth toward the idea of children. After a few days of deliberation I chose a man identified only by a number, which I committed to memory, like a password to a secret account. At night I dreamed of babies, round-cheeked and gurgling, arms that wound around my neck and heads that nestled against my chest, a dream-weight so real that I grieved when I woke to find it gone.

The doctor's office was decorated in shades of white. The front counter was built of sheaves of paper into which little alcoves had been carved; on each alcove rested a tiny, perfect, ceramic egg. At least I think they were ceramic; I never touched them, although I stared at them each time I visited and was fascinated by their whiteness and perfection. They were aspirational eggs, the eggs all of us, the female patients, wanted to have. There was no object representing perfect sperm. The male patients I saw in the waiting room didn't linger; they quickly checked in and made their way to a room down the hall, where everybody knew and tried not to think about what they were doing. Meanwhile the women sat in our stretchy yoga pants, which were easy to pull on and off; we sat and stared at the eggs.

My doctor was thin, with a luxuriant moustache and a ballpoint pen he clicked incessantly during the appointments, a nervous tic that was suggestively phallic, and I told him so. He looked down at the pen in his hand as if he'd forgotten it was there. "I can see how you'd interpret it like that," he said neutrally, with the disengagement of a man who'd heard a lot of wild statements from hormonally turbulent women over the years. I didn't like him much. But the same qualities I disliked—his arrogance, his statistically exact and carefully phrased answers, even the painstaking diligence with which he rubbed his hands with alcohol gel before examining me—seemed to testify to his medical competence, and were therefore reasons to return to him, even though month after month I failed, under his care, to become pregnant.

Maybe the problem was me and my imperfect, non-ceramic eggs. Maybe they wouldn't accept my donor's sperm, despite the warmth he had expressed in his file, indicating that he wanted to share the gift of life.

Maybe I'd waited too long.

What began as a simple set of procedures grew in complexity and cost. At the doctor's direction I took pills, then hormone shots, and my belly ballooned, taut against my clothes like a sausage in its casing. Javier, over lunch at a Japanese place, suggested I lay off carbs. "I don't even miss bread," he murmured unconvincingly, chopsticking his sashimi. I said it sounded like a good idea. I didn't tell him why my breasts and stomach were so swollen, or why I'd given up caffeine. I didn't tell anyone anything. I felt embarrassed by my body, as if it revealed to anyone who looked my yearning to have a child, my weird relationship with Wheelock, my particular and error-filled life choices. I excused myself from the table and gave myself a shot in the abdomen in the restroom, swabbing the skin, pinching it, feeling the needle prick. There was something satisfying in this action, the tiny metal instrument disappearing into my body for a moment. It was an offering I made to a greater pain: it said I was ready for more.

I got used to the ultrasounds quickly, and the invasion of the doctor's wand grew mundane; we both examined the black-and-white follicles inside my body with academic interest. He measured; we waited. After days of injections and monitoring, my eggs were ready for retrieval. The nurse said I would be anaesthetized and asked who would take me home afterward. "I'll take myself home," I said. Without raising an eyebrow she made a notation on my chart. I'll always love her for that, this nurse named Natalie whom I never saw again, for not thinking it was a big deal that I'd be going home alone.

I slept through the procedure, woke up, ate applesauce, went back to the apartment. Several days later the doctor called to inform me that we'd created some beautiful embryos, top-grade, a phrase that reminded me of the sirloin at *The Meat Market*'s restaurant. His voice was warm at last. I listened on the phone for the click of his pen, but didn't hear it. Which seemed, at that moment, the most exciting development: the news was so good that he'd put down his pen.

23.

Sometimes, as I charted my monthly cycles and injections in a little notebook, I thought about Marianne, who'd had her children so casually, so accidentally, and I was consumed by jealousy, a feeling that seemed all the more powerful because it was irrational and unfair. In these moods I was more angry at her than ever for her unhappiness as a mother—she'd felt burdened by a situation that I would've given anything to undertake—and I spent hours mulling over the injustices of my childhood, Marianne's temper and frequent absences, her lack of interest in Robin's music or my schoolwork. I began to wonder if her disinterest in us had had long-reaching consequences. Other women our age had families and lived in houses with spouses and retirement accounts, whereas I had a swollen belly, bruised at the injection sites, and Robin had wolves and a barn full of pianos. Why did we live these strange lives? It must be our mother's fault. My concern for Marianne's state of mind shrank, as blame bloomed in its place.

In the vigorous, almost buoyant state of this anger—for which I can see now the hormone treatments were at least partly responsible—I'd call my mother and render accusations, spilling them over the phone in partial and stuttered sentences that were greeted with silence. Marianne didn't react, she didn't defend herself or even seem upset; she had no idea what I was talking about. It was as if I'd called to give her the weather forecast for a place far from where she lived. What did she care about a blizzard in Montana, rain in the Philippines? It had no bearing on her life. She responded, if she did at all, with complaints about the upstairs neighbor whose footfalls were too loud or the landlord who wouldn't fix the leaky faucet in her bathtub.

After these calls I inflicted myself on my sister, wanting her to join me in my anger, share my victimization. Robin only occasionally answered the phone, and when she did pick up she was often out of breath. I hadn't told her about my fertility treatments, or even my desire to have a child, and I understand now how puzzling and irksome my behavior must have been without this context—or even might have been with it. She must, I realize, have shown great patience with me. She listened to my complaints and never told me to shut up, or that I was wrong.

"She's a narcissist," I said once, remembering as I said it that Marianne had once claimed the same of my sister. "She should never have been a mother in the first place."

"Then where would we be?" Robin asked drily.

She didn't defend Marianne. But neither would she add her own criticisms, and the only time she argued with me was when I talked morosely about how our lives were off track, how with different parents and a different childhood we might have been successful, might have been happy.

"Speak for yourself," she said testily. "What are these terms you're using—*happiness, success*? You want to have a home in the suburbs, and a husband in a business suit? Go find one."

"Everyone is married already," I said, starting to cry, as the phrase *home in the suburbs* conjured for me images of women who spent their days strolling children to the park, hauling them in and out of grocery store carts and whacking their hands away from sugary choices in the cereal aisle, lives that during my time in Briar Neck would have struck me as banal and that now seemed perfect and full.

"Then steal someone else's husband," my sister said. "People do it all the time."

I laughed, though I was pretty sure she meant it as a serious suggestion. On the other end of the line the silence was preoccupied. Once she was actually on the phone, Robin was always doing something else at the same time, and if there was a pause in the conversation I never knew whether she was taking her time to respond or hadn't heard me in the first place. This time I heard the subway-like swoosh of wind, indicating that she was outside, and a sputtering rumble that sounded like her truck engine. "What's happening?"

"It's Catherine of Aragon," Robin said. "She's hurt." My sister had named a number of the wolves after Henry VIII's wives. A different pack was named for deadly plants (Nightshade, Belladonna, Oleander) and still others for weapons (Blade, Arrow, Spear). She spoke of them as if about friends: *Blade caught a rabbit today,* or *Jane Seymour has a limp.* When I asked why the names she chose were so dark, she told me I had no sense of humor, which, at the time, was probably true. Now her voice lifted with concern—for the wolf, not for me. "Last week I noticed she wasn't putting weight on her back right leg. Today it seems her back left leg too."

"Do you think her legs are broken?" I said, not knowing what else to suggest.

My sister's breath chugged in my ear, suggesting that she was moving fast in some direction I couldn't guess. "We don't know. I have Michel up here"—I didn't know who Michel was, and didn't ask—"to shoot her with tranquilizers. We're taking her down to a large animal vet in Montreal. *Tu es prêt?*" she finished, evidently speaking to Michel. There came a sound of heaving and scraping, presumably an animal crate, and muttered remarks and instructions, and truck doors opening, slamming shut again.

"Well," I said, deflated. "Keep me posted. Good luck to Catherine." There was no more noise; I didn't know if Robin had hung up or just shoved the phone into her pocket or if the spotty mountain reception had cut out. She wasn't, as a rule, one for goodbyes.

24.

I was excellent at making embryos. Having embryos made for me, behind closed doors, by the embryo elves. I'd outsourced the most basic form of production, become a mogul with a factory assembly line. The doctor showed them to me through a telescope, their surfaces marbled and foreign, like pictures of the moon. "These are grade-A blastocysts," he told me. "You should be proud."

I blushed, weirdly, shy in front of a man who had probed inside my body for months. I said, "Thanks," as if I'd done the work of creating them myself, although I hadn't; he had done it, in his lab, so really, he was complimenting himself. My work had been to learn the vocabulary of blastocysts and retrieval, to haunt internet bulletin boards where women talked about their partners having *good swimmers* or *poor swimmers,* where they wished one another baby dust, where beneath their optimistic screen names (rainbow412, momtobe16) ran a ticker of acronyms and symbols that summarized their journey, ever-continuing, toward motherhood. *TTC 2 yrs, angel baby 11/10 10 wks, always in my heart, IVF #2 scheduled April!*

I always read and never posted, couldn't bear to assign myself a name, to join the parade of superstition and optimism and failure. But I studied the chat rooms with the same obsession I'd once brought to my schoolwork and to films; I collected the tidbits of knowledge there and did what I could with them; I took whatever supplements people recommended. I drank green tea, and then I abandoned green tea and ate pineapple and yams. I read about the importance of reducing stress, which would poison my body and make it hard for the embryos to implant—they could sense stress, the embryos, as dogs smelled fear.

"You've got a great yield here," the doctor had said. "We can work on this for a while."

My days were spent between the editing office and the lab, structured by doctor's appointments and hormone supplements, by blood tests and measurements of the thickness of my uterine wall. I'd never been so closely monitored, so attentive to my body's shifts, never had blood so frequently drawn. One day, in a fit of self-pity, I confided the situation to Elena, who shook her head without any sympathy at all.

"Oh, chicken," she said, "what a waste of time. You want a kid, go sign up for one. They're bursting with them at social services." She shook her hands in the air, to indicate all the rooms bursting with children. She thought I should adopt and do something right for the world instead of spending my "rich person's money" on grade-A blastocysts. Later, she came downstairs to my apartment clutching a *New York Post* article about Romanian orphanages where babies suffered cruelty and neglect.

"If you're so determined to be a mother," she said, "choose one of these babies who needs it. Or an older kid. Nobody wants the older ones. You could have five of them by tomorrow. Or so I'm told."

"Who tells you?"

"People," she said. "The news. Everyone knows about the older kids."

Part of me thought she was right. I lingered over the article for a long time. Those poor Romanian babies tugged at me, left alone in their cribs, their heads flattened against the mattresses, their cries ignored. Meanwhile I ran through the embryos like a gambler on a losing streak. The yield shrank to nothing. I signed up for a class on adoption. Increasingly the doctor was away, on vacation or at conferences, and somebody else filled in for him at my appointments. I believed this was because he didn't want to see me and my unlucky body that wouldn't accept his beautiful blastocysts. In the waiting room I sat silently with other women as we leafed through magazines and checked our phones, everyone yawning because we weren't drinking caffeine. Nobody made eye contact because we didn't want to see our sadness embodied in another person, where it was so stark and hard to ignore.

I filed an application with an adoption agency and tried again with the doctor; this time the yield was *moderate but respectable.* I thought perhaps my body would be less intimidated by the bounty this time, freed of too-high expectations. We still had some lovely blastocysts, said the doctor, admiring them like pageant contestants. But my body said *No thank you* to the lovely blastocysts, expert by now in refusal.

I read a news article about surrogacy in India, how Europeans and Israelis and North Americans were paying Indian women to carry their babies, a fraction of what it cost elsewhere. In the accompanying photo, a young, beautiful woman sat in a chair by a window, looking at something we couldn't see, her expression serene. Or maybe she was exhausted. Or else quietly miserable. *Exploitation or opportunity?* read the caption. I pictured my embryos on a plane to India, off to meet a stranger whose bodily climate was more receptive than my own, and I felt a deep disturbance, the unstable shifting of tectonic plates. Sometimes I wanted to escape on a plane myself, to ignore as if they'd never mattered my body, my fever for motherhood, my moods. And yet my craving remained, circulating in my blood, and each month I returned to the doctor's office, unable and unwilling to leave my hope behind.

25.

My sister called to ask me for money. I was trying to meditate when my cell phone went off. I hated meditating, it was the least calming part of my day, and I grabbed at the phone on the first ring. As I said hello I could feel the irritating rub of some little silver balls my acupuncturist had glued to my ear, whose purpose I'd forgotten. She'd also tried moxibustion—affixing a little stick to my belly and then lighting it, so that it smoked, incense-like, over my belly button—and cupping, sticking heated glasses on my skin. I disliked our sessions intensely, but at least she never talked about my yield.

"Catherine of Aragon is paralyzed," Robin said. I told her I was sorry to hear it. For once she didn't seem to be speaking while simultaneously doing something else outside, and I noticed the quietness of the cottage behind her. I thought about a lecture I'd gone to in graduate school once, about the presence in film of "room tone"—the aural fingerprint of the production space, caused by the position of the microphones in relationship to the physical boundaries where filming took place. It was important to record spare moments of room tone for use in editing. The professor giving the lecture had constructed an entire theory of room tone, the specifics of which I couldn't remember and probably hadn't understood in the first place. What I did remember was her playing moments of silence from famous films—*Casablanca, The Seventh Seal*—without the images, some lush, some crackling, a soundtrack that was both nothing and not nothing, as we sat in the room and listened. She was building an archive of room tones, a treasure trove of background noise. A few of the students rolled their eyes. Others said it was the best lecture they'd ever heard; two of them later formed a band called Room Tone, which played cover songs punctuated by moments of silence.

My sister's room tone was cool. De-peopled. I had the impression that she was home by herself, a rare enough occurrence. "I know you must have money," she said. "You didn't pay rent for all those years." I'd never thought that Robin was paying attention to my finances. When I left Wheelock I did have a chunk of savings, but the treatments had almost drained it, and now I was living paycheck to paycheck. I hadn't paid much attention to Robin's finances either; from what I'd gathered, her inheritance had covered the land she bought but not much else, and her wolf project survived on donations.

"I want to ask you to help this wolf," Robin said. She wasn't requesting a loan but a gift, and I appreciated her directness. "We're bringing in a specialist to treat her with high-dose antibiotics and daily acupuncture and physical therapy. I already spent a lot on a surgery that didn't work. I thought you'd want to help her."

I had no particular affinity for the wolves; they scared me, and whenever Robin had gone to feed them—from what I understood, she threw frozen roadkill into the enclosures and watched them tear it apart—I'd made myself busy elsewhere. No matter how tall the fencing, or how sturdily anchored in the ground, part of me believed that the wolves were capable of breaching it, and that they didn't wish us well.

Now she waited for me to make up my mind. I looked around at the apartment, littered with evening primrose oil supplements and pamphlets from adoption agencies and visualization tapes. My room tone was a cluttered cage. *The Meat Market*'s current season was wrapping up; once it finished, I was scheduled to start yet another treatment cycle, with my last remaining embryos, and I dreaded the possibility of more failure, as well as the discussion with my doctor about whether it was time to give up.

"I'll give you whatever you need," I told her, "on one condition. Can I come stay for a while?"

"You can stay here whenever you want," Robin said. "You don't need a condition."

But I did; I needed to feel that in one area of my life, however small, I had struck a bargain of my own devising.

26.

I landed in Montreal in dark mid-March, the city a wreck of slush puddles and salt-crusted sidewalks. Gritty snow was piled everywhere, studded with cigarette butts. I spent two days with Marianne, which were uncomfortable for both of us. At the beginning of my visit I mentioned her mind wandering and suggested she might see a doctor. She was furious.

"You think I'm senile," she said. "An old woman halfway to the grave."

"I worry about you, that's all."

At this she narrowed her eyes, blatantly skeptical. We ate a stiff meal at a diner near her apartment, Marianne introducing me to the waitress as "my daughter who thinks I'm insane," and when I left she acknowledged my departure with little more than a curt nod.

Robin met me at the bus stop in Sainte-Agathe looking wan and thin, dark circles grooved beneath her eyes. She'd cleared the house of people, wanting to keep the environment calm, and built Catherine a special secured kennel right off the kitchen. I'd never been so close to a wolf before, and I was nervous, but the wolf was more dog-like than I'd expected. It probably helped that she was lying down, on a bed, like a patient in a hospital. Her legs were long and spindly and delicate, with large paws that made her look puppyish. Though she was a grey wolf, up close her fur was surprisingly varied in color: some threads silver, some white, the occasional strand of reddish brown. She had enough room to pace, if she could have paced, but instead she lay on her side, her yellow-green eyes flickering with constant movements that were hard not to read as confusion and anger. In order for the veterinary specialist to treat her she had to be sedated, Robin told me, and she had come to know when the drugs would be administered and to rumble throatily with defiance and fear.

My sister couldn't sleep. Her hair looked greyer than the last time I'd seen her, her long braid shot through with it, though it had been less than a year. At night she smoked and paced the house as if walking for the wolf who couldn't, her footsteps creaking on the old wooden planks of the stairs. At first the vet had thought it was a nerve injury, but now she'd decided it was a bacterial infection caused by eating rancid meat—alas, a common habit of wolves. Apparently they liked to cache the carcasses they couldn't finish and come back to them later, after they were rotten. The vet, a known expert in such cases, made regular trips from New York State to administer antibiotics and stipple the wolf's body with colorful acupuncture needles. I watched her do it, wondering if the wolf hated acupuncture as much as I did.

While the vet placed the needles Robin would sit on the floor, cradling Catherine's head in her lap and speaking softly to her, words I couldn't make out but whose tone was tender. I remained on the other side of the kennel; I was still scared of the wolf, even when she was sedated. The wolf bared her sharp teeth, making a noise that was part whimper, part growl. In response, my sister sang Beatles songs, folk songs, "Au Clair de la Lune." The vet stood, her work with the needles finished. "Now we wait," she said.

Robin stayed with the wolf as much as she could. When she had to go work a shift at the restaurant she made me sit by Catherine in case of emergency, with the vet's cell number scrawled on the wall. "Keep her company," she said. "Talk to her. They're social creatures."

I sat by the kennel, every twitch of the wolf's limbs or fur making me flinch. I watched her chest rise and fall, thinking I should find some mystical meaning in it, some deep thoughts about wilderness and beauty, but all I felt was the gradual waning of my fear into something more mundane. "So, Catherine," I'd begin awkwardly, "how's it going today?" The wolf never raised her head, ignoring this question, which seemed what it deserved. When Robin talked or sang, it seemed natural for her to do it, but when I was alone with Catherine it felt absurd, making small talk with a wolf. One afternoon I hit upon the idea of reading out loud; I'd found a book about wolves on Robin's shelf and I thought I'd learn about them. Opening the book in the middle I started reading a section about a German officer named F. W. Remmler, who'd trained eagles to hunt wolves, apparently a traditional practice in central Asia. To teach the eagles he dressed children in leather armor and attached strips of raw meat to their backs. When the eagles were able to knock the children down, they moved on to wolves. Later, Remmler moved to Canada and lived out his days on a wilderness preserve located on an island in Lake Erie. Horrified by this tidbit of information, I stopped reading, put the book back on the shelf, and never opened it again.

I preferred when Robin gave me other tasks to do. I took over the cooking, the grocery shopping, answering the phone. Occasionally I called Marianne, wanting to repair the damage my visit had done; I gave her updates on the wolf, to which she responded with updates of her own. Some of her news was ordinary (the weather bad, her health bad) and some of it peculiar (she couldn't find her glasses, and believed someone had stolen them while she slept). Often she'd tell me the exact thing she had the day before; our conversations were eddies, swirling around the same few topics, but I knew she'd be angry with me if I pointed out the repetition. I dreaded these calls without being able to stop making them, and I often had the sense that Marianne dreaded them too, but couldn't stop herself from picking up the phone.

Before returning to the US, the vet trained Robin to perform Catherine's physical therapy. Robin made me sit on the floor and hold the wolf in a kind of harness while she manipulated her legs, pressing up on each back paw in turn, bending the leg and then straightening it. The wolf smelled funky and strange, like forest and fur and metal all combined. Though she was sedated, she wasn't unconscious, and I believed I could sense an agony of energy suppressed. It felt like holding back an avalanche.

Robin wiped her hands on her pants. "Done," she said. "Good job."

"Thank you," I said.

Robin rolled her eyes. "I wasn't talking to you," she said.

That night, as we ate dinner—I'd managed to produce an edible if unremarkable chili, which Robin swallowed without comment—she passed the keys to the pickup truck across the table. "Bernard's coming on the bus tomorrow afternoon. Gets in at three."

"Okay," I said. "But I thought you didn't want visitors these days."

"Bernard's not a *visitor*," she said. "He's family."

I wondered exactly what she meant by that. "Are you guys still—you know, whatever?"

"*You know, whatever?*" my sister mocked me, and I flushed. I knew she was exhausted from worry and lack of sleep, and yet I couldn't help but feel wounded. Her moods reminded me of Marianne's, how she'd sighed with annoyance at us when we were children, and the familiarity pierced me with hurt while also making me feel at home.

. . .

When he stepped off the bus Bernard was wearing a red-and-black-checked jacket and a dark blue hat, which he took off in the truck to release a great profusion of hair. He looked very much like his old self in the Tunnel days of weed selling and international hip-hop. I was so surprised that I kept turning my head to look at him and a couple times he reached over to the steering wheel, afraid we were about to go off the road.

"I'm sorry," I said. "It's just that last time I saw you, you were bald." I didn't add that I'd assumed he was shaving his head because he was losing his hair.

"I needed the insulation," he said, lighting a cigarette. I rolled down the window, and the cold air cut through the car loudly, making conversation impossible. With all that hair he looked younger, his brown eyes soft and large, and he seemed to have put on some weight, too, not muscle but a layer of padding, like an animal that had fattened itself for winter. He finished his cigarette quickly and crushed it into the truck's ashtray. When I rolled up the window, we could hear each other again.

"So how's our girl?" he said. "On the phone she's been sounding kind of wild."

"She's stressed," I said. "Really worried about Catherine's condition."

"Yeah, she told me," Bernard said, nodding. "She's got no boundaries when it comes to those animals, man. Imagine if she had a kid."

"Imagine," I said, with an involuntary twinge in my body.

"No telling her anything, though. Never has been."

"True," I agreed. Then I added, softly: "She's spending a lot of money on vet bills." It was a kind of test balloon for his disapproval. I wondered if, as a guy who'd spent time in prison, who'd grown up in foster care, he saw her choices as ridiculous, indulgent. I realize now that I was testing his judgment of me, my own ridiculous expenses and indulgences. But if Bernard thought Robin spending money on a wolf was stupid, he didn't show it. He seemed to accept it as a normal part of Robin's life, as normal as having built a wolf preserve to begin with. He only nodded and said, "That vet from New York is expensive. Supposed to be the best though."

"Don't you think——" I began, and stopped. "Maybe——"

Bernard turned to me and smiled. "I'm going to stop you right there," he said. "You better not second-guess Robin." When I parked in front of the house, he opened his door and stepped out, then turned around and stuck his face back in the truck, right up close to mine. I could smell the smoke and sweat on him. "Not if you value your *life*."

27.

On the tenth day of acupuncture and physical therapy, the wolf stretched her left back leg three inches, all by herself. Robin was elated, couldn't stop talking about it, drank three glasses of wine at dinner, smiling with chapped lips. We were eating a roasted chicken Bernard had made—he'd taken over the cooking as soon as he arrived, much to my relief—and talking about the wolves. As I stood up to clear the plates, the world suddenly sloped and the clutch of forks and knives in my hand clattered to the floor. I sat down next to them, trying to focus the blur.

Bernard was by me instantly, resting a large hand on my shoulder. "You all right?"

"It's just my vertigo," I said. "It still comes back sometimes." The wall next to me shimmied, then stilled. The nurses had told me to find a fixed point and stare at it—closing my eyes would only make it harder to stabilize myself, they'd said. You can't rely on your inner compass when your inner compass is broken. The wall was composed of blue painted planks and I found a knot in one and stared at it, a tiny whorl that seemed, the longer I looked at it, to grow both larger and more meaningless, an expanding and arbitrary universe, as a word looks stranger the more you fixate on it, trying to remember how it's spelled and what it means.

Robin glanced at me and then got up, clearing the plates herself. Bernard kept his hand on me, and this comforting weight, more than the knot in the wood, steadied me, fastening me to the ground. After a while I was able to sit back up in the chair, and my eyes focused on my sister, as she dried her hands with a towel, the dishes already done. She raised her eyebrows at me, asking if I was all right, and I nodded.

"Does that happen a lot?" Bernard said.

"Sometimes," I repeated. I felt like I ought to say more but the words were beyond my reach, slipping away through some dark water, tangled with weeds.

Hours later, unable to sleep, tired of listening to every creak and groan of the house, I went downstairs and poured myself a small glass of Robin's whiskey. Standing in the kitchen, I heard a moaning sound. For a second, I thought it might be the wind, but when it came again, I knew it wasn't. In my sock feet I padded over to the kennel where Catherine was housed. It was just before dawn, the sky sooty. The wolf was asleep, and my sister lay beside her, one arm flung across the wolf's neck. One leg was pressed against the length of the wolf's back. The moaning was coming from Robin, in her sleep, and I didn't know—still don't know—whether she was in pain or having a bad dream. The wolf's eyes flickered open, and she gazed past me as if I didn't exist.

The next day everything looked strangely crystalline, the sparkling delineation of objects made that much more extreme by the sun, which came out in full force after days of clouds. This happened to me sometimes after a fit of vertigo, as if by re-centering itself the world grew more solid, and sharp, and clear. For the first time, I walked with Robin to the wolf enclosures and watched her throw frozen deer haunches over the top. The wolves sprang instantly to the meat, tearing it apart one at a time, according to the hierarchies they'd established. My sister watched them intently, one hand gripping the fence.

Inside, I sat with Catherine in my lap while Robin manipulated her limbs, and the wolf licked her lips, which Robin said was probably a request for food and indicated that her appetite was returning. That night, we ate quickly—sandwiches Bernard had picked up in town—and standing up. Then we separated. I lay down with a book but didn't read it. After a while, smelling cigarette smoke, I went out to the back porch, where Bernard sat drinking tea and reading *What's Bred in the Bone*. I reached out my hand for a cigarette and he gave me one, which I inhaled along with the cool night air. For months I'd been treating my body as a scientifically controlled environment that could be contaminated by the slightest misstep—a sip of coffee, a French fry—and the trashy taste of nicotine was deeply satisfying. Maybe, I thought, I'd give it all up. Move to Australia and live on a beach, until I shriveled to a happy, wrinkled husk. Or maybe I'd move back to Montreal and become one of those old ladies I used to see in our neighborhood, stepping carefully around the slush in their orthopedic shoes, carrying plastic bags from the supermarket with one apple, one can of soup.

In the yellow porch light above Bernard's head moths swirled curiously, as if they too liked the smoke. "Are you enjoying it?" I said.

He frowned. "Robin gave it to me. She said it's her favorite book."

This was news to me. "And?" I said.

"I hardly understand it," he said. "I should have stayed in school."

"You could always go back," I said stupidly.

He shrugged, then leaned forward. "There's an angel and a demon in this book," he said. "And the demon believes that adversity can make a person stronger, and the guy whose life it's about has terrible things happen to him, right, war and Nazis and all kinds of stuff, and I don't know? I think adversity is just stuff you'd avoid if you could."

"Seems sensible," I agreed.

"Your sister is kind of like this demon," he said. "She thinks we have to be tested."

"What do you think?"

He closed the book as if he'd won an argument with it. Then he turned to me, business-like almost, formal, as if he'd been waiting for this moment, had prepared for it. When he was young, he said, speaking as if to a stranger, he and Robin went to Europe. On the plane, they cuddled under a blanket, kissing, ignoring the annoyed looks of other passengers. He was in a kind of trance, although probably it was partly the drugs he was taking. He was always in a fog in those days, a combined fog of drugs and of being in love with Robin, who was his sun and his moon. I remember him saying this—*She was my sun and my moon*—as an adult now, a grown man with scarred cheeks and sad eyes, and I remember how he smiled at his younger self without any mockery. He was happy, I thought, to have once been young like that.

He'd never been out of the country before. He'd had no idea, he said, that cities could be so old. They saw churches dating back to the middle ages, castles built of grimy rock crumbling under the weight of centuries. He kept expecting knights to burst forth on horses, like he'd seen—where had he seen this image? He hadn't grown up with books and couldn't name a single movie where he'd seen a knight. It was just a thing in his head, a seed planted by an invisible hand.

Robin seemed to know everything, where to go, what to eat, she made friends easily, she played her music easily. He admired her even more than he had at home, and tried to imitate her fearlessness. While she was rehearsing, he walked around the cities, trying to score drugs and just looking around. Before long, he had his own way of navigating, speaking the universal language of drugs. He could always find someone to get high with, and they usually had friends, and even if they didn't know much English there was a shared code of spacey laughter, of cash passing hand to hand, of nods that meant *Thanks, man.* He'd found his people and they were the same in ancient Europe as they had been at home.

One morning he woke up—okay, it was the afternoon—and the little man from the orchestra was yelling at him about Robin. It took some time for Bernard to understand what had happened, which was that Robin was blowing off rehearsal. It didn't seem like that big a deal to him. Everybody blows things off sometimes. Maybe a sober person would have picked up on the situation just a little bit quicker. The little man was at pains to impress upon him the fact that Robin hadn't been seen in some time. Didn't you notice? he said. His lips fired spit in Bernard's face. Didn't you notice she was gone?

Bernard had not noticed.

The little man couldn't believe that Bernard didn't know where she was. That she hadn't confided her plans to him. It took Bernard some time to believe it himself, and even longer to understand just how adrift he was. Without her, he had no reason to be in Europe, no place to stay, no itinerary. All he had was the cash in his pocket and his passport.

"So you see," he told me all those years later, smoking another cigarette. "Robin saw I was lost, and she gave me that gift."

"What gift?" I said.

"She made me figure out how to get home," he said, "she tore me out of the fog. I was"—he searched for the word for a long time, and we both waited patiently—"complacent, and she took that away from me. It was a gift."

I thought this was absurd. He'd had to find his way home and later wound up in prison because dealing drugs was the only way he knew to make a living. In what chapter of this story did Robin's behavior offer him any benefits? Not for the first time I marveled at Bernard's acceptance of her, his seemingly limitless forgiveness.

"She abandoned you," I said, "and you think it was a gift?"

He smiled at me and stubbed out the cigarette on the doorsill, spraying sparks into the dark. "I know it was," he said.

28.

"So what do you want?" Robin said.

"How do you know I want something?"

"You always want something, even when you don't know what it is," she said.

It was my last night, and the two of us were sitting in the kitchen, Bernard having made himself scarce.

"I mean, everybody does," she said, lighting a cigarette. "You're just more hung up about it than most people. You seem to think wanting anything is a character flaw. Marianne says it's because of your father leaving."

"What are you talking about?"

"She thinks that because Todd left when you were a child, you want to prove that you don't need anyone. You can't ask anybody for anything. You shut yourself off to prove you can't be hurt."

"I was with Wheelock for years."

"Exactly," my sister said. "You picked a machine of a man."

I picked up one of her cigarettes, smelled it, put it down. "He hurt me anyway."

"I know," Robin said.

"Anyway, you're the one who's shut yourself off. You live up here with your wolves and your visitors. Who's Derya to you, or Bernard? They come and go, nothing permanent. Maybe that's because of *your* father."

She shook her head, not the slightest bit riled. I couldn't make a dent in her. "I have the life I want," she said. She smoked her cigarette and tipped the ash into a beer bottle on the table. Then she added, quietly, "Poor Marianne. She tried."

"*Poor* Marianne?" I said. "She drove everyone away."

"I know. But she wanted us to be happy, in her own way. Don't you remember how she kept bringing those men around? Trying to find us new fathers."

"She was making us audition for them, perform like little marionettes."

"We weren't auditioning. *They* were auditioning."

"Even Hervé?" I said.

She didn't answer that. "I'm just saying you always think you have no power in any given situation. That's your problem."

I didn't know if this was true, or how to answer, so I said nothing. I noticed that her teeth were turning yellow from smoking, and laugh lines starred around her eyes. I saw these details but I couldn't register them, really. No part of her aging seemed real to me; she would always be my little sister. She put out her cigarette, then lit another, watching me.

She was right that I wanted something. I'd hesitated over the request for days, brooded and questioned it, and I couldn't get it out of my mind. It seemed a ridiculous, impossible thing to ask. And yet I'd watched my sister cradle a wolf in her lap, sleep with it at night. If anyone could understand the necessary presence of the ridiculous, could imagine cravings that others might find absurd, it would be her.

"I want a child," I said. "It's the thing I most want."

"Go ahead, then. Get yourself knocked up."

I thought about a woman I'd overheard talking on the phone at my doctor's office. She was crying. "People keep telling me the body knows what to do," she said through her tears. "And I keep saying *my body* doesn't. *My body* is a dumbass."

I wanted to tell Robin, *My body is a dumbass.* "It's not so easy."

"So adopt one," she said airily. "Aren't there a million girls in China or whatever?"

I sighed. I wanted to talk to her about the impulses of the body, about a desire so deeply rooted it felt cellular, but I didn't know where to begin. Instead I said, "It's not like picking up a liter of milk at the store."

There was a moment of quiet. A distant look came over my sister's face, an almost ghostly absence, as if she subtracted herself briefly from her body, and then returned to it. And then, in one of those quicksilver moments of comprehension that dated back to our childhood, she nodded. "You want to do it a different way," she said.

I nodded, too. I explained it all as carefully as I could, the process, the time, how it would work, what the arrangements would be. She listened and said nothing. And nothing. And nothing.

I folded my hands together. I couldn't beg her. She had to say yes or no on her own.

"Are you thinking about it?"

"I'm thinking about it," she said.

We went to bed. I sat up in the small bedroom, my eyes moving over a book I found on the shelf, thinking about the clinic in New York, the nurses in their dark blue scrubs, the tight-lipped women in the waiting room. The smell of cigarettes in the house told me that my sister was awake too. The room was cold, and I pulled a sweater on over my pajamas. The night waned; the sun came up; it was morning, and I couldn't bring myself to leave the room. Then Robin knocked softly on the door, came in, and sat down on the bed. She said yes, she would do it, she would help me have a child.

29.

On a frozen morning in early December, Marianne disappeared.

Robin called to tell me, and I got on a plane. When I landed in Montreal, the afternoon was brilliantly sunny, but by the time the taxi reached my mother's neighborhood, the short day was already gone. In front of her building a bicycle had been chained to a parking sign, its wheels lumpy with snow. Next door was a storefront I hadn't seen before, displaying clothes that looked quirky and chic. Robin and Bernard were both already there: my sister pacing, Bernard in the kitchen making tea, which I knew would offend my mother, if only she were present to be offended. She'd called Robin several days in a row the previous week, leaving voice mail messages that were nothing more than a series of long-winded complaints. She was upset about the traffic on her street, about the noise her upstairs neighbors were making. I asked Robin how Marianne sounded when she called back, was Robin able to calm her? My sister shook her head. She hadn't called back. By the time she got around to it, Marianne wasn't answering the phone. She and Bernard had driven down last night to find her gone.

Bernard brought us the tea in our mother's tiny cups. They looked like doll's cups in his large hands, profaned by his yellow, cigarette-stained fingers. After delivering the tea he stood to the side, waiting like a butler, his eyes fixed on Robin. She and I made a list of places to look, called the police and hospitals, then divided up neighborhoods and got to work.

I visited Marianne's favorite diner, where she sometimes had cheap meals and passed the time with the waitress at the counter. I held a picture of her from the previous Christmas, smiling a pained smile. It barely looked like her. In person her eyes had a wicked, vital gleam. But in still photographs she could have been any middle-aged lady, with her short hair, her glasses, her age-spotted hands. Once she'd held them out to me, bitterly. "I never feel old except when I look at my hands," she'd said. "Life makes you into a monster." The waitress, when I showed her the picture, only shook her head, as if she didn't recognize my mother at all.

It was impossible to say where she might be. I wandered along Mount Royal, in and out of places that probably hadn't changed much since she was a girl: a bookshop, a music store that still sold vinyl records, a café. It was windy and dark, winter's raw edge carving the air, and I hoped that wherever she'd gone, she was inside.

I called Robin. "Anything?"

"No, you?"

"No."

I took a taxi to Carré St-Louis, which my mother had always said was the prettiest spot in Montreal. When she was a girl she'd dreamed of living there. It made me think of Claude Jutra, who'd lived there, and whose film *Mon Oncle Antoine* my high school history teacher had shown to us just before Christmas break one year. In the eighties the filmmaker, suffering from early-onset Alzheimer's, had been found dead in the St. Lawrence River. There was a note in his pocket that read *Je m'appelle Claude Jutra*.

Snow was falling now, fizzy and yellow under the streetlights, and I stood on a corner hoping my mother would magically appear. Instead I saw a man asleep on a bench, under a dirty blanket, and a woman walking her dog, begging it to hurry up and finish its business.

Robin called. "Anything?"

"Nothing," I said. "You?"

"Nothing."

It was the police who found her. She'd boarded a bus to Trois-Rivières and taken a room at a small hotel. Why did she go there? She wouldn't say. In her purse was a pack of cigarettes and several boxes of Glosette chocolate-covered raisins. When the Glosettes ran out, she tried to shoplift more from a dépanneur. She was not a discreet thief. When the cashier questioned her, she became argumentative, and the police were called. She wouldn't give her name, but the officer had read the bulletin about a missing woman in Montreal, and he found her identification in her pocketbook.

Whatever else she'd done in Trois-Rivières, she kept to herself. The hotel, not far from the bus station, was grimy and run-down. There was a small television in the room, a shower stall cloudy with age, a coffee maker. I know this from reading online reviews, not from my mother, who never spoke of it. When the police officer arrived at the dépanneur, she went with him obediently, like a criminal who understood that the gig was up. But she wouldn't speak to him. I don't know whether this was because she didn't want to tell him anything or because she herself didn't know the answers to the questions he asked.

Robin and I picked her up at the police station in Trois-Rivières. They'd brought her some tea in a paper cup, which she was sipping with an air of disgust. Her winter coat was draped over the seat behind her. She was wearing a blue cable-knit cardigan with a silver brooch, and seemed none the worse for her escapade. When she saw us come in, she frowned.

"We're here to take you home," my sister said. "It's time to go."

Our mother set her tea down, and stood. "It took you long enough to get here," she said.

"You were the one who went away."

"You always say that," our mother said angrily. "I think you almost believe it's true."

"It *is* true," Robin said, annoyed.

I put my hand up to stop them arguing. "Marianne," I said, "you should be nicer to Robin."

"Why?" said our mother, her voice trembling with complaint.

"Because she's pregnant," I said.

Our mother shook her head. "That has nothing to do with me," she said.

Over the months that followed, as our mother's condition worsened, I came to believe that if she could have, she would never have returned from Trois-Rivières. She would have left of her own volition, when she was still able to do so. She knew what was coming for her, and she boarded that bus with the last vestiges of her defiance. When I grieve for her, as I still do, I think about how much she would have liked to engineer her own exit, to exert in her final days a control over her life that had so often been denied her; I think about the last and greatest loss, how it must have pained her, how badly she wanted to hold on to it. Her pride.

30.

Robin was three months along. During the summer she'd stayed with me in New York, leaving Bernard and Derya in charge at home, and conducted the business of treatment—paperwork; medications; implantation—with the same efficiency she'd shown when finding me an apartment. Elena and the other neighbors greeted her with warmth that made clear I'd always been their second choice. When they invited us over for drinks and dinner, Robin asked for water; she'd quit smoking and drinking. "I will be a temple," she said with mock seriousness, waving a hand across her body.

We went to a different clinic than the one I'd used before—I wanted a change, hoping for better luck—and this doctor was a slender, dark-haired woman whose bedside manner was even more impersonal than the first one's had been. She asked nothing about our situation—we could have been a couple, for all she knew—and spoke only in numbers: these were Robin's levels, these were the days on which we were to come back for testing. On the forms required, Robin gave her date of birth; described her health as excellent; answered the questions about *previous pregnancies* (one) and *children* (zero). I wanted so much to ask her about that *one,* and yet I couldn't bring myself to do it; it was like a wall I kept walking toward, pressed my palms against, and then turned away from.

But she knew I had seen it; she must have known I was wondering. If I understood anything about Robin, it was that she would not be pushed; she would only offer what she was prepared to offer, and no more.

I remembered her postcard from Sweden—*Don't look for me*—and didn't ask.

The first doctor sent over my last remaining embryos. I didn't ask the second doctor what she thought about them; I didn't want to hear her say they were lovely or not. On transfer day Robin and I took a taxi to Midtown together. I remembered the days when I'd leaned back and crossed my fingers, trying to be calm. Now it didn't matter whether my body was a stressful environment; I could be as anxious as I pleased, and worry grew inside me like a weed, easier to nourish than hope. At the clinic, my sister closed her eyes, her long hair trailing down her chest. The nurses had given her a mild sedative, and she smiled like a saint. When they came back to check on us, she was snoring.

Two weeks later we returned for a blood test, and the nurse called in the afternoon to say that Robin was pregnant. Detectable levels of HCG were present. Robin proposed champagne, "for you, I mean." I said it was too early to celebrate, that we should wait for a few weeks, to be sure it was real.

"How much more real could it be? *Detectable levels of HCG* sounds confirmed to me."

"It's too early," I said.

"When will it be late enough for you? When the thing is coming out of my body?"

"Don't call it a thing," I said. I was in tears.

Robin held up her hand. "Lark," she said, "this just started, and you're already driving me crazy."

My inclination was to tell no one of our plan, to cradle it inside, in the same tender place it had lived before. I wanted to protect myself from the possibility of more failure. But my sister wasn't like me; she turned my fears inside out, and wouldn't hide anything. She told Bernard, she told Derya; she told our mother, who listened to the story with an impatience she didn't bother to conceal.

"I don't know why you're telling me this," she said at last. "You've always done whatever you wanted anyway."

"We're not asking you for permission," Robin said. "We just want you to know you're going to have a grandchild."

I winced as she said it, at the certainty in her voice. Our mother's eyes narrowed, and her hands shook as she raised her teacup to her lips.

"Neither of you knows what it is to be a mother." Her bitterness

was permanent, like a bone that had broken in her and healed crookedly; it couldn't be straightened now. "Marianne," I said, and reached
out my hand to her. She didn't take it.

"Don't bother, Lark," my sister said. "You'll never change her mind."

It was true that I couldn't change it, but her mind was changing
all the time anyway, its territory ever shifting, like a beach as the
water came and went. She was pleasant one day, hateful the next.
She was always nicest when she forgot who we were.

31.

For a few days after Marianne was found, I stayed with her, Bernard and Robin having gone back to the Laurentians, and I could tell
I was getting on her nerves. She didn't like to see me in the morning,
asleep on the couch, when she was preparing her tea. She still began
each day with the newspaper, although I noticed that sometimes she
picked up the previous day's edition, if it hadn't been cleared away,
and read it without noting the repetition. Other times she sat in
silence, looking out the window as her tea cooled, thinking I don't
know what thoughts.

One day as I came out of the shower I found her searching
through my suitcase, which I kept in a corner of the living room,
my things jumbled inside. She glanced up at me, not seeming to feel
any guilt. "Aha," she said, holding up my digital video camera like a
piece of incriminating evidence. "What are you doing with this?"

"I don't know," I said. I threw my towel on the couch, which I
knew annoyed her, and dressed quickly. "I usually carry it with me.
In case."

"In case of what?" she said, like a lawyer badgering a witness.

"In case I want to use it," I said. At Robin's, I'd occasionally done
some filming. I shot the trees whipping during a storm, the outside
of the barn, random moments that seemed, when I looked at them
again back in New York, to have captured none of the spirit of the

place, and which I then erased. My mother was turning the camera over in her hands, gingerly, as if it might explode.

"Remember when you filmed me before?"

I'd never shown her the footage. I felt a pang now, though I wasn't sure why; because I'd thought she wouldn't like what I'd filmed, or because I'd stopped editing the footage, finding it too depressing.

"Let's do it again," she said.

For the next few days, we filmed. It was the first thing she wanted to do in the morning and the last thing before she went to bed. She arranged herself on her sofa, put on her lipstick, and presented herself to the camera. She didn't want me to ask questions. She had many things to say, and opinions spilled from her as if she'd long been denied them. She thought women these days were becoming too much like men. She thought we should all be concerned about the coming plague as global travel brought germs to North America on planes. I didn't remind her that I had worked extensively on plagues. "It's retribution," she told the camera—unlike most subjects, she was very good at talking to the camera and not to me—"for the hell we inflicted on the First Nations. Smallpox and all the rest."

From smallpox she meandered into a discussion of her own health, and then told a story about a girl she'd known as a child, who had died of meningitis, and from there to a lengthy condemnation of a pharmacist in the neighborhood who had left her husband for another man. "She thinks she deserves something better," she said, "but she doesn't."

When I could get a word in, I asked her about herself, about the years of Robin's and my childhood, even, with some hesitation, about Hervé, but the answers I received bore no relation to the questions. She seemed to be responding to some inner inquisitor whose voice was more commanding than mine. Sometimes she stopped mid-sentence and shifted to a different topic, as if she'd been interrupted and redirected. Sometimes, after speaking at great length, she would glance at me, surprised and almost abashed, as if she'd forgotten I was there. But if she'd forgotten, then to whom had she been speaking?

This time I was more judicious setting up the shots. The filming happened to coincide with a string of sunny days, so her apartment was brightly lit and cheerful, and she dressed with care, each day wearing a different blouse and necklace, matching earrings. She turned to the camera as if it were the audience she'd been waiting for all her life.

I got a testy email from Javier, who was my producer on a new show, a docu-soap about a mother-daughter team who had once been rich but now were cash-poor and attempting to mount a comeback by starting a gourmet dog-food business. They cooked the food themselves in the kitchen of a model home in Phoenix and based it on their own diet, which was Paleo-organic. Their house was full of dogs, who jumped on the furniture and slept in the beds; at Costco and Whole Foods they sat upright in carts, gazing down the aisles. The barking made editing a nightmare. But the women were surprisingly funny and I missed the hours I spent capturing their barbed banter, how the daughter would smack her mother's jutting hipbones to move her out of the way, or drop foie gras into a blender and say, "Well, here goes nothing. Four hundred dollars of nothing." I'd pled a family emergency when leaving, but we were on deadline and the network was impatient. *Unless you're missing a limb,* Javier wrote, *it's time to come back. And even then it might depend which one.*

Marianne had tired of the filming and she had a slight cold that made her even more querulous than usual. She lay in bed all day, and when I offered to bring her soup or tea she scowled and told me to leave her alone. I don't know why I lingered where I wasn't welcome. Robin didn't want me to visit either. She didn't want me hovering over her, obsessing over her body "like it's your rental property," she said. I'd spent a night at the cottage and even that was too much for

her. She went to bed early, after which I found Bernard and interrupted his reading, not wanting to be alone.

He put down his book and asked me, "What are you going to
call it?"

"It depends," I said carefully. Of course I dreamed about the future,
my arms cradling a body that couldn't yet be held. But I couldn't
speak about it, or about how often the dreams turned to nightmares
in which the baby came to harm, and it was always my fault—there
were car accidents and earthquakes and sudden gaping chasms in
the ground and each time the baby slipped from my arms and fell
away into a nothingness that was the only thing left when I woke up.

"Do you think it's a boy or a girl?" he said.

We'd told the doctor we didn't want to know. "I have no idea,"
I said.

"I think it's a girl," he said.

"Let's stop talking about it. It makes me nervous."

"Okay," he said. "But can I ask you one thing?"

I buttoned my lips, nodded.

"Can I come visit her?" he said.

"Of course," I said, and he smiled.

"I had a little sister," he said. "They took her away. I was good with
her. But I was too young to take care of her, and my mom, well, you
know how she was."

I looked at him closely, but his face was as untroubled as ever,
as strangely serene. "I didn't know you had a sister. What happened
to her?"

He shrugged. "Don't know," he said. "She went into foster care
and then got adopted. My mom never found out where she was put.
We always thought maybe she'd come looking for us, but she didn't.
I guess she doesn't even remember us."

I tried to fathom the sadness of this, but couldn't: it was a dark
well, so deep I couldn't make out its bottom. But it explained something to me about Bernard: his softness, and his friendliness to and

need for women, and how some part of him seemed stuck in child-hood, mired there. As if he was still waiting for her.

"Robin never told me about that," I said.

"She doesn't know."

I was puzzled. Why had he told me and not my sister, to whom he'd been so much closer, and for so long? Later, I decided that he'd withheld it from her out of some instinct for secrecy, understanding that she craved distance from him as much as she brought him close. In this, as in other things, he knew her well, which was one of the reasons they'd each stayed part of the other's life.

"I hope she remembers you," I told him.

He shrugged. "I don't," he said. "It might make her sad."

I asked if he'd looked for her, what her name was, what she'd looked like, but he was done with the conversation; standing up, he told me with gentle finality that it was time for bed.

32.

Robin and I planned to move Marianne into an assisted-living facility. A spot would open the following month, with a kitchenette and a private bath. She could make her tea; she had a view of a field where deer, we'd been told, could sometimes be seen. Did she enjoy nature? The director had asked when we took the tour. We shook our heads; she didn't. The director looked stricken. "Our residents find this view quite soothing," she said anyway.

What did our mother enjoy? It was a question we'd spent our lives not answering. She liked complaining about the world, about us. Finally Robin said, "She likes to read the news," and the director was able to promise a daily newspaper delivery, so we all moved on.

Then we met with the doctor who'd evaluated Marianne's condition and would supervise her care. Robin said, "Isn't it too early for her to be like this? She's not even sixty."

The doctor, a genial, bearded man, smiled patronizingly and said, "It's never too early for most things."

"What's that supposed to mean?" Robin said.

The doctor's voice was bland. "It means things happen when they happen," he said.

In preparation for the move, I helped Marianne organize her belongings. There wasn't much to do; she'd already discarded so many. I wanted to be useful, to ease her transition from one place to the next, but instead we fought constantly. Every time I touched anything she yelped as if I were going to ruin it. I gave up, shouted at her that she was being unreasonable, and left the apartment. When I came back, she was contrite, and she sidled up to me like a child. "I'm sorry," she said stiffly.

I put my arms around her. Awkwardly I kissed her head. What came over me, that I kissed my mother's head? We had no fluency in affection; it was a language we'd never learned to speak.

That was the last time I saw her.

I flew back to New York and went to work. When I returned to Montreal several weeks later, for the scheduled move, I rang the doorbell at Marianne's building and received no answer. This in itself wasn't unusual, even when she was home and expecting me. Her hearing was fine, but when caught up in a task—reading the newspaper, folding laundry, even looking out the window—she seemed to shut the world out so completely that nothing could penetrate her attention. I'd finally taken her keys and copied them so that I could get in whenever I wanted to. This was a Wednesday evening, around nine, and I hadn't eaten. I stood on the stoop of her building, watching the restaurant across the street, which was, as always, empty. How they survived, I had no idea. Marianne believed they were running an illegal business for which the restaurant was a front—drugs, she said, or laundering money for one of the biker gangs—and I'd told her she was being dramatic, but in fact she was often right about things like this. Even when her brain was confused, her pronouncements were sharp. It made her dementia harder to grasp, because it alternated with such lucidity.

After waiting a decent interval, I let myself into the building and climbed upstairs. The morning newspaper lay folded on the mat outside her apartment door: this was the first sign that something was wrong. When I opened the door, I could feel the silence. My mother was often quiet, but this quiet was different.

She had died in her sleep. She was lying on her back, her hands at her sides, her face without expression.

I called Robin, and Bernard drove her down. I waited for them in the living room, as if I didn't want to intrude on my mother's privacy even after her death. Spooked and frozen, I sat on the couch for two hours with my hands on my knees; I didn't know what else to do.

The three of us gathered in her apartment as we had the day of her disappearance. Later, the doctor said he thought it was an embolism. I wasn't sure. I didn't think she'd taken pills or anything but somehow, I felt, she'd done it on purpose. With the same defiance that had fueled her whole life, the same anger and independence, she had lain down and willed herself not to wake up.

33.

Nothing surprised me more than the way Robin fell apart when our mother died. One minute she was full of energy, a bombastic and self-determined person who seemed to do and think whatever she wanted, and the next she was couch-prone and immobile. She *stopped*. I was so shocked by it that my own emotions skittered into a dark corner, hiding, and I didn't retrieve them for a long time. I'd grown used to the energetic, capable Robin, and suddenly she was replaced by a Robin who wept all day and refused to leave her bed.

I took charge of the necessary tasks. We buried Marianne in a small ugly cemetery in Laval, where years ago she'd bought a plot for reasons that were unknown to us. So much of her remained a mystery. She'd left instructions about the service, indicating that under no circumstances were we to contact the family from whom she'd been estranged since her adolescence. *Do not burn me,* she also wrote, so we didn't. We wore dresses and high heels and the wind sliced our stockinged legs. Her old boyfriend the dentist came, and a couple of her friends from the neighborhood, and they pressed our hands and then scurried quickly back to their cars, eager to get out of the cold. I thought we should play music, or sing, or say something. I remembered how, at Worthen, Robin had taken charge of the funeral for Emma's cat, how she'd sung a Beatles song. I didn't suggest she sing now; she could barely stand up. She leaned against me, her pregnant belly curtained by her unbuttoned coat, swiping at her runny nose with the palm of her hand. I kept giving her tissues and she kept losing them. We couldn't decide on an inscription for the tombstone so we only put Marianne's name and the dates of her life, the barest bracket of a person, and then we went back to her apartment and Bernard and I drank whiskey and Robin lay down on the couch, crying. I sat down next to her, patted her shoulder, but I could feel her tense; my touch was no comfort. She kept her eyes closed. I looked helplessly at Bernard, and he got up and turned on the radio; a piano sonata came into the room, low and delicate, but it seemed to enrage Robin, who sat up long enough to say, "Turn that fucking thing off," before lying back down and resuming her tears.

I sent her back north with Bernard and emptied the apartment by myself, donating Marianne's possessions to the church down the street, which was hosting a rummage sale. There wasn't much to give. She'd occupied the apartment like a hotel room. In her dresser I came across a loose color photo of a beautiful young girl with her long hair in a braid, and I stared at it for a long time, wondering who she was. When I turned it over I realized it was the stock photo that came with a store-bought frame, which I found in a different drawer, empty. At last I cleaned the apartment and gave the key to the landlord, who took it indifferently, as if Marianne hadn't lived there for years, as if she hadn't just died, and then I sat in a bar down the street with a double shot of vodka, dry-eyed and queasy with colorless grief. An older man winked at me and sent over a drink. I refused it and he called me a whore and a dyke and so I left the bar, relieved that my moment of mourning had turned ugly; otherwise, I might have sat there all day.

When I got home to Brooklyn, I told Elena that our mother had died, and she brimmed with condolences, bringing over a casserole and a bottle of wine. She talked about her own mother, how good she was, how strict yet warm, how the moment when a daughter loses a mother is when her heart splits open forever. I sat and listened, feeling numb and a bit provoked; I didn't think any of what she said applied to me and Marianne.

"You need to cry, little lamb," she told me, folding a hand around mine.

"It's complicated," I said. "My mother——"

She squeezed my hand so hard that tears did come to my eyes. "She was still your mother," she said firmly.

I almost preferred the guy in the bar, calling me names.

Work soothed me as it always had. The mother and daughter were having a semi-scripted falling-out over their differing visions of the dog-food company's future, and I was heightening the drama in their tense meetings with potential distributors and store reps. In the B storyline the daughter was dating a waiter at a Mexican restaurant and the mother thought he was only into her for their money. The daughter said she was paranoid and racist. Everyone drank a lot of margaritas and said stupid things. The daughter wore revealing tops that were forever threatening to slip an inch too low, even for cable television. Her mother told her she dressed like a desperate prostitute and the daughter said she'd learned from the best.

"Is that supposed to be me?" the mother said. "*I'm* the best desperate prostitute in your life?" I cut away before they both started crying.

One night on the Lower East Side I had dinner with Olga, who was once again in town, and told her about Marianne and Robin. She observed that it sounded like a turbulent time, and I said she was right.

"And yet you don't seem unhappy. Your life is moving, it isn't stagnant," she said, with the knack she'd always had of seeing something from a distance that I couldn't see myself. Then she asked about my work. Since we last spoke she'd lost her disdain for reality TV; she'd decided it was an important and evolving art form. I reminded her that I'd told her as much before and she looked at me blankly.

"Everybody knows it is not reality, it is created, and yet it is the very blurring of the lines between the real and the not-real that is the source of its appeal," she said, lecturing me as if I hadn't told her the same thing.

"Yes," I said. "Also the people are good-looking and behave badly."

She tilted her head and began telling me about her current book project, *The Epistemology of the Cut,* in which she was examining conventions of editing, how we accepted the abrupt displacement in space and time as a given of narrative when in fact it was a construct. As with so many things, she said, we act like something is natural when it is artificial, and vice versa. "What is artificial?" she said loudly, raising her voice as if we were having an argument. "The terminology itself is critical," she said. "Is it a cut or a joining together? Did you know that they sometimes call it that?"

I said I did, but I don't think she heard me. She was talking about Althusserian rupture. I let her voice flow over me, thinking about how Althusser, the literary theorist, had gone crazy and killed his wife. Wondering why I remembered Althusser's crime, I then thought of a scene in *Vertigo* when Jimmy Stewart stares at a coiled bun at the back of a woman's head. The film treats this moment like the discovery of an important truth, though it turns out to be a fiction constructed by his villainous former friend. The feeling of a crucial secret being exposed hangs in the camera's gaze, even after the story dismantles it. Maybe this was what Olga meant by epistemology. Or maybe I was just as strange as Jimmy Stewart, preoccupied with details like the coil of a woman's hair at the nape of her neck. I heard Olga say something about reproduction, and I startled, thinking she was talking about Robin. But Olga, who'd never had any interest in children, had greeted the news of my sister's surrogacy with a simple nod. Now she was talking about Walter Benjamin's essay "The Work of Art in the Age of Mechanical Reproduction." I stopped trying to follow her train of thought, or rather I acknowledged to myself that I'd stopped following it a while ago, and I drank my tea and admired Olga in the candlelight, the rapid movement of her ideas, how she pulled at their strings and made them dance at her command.

That evening when I got home there was a message from Bernard, who'd never called before, saying Robin wasn't doing well.

"Is the baby okay? I can't really leave right now," I said when I called him back. "We have to finish this episode by next week, and I'm working twelve-hour days. I'll be there in two weeks."

"Yeah that's cool," Bernard said, sounding unhappy. "I guess I'm just thinking, I don't know, not sure about where Robin's head will be at in two weeks."

"What do you mean?" I said. "What's happening there?"

There was a pause, then audible suction, the room tone taken over by Bernard's lengthy interlude with a cigarette. "She's kind of wigging out, I guess," he said.

"More than when I left?"

Another silence, another slow intake of breath. "She wants to sleep with the wolves," he said. "Like she did when Catherine was sick? But none of them are around."

"So?"

"So she's out looking for them," he said.

I closed my eyes, rubbing a furrow I could feel cutting deep between my eyes, unable to smooth it. "What are you talking about?" I pictured Robin wandering the chilly woods in a white nightgown and bare feet, like some deranged Victorian heroine, howling for the wolves.

"Also she's not eating right," he said.

"Well, it's okay for her to have a little junk food," I said. "This is a rough time."

"I'm not talking junk food."

"Then what?"

"Stuff that's not even food. Paper. Pebbles."

"Robin's eating rocks?"

"What she really likes is dirt. Other day I come in the house, she's sitting at the kitchen table eating dirt out of a bowl, with a spoon."

"What the hell? That's insane."

"Like I said," Bernard said. "Wigging."

34.

Javier told me that if I left I wouldn't have a job, so I didn't have a job. I tried not to think of my dwindling bank account; instead I flew to Montreal, rented a car, and was in the dark mountains by evening. I rolled the windows down as I pulled up, listening to the crunch of gravel that warned of my approach. The lights were off. Bernard greeted me at the door, where he'd apparently been watching for me. We hugged quickly, and I smelled his nicotined breath and the better, woodsy smell of his sweater. Only the lights in the kitchen were on, and that's where he led me, both of us tiptoeing, like parents trying not to wake a child.

"She conks out early," he said. "That's one good thing."

"How was today?"

He shrugged. "Same as yesterday."

I rubbed my forehead again, that same unsmoothable spot. On the dog-food show the daughter had once gone to a raucous party with her Mexican boyfriend's family and been served menudo with tripe in it, and she'd embarrassed her boyfriend by throwing up and then locking herself in her car. Later, she'd told the camera, "I'm so sorry. I was out of my zone."

I too felt out of my zone. I looked at Bernard, and we smiled weakly. He put his hand over mine, a more welcome touch than Elena's had been, and one more likely to make me cry.

"I did this to her," I said, by which I meant the pregnancy.

Bernard shook his head. "She's always had a weird streak," he said without judgment. He rolled up his sleeve and showed me a scar on his forearm, just below the elbow. "Took a chunk out of me once," he said. "That was back when we were abroad."

"She bit you," I said. The mark on his arm was puckered and faint, a ragged hole that had closed up over time.

"Nope. Corkscrew," he said. "We were arguing in a park. She dug right in there." His tone held a little admiration, a little nostalgia, only a little hurt. "I had it coming, kind of," he said.

"Do I?" I said. "Have it coming, I mean."

He wouldn't look at me, which I took to mean he thought I did. I traced the scar with my fingertip, then drew my hand back. His skin was warm to the touch, and I was shivering. It was always so much colder here than I remembered.

Upstairs, I crept past my sister's room. The door was shut and I opened it, half-hoping the creak would wake her, but it didn't. I could see her huddled lump in the darkness, and hear her raspy breath. I stepped inside the room and sat next to her, pressing my palm against her forehead, which was damp with sweat. Although the room was chilly, she'd flung most of the covers off and heat came off her, along with a pleasant yeasty smell, like rising dough. I felt that she must've known I was there, even in her sleep, and I got in beside her, pulling the quilt over me, warmed more thoroughly by her body. I touched her shoulder, her elbow. She turned on her side, her back to me. My eyes got used to the darkness and I felt lively and clear and awake. She had the window cracked and its little lace curtain fluttered, then stilled. As I lay there she nestled against me, curving the small of her back, and I arranged myself around her, watching her as she slept.

In the morning she woke up slowly, wiping crusts of sleep from her eyes, and propped herself against the pillows. "What are you doing here?"

"I was worried about you. I heard you're turning into a lunatic."

"I might be," she said. "You should watch out."

"I'm sorry," I said, putting my arms around her, but she shook me off. "I'm sorry I'm putting you through this."

"It doesn't matter."

"It does matter."

"What I meant was," she said, "it's too late to worry about it."

She sat up and pressed her head to her hands. The effort seemed to exhaust her, and she lay back down. I brought her tea and toast in bed and then suggested we go for a walk, and she followed me around the property, her steps slow, draggy. We unlocked the barn, and she sat down at a piano but said she didn't feel like playing.

Bernard made us chicken noodle soup and I forced Robin to eat it, spooning it into her mouth. She grimaced as if it were poison. Regular food tasted terrible, she said, like metal in her mouth. She craved burned matches and stones. She showed me a little grey rock she carried in the pocket of her jacket, clean from licking.

"You can't go around eating bowls of dirt, though," I said.

A little time on the internet had informed me that Robin's disorder was called pica, and that it sometimes occurred during pregnancy. The word *pica,* I learned, meant magpie, a bird that would eat almost anything. I remembered how I used to think of myself as a magpie, collecting tidbits of information like shiny objects; but this, I also learned, was folklore. It turned out magpies didn't like shiny objects. Scientists had performed an experiment proving that magpie thievery was a myth. *The magpies have been exonerated,* one scientist had written. When I told all this to Robin, she was unimpressed. She asked me to look online for clay that was safe to eat.

I said no. Instead I took her to the doctor, who recommended iron supplements and gentle exercise. So we walked, circling the property every day, Robin's face round-cheeked, windswept, and troubled. At night I slept in her room, sometimes in bed with her, more often in a sleeping bag on the floor, and throughout the night, waking, we'd murmur little things. *It's going to rain tomorrow. Remind me,* we said. *I need to pull the tarp over the woodpile. Don't let me forget to buy milk.* Sometimes we fell back asleep mid-sentence, so that we just murmured to one another, *Don't let me forget.*

35.

I'd brought my computer, and I spent some time editing my footage of Marianne. I stitched together her pauses, her stutters, the instants when she looked up at the ceiling or out the window, gathering her thoughts, or trying to gather them, and failing.

My sister didn't understand how I could spend hours at a time looking at our mother's face, listening to her voice. But I was absorbed. I found patterns and rhythms; just before Marianne changed subjects, I noted, she'd glance sideways, out the window, as if aware of some sound the camera and I couldn't register. When she talked about her parents she licked her lips, and then when she gossiped about people in the neighborhood she pressed her lips together, firmly, as if condemnation brought her back to surer ground. I noted the moments when her eyes grew distant, interior; and then the moments when they sharpened again, often in anger, which seemed the surest route back to lucidity for her. I tried to cut at these exact moments, the pendulum shift between hazy departure and focused return. I took out the stories themselves, the useless clutter of her anecdotes, and edited the footage down to a steady stream of her face as she lost and regained her concentration. I took everything I'd learned in reality TV—the attention to the minute shifts in human expression, and how these signaled mystery, drama, emotion—and applied it to my mother. It was a study of her effort to keep her mind from changing. Eventually I composed a six-minute film called *Marianne Forgets.* Robin refused to watch it; Bernard sat through it politely and then said he didn't understand what it was about but that Marianne was a nice-looking lady.

Everything in my life felt paused, tensed with waiting. When I think about that spring now, I remember Robin's moods, her vagueness and torpor, her frequent crying, and then her less-frequent crying. I remember the birds. I'd spent my life indoors, in the buzzing fluorescence of editing bays, my ears garlanded by headphones. At Robin's house, sleeping with the windows open, the birds woke me. I learned to identify the finches and cardinals and swallows. The little brown larks. Once as we were walking Robin told me she'd always hated her name. "It's so ordinary," she said. "Robins are everywhere. Puffed out with their boring red chests. And the name is so dated."

"Lark isn't so bad," I said. "It's a bit hippie, though."

"It's never suited you at all," she said. She was right, of course. The robin is common, grounded, unremarkable; the lark is a slip of a bird, known for melody and flight. We should have traded but we'd each held on instead, and now it was too late to change.

36.

I brought Robin things I thought would please her: a body pillow, comfortable maternity clothes. She used the pillow but disdained the clothes, preferring men's jeans and plaid shirts that had been left behind by who knew which previous guests. The only thing she asked me for was a full-length mirror, which she hung on the back of her bedroom door. As her belly grew and her mood lifted, she started staring at herself in it. When I knocked, I sometimes found her naked, turning from side to side, examining all the angles. "Look at this," she said, not proudly but impartially interested, as if her body belonged to someone else.

"You look beautiful," I said, which was true.

Robin wasn't after compliments. "I'm like an *incubator.*"

She said she could feel the baby move, but when I asked to put my palm to her skin, nothing happened. The baby seemed to dart and hide from me like a fish in an aquarium tank, and I tried not to show how much this pained and concerned me, as if the baby, like all those blastocysts before it, sensed there was something wrong with me.

"I feel like I'm swimming underwater all the time. Like I'm growing gills. You know?"

I didn't know. She sent me these postcards from the world of pregnancy, and I received them with a combination of curiosity and gratitude and envy and sadness. When I looked at her pregnant body, I felt a fascination so intense, so physical, that it was almost akin to lust. At one point I asked if I could film her, to record the baby as it grew, and she shook her head and told me I was staring at her too much already. I would, she said, just have to remember it on my own.

"Think about Marianne," she said now, "at sixteen, and then again at twenty. With two different guys."

She was staring at her belly button, which protruded like a pebble perched on a mountain. Bright blue veins plotted her stretched skin. I saw tears in her eyes.

"No wonder she was such a fucking maniac," she said.

Bernard went back to Baltimore; maybe he worried about intruding on us, or maybe he needed his own distance. Until he left, I hadn't realized how strange it was to be alone with Robin; we'd grown used to living as a triangle. The house felt too big for the two of us, and we knocked around inside it, loose and adrift.

One night we were sitting outside after dinner. Always hot, Robin's cheeks were rosy, despite a chill in the air that had sent me inside for a sweater. Earlier it had rained and now when the wind blew the fir needles shook the remaining drops off. Robin was talking about sleeping outside that night, and my stomach dropped uneasily. She saw me frown.

"Don't be uptight," she said. "It's so stuffy inside." She kept all the windows open, sometimes even the doors, and the house was drafty and eerily open; one morning I'd come downstairs to find a swallow picking at some crumbs on the kitchen table. "Maybe I should have the baby here. Just lie down on some hay in the barn and let nature take its course."

From her lifted eyebrow I knew she was saying this to provoke me. We had a doctor at the hospital in Rivière-Rouge. I'd timed the route; we could reach a sterile medical environment in twenty-five minutes. But fear still gripped me, an anxiety and confusion that hadn't been lessened by the forms I'd watched Robin fill out at the doctor's office, listing a previous pregnancy that hadn't resulted in a child.

"In Sweden," she said now, "they spend practically the whole summer outside. Kids run around naked. It's . . ." She rubbed her palm over her belly. We were sitting in Adirondack chairs Bernard had scavenged from a yard sale in town, and I remember rubbing the flat armrests of mine, instinctively imitating her.

"*Summer with Monika*," I said, thinking about how we'd watched the Bergman movie together before she left, Robin saying it was boring and couldn't we watch *Independence Day* instead.

"Monica?" Robin said. I was sure she didn't remember the film or her own complaints about it. After she disappeared for those six months, every conversation we'd had tripled in significance for me; I'd combed through them, sifting each word through my fingers. But Robin was off traveling, exploring, whatever she'd done; she likely hadn't given them any thought at all.

"The summers there are so bright," she said. "They all sail to the islands and then build fires and cook and chat. The light makes people crazy, nobody ever wants to go to bed."

In the silence that followed a few raindrops fell, a quick light shower that ended as soon as it began. She shifted in her chair, moving her hands from her belly to the armrests, and I thought about how I used to hear her fingers tapping when we lived together, rehearsing whatever music she was learning at the time. Instead, now, she stretched two fingers out as if holding a phantom cigarette between them.

"Is that what you were doing—sailing around the islands?"

"A little. I met some people. Hung out various places. Busked for money, singing."

"Sounds fun," I said, unable to keep the acid from my voice. I was thinking of my calls to police, the postcard she'd sent from Ytterby—*Don't look for me*—and my own sleepless nights. How I'd flailed at work and school.

She spoke as if she hadn't heard me. "But when summer ends everything changes. People go outside, sure, but they avoid each other. Nobody would look me in the eye. They all keep their distance. I felt like I didn't exist. It scared me."

"And that's why you came back?"

Years later, great and heavier, my sister shook her head, and a strand of hair caught on her lip. She drew in her breath and then tilted her head back; she stared at the sky as she exhaled.

"No," she said. "I was going through something like this. Strange to think about it now."

It took me a moment to understand what she meant by *something like this*.

"What?" I said. Even though I'd seen the paperwork, the information was hard for me to take in. I wasn't sure which was more difficult to grasp—that it had happened to my sister, or that she hadn't told me about it. Both.

"I wasn't far along like this," she said. "It was just at the beginning.

I left the tour because I wasn't sure what to do, and I wanted to be by myself. To figure things out."

I looked at her, but she was staring straight ahead at the inky line of pine trees, the darker sky above them. "So you and Bernard—"

"I didn't tell him. You know how Bernard was—like a puppy. He wasn't capable of carrying a weight like that." I remembered Bernard as a young man, and knew what she meant—how guileless he'd been, how gentle, how vague.

There was another chair nearby and my sister got up and dragged it over, declining my offer of help, and put her feet up on it, then rested her hands on her belly. "I never wanted to be a mother," she said. "Still don't. No offense."

I tilted my head to say, *None taken.*

"Of course I keep thinking about it lately," she said, looking down at herself, her changed body. "It was a weird time. I left the tour because it didn't seem important anymore. All that practicing, all that jumping through hoops, for what? To please other people. I was so tired of my life. In a way what happened was just an excuse to abandon it. I left and I just . . . wandered for a while. It felt good. My whole existence up to that point, people had been telling me what I should do. Mrs. Gasparian. Boris. Everyone at Juilliard. Even you."

I bit my lip against the words I wanted to speak. I would have apologized or explained; I would have said that I was only trying to take care of her; but I knew she didn't want me to say anything. What she wanted was silence.

"In Sweden, I felt like whatever happened should be my own plan. I would get to decide, me and only me. Eventually I made up my mind that I'd have the baby in Sweden and give it up—I thought I'd leave it at the doorstep of a church or something, like in a book. Growing up in Sweden seemed like a good life. The kids looked pretty happy there."

She still wasn't looking at me. The weight of what I'd asked her to do, of what I hadn't known, settled on my chest. My vision smeared, a dirty lens.

"I made money busking for a while, staying wherever, and then it got colder and darker and less fun. My clothes didn't fit anymore and the whole thing started to seem more real, and scary. Then I got sick. I was staying in this hostel and one night I woke up in bed and there was blood everywhere. I had terrible pain and I couldn't even think or breathe. I got up and crouched in the bathroom and there was more blood. Two girls from Belgium came in and one of them started screaming but the other was great, she took charge, and she kicked the other one out and she held me for a while and then we went to a hospital—I don't even remember how we got there. This girl from Belgium stayed with me the whole night, holding my hand and singing these Belgian folk songs. Oh, man, she had a terrible voice."

I reached out a hand to touch her and then drew it back: her arms were crossed over her chest, her palms on her shoulders, and the look on her face was inward, private.

"At some point they gave me drugs to knock me out and when I woke up I was alone. It was over. By the time I got back to the hostel the girls from Belgium were gone. I never even knew their names. It took me a while to sort through what had happened. I spent two more months in Sweden in this state of—suspension, I guess."

I thought about how starved Robin was the day she returned to the Tunnel, how when I pulled the thick wet sweater over her neck, I was startled by the rise and cut of her bones. There was almost nothing left of her. And then I recalled my own feeling of suspension in New York after I left Wheelock, how I'd called no one, spoken to no one, because I didn't know what I would say.

Robin looked at me for the first time. "And then after a while I just said *Fuck it* and came home."

"I remember," I said.

"Listen. It's not like I was heartbroken or traumatized for life," she said. Her voice was clear and unwavering. "You shouldn't think that."

I nodded. "But why didn't you tell me?"

"It belonged to me," she said, and I understood she meant not the baby but the experience, the secret she'd kept, and even the telling of it now. Her face softened, and she held a hand out to me, and I took it.

"Do you think about it a lot?"

She tilted her head. "I don't know," she said. "Do you think about your thumbs, or your lungs, or anything else that's a part of you?"

She didn't mean for me to answer, and so I didn't.

"I'm thinking about it now," she said.

I gripped her hand. We sat quietly as a steady rain began to fall. I couldn't stop thinking about my sister at twenty, alone in another country; sending me a postcard telling me where she was, a note that contained its own contradiction, that said both *I am here* and *Don't look for me.* I wished I could have been there with her. As we sat together, I remembered Olga lecturing in an almost empty hall at Worthen; she was talking about Eisenstein, the great Russian filmmaker, and his theories of dialectical montage. He was interested in editing for contrast as well as continuity. If you juxtapose two images, he said—or Olga said—no matter how different, the viewer will make meaning from the montage. The second image in the sequence will alter the meaning of the first. It was, I thought, how memory worked: yoking disparate elements together across time. My sister next to me now changed how I thought of her then. My sister next to me changed how I thought of myself.

"This time is different," my sister said as the rain fell harder.

"Yes," I said. I moved close to her and pressed my wet cheek against hers.

37.

She was overdue. According to the nurse, this was common— "Don't worry about your little lazy one," she said, and I frowned— and Robin rolled her eyes. After patting her hand condescendingly, the nurse left the examination room. Robin made a low growling sound of aggravation, whether at the baby or the nurse or myself, I couldn't say. In the final weeks of pregnancy she'd entered a new stage, of constant misery; she slept fitfully, raised on pillows because of her heartburn, went to the washroom every ten minutes, asked constantly for food but didn't eat it. I got used to hearing her pad restlessly around the house at night. Then I woke early one morning feeling strange, murky with prolonged rest, and realized I'd slept the whole night through for the first time in ages. The house was silent. I was terrified when I looked in her bed and didn't see her there, or in the kitchen, or anywhere else.

I went outside; it was just before dawn and the sky was milky, drained of color. I tramped through the wet grass, which we weren't good at keeping mowed since Bernard left and which lashed at my ankles and calves. First I looked in the barn, but she wasn't there. The swallows were up, though, busy at their tasks in the rafters. The air smelled of mildew and hay. Another piano had recently been delivered, from a church in a nearby town that was being demolished; it was missing several keys, and it leaned against one of the walls like a drunk collapsing after a hard night. The day it arrived, Robin had played it for hours, producing jangly, ugly music, full of gaps and off notes, a wrong-footed sonata that was painful to the ear but that she seemed to enjoy. I'd asked, tentatively, if she had any interest in moving one of the pianos into the house. "These derelicts?" she'd said. "These are for falling apart."

At last I found her, slumped over by the wolf enclosure, and for a long, terrible moment I worried she was dead, or dying. At the corner of the fencing that housed Catherine of Aragon and her pack, she sat on the ground, leaning back against the wire, legs outstretched, her head tilted grotesquely to the side, like a broken doll. When she heard me coming, she opened her eyes.

"Jesus Christ," I said. I knelt down next to her on the cold, wet ground.

When she smiled at me, her face was calm. "I can't sleep in that house anymore," she said. "It's airless."

I began to argue—she had every window and door open, we were practically sleeping in a lean-to—but when I saw how content she looked, I changed my mind. "So you're all right," I said.

She nodded, and uncurled her fingers from the wire mesh of the enclosure. "They came and licked me," she said. "For a while, they slept next to the fence, three of them. We fell asleep together." The wolves, her better companions, had given her the comfort she needed.

The next day was hot and dense and we went for a walk together, Robin breathing hard. I could smell her sweat. I kept reaching out my arm, in case she wanted to take it, but she didn't.

We were heading for the forest canopy, hoped the air would be cooler there.

I was telling Robin about the cache of old films found in the frozen landfill in Dawson City, though I knew she wasn't really listening. I think I was talking to the baby as much as to my sister, trying to teach an unknown person to recognize the sound of my voice.

Then Catherine came running out of the woods, her half-hobbled gait unmistakable.

Later, I suspected it was Robin herself who'd opened the enclosure, so agonized by her own claustrophobia that she couldn't stand fences anywhere. But when I asked, she denied it, and I think it's possible she genuinely didn't remember. We eventually found Catherine howling at her packmates from the outside of the fence; if she wanted to roam, she also wanted to return to her kind.

But at the time I didn't know what Catherine was doing there or why she was running toward us, and panic burned my throat like bile.

The wolf came close and then closer, her yellow eyes fixed yet unseeing.

Vertigo hailed me: a spell of muddy sight, graspless touch. When I grabbed Robin she went down hard, and I was so upset that I barely registered the wolf go past us, continuing on her errand, whatever it was. For some time Robin couldn't get up; I kept apologizing to her, which she ignored. When, eventually, she made her way to her feet, all she could talk about was Catherine. She wanted to go look for her; I asked her about the baby and she frowned at me emptily, as if she'd forgotten there was one. I put my hand on her belly and she swatted it away.

"Can you feel it moving?" I asked.

"I never feel it in the daytime," she said.

Then she bent over, grabbing her knees with her hands, sucking her breath in hard, unable to hide the pain.

"We have to go," I said.

"But Catherine—"

"Now," I said, and when Robin stopped arguing I knew the pain had to be intense. We inched back to the house, my sister leaning her weight against mine. I drove to the hospital, my palms sweating against the steering wheel, Robin groaning at every brake and turn. She panted shallowly, and her eyes were unfocused and glassy. When I asked how she was doing she told me to shut up. Despite my urgent calls for help once we arrived at the hospital, the nurses didn't seem excited. They timed the contractions and told us we'd come too early, and though I described Robin's fall one of them shrugged and said it would be rare for such an incident to do damage. Eventually they left us to our own devices. The maternity ward was oddly deserted, with no other patients around, a desolation that felt ominous. I turned on the television in her assigned room, then turned it off. Robin kept shuffling up and down the hall, every so often banging her head against a wall. I brought her ice in a cup and she chewed it violently; they wouldn't let her have any food.

We waited for her water to break, but it never did. What happened was that she fainted in the hallway, grabbing onto a wheelchair on her way down and whacking her head again. I caught her just before she hit the floor. I don't remember screaming, but I must have, because the nurses finally came running, and then they took her away without saying a word to me.

For a seemingly endless hour I waited in the hallway by myself. I didn't understand why I couldn't see her and no one would explain anything to me. At last I was granted permission to enter the operating room where my sister had been prepped. I was given a surgical mask and gloves and gown and I saw her lying on a gurney, pale and limp, her eyes closed. They'd decided to cut her open.

I held her hand. I talked to her about our childhood, about Mrs. Gasparian and the Dean Smiths and the track team at Worthen, about Bernard and Catherine of Aragon, trying to stitch our lives into a story that would hold her fast to me. I don't know if she heard anything I said. I smelled burning flesh. I saw a small dim form being carried to the other side of the room. *What's happening?* I said or think I said, but no one answered. Robin's eyes were still shut, and the doctor was closing the incision. My sister's body remained motionless in what seemed like a permanent way. I was holding her hand, but she wasn't holding mine.

"You can let go now," the doctor said. "We'll wheel her to recovery and she'll wake up there."

I let out a long-suspended breath. Later, I would find Robin, groggy and dry-mouthed from drugs, and she would smile at me winningly, cheerfully, because she was confused and high. I would spend the night with her, listening to the steady, medicated rise and fall of her breath. Two days later we would drive home. But first, in the operating room with that burning smell, I held the warm body of my baby, legs skinny and long, fingers curled into fists. Red and fragile with combustible life, she opened her mouth and cried.

PART FOUR

After

I never wanted my mother as much as I did after my own child was born. It was an absurd desire, born as much from nostalgia and exhaustion as it was from any memory of tenderness in Marianne. But I wanted so much to thrust my baby into her arms; I kept thinking that it would have softened her somehow, would have made up for everything between us that was lacking. *Nostalgia is a romance with the fantasy of loss,* Olga had lectured back at Worthen, and at the time I thought of this as a condemnation; now, older, I thought it was a virtue, because in missing my mother I found her again, made a space for her in my days instead of trying to evade her memory.

Robin told me I was being sentimental, and I'm sure she was right. Though it was my sister who endured the hormone changes of pregnancy and after, I was the one whose emotions wavered and sprang, buoyant one minute, sinking the next. In the first months after the birth, which we spent in the Laurentians with Robin, I cried every day and most of the time I couldn't have said why. My sister, by contrast, snapped back to herself. Some part of me had worried that it would be hard for her to give the baby over, but she wanted very little to do with her. She returned to the wolves and her job at the restaurant, and her eyes were steely again, composed. Derya came to visit, and they played music in the barn together. I brought the baby to hear them, but she was cranky and disinterested and whatever image I'd held in my mind of some mystical moment of communion evaporated in the humid air, which kept giving her diaper rash.

When Bernard came back from Baltimore, he held the baby in an inexpert grip that made me nervous, but the look of pleasure on his face when she curled a hand around his finger was lovely and pure. He gave me, shyly, presents for her—two books and a fleece blanket, which I spread out on the floor in the living room, a stage for the baby as we admired her. I invited him to come see us in Brooklyn sometime, and he blushed and said he'd like that. Then he withdrew, making himself useful around the property, most comfortable, or so it seemed to me, at the periphery.

Both Derya and Bernard hovered around Robin as they always had, and I understood that things at the cottage would continue however she wanted them to; she knew how to bend the world to fit her needs.

I thought often of Marianne as she would have been at sixteen, weighted down by motherhood, and the hardest thing to grasp was that I'd never see her again. Sometimes I watched the film I'd made of her, and Robin finally watched it with me once, her head tilted to the side.

"God, I look like her," was all she said, and it was true; they had the same eyes, the same face, its sharp angles softening with age.

The baby was fascinated by the images flickering on the screen, one of the few things that quieted her, so we held long marathons with old black-and-white movies I loved: comedies by Preston Sturges and Howard Hawks, musicals with Fred and Ginger. I showed her Joel McCrea and Veronica Lake on the road in *Sullivan's Travels*, Cary Grant looking for the intercostal clavicle in *Bringing Up Baby*. I wanted her brain to be filled with happy things. Mostly I fell asleep with her on my chest, waking to the strains of "Shall We Dance" as yet another leaky diaper dampened my shirt.

When the movies weren't playing she was a cranky baby and not beautiful; her face was red and bumpy, with scaly patches of dry skin, and a blister on her top lip kept popping and re-forming. Her hair was a nondescript pale color and her legs and arms were skinny and elongated. She looked nothing like the picturesque chubby babies that had once dominated my dreams. She looked like a baby monkey doing her best in a difficult situation. The doctor said she was fine;

she was gaining weight and producing dirty diapers, and what else did I want from her? He rushed out of the room before I had time to unfold the creased paper on which I had jotted my millions of questions.

I named her Scottie, after Jimmy Stewart's character in *Vertigo,* which Robin told me was deranged. "This is her life model? A mentally ill cop with women issues?"

"I love Jimmy Stewart."

"You could have named her George Bailey. Or Liberty Valance."

"I never realized you knew so much about movies."

"Everybody knows those movies."

"I think Scottie is cute," I said.

"You should name her Midge, after Barbara Bel Geddes. She's the only decent person in that movie."

"A midge is a kind of insect, it's an ugly name."

"Well, she's not exactly a beauty," she said.

I nestled the baby against my chest and said, "It can't matter to you, Robin."

"You're right," she said.

Later, I told her that I wished I could've asked our mother for advice about Scottie, and she laughed. "Marianne would have fixed herself a cocktail and ignored you," she said. "You forget everything bad now that she's gone."

It was true. I forgot everything bad, now that she was gone.

2.

Two years later I was back in Brooklyn. I'd rented another apartment in the same neighborhood and still saw Elena regularly. She was always offering to babysit but this mostly involved her smoking on my couch while telling Scottie that kids in her day behaved a lot better, so I didn't take her up on it much. I had a job on a show about dating after divorce, starring a grizzled heiress who'd survived three marriages and was looking for true love the fourth time around. She wore long fake eyelashes and her facial expressions were muted from all the Botox she'd had. But she was great at dismissing her suitors with a single, cruel line of judgment. Of one she said, "He's like if you took a slug and poured salt on him, then put him in a suit."

My daughter had grown into a sturdy, excitable girl with curly blond hair; she looked nothing like me or Robin and everything like the father none of us knew. I taught her that I'd asked for her and Robin helped me bring her into the world, which she took to mean that I had ordered her online, as I did diapers; she demanded to see the cardboard box in which she assumed she'd arrived. She was no longer interested in movies, wouldn't sit still for anything on-screen, and when I tried to show her the films I wanted her to love, she ran out of the room, clutching her toys for dear life. I had years' worth of tidbits to share with her but when she asked me questions they were always about subjects—why people got old, why yellow was yellow and blue was blue—on which I had no answers prepared.

Robin came to visit for Scottie's third birthday. Still waitressing at the restaurant, she complained relentlessly about the customers and their dumb requests and low tips, though I believed she must have enjoyed it, because Robin never lasted long at anything she didn't enjoy. She was happiest talking about the wolves: she was introducing new pups to the pack and could go on for hours about their eating and grooming habits, and how the older animals were teaching them to belong. She treated my daughter with an absent-minded brutality that roused intense devotion. If Robin told Scottie to be quiet she would sit silently in a corner, obedient to my sister as she never was to me. At night she clamored for Robin to tell her stories and begged Robin to sleep in her bed. When I went in to check on them, I found her curled against Robin, clutching the tail end of my sister's braid in her little hand. Robin, holding her other hand, was breathing into the curled shell of her ear. The brutality was a pretense.

Sometimes I wondered if there were vestiges of physical connection between them, some trace element of Scottie's origins inside Robin's body, her citizenship there. But Robin, when I tried to talk to her about this, told me I was being ridiculous. Anyway it was me Scottie ran to when hungry or hurt, me whose eyes she sought for reassurance when Robin told her some outrageous tale. I was the first person she looked for when she woke. Robin was the beloved guest, all the more adored because she was known to leave.

For Scottie's birthday Robin gave her a box full of sticks she'd collected from around her house in the Laurentians. "What do I do with these?" Scottie asked, and Robin said, "Build, poke, I don't know." Scottie gazed at them in confusion, city girl that she was, but because they came from Robin she weighed them in her hands like treasures. The day after her birthday they went together to the park and dug in the dirt with the sticks and then flung them at each other, as the other mothers watched disapprovingly, imagining eye injuries and head wounds. It was a grey day and muddy and their shoes squelched as they ran. I took out my camera and filmed the whorls in the mud, the sticks traveling in the air. The sound of their voices rose and fell off-screen, music to remember them by.

Acknowledgments

Thank you to my colleagues at Lafayette College, where I started this book, particularly Lee Upton, my dear friend and model for how a writer and teacher should be. Thank you to the English Department at McGill University, where I finished a draft during my time as Mordecai Richler Writer-in-Residence. Thank you to the Creative Writing Program at the University of British Columbia for your trust in me.

Many people generously read drafts and offered perceptive, helpful comments: thanks to Natalie Bakopoulos, Ariela Freedman, Peter Ohlin, Karen Olsson, Liz Van Hoose, and especially Amy Williams, who saw what I was trying to do from the start. This book, like my others, owes so much to the steadfast support of Gary Fisketjon and Sarah MacLachlan.

Thank you to Bianca Falbo for helping me learn about wolves; Chris Reynolds and Tracy Pratt-Stuchbery for sharing their experiences as pianists; Nandini Sikand for talking me through developments in documentary film; and Eileen Finkelstein for teaching me about editing for reality TV. Any errors or artistic liberties that remain are, of course, my own.

Certain aspects of Robin's home in the Laurentians owe a debt of inspiration to Hélène Grimaud's memoir *Wild Harmonies: A Life of Music and Wolves* and Neko Case's album *Middle Cyclone,* but the details of her life, her character, and all scenes are entirely my invention. Olga's work on nostalgia is informed by Svetlana Boym's *The Future of Nostalgia,* though her character, life story, and quotes are fiction.

My father showed me old movies and talked to me about John

Acknowledgments

Grierson and documentary film and taught me that to be a writer and artist was something of value. My whole family has supported every aspect of my writing life since I was a child. Stephen and Peter have continued to make space for my work, even when it takes me away from them, and I am grateful for them daily.

To my devoted mother, my sister, and all the women who have been like mothers and sisters to me: thank you.

A Note on the Type

The text of this book was set in a typeface named Perpetua, designed by the British artist Eric Gill (1882–1940) and cut by the Monotype Corporation of London in 1928–30. Perpetua is a contemporary letter of original design, without any direct historical antecedents. The shapes of the roman letters basically derive from stonecutting, a form of lettering in which Gill was eminent. The italic is essentially an inclined roman. The general effect of the typeface in reading sizes is one of lightness and grace. The larger display sizes of the type are extremely elegant and form what is probably the most distinguished series of inscriptional letters cut in the present century.

Typeset by Scribe, Philadelphia, Pennsylvania

Printed and bound by Berryville Graphics,
Berryville, Virginia

Designed by Betty Lew